Speared By You

Chicago Steel
Book 4

Jessica Buss

Dedication

For Grandma Raine
My example of never giving up.
Strong. Determined. Sacrificing. Dedicated. Selfless.
Fellow smut reader.

Chapter 1

Tristan

May 2005

Stretching my arms high above my head, I look over at my alarm clock, which reads five a.m., and release another yawn as my body attempts to wake up. Since I was five, I've been coming to the arena to skate or practice at least a few times a week. When I was a preteen, my practices moved to early morning before school, and by the time I was in high school, it was still early, but it was every day. Ice time wasn't cheap, but our parent booster club set up ample fundraising opportunities to cover it and travel trips each year.

The drive to the arena was a blur. Reaching down, I tie my skates without thinking. After this many years, it's become second nature and I could probably do it in my sleep.

With the arena empty, I savor the quiet peace it offers. This, right now, is my favorite time of the day.

It's when I feel most centered and like myself. Today I need that because it is a big day. It's my high school graduation. That might seem trivial when you are looking ahead to your future and it's as promising as mine. But I can't deny the impact high school has had on my life.

Before stepping out onto the pristine, freshly resurfaced rink, I inhale deeply. Sucking in the cool air wafting around me, I feel transported to another place. To me, the arena is magic, always making me feel alive and invigorated. It is where I find solace, no matter what is going on in my life.

My skates slice against the ice like a hot knife to butter. Everything about being here is energizing. From the familiar push and pull on my leg muscles to the ease with which I perform crossovers and stops, skating to me is almost a religious experience.

Letting my eyes linger around the arena as I do laps, I'm drawn to the ever-present championship banners that hang from the rafters. Over the years, our town has amassed quite a few. The earliest is from decades before, right around the time they constructed the arena. There is a long-lasting legacy of hockey excellence that has called this arena home, and now I'm part of that. I'm skating into the history books. Hopefully, my chapter will be longer than a few pages. But only if I'm lucky.

Is Lady Luck real? Until recently, I wasn't sure. But now? Now I'm positive she is, because I'm one lucky son of a bitch. In addition, I also know it took my dedication, persistence, focus, skill, and stamina to get to my dreams. Luck was only part of it.

While my graduating class will be thinking about college and frat parties, and walking across that stage today to celebrate receiving their high school diplomas, I'll be celebrating something else. Yesterday, I was drafted to play professional hockey with the Boston fucking Storm. I, Tristan Murphy, just signed to play for the team that's amassed the most Stanley Cups since its inception in 1893. Since I was small, this has always been my dream. And let me tell you, it feels fucking fantastic.

After I finish my skate, I return home to get ready for the day's festivities. I need to shower because even though it wasn't practice, I still worked up a sweat. All dressed, I look in the mirror to check my tie, and my mind instantly goes to hockey and being back on the ice.

"Tristan, are you ready to go?" my mom shouts up the stairs, knocking me from my daydream.

"Just about," I holler back.

I pull my black robe on, making sure I look good before I zip it closed. "Let's go!" I tell myself as I take one last look in the mirror. Clomping down the stairs, my parents come into view. Both wear a sappy, awe-struck look plastered to their faces. My mom clasps her hands together, and I watch as her eyes grow misty.

"No tears today, Mom," I caution. "This is a happy day. I'm finally done with school."

My dad mumbles under his breath, "Hallelujah." I laugh and Mom scowls.

Once I reach Mom, I pull her into my chest. She hugs me for a second before swatting at me. "I'll have you know," she warns, "these... these are happy tears, Tristan. I can't believe my baby boy is all grown up."

"Well, believe it. In a few months, I'm headed to Boston to begin the next phase of my life, and I can't wait."

Dad's firm grip presses on my shoulder. "Don't grow up too fast. Being an adult and on your own is harder than you think."

Sure, Dad. I laugh because right now I'm unstoppable. "Noted. Ready to go?" I ask them before we head out.

Three hours later, after graduation commencement has concluded, Steph and I leave our high school's football field to find our parents. Thankfully, it's a nice day that isn't too hot, or the ceremony would have been worse. "That was so boring," I whine to Steph as we head over to our designated meeting spot.

"It was like the staff was trying to torture us one last time. Did it really need to be so long?" she complains as we pass all our classmates that are being forced to pose for pictures. Nudging her, I see the torture already being inflicted on our friend Franklin. He's usually a chill guy, but right now he's having an animated conversation with his mom. Steph laughs and I squeeze the hand I'm holding.

"I don't know what you're laughing about. You know that will be us as soon as we find our parents."

"Don't remind me." She groans.

I stop walking and pull her to me, giving her a kiss on the lips. "I love you, Steph. We're in this together, right?"

"Yes, we are."

"Good. Then I guess we'll just have to make it fun," I rationalize. She nods and smiles back at me. We get that this is supposed to be a big day for us. But it's just high school, and the next stage of our lives is way more exciting.

Dating since the week before our junior year, we've taken a million pictures and shared hundreds of memories. Basically, we are inseparable. I know there will be thousands more, but right now, we are over it. We're hungry, tired, and running low on patience. "It's six o'clock, don't we have reservations at Cibo?" I groan impatiently.

My mother flitters here and there, trying to fix hair, ties, and poses as my dad takes the millionth photo of the day. "Margie, leave them alone. Tristan's right, we need to get to the restaurant."

Following dinner, Steph and I change into something more comfortable. Then we head out to a few after-graduation parties. But nothing really holds our attention, so we head to our spot. It's nothing fancy, just some vacant land tucked back in the woods, right on the outskirts of town. It's extremely private. Over the past two years, we have spent many hours here. Not all of it was having sex, although that certainly happened. A lot. In fact, we've perfected the backseat hookup. Tonight, we don't waste any time undressing. It's a warm night and we've got our windows cracked to let off the heat we know we'll generate between our bodies. Since we've been together since we were sixteen, we've shared all our firsts with each other. Meaning we fumbled through it all, hoping for the best. It's gotten better, for sure, but I know there's more to learn.

"Are you excited about this fall? For Boston?" I ask while we're lying in the backseat cuddled together. Steph's warm skin is pressed against mine and there is no place I'd rather be. I bury my nose in her hair while I wait for her to answer. *She smells incredible, like always.* And I press a gentle kiss to her temple because I can't help myself.

Steph sighs. "Yes and no."

"What do you mean?" I ask nervously, holding her tighter. *What is she going to say?* Steph has always been so positive about us moving. I hate that at the last minute, she could change her mind. I have to go to Boston, but she could decide to go to any of the other schools that accepted her. *But where would that leave us? She has to go to Boston.* Dread weighs heavily on my heart and I'm sure the color in my face has drained.

"Well… with you playing professional hockey and traveling all the time and me busy with school, I'm afraid we'll hardly see each other." She buries her head in the blanket. *We have a plan. We've talked about this several times.*

Uncovering her head, I ask, "Steph, can you look at me? Please." When she finally makes eye contact, I remind her, "Yes, we will both be busy and going in very separate directions, but we are a priority. We have to make the time we have together extra special and meaningful." I give her a chaste kiss, making sure she's heard me. "Okay?"

Only nodding, she can't hide the worry pulled tight across her face. "Baby, tell me what's wrong," I push.

Pulling back and putting some space between us, I look deeply into her gorgeous brown eyes.

She sniffles, then confesses what is weighing on her heart. "Everything's changing, and I hate change." Pulling her tight to my chest, I stroke her long chestnut-colored hair. "It'll be fine, I promise. You'll see."

"I hope so," she whispers. *For her, I'll make it right. I'll do whatever I have to do.*

Chapter 2

Stephanie

The summer flew by, and it's now time to pack everything up and head to Boston. Both classes and training camp start next week, and I know we'll expect to start strongly. These last few months, both Tristan and I have tried to pack in as many activities as we can. I know we'll be in the same city, but I have a horrible nagging feeling I will hardly see him. And to be honest, the thought of that is making me panicky. So to address that, this summer, we've done family dinners at both his and my house. We've taken my little brother Jeremy out to the movies, bowling, mini golf, and hiking. Wanting to stay in peak physical shape, Tristan spent hours a day on the ice, working on conditioning and drills that would better prepare him. I got a paid internship working for a small non-profit. When I wasn't busy restocking supplies or answering the phone, I was the office's runner.

Although I wasn't there long, I could see some of the inner workings of the charity. And the experience unveiled a future career path to pursue. Someday, I want to run a non-profit for the benefit of fighting breast cancer.

During our sophomore year of high school, doctors diagnosed my mom with an aggressive form of breast cancer. Even after a double mastectomy and chemo, the cancer spread in her body and she passed away a few weeks before summer break after my sophomore year. Every member of my family dealt with it differently. My dad, who'd lost the love of his life, basically shut down. He still went to work and financially provided for us, but without my mom there, he was not emotionally available anymore. My little brother Jeremy was still in elementary school, and his way of handling it all was to act out. Let's just say those last few weeks of school before the break were trying. Dad and I hoped that summer break would give him the time to process what had happened. But it wasn't enough or what he needed. The year following Mom's death, Jeremy received an in-school suspension twice and more detentions than I'd care to mention. When he got into junior high a year later, thanks to Tristan coming into our lives, he had worked most of his anger out.

Tristan was an absolute godsend to my entire

family. We were drowning in our despair and he rescued each of us. He helped my dad around the house when chores, like mowing the lawn, began piling up. With Jeremy, Tristan would take him running when he was angry and let him vent. While the boys were out on their excursions, I found the time to journal. Right after my mom had passed, one of my favorite teachers, Mrs. Harrisburg, recommended the idea and it stuck. No matter what I was feeling or thinking, I knew it was safe and protected in my journal. It was like writing a love letter to my mom, telling her everything that was happening in my life. And the journal was a gigantic piece to my healing, but the other was Tristan. For me, he showed me love and grace. When we'd met, he knew I was broken by what had happened. Instead of giving up, he patiently helped me piece myself back together.

* * *

The drive to Boston isn't bad.

Not long after we leave Concord, our hometown, I ask in the most annoyingly nasally voice I can manage, "Are we there yet?"

"Not yet," he answers.

After less than a half an hour stuffed in Tristan's truck, thanks to traffic, I'm ready to stretch my legs. My butt is sore. I'm glad I'm not driving, because if I were, I couldn't have kept shifting, trying to work the charley horse in my ass free. Watching the road signs fly by my window, I see one advertising a coffee joint and what exit to take.

In a sweet voice, I ask, "Can we stop for coffee and pee break, please?"

Focusing his eyes on me, I can almost hear the questions tumbling through his brain. *What are you up to? Are you getting me a coffee? How about snacks?*

Tristan focuses back on the road, takes the correct exit, and steers us over to the gas station with an attached coffee hut. Smiling, I hop out, "I'll be back in a minute. Need anything?" Tristan just gives me a smirk.

Ten minutes later, I return with an empty bladder and arms loaded. Two piping-hot vanilla lattes, a giant bag of kettle corn, and a variety of our favorite candy bars.

Laughing, Tristan asks, "You think you got enough?"

"Do you think we need more?" I ask, faking concern. I know I went a little overboard, but I'm a stress eater when I'm nervous, and if anything qualifies as a time to be stressed, it's now.

Tristan gives me his steady smile. "It'll be fine, babe."

I hand him his latte, and he thanks me before taking a sip. "Ready?" A head nod is all he gets, as I'm busy crunching away on the delicious, sweet and salty popcorn I bought.

Pulling into traffic in Tristan's truck with the 4x8

U-Haul trailer stuffed full, we're back on the road to our next adventure. When we finally arrive in Boston twenty minutes later, we head to the studio apartment he rented so he can sign the lease and get his keys. All I can say is it's small. After a visit to a furniture and home goods store, it will be much homier.

Once everything's moved out of the U-Haul, we load my things back into the truck. A stop at U-Haul to return the trailer before we head to my dorm is on the agenda after we have lunch. By the time we're done moving me in, it's mid-afternoon and we've got a handful of things left to do.

By the end of the day, when Tristan pulls up to my dorm, I can barely move. Everything hurts, and the idea of sleeping in tomorrow sounds incredible. Thank you to whoever designed my first-semester schedule. This schedule angel of mercy selected an eleven-fifteen for my first class of the day. *Hallelujah.*

Looking at his dash, my mouth falls open. "I can't believe it's ten already."

"We were pretty busy today. Thank you for helping me move in and getting my apartment to look less empty. Your idea of visiting the home goods store was a good one, even if I grumbled a bit."

I scoff at him and say, "A bit? I think the complaints coming from your mouth were not just louder than that two-year-old we saw, but they were more frequent too."

He shakes his head no before he finally smirks at

me. "Well, at least it's done, and I don't have to go back there anytime soon."

Rubbing my tired eyes, I say, "I should probably go. I want to unpack at least my clothes before I go to sleep. And I need to find my toothbrush."

Tristan yawns. "Yeah, I should probably at least find my toothbrush and lay out my hockey stuff for my meeting with the Storm staff tomorrow."

He runs his hand through his hair, a dead giveaway he's feeling anxious. Grabbing his hand, I stroke my thumb against his and remind him of a few things. "The Storm drafted you. You've got this. Will it be hard? An adjustment? Will you have to earn your spot and their respect? Hell yes. You'll have to do all that and more. But, Tristan, you are the bravest man I know. You have nothing to be worried about or anxious over. I believe in you."

Tristan squeezes my hand and then tugs me in for a kiss. After a few moments, he pulls away and rests his forehead on mine. "I love you, Steph. I know I wouldn't be here without you pushing and encouraging me. Thank you."

He gives me another kiss before I pry myself from my seat. "Night. I love you," I murmur.

"I love you too, Steph."

Chapter 3

Tristan

The feeling of stepping onto the ice for the first time as a professional athlete is surreal. I've dreamed about this moment. I've thought about how I'd feel and what I'd think. Other than *this is a fucking incredible experience that I will remember always*. Words escape me. The cool blast of wind I feel on my face as I skate lap after lap is the wake-up call I need. Instead of feeling overwhelmed and anxious like I'd expected, I'm surprisingly calm. It's like my skates cutting through the ice puts me in a Zen-like state, where nothing permeates my temperament.

Taking shots at Doogan Hudson, our goalie, and one of the best in the league, is thrilling, especially when I hit the upper corner and he misses it. I'm on top of the world as he shouts to me, "That's your first and last rookie!" I laugh, giving a chin raise, letting him know I heard him loud and clear. But just as with any rookie in the NHL, I have a big ego, and I'm determined to catch Doogan off again.

Training camp is brutal, but I think I show well. At least the coaches don't yell at me too often. In fact, they pull me aside toward the end of the week, and Coach Phillip definitely has some constructive criticism. Not everything is negative and much of it I expected, seeing that I've never played at this caliber before. He recommends visiting our team's trainers to set up a workout plan that will highlight strength training and build my cardio. If I don't improve both, I'll struggle to keep up with "the big boys."

Stephanie

By the time I get up and ready for classes on Monday morning, Tristan is already at training camp. On my first day, I'm already learning how college differs from high school. After my first class, I already have a paper to write before the next session. *Holy crap.* It isn't that the assignment seems hard; it's just I wasn't expecting it. Guess that's the price I pay for coming into my freshman year with college credits. Between AP classes and earning college credits while still in high school, I set myself on track for graduating early, hoping I can finish my degree in three years.

On my way back to my dorm following dinner, my phone rings. It's Tristan and my heart flutters.

"Hi," I gush into the phone.

"Hey, babe. Have you had dinner yet?" he asks.

"I just finished and am walking back to my dorm now. How was your day?"

Letting out a deep breath, his voice shakes. "I'm not going to lie. It's tough, Steph. Going from being at the top of the food chain to clinging to the bottom isn't something I was prepared for." His admission weighs heavily on my heart. He sounds defeated after just one day.

"I'm so sorry to hear your day wasn't great. What can I do to cheer you up?"

Tristan's answer is only two words. "Look up." There, standing in the front of my dorm, is the most handsome man I've ever seen. Sure, he looks exhausted, but that doesn't diminish the yumminess factor one bit. He's not wearing his usual backward ball cap. Without it, his sandy-brown hair's tousled, making him appear even more wild and sexy. Tristan's wearing a black Boston Storm hoodie with athletic shorts that show off his summer tan and the incredible definition of his legs. It's tough to miss all the female attention he is attracting. Despite it, his mocha brown eyes remain fixed on me. *Take that, self-esteem.* I plaster a goofy smile on my face.

"Tristan," I say as I jog the remaining way to him.

He wraps me in his arms, picks me up, and hugs me tightly.

"Surprise," he says above my ear. Once he's done, he sets me down and pulls me in for a toe-curling kiss. Some passing students whistle, reminding us we aren't alone.

As we pull apart, I say, "I'm definitely not complaining you're here, but why are you?"

Tristan pouts his lip, trying to look like I hurt his feelings. Expecting an answer, I just smirk at him. "After that practice, I just needed to see you and hold you for a bit. Today rocked me to my core, and I know it's meant to. I just needed a Steph pep talk before I return tomorrow for another helping of ass-kicking."

It's hard not to laugh, and I swear I try, but in the end, when he adds a grin to his comments, a laugh escapes from my lips. My hand flies up to my mouth, trying to stifle it, but I just end up laughing into my hand.

"Is getting my ass kicked funny to you?" Him trying the mock anger only makes me laugh harder. Tears are building up in my eyes and my stomach tightens.

"S-s-sorry," I manage to get out.

"And to think I brought you a chocolate dessert. Guess I'll have to eat it since you'd rather laugh than comfort me."

My ears perk up when I hear chocolate. Finally getting my laughter under control, I say, "I'm really sorry for laughing, Tristan. I didn't mean to hurt your feelings. I'm also sorry camp didn't go how you hoped, but I think it's an opportunity."

"An opportunity?" he questions.

Nodding, I explain. "Yes, an opportunity. Playing for the Storm is a childhood dream, and it's within reach. You already made the team, now you just have to work hard and show them you want a spot. If you say you're at the bottom of the bracket, I believe you. Even though it seems unlikely. You are going to have to push yourself harder. Ask your coaches and your trainers what to do to make yourself more of a threat on the ice, not just against your opponents, but for spots on those starting lines. Shake things up in the best way possible."

Tristan leads me over to a bench, and after we sit down, he pulls a slice of chocolate cake and two forks from the bag he's been holding. My mouth waters. "Is it too late for one of these?" he asks as he pulls a large bottle of Frappuccino out.

"Nope, I still have some homework I need to work on tonight."

Sitting back on the bench, cuddled closely together and sharing the deliciously decadent cake, is the perfect way to end the day. "This is divine." I let out a moan.

"Steph," Tristan cautions in a deep growl.

"What?" I ask, unaware of what I've done.

Leaning forward, he nibbles at my lips and then

whispers, "You moaned, and you know what that does to me. Since we're in public, I'm trying to keep things G-rated, even though I'd much rather be inside you."

That sounds amazing. "I'd love to take you up on that, but we have one major roadblock: my roommate. And she's home."

Tristan drops his head and lowers his voice. "That sucks." Then, in an instant, his head whips up. "We still have this weekend, right?" He's filled with so much hope, it makes me smile even more.

Leaning in, I whisper in his ear, "We do. I reserved the entire weekend for all the sexy shenanigans you can dream up." Tristan breaks out into a smile that makes me willing to reconsider the risks associated with park bench sex. But I'm quick to remember that neither one of us needs a public indecency scandal if we're caught.

Instead, Tristan wraps his arm around my shoulders, pulling me in tight. "I'm looking forward to it."

Chapter 4

Tristan

By Friday afternoon, I'm exhausted and achy. Since the season hasn't officially started, Steph plans to come over tonight to stay the weekend. Waiting for her, I realize I'm giddy with excitement. I can't wait to see her. We've been joined at the hip since we started dating our junior year of high school. As things progressed physically, we experienced every first together. Which was a challenge because we always had parents around. Not to say we didn't find time to have sex, but it was often rushed or in my car somewhere off a beaten path. We never could explore. And now that I have my own place, we're both looking forward to the freedom it provides.

* * *

Stephanie

The day has finally arrived. I feel like I've been dreaming of it for years. It will be Tristan's and my first sleepover. When my roommate invited me to the mall earlier this week, I found a special outfit for the evening.

At five sharp, Tristan picks me up from my dorm, and he looks as excited as I feel.

"Hi, babe," he croons, an enormous smile on his face.

"Hi," I answer back.

"You ready for this?" he asks.

I smile widely, then gush, "So ready for an entire weekend alone with you."

Tossing my bag in the back seat, I climb in. Since it's the beginning of the semester, I don't have much homework that I need to finish before classes next week. As I sit in the car on the way to his apartment, my stomach flutters as my excitement builds. It feels like we're playing a version of house. And I can't wait. We make a quick stop to grab dinner before we make it back to his place.

When we arrive, my excitement turns to unease. Tonight feels like it's my first time again. Walking up to the door, my trepidation grows. I know what's going to happen, and because of that, I'm suddenly a nervous wreck. I fidget, feeling awkward and unsure. I tap my foot nervously, needing to rid myself of all the extra energy I feel coursing through my body. I'm sweating like a sinner in church, and I wipe my palms against my jeans.

He unlocks the door and lets me in. "Ladies first," he says. Glancing over at Tristan when he walks by, I notice he's as calm as can be, wearing a cheerful smile on his handsome face. It makes my stomach flip. *Why am I nervous?*

Sensing my nervous energy, Tristan comes closer before he asks, "Babe, what's wrong?"

Shifting in place, I mumble, "I'm nervous."

"Nervous about what?" he questions, concerned.

Dropping my voice to a whisper, I hesitantly answer, "About tonight."

He pulls me in for a hug and kisses my head. "What about tonight?"

Ashamed at what I'm feeling, I step back and look down at my interlocked hands. After a minute of silence, Tristan leans over, kisses my cheek, then asks, "Steph, can you look at me?"

Slowly, I turn my head and there, staring at me, is the man I've loved since I was a teen, and he's wearing the sweetest smile. Tristan is everything, and I can't believe he's mine. Sitting in silence, he lets me collect my chaotic thoughts. "Tristan, this is our first full night together. Aren't you nervous?"

His smile widens, showing his perfectly straight white teeth, and he shakes his head no. "I'm excited, Steph. I've been waiting for so long to fall asleep with you in my arms. To finally make love to you without worrying we'll get caught and grilled by a parent over contraception."

His confession makes my heart race. Everything he's mentioned is true, and I'm definitely looking forward to undisturbed time with him. I'm just nervous about how we'll fill all that time. We're both pretty inexperienced. Veering from inserting slot A into slot B to rock my world is intimidating. The pressure is intense and my insecurities pile up. In weeks, he'll be surrounded by hundreds of women who are more than willing to expose him to all the flavors of the world. And here I am, a vanilla-flavored Pollyanna. My stomach tightens. How do I share those fears without sounding ridiculous? Will he decide after a few months in the league he wants someone who's more than me? You know, in every way. I know the temptation has to be strong when you're never home and opportunistic women are always throwing themselves at you. My feelings sit heavy in my chest, and suddenly tears cover my cheeks. Feeling embarrassed, I swipe at them, hoping to erase the evidence of my insecurity before Tristan notices.

But observant as ever, Tristan catches a tear and he nudges my head up so he can look into my eyes. I sniffle, then wipe at the tears still falling. "Steph, what is really going on?" Grabbing for my purse, I find a tissue to wipe my eyes and blow my nose.

"I'm just worried I'm going to lose you," I confess. Wrapping me in his muscular arms, Tristan kisses my head, then utters reassurances to me.

After I've calmed down some, Tristan pulls back. "Steph, there will only ever be you. I don't want anyone else. You mean everything to me. I'm sorry you're worried about this. I love you so much. What can I do to convince you?" He kisses my knuckles and then looks into my eyes. Still overcome with fears, I remain mute. "Do you need me to show you how much I want you and only you?"

I nod. "Please."

He leads me back to his bedroom. It looks different from when we moved him in. His bed is covered with new bedding. Scents of vanilla waft through the air, and I notice all the candles. He gently lays me down on the bed before he takes his time loving and worshiping every part of me. And it's perfect.

As he cuddles me in his arms that evening, he tells me, "I got something for this weekend." Pushing off his chest, I peer at him. "Over there. It's wrapped on my dresser." When I climb from the bed, I feel his gaze on me, making me feel incredible. Stepping over the pile of clothes he dropped on the floor as he stripped us, I grab the package he mentioned. Crudely wrapped in a hodgepodge of paper, it feels like a book. *Why would he get me a book?*

Flipping it back and forth, looking for clues, I tentatively ask, "What's this?"

He smirks. "Just open it. I think it'll make our weekend even more exciting and fun."

Peeling back the paper, my eyes fall on a black-and-white photo of a couple having sex.

"Oh!" I gasp. His eyes are dancing when I look up at him through my lashes.

Slowly, I flip through the pages of the book, *The Pursuit of Great Sex*. It's filled with a plethora of unfamiliar positions, and instantly I'm intrigued.

"It's like a how-to manual?" I ask, and Tristan eagerly nods. I give him a questioning look and worry flashes across his face.

He rises from the bed and approaches me. "Do you not like it?" I shake my head because that isn't it, but his worry turns to a frown. "I'm sorry. I thought that would be fun to explore together." He reaches for the book, but I hold it tight.

"Tristan, I'm not upset. I was going to ask you which position you want to try first."

"Really?" he barks out in a relieved tone.

Nodding, I smile at him and confess, "Since we're showing off what we brought for our wild weekend, I got something too."

Tugging me to him, I feel his cock harden between us as he growls, "You did?"

I swish my hips, rubbing against him, and kiss his lips. Pulling away, I say, "Give me a sec and I'll show you." Grabbing my bag, I duck into the bathroom to change.

Let's just say my new silk and lace nightie with matching G-string is quite a hit. It doesn't stay on long. But the hungry look in Tristan's eyes makes it worth it.

Chapter 5

Tristan

My first year in the NHL has a steep learning curve. Not only do I spend a huge amount of time reworking my physical training regimen with the training staff, but I also have the team dietician to help me tighten up my eating habits from a teenage boy's to a professional athlete's.

Learning how to rebuff the advances of puck bunnies so I don't come across as an aggressive asshole could be an entire college-level course. They are relentless in their attempts, which gets old really fast. If saying no and storming off makes me an asshole, I'm okay with that. They don't listen, and it doesn't matter if you're single, dating, engaged, or married. Each time they approach me, I easily reject them. No one will ever compare to Steph. She is all I will ever want.

After each game, every one of my teammates gets

offers. It's sickening to watch some guys, knowing they're cheating on their partner back home. But I learned early on not to get involved. I only need to worry about myself. Knowing I have Steph at home makes rejecting the piranhas easier. I'm simply not interested. Most nights I escape without confrontation, but those ladies are aggressive.

When I'm in town, Steph comes to most of the games to cheer me on. It feels incredible to have her in the stands, cheering me on. I can't wait until I can make the name on the back of the jersey she wears permanent. I haven't bought a ring yet, but I know she's my forever. The right time will present itself. Maybe then she'll want to be in the family box. I understand if she doesn't though. Some wives and girlfriends (WAGS) are so over-the-top, that I completely get why she wants to keep her distance.

One of my teammates, Lance, who has been on the team two years longer than me, just got married over the summer. His wife, Becca, is great. She, too, doesn't like the WAGS, and often Steph and Becca watch the games together. Decked out in their tight ripped jeans and Boston Storm jerseys, they holler and cheer with the other die-hard fans. Following the games, they always meet us in the players' tunnel. The hug and kiss I get from Steph lights my body on fire. It's probably all the extra endorphins running through my body. But more than once, I've warned Steph I'm going to sneak her into one of the unused training rooms and have my way with her. Saying things like that with my voice dropped low always makes her squirm. The telltale shivers that break out across her body confirm she's as into the idea as me. Often, she'll whisper back, "Promise?"

My second year in the NHL goes eerily similar to my first. I continue with my strict diet, along with the strength and weight training. By the end of the season, trainers and coaches have commented many times on how I've impressed them, not only with my skills and level of play, but by my unstoppable endurance. When pulled for a line change, unlike many of my teammates, I'm not winded at all.

During the last few months of season play, I move to the starting line with Lance, Cooper, Max, and Fletcher. Doogan, our main goalie, is still killing it as our starter, setting records left and right. Our team does well and makes it all the way to the semi-finals of the Stanley Cup. The only reason we don't go the entire way is that we're a fairly young, inexperienced team who still has some kinks to work out. In our last playoff game, Doogan almost gets a shutout, but our defense became complacent, allowing one too many opportunities past them.

During my second year, I also start getting some sponsorship opportunities, making my days home in

Boston busier than ever. Thankfully, Steph is understanding. The reason I sign on with so many is because I'm saving up for a ring and a bigger place. Plus, I know once we're married, we'll have additional expenses, as Steph is still in school and had talked about graduate school.

While I'm busy with games and sponsorship deals, Steph finds a local non-profit that works with breast cancer survivors and their families. Not only does Steph volunteer to help with activities and fundraising. She's even spearheaded one of their biggest events, a 5K, to raise awareness. The run coincides with a Saturday that I'm in town and without a series. Because of how it unfolded, that day will forever be burned into my memory. It's one of the proudest I've ever been of Steph.

Throughout the day, I meet some incredible people and hear amazing stories from many survivors. I also hear from both the charity's employees, volunteers, and survivors how amazing Steph is. I already know that, but it's fantastic to hear that she's making such a difference with something she truly feels passionate about. It's inspiring to see Steph embrace helping women who are fighting against the same disease that took her mom from her as a teenager.

Steph is in her element as I watch her at the event. She is confident, eloquent, kind, and, above all, loving. The thing I hear repeatedly is that Steph uses her own grief to help build bridges with those who are suffering because of breast cancer.

"Tristan, there you are." Steph tackles me as I make my way onto the park strip as everything is being dismantled after the run.

I pick her up and hug her tight. "Hey, babe. This was incredible. I'm so proud of you."

"Thanks." She squeals before she plants an excited kiss on my lips. Not wanting to let it get out of hand—we're in a public park and some of the people from the non-profit are still milling around—I pull away and set her down.

"What needs to be done before you can get out of here?" I ask.

Pointing over to a nicely arranged stack of boxes, she says, "I need to drop those off at the office and then I'm yours." We load the boxes into my car and deliver them to the employee who's there working, then head to my apartment for the rest of the night. Steph has some papers to finish for next week because finals are approaching, but I convinced her to stay the night so I could give her a massage and work out all those knots she was bound to have after orchestrating the fundraiser.

Chapter 6

Stephanie
May 2007

Watching Tristan's success in the NHL is incredible. He works so hard to move up to the starting line, and he receives many accolades from his coaches and trainers because of his work on and off the ice. When the season ends, and classes are done, Tristan uses his sponsorship money to treat us both to a much-needed weeks' vacation. Neither of us had been there before, so we go with a friend's recommendation of Maui. And it does not disappoint. We stay at a rental in Kihei. From the complex we're in, we can walk to the beach and many local restaurants. On our first night on the island, after grabbing fish tacos from an incredibly busy Mexican café, we walk to the beach and enjoy our first Hawaiian sunset. It's magic.

The next morning, Tristan gets up early and goes for a run on the beach. I sleep in, and it's heavenly.

When I finally wake up, it's to birds chirping outside my window. Stretching my hands over my head, I breathe in the warm air. Tossing off the thin comforter, I step out onto our private lanai and watch as the birds flit around, looking for breakfast. My stomach growls in response, letting me know I'm hungry too. Heading back into our rental, I make sure I shut the screen door so I don't let any uninvited wildlife in. I heard geckos often make it inside people's homes, but they're harmless.

Crossing over into the kitchen, I see the owners left us a basket of Hawaiian goodies: sunscreen, a map of the island, a pineapple, macadamia nuts, Hawaiian coffee, Maui Caramacs, and papaya. The pineapple has a tag on it that says if you can tug a leaf loose, it's ready to be eaten. So, I do just that, and to my surprise, it pulls out easily. Never having cut a pineapple before, I do my best to get all the eyes off the delicious-smelling fruit. Just as I chop the last piece, the door opens, and in comes a sweaty, pierced, naked-chested hunk of a man. Tracing my eyes over all the places my hands and tongue visited the night before, my body buzzes with excitement and anticipation of what could be. Tristan senses the energy in the room and licks his lips. Standing there in a thin tank top and lace panties, I know it's no secret he turns me on.

Shutting the door and moving toward me, Tristan's movements are quick and stealthy, kind of like a jungle cat. When he's inches from me, I reach out, hook my finger into the drawstrings of his shorts, and pull them down. He kicks them off and toes off his running shoes. Then he steps up to me and presses his hard cock into my stomach. Lifting a hand to one of his nipples, I toy with the barbell piercing the nub.

"Steph," he says on a groan.

Shortly after we got to Boston, we began exploring our sexuality together. During that time, we discussed everything we were interested in; from types of sex, the use of toys or aides in the bedroom, and personal tastes or desires. Tristan had been surprised that I'd always found pierced nipples on a well-sculpted chest a major turn-on. So, for my birthday, he'd gotten them both pierced with silver barbells. But he soon learned after they'd healed, it wasn't just enjoyable for me. Having them sucked and tugged a bit became something he craved. The moans I could elicit from him just from nipple play alone was empowering.

He lifts me up, and I wrap my legs around his trim waist and rub my lace-covered center up and down his cock, earning a deep, sexy growl that only encourages me more. Stalking to the bedroom, Tristan tosses me on the bed. Giggling, I push myself back toward the pillows. My wild, dirty-blond hair covers my face and I sweep it out of the way at the same time Tristan tugs my panties down my legs. With the flick of a wrist, the small damp scrap of fabric flies over his shoulder and he smirks. Desperate for him, I open my legs wide. He crawls onto the bed and moves toward me. When he drags the head of his cock through my already damp folds, I release a breathy noise that is supposed to sound like a please, but comes out more like a whimper.

Needing to move things along, I lick the palm of my hand, which tastes amazing from the pineapple I just ate. Lowering my hand, I wrap my fingers around his throbbing, hard-as-steel cock. Using the moisture from my saliva, I stroke my hand up and down him, jerking him off. "So fucking good." Tristan groans as I pump him. His hips thrust forward, chasing the feeling I'm pulling from him.

"Steph, I need to be inside you now." I nod, then line us up. Placing my hands on his hips, I encourage him to thrust forward. When he finally does, he bottoms out entirely. My body rewards him with a panting moan.

"That feels so good. Please don't stop."

Gritting his teeth above me, he thrusts his hips wildly. Wanting to control the direction of his thrusts, I dig my fingernails into the flesh above his ass cheeks and pull him into me. His punishing pace and heady thrusts drive me higher and higher. "Almost there. Don't stop," I whine, desperate for the amazing release I know is coming. After a few more thrusts, Tristan pushes me into ecstasy. He follows closely behind me with a roar that sends goose bumps across my heated body.

Over the years, we've learned everything about

each other. We figured out what works and what doesn't. Tristan knows my likes and dislikes, and I hold the same knowledge about him. Our sex life is always good. It's the other parts that sometimes struggled. Living in the same city but separately is difficult. His travel schedule means he's gone a lot. And my school responsibilities make getting together when he is in town extra stressful for me. I always have to make sure assignments, projects, and tests are finished or mostly done before he's back in town. I get a set amount of time because of practices, meetings, and media obligations. He also landed a few great sponsors that demand time when he's home. Occasionally, I have my feelings hurt because I don't feel like a priority. During these times, I question if it's worth it. But when it comes down to it, I love Tristan, and I want to be with him forever. We just have to figure out how to balance it all. Being here in Maui helps with that. I have his undivided attention for seven days, and it is magical.

On the last day of our Hawaiian getaway, I'm like a grumpy cat. I do a lot of frowning and complaining. I don't want to go back to Boston and deal with all our commitments. Over the years, it's gotten worse. I'm ready to be with him one hundred percent of the time. But with one more year of school for me and an undetermined number of years left in the league for him, things are uncertain. Understanding that what I want isn't feasible doesn't deter me from hoping.

Another issue is the constant back and forth from

his place to mine. It's getting old, but we haven't had a conversation about what comes next. My father isn't too traditional, but Tristan's parents are adamant that we not live together until we're married. I guess what they don't know won't kill them, because I practically live with him now... well, when he's in town, that is. If it were up to me, we'd be married and living together already, but I don't know if Tristan is thinking the same. So, out of respect for our parents, we maintain separate living spaces, which isn't too hard because I'm still in school, and room and board are part of my tuition. With graduation looming, I know I'll either have to find an apartment that I'd never be at, or we could get married, which we've talked about doing for years.

Chapter 7

Tristan

Waiting weeks to ask Steph to be my wife almost kills me. In fact, as soon as I had the ring, I wanted to propose. But I want to make it special, and we already planned our Maui trip. The timing is perfect. I'm sure I can make something special for her.

We've been so busy running around the island and enjoying ourselves. The night before we leave, while I'm repacking my bag, I come across the ring box I'd carefully hidden until my big surprise proposal. *Fuck. How had I forgotten about it? What am I going to do now? Should I wait until we're back in Boston? No.* The thought of that doesn't sit right. After all, we're on a tropical vacation. It's the ideal backdrop. Kicking myself mentally, I can't believe I blew this. Some might say I forgot, but that isn't quite accurate. In my mind, Steph is already mine. And I'm hers. The act of getting married is just making it official in the world's eyes.

That night, as I lie in bed, listening to the waves crash on the beach, I plan the proposal. It all starts with one particular section of beach that we love. Each night before sunset, we visited this spot. On the second night, sitting on the fallen Kiawe tree, I pronounced it our spot. Wrapped around each other, we'd watch as the sun slowly dipped beneath the horizon. We marveled at the magnificent colors the sky displayed. Every night was different, yet still breathtaking.

And while she slumbers next to me, my plan comes to light. That tree, that spot, will be the perfect place to ask for her forever.

* * *

The next morning, I wake up before the sun rises. Seeing that it's still so early, I opt for a run through Kihei while Steph sleeps. I plan to stop by the café we discovered earlier in the week and grab something for my sleeping beauty.

As I traverse the streets of Kihei, the sun breaks over the horizon. Soon birds become busy with their morning activities and the air is full of happy chirping. Running past the yellow, pink, and red hibiscus while the waves crash on the beach across the road is something I'll miss when we return to Boston. Trading tropical paradise for a cold, sterile gym at the Storm complex sounds less than appealing. But Hawaii doesn't have a professional hockey team, and since I'm still a newbie, transferring off the team would be a huge mistake. To rectify this, I vow to bring Steph back here. And often.

Once I finish my run, I stop and grab breakfast. Banana and macadamia nut French toast for her and a breakfast burrito for me. The unit is quiet when I enter it, but there on the couch Steph sits curled up, absorbed in a book. My guess is it's a romance, as that's a particular favorite of hers. Hell, I'm not complaining because often it gave her some pretty wild ideas for the bedroom. And all but a few of them I'd totally been on board with. The idea of using hot wax makes me twitch, and I'm not really comfortable with devices for my cock. That'd be a hell no to a cock ring or chastity cage. Steph had once read a book where the cage was used. Not only did it sound like a medieval torture device when she read some of the book to me, but just the thought of it unearthed terrifying fears within me. What if it got stuck and you couldn't remove it? Can you imagine that ER visit? *No, thank you.* That is definitely not how I want to make the papers.

Watching her, with her completely oblivious, I notice the sultry look on her face. And that she's holding her breath. *I bet she's reading a steamy part.* Steph finally releases her breath, bites her lower lip, and touches her chest. Her cheeks flush with an adorable pink hue.

I can't help but be amused as I continue to watch her. When she switches her position, her eyes land on me and she gives me a sexy smirk. *Am I about to get lucky?* Thank you romance authors for your ability to inspire my woman with your words. Looking at her, it's hard to miss the fire behind her mocha eyes. And when she licks her pink lips, I do the same. She sets her book down and slowly walks to me. With each step, I feel more blood rush to my groin. When she reaches me, she takes the bag from my hands and sets it on the counter. Then she trails her fingertips down my sweat-soaked t-shirt. When she lowers herself in front of me, time stops. As Steph is pulling my shorts and boxers down my legs, a gust of wind comes through the screen door. Although it isn't strong, it's enough to remind me I'm sweaty from my run.

Steph leans in and is about to wrap her luscious lips around my cock when I pull back. Enough blood is still in my brain screaming that I need to shower before my woman tastes any part of me. "Babe. Stop," I rasp. Her eyes flick up at me, questioning. "I need a shower first," I tell her as I'm pulling her up. Kissing her, I whisper against her lips, "Want to join me?"

Not even giving her time to answer, I kick off my shoes and strip off my clothes before throwing her over my shoulder. Steph slaps my butt with her hand and giggles, and the cheerful sounds bounce off the walls of the unit, making me smile.

Following a quick rinse, I back Steph up to the

tiled wall. She's close enough that the warm spray can reach her, but it isn't close enough to be problematic to my plans. While I kiss her, I trail my hands up and down her curvy body, enjoying each dip and rise. Separating our bodies slightly, I move my hands up to her breasts and caress them. Circling her nipples, I pluck and pinch them until she pulls back and lets out a loud gasp. "More, Tristan. Please." The sound of her begging registers in my balls, forcing them to grow tight. *Not yet.*

Knowing I need to give myself a slight reprieve before I blow my load, I step back and look at her. "You are beautiful. I love you." Her eyes are soft, reflecting the love I feel. She pulls me into a soft, gentle kiss that means everything to me. She is everything to me. Despite all the time I have to be on the road, away from her, I know she is my home and someone I want forever. Just the thought of that reminds me of the ring I have in my bag and the proposal I've planned.

Suddenly filled with excitement, I move our kiss into the risqué, nipping at her lips. Leaning down, I lift her to my waist, wrapping her sinfully sexy legs around my waist. Sliding her back an inch, I line us up and thrust into her, placing one palm on the wall to steady us before I become a savage. Her slick, wet channel grabs and squeezes me tightly, driving my desire for her to new heights.

I pump my hips, thrusting in and out of her like a piston running at full steam. I feel a familiar tingle run down my spine, and I know I only have moments to make her come first. I slip the hand that isn't supporting us to her clit and make quick circular motions, every so often flicking and tugging her pulsating nub. Steph's body gyrates against mine as she chases her own high. When she finally explodes, the stranglehold she has on my cock makes me see stars. Then my own cataclysmic orgasm rips through me. When I can finally feel my body again, my knees are weak, and I press my body into her, stabilizing us. Our labored breathing syncs as we savor the sated feeling that's overtaken our bodies.

Hours later, when we were all checked out of our unit, we find our way to our favorite stretch of beach for a walk. Hand in hand, we talk about what we enjoyed the most on our first trip to the islands. We make vows that we'll visit again soon.

When we come upon the fallen Kiawe tree, Steph climbs on it and takes a seat. As her sun-kissed legs hang down, I walk around the tree, meeting her on the other side. She gives me a curious look as I nudge my way between her legs. Running my hands up and down her smooth, tan legs has a calming effect on me. Looking at her, I know this is the right moment. With her blond hair blowing in the warm breeze, and the air smelling like plumeria and sea salt, it's perfect. I lean in and place a tender kiss on her lips. She sighs. More than ready, I break the kiss and step back. Then I drop to one knee. Realization is instant. Steph's eyes bulge and her hand flies to her mouth. *I surprised her.* I imagine everyone will think I should have waited until she was done with school, but I'm impatient. When she says yes, I can finally make her mine. Mrs. Stephanie Murphy. *Yes, that sounds perfect.*

"Steph. I love you. I knew there was something special about you the moment I met you. I've known for years you are the woman I'm meant to spend my life with. You are all that I'll ever want. I waited until I was sure I could provide the life you deserve to ask you the most important question of my life. Babe, will you marry me?"

It's short, sweet, and to the point. Steph seems stunned, but I catch the nodding of her head, so I'm assuming that's a yes. Standing up, I retrieve the solitaire ring from my pocket. It's simple and small. And I plan to upgrade it once I'm making more money. But I know Steph won't care because all that matters is the commitment were making.

Steph gasps, then says, "Tristan, it's gorgeous." Sliding the white gold solitaire onto her finger feels surreal. Tears fill her eyes and the most beautiful smile graces her lips. *How did I ever get this lucky?* Wiping at her eyes, she laughs. "Why am I crying?"

Pulling her into a hug, I laugh with her. This is the beginning of our forever. Finding each other so young will allow us to grow up and old together. It is a future that I look forward to. Climbing up onto the Kiawe branch with Steph, I wrap her in my arms and we watch families spending the day at the beach. It's impossible not to wonder how long it'll be before we'll be back, and with a family of our own. I'm not in any rush to add kids to our dynamic, but I've always assumed we'd have some. Steph and I have talked a little about it, and we both decided that it's something to consider much later in life.

That night, before we board our flight back home, we call our parents and share the joyful news of our engagement. Everyone is excited, and we couldn't be happier.

Chapter 8

Stephanie

Coming home from Maui has been depressing. Immediately, we are sucked back into all the stressors of daily life, and before I know it, I'm completely overwhelmed. Tristan is constantly at the gym or training to make sure he's in shape for the season. At the end of the school year, I secured a summer job that allows me to live on campus during the break. When I'm not working, I'm inundated with everything wedding related. Like many women, I've dreamed of my wedding since I was a little girl. Tristan and I agree that we'll wait to tie the knot until after I graduate in the spring.

For next semester, I've been lucky to score one class with my roommate, Emily. We aren't the same major, but we've both put off a science credit. When it was time to register last spring, we both selected earth science, hoping we might end up together. I also scored a few classes with Erika. She's also an accounting major trying to fast track her degree. We meet for coffee every week to keep each other accountable. Our advisor introduced us our freshman year, and through the years, we've formed a friendship of sorts. We don't go do things on the weekend, like Emily and I do, but she's a good sounding board for school and talking about future career endeavors.

On top of all that, I make a visit or two to the school's registrar to make sure I'm still on track to graduate early. With summer fading away, I know next year will look remarkably different. Tristan and I will be married and finally living together.

Hopefully, the internship I've secured for graduation requirements will give me great experience and help me find a job. For it, I'll be shadowing a CEO of a non-profit. Their mission is to ensure everyone in the community has access to basic medical care. As part of my internship, I'll help coordinate a multifaceted health event. The event will assist with dental checks, vision checks, and basic medical screening. I'm really looking forward to it, even though it's daunting.

When the summer ends, so does my stay in the dorm. Before the spring semester ends, my roommate and friend, Emily, who is an English major, suggests we live in an apartment near campus. We move in the weekend before classes begin. As I unpack my various boxes, my phone rings. I answer without looking. "Hello."

"Hey, babe," Tristan rasps out. *He sounds exhausted.* Despite that, my heart still flutters. *I miss him.* Because of our hectic schedules, I haven't seen him much lately.

"Workout done?"

He laughs. "First one, yeah, but I'm starving and wondering if you want to grab lunch before I have to meet the guys for the next punishing session."

My stomach growls loudly and Tristan laughs. Looking around the room, I see that I'm nearly done. "I'd love to meet you. Where and when?"

"Great. I'm going to hop in the shower and then head your way. Meet you at that deli close to your dorm in half an hour?"

That'll work perfectly. I can finish unpacking before I have to leave. "You got it. See you soon. Love you."

"Love you too, Steph."

The final unboxing goes faster than I thought, and I break down my boxes to put in storage before I have to leave. It's a nice day and I walk over to Deli Co., a cozy family-run deli that is amazing.

While waiting for Tristan to arrive, I pull my class schedule from my purse and study it. I don't have a heavy load this semester, but I've heard that the course work demands a lot of your time. Worries and fears plague my mind. *How am I going to manage it all?*

Lost in thought, the bell above the door chimes and I look up to see Tristan approaching. He's wearing a million-dollar smile, even though I know his entire body hurts. The scent of Bengay permeates the surrounding air, and I smirk.

"Sore?" I ask.

He smirks. "Just a little."

We order our sandwiches and take them back to a semi-private table.

"How did moving and unpacking go? Was Emily already moved in? How's the apartment? Is your room bigger than the dorm rooms?" He fires questions at me before taking his first bite.

Shrugging, I reply, "It went fine. I'm more than ready to get married and live with you."

Tristan smiles. "You and me both, babe."

* * *

By the time November hits, I'm completely exhausted. Surrounded by books, I continue working on the paper that is due for my English Lit class. After three hours of sitting in this chair, I need to get up and move.

"Ahh." I moan as I stretch my arms above my head. When I stand up to grab a snack, I notice my foot has gone numb. "Oww," I whine as I put weight on the tingly body part. After a quick pee break, I settle back in for another few hours of work.

The phone rings.

Looking at the clock, I see it's ten at night. *Who is calling me?* Picking up my phone, I see it's Tristan.

He's on the road. He left this morning for an away series.

Surprised, I answer, "Hello."

"Hey, Steph. How are you?" There's noise in the background and I wonder where he is. Someone near him shouts, "Murphy, you headed to the bar?" Tristan apologizes and answers back, "Nope. I'm on the phone with my girl." One of his teammates makes a dramatic sigh, and I laugh.

Once the noise disappears, Tristan speaks again. "Sorry, Steph. I was just walking into the hotel after a team dinner."

"It's okay. It provided some entertainment for my evening," I quasi-joke.

He groans. "Not a good night?"

Looking around my desk at all the opened books and knowing I still have hours to put in before I finish my paper, I grumble, "I am so ready to be done with college. This paper I'm working on is the worst. I'm never going to use this stuff in the real world, so why do I have to prove I have a working knowledge of it?"

"I wish I had the answer for you, but I don't. What I know is that you are so close to finishing, and I am so proud of you. It won't be long. After spring semester, you'll have your diploma."

Letting out a deep breath while I rub my temple, I say, "Thank goodness. I'm not sure I'd make it much longer."

"Well, I don't want to take up your productive evening, but I wanted to tell you I love you."

"I love you too, Tristan," I gush. "Thanks for calling. I don't know how you knew, but I needed to hear your voice."

After we hang up, I put in another few hours before throwing in the towel. Tomorrow is a relaxing day. I only have my internship in the afternoon, so I can sleep in and do my last read through before I turn in the assignment. *Small miracles.*

It seems like the rest of fall semester is monopolized by my internship and finishing papers or projects. I have time for nothing else. Relief from my constant guilt at being unavailable or pulled in too many directions only comes on the weekends when Tristan is on the road. At first, he tries to be understanding and will grab dinner for us, even offering to rub my shoulders as I type papers on my laptop. But that only lasts so long. Instead of coming over for the entire weekend and being completely immersed in him like previously, I now struggle with balancing it all. It feels like all I do is run back and forth between his apartment and campus.

It doesn't take long for Tristan to become resentful of my lack of attention, which leads us to fight. We've gotten into a pattern. Every time he returns home, I get agitated and stressed out. I dread the self-imposed pressure I always feel about getting everything done so I can be available all the time. I know that sounds terrible, but I'm exhausted from juggling everything.

A few weeks before winter break, he starts sending me texts, reminding me he's going to be in town. I'm sure he thinks those "helpful reminders" are just that, but to me, they aren't. Instead, they put me on edge. I never say much about all the stress I'm under, because I'm not sure Tristan will take me seriously. So, I never give him the chance to prove me wrong.

The Thursday before finals week, I get one of his "helpful reminder" and it sends me over the edge. I'm already stressed from finals, and I haven't been feeling well. I feel like I'm neglecting my internship because I called off the last week to study. This semester is kicking my butt. I've done my best to stay ahead of assignments, but sometimes when working in a group, I just can't manage that. Reading Tristan's text, chills cover my body and my stomach cramps. *How would his expectation of spending time with me work with my study needs?*

TRISTAN

Are you coming over this weekend? You know I'm in town.

ME

Yes, I'll be there. I have a group project on Sunday that I have to work on, so I'll leave after breakfast.

TRISTAN

So, does that mean you're coming to my game Saturday night? We could go out afterward.

That would be nice, but I can't.

ME

Yes. I was planning to go to your
game if you can get a ticket. But I
can't go out afterward. I need to finish
a paper on Saturday night that's due
Monday.

TRISTAN

Can't you do that Friday since you
already told me you couldn't make
that game because of your internship
and study group?

ME

I plan to go to the library Friday after
my internship. I will meet with my
study group and then start my paper
for the group project. Likely, I'll have
to finish it Saturday night after your
game because I'm meeting the group
Sunday.

TRISTAN

Maybe you should just stay home this
weekend and I'll see you next time
I'm in town.

Grinding my teeth together, I type my response,
knowing it'll probably cause a fight.

ME

That isn't fair. I have a lot on my plate.
I'm trying to balance my internship
requirements, earn good grades in my
classes so I can graduate, and plan a
wedding. I'm overwhelmed.

Tristan doesn't respond.

Five minutes later, there's still no answer. My heart clenches and my stomach drops. *Really? He's ignoring me?* All he ever has to worry about is chasing a stupid puck around the ice. He doesn't know what it's like in the real world. He wouldn't survive it. I balance it all so that he never has to worry if I'm available for him while he's in town. While he's gone, I stay up later, pass on things with friends, and stress myself out just so that he doesn't have to be inconvenienced by my trying to graduate a year fucking early. I wish, just once, he'd acknowledge everything I do to make his visits home as relaxing as possible. Because I'm sure if I didn't, he wouldn't know what to do and we'd end up constantly bickering. What a childish, selfish asshole.

> **ME**
>
> Tristan, are you there?

Again, no answer.

Screw him.

A half an hour passes and I still don't hear from Tristan. Wiping fresh tears from my cheeks, I head toward the library to meet my group for a project we've been working on for weeks. The final project is due next week, and we're doing most of it tonight and putting on the final touches on Sunday. Our entire group is anxious about the assignment, as it's forty percent of our semester grade. Since we're all seniors and this class is required to graduate, we need to do well on it. But instead of being able to focus on that, anxiety plagues my mind about what's going on between me and Tristan.

As I walk across campus, I notice it's colder tonight than it's been in weeks, and it seems to pass straight through my black pea coat, chilling me to the bone. My teeth chatter and I stuff my hands into my pockets, wishing I'd made better clothing choices this morning. Instead, I'm wearing a long wrap dress that covers most of me but isn't doing anything to fight off the winter wind. "Man, it's cold out," I mumble to myself just as I hit a piece of icy sidewalk. Hoping to remain upright, I throw my arms out as a squeak falls from my chapped lips. Still standing, my heart thunders in my chest. *That was close.*

"Are you okay?" a deep voice questions. Carefully turning around, I see it's Jake from my study group, and I breathe a sigh of relief.

"Yeah, I'm fine. My mind was elsewhere, and I didn't see that icy patch," I admit.

Jake steps up beside me. "I'll walk next to you in case there are other slippery spots. That way you can grab on to me instead of falling."

"That's really nice of you, Jake. Thank you."

He smiles. "It's no problem." Another classmate and friend, Erika, joins us and we brave the slippery sidewalk on our way to the library.

"I should have worn my skates today." She laughs

and then turns to me. "Hey, Steph. Are you a good skater?"

Shrugging my shoulders, I answer, "I'm decent. Why... are we going to test out your theory tomorrow?"

She sticks her tongue out at me. "No. Considering who your fiancé is, I just wondered."

"I can hold my own, but Tristan is definitely better than me."

Jake stops. "Wait. Your fiancé is who, exactly?"

Quietly, I admit, "Tristan Murphy."

His mouth falls open, and he stops walking. "Wait, you're getting married to one of the best players on the Boston Storm? How did I not know that?"

I laugh. "It's okay, Jake. Most people don't know because I don't scream it from the rooftops. Tristan and I have been together for years, and we're pretty private."

"Ummm. It's pretty cold out here. Can we keep moving?" Erika begs.

"Definitely. Let's go."

Our study group is incredibly productive, but we still need to meet on Sunday as planned to finish things up. After everyone leaves, I settle in to start on my final paper for my business ethics class. I'm making good progress on it until I hear the familiar chime that it's closing time. Cleaning up my notes and laptop, I shove them back into my bag. My hand skims across my phone and I pull it out, wondering if Tristan ever replied. He didn't, and my heart sinks. An eerie feeling washes over me as I pull on my coat. Tugging the waist-belt tight, I notice I'm still chilled.

Wishing I had a car, I do my best to power walk across campus. I'm almost to my dorm when I again slip on an icy patch I missed. My stomach rises, then falls like it's on a roller coaster, and I do my best to brace for impact. I fall but am lucky I land more on the frosted grass than the sidewalk. *Why am I so distracted?*

"Tristan," I say to myself as I get up off the cold, slippery sidewalk. Why is this interaction with him troubling me so much? *Because he's never done this before.* He ghosted me when he wasn't getting his way. As far as I'm concerned, it's immature, but that doesn't make it hurt any less. I'm sad, frustrated, and angry. I bend over backward to make myself as available as I can, and he can't be sympathetic to finals?

As I enter my door, I grumble to myself, "I don't understand." My meeting with other groups while he's in town hasn't bothered him before. So why is it now? Usually, I try to schedule it for a time when he's going to be busy, so it doesn't take away from us. But this weekend, it couldn't be helped. And instead of being understanding, he turns into a toddler throwing a tantrum. Pushing into my room, I tell myself, "Maybe I don't need to go see him this weekend." He did kind of dis-invite me anyway. It would give him a taste of his own medicine. See if he likes it. Am I bitter? Yes. Yes, I am.

Chapter 9

Tristan

"Yo, Tristan. Keep your head up," Jamey hollers at me as we skate onto the ice for warmups. Clint Jackson, also known as Jamey, is the captain of the Boston Storm and the biggest encourager we have in our organization. It's no surprise they selected him for the captain. He's not only an amazing hockey player, but he spouts wisdom just about every time he opens his mouth. Usually, I appreciate it. Today, I want to get out of earshot of whatever happiness he's peddling. Jamey must have some magical homing beacon alerting him to any teammates with a shit attitude, because today that motherfucker is focused on me. And he isn't wrong. My mood is shit.

After my tense texts with Stephanie on Thursday, I haven't talked to her. Is my behavior childish? Yes. Do I care? I'm struggling to. I know I've hurt her, but everything that I thought was so sure is now in question, and I don't know how to handle that. I love her and I don't want to be a selfish jerk, but I've been focused on my dreams for so long, sometimes I find it difficult to consider others. And I understand my response was crappy, but I'm worried I'll only make it worse if I try to apologize.

As I sit and stew over the right thing to do, it hits me. This was our first real disagreement, and I'm having a hard time getting over it. Without a doubt, though, I miss her. She's my person, and instead of having a grown-up conversation about prioritizing our relationship, I'm doing the opposite. I'm childishly ignoring her, wanting her to be the bigger person. I'm scared and I feel like shit. In fact, this whole situation has screwed with my head. All weekend, my ability to play hockey was laughable. Basically, it's a steaming pile of garbage. The longer our silence stretches out, the worse I feel, but no matter what, I can't make myself take the first step. Being stubborn is a trait we both have.

The part that makes me the most frustrated is her implied accusation that I don't appreciate how overwhelmed she is. I know she's busy and has a lot on her shoulders, but we don't get that much time together, and when I'm in town, I want to enjoy the time we have. And yes, I understand that our time still has to be scheduled around my hockey commitments. If I could just ditch practice, I would. But I can't. That's not how it works in the big leagues. It's tough because I have no wiggle room. This is my job and there's nothing I can do about it. This is my foreseeable future: hockey and Steph. Or at least that's what I want it to be.

During a water break, Jamey skates toward me. *Here we go.* Trying my best to hold in any muttered curses, I mentally prepare myself for whatever bullshit he'll be preaching.

"Tristan, you okay?" he asks while removing his helmet.

"Sure, Jamey, why do you ask?" I answer, hoping he'll leave it at that.

He pulls his hand through his sweat-soaked hair, pauses, then clears his throat. "Can I be honest with you?" *Why does he sound unsure?*

This conversation has already veered into the unknown. Jamey doesn't get emotional when he's giving advice. He is more to the point, like a day-of-the-week advice calendar. "Sure," I hesitantly answer.

"You have more talent in your pinkie than half these guys here. Hell, half the league. But you've been distracted since this weekend. And your game has suffered. What's going on?" *Shit. One terrible weekend and I'm already getting dragged over the coals. Can't a guy have an off day or three?*

"Fuck. I was hoping it wasn't that noticeable. I had a fight with my fiancée and it's messing with my brain."

Jamey sets his gloved hand on my shoulder. "I'm sorry, man. That's tough. My advice is to talk to her.

The longer you go without working it out, the worse it'll be for you both, and it will continue to affect your game."

Dropping my head to my chest, I mumble, "I know."

"If you need anything, you let me know. I'm great at the beer and pool distraction." He smiles wide and I match it.

"Thanks, man. I really appreciate it."

For the rest of practice, I force myself to stay present. Once I'm done with my post-practice workout and shower, I'm going to grab lunch and head over to Steph's. Hopefully, she'll talk to me. We need to work through this. I need my girl back.

I don't know how she managed it, but Steph only has two classes on Monday and they are both early in the morning. By lunchtime she's back in her on-campus apartment she shares with Emily.

After pressing the doorbell, I wait a few seconds.

Steph answers the door, shocked to see me. Her face scrunches up as an "oh" falls from her lips. It's then that I notice her bloodshot eyes and tear-stained cheeks. *Did I make a mistake in coming? Am I making things worse by coming here?* Hurting her is the last thing I want to do, but I need to make things better. She means everything to me.

"I brought lunch and an apology," I explain while holding out the bag with the still-warm Italian sandwiches I grabbed on my way over.

Stepping to the side to let me in, she mumbles, "Okay."

As if we're strangers, an uncomfortable silence surrounds us, until I ask, "Am I interrupting anything?"

Shaking her head no, I see the last few days have been hard on her. The pale skin and sunken eyes confirm it, and I feel terrible knowing that she's struggled too. Her normally radiant eyes look dull and distant. Her smile's forced and pained. The sing-songy voice I love so much is hesitant and strained. My stomach breaks the awkward silence by growling loudly. Steph laughs, the sound chasing away the chill between us.

"You must be hungry," she says. "Didn't you just have practice?"

Holding up the bag in my hands, I answer, "Yes, we did, and yes, I am famished. And I took a chance and brought you something too." Setting the food on the table, the aromas of Italian spices and freshly baked bread waft out of the bag.

"Give me a second. I need to go turn off my laptop. I was working on a project."

Sitting at the table, waiting, I'm a mix of emotions. *How is this conversation going to go?*

Chapter 10

Stephanie

When my doorbell rang, it surprised me. I wasn't expecting anyone, especially since Tristan and I still weren't talking. But there he stood, looking as horrible as I felt, armed with lunch and the promise of an apology. What I want more than an apology, though, is a conversation. If we don't talk about what caused our argument, we'll just keep repeating it.

After lunch, my first actual meal in days, we settle on the sofa. Tristan notices I'm seated on the other side and frowns. "Steph, why are you all the way over there?"

"Because this is our first big fight and I know we need to talk it through, and that won't be so easy if you're getting handsy."

He grins, but when he notices I'm serious, his head drops and he quietly agrees.

Trying to remain calm, I say, "Tristan, these last few days have been absolutely horrible. When you stopped talking to me Thursday, I knew you were upset with me, but you left me in limbo. I didn't know what to do or think. Were we over? Would you finally reach out?"

Tristan's head whips up, his eyes cloudy, and he scoots closer to me, grabbing for a hand. "Steph, I am so sorry. I was really upset with you. It felt like you were putting your schooling before me. I'm only in town so often and I didn't understand why you didn't want to spend time with me."

Reaching out and grabbing his other hand, I squeeze it. "I always want to spend time with you, but I can't ignore my school requirements. I'm graduating in May and these are my last classes. I need to do well and I need you to support me and not give me a hard time for choosing to make that a priority. I've never guilted you into skipping practice or not going on a road trip to spend time with me, have I?"

"No. But that's my job. I'd get in trouble with the team if I did that," he defends.

"And school is mine. If I don't do the homework, projects, etc., I could fail my classes and not graduate," I shoot back.

Tristan flops back on the couch, the realization of what I've said finally registering. "I'm sorry. I get it, I do. I just miss you, and it felt like we weren't going to spend any time together and I got angry over that."

Crawling across the couch, I climb into his lap and pull his lips to mine. After I give him a soft kiss, I pull back and say, "I miss you too, and I'd much rather be spending time with you than doing homework. But the end is in sight."

Tristan wraps his arms around me and holds me tight to his chest. "I love you, Steph. I'm sorry I was a childish asshole."

Making sure I make eye contact, I remind him, "No relationship is perfect. All couples fight. It's how we resolve them that speaks volumes. In the future, can you promise me you'll tell me what you're thinking?"

Placing his lips on mine, he mutters, "I promise." Then he kisses me like it's been months since we've seen each other.

"Can we make up now? I heard make-up sex is the best," he asks while waggling his eyebrows and squeezing my sides.

Still cuddled into his chest, I tell him, "I'd like that. And, Tristan?"

"Yeah?"

"Thanks for coming over and making the first step. I love you."

Without another word, he stands up, cradling me in his arms, and heads off to my bedroom. Kicking the door closed, he gasps at my bed, and I laugh. It's covered in school work. "You weren't kidding," he mumbles.

"Give me a second to clean it up before..." I say.

"Before I dirty you up, right?" His deep, husky laugh makes my body hum. I gather all my things, putting them away, before Tristan tosses me on the bed. A giggle escapes and a huge smile appears across his handsome face.

"Are you going to strip for me?" I ask.

Tristan reaches over his head and pulls his shirt off, leaving him in low-hanging worn jeans that reveal the treasure trail that I love to trace with my tongue. "No, I'm going to strip you and show you how much I've missed you first." My heartbeat soars and my thighs squeeze together. "Are you wet for me?" His growled question renders me mute.

When I nod, his eyes shine with excitement. Grabbing my leg, he pulls me toward the edge of the bed. He runs his hands up my legs until he reaches my thighs. He squeezes them before trailing his fingers over to my zipper. "What do we have here?"

I squirm in place as he opens my jeans. In seconds, he has them peeled off. "Please," I moan when his hand returns to my center. Skimming his knuckles against my folds through my satin panties almost propels me off the bed. It's a delicious mixture of heat and friction, and it's addictive. "More, please."

Tristan leans forward and nuzzles his nose against my fabric covered pussy. "You smell just like home." Grabbing my panties, he tugs them down. "Now, what do you taste like?" Shivers spread across my entire body as his hot breath hits my damp flesh.

Spreading me open with his hand, he licks me from back to front.

"Ahhh. That feels so good."

He continues on with his languid licks, focusing on my clit. Running his teeth over my nub before sucking it into his mouth feels divine. When he slides two fingers home, I tighten around them. "Damn, Steph." My body lubricates them as he continues to thrust them into me. I can feel my orgasm brewing as he curls his fingers and brushes against my G-spot.

"Right there, Tristan," I pant as my legs shake. He continues to lick and suck at my center. My back arches and my eyes squeeze closed as my orgasm tears through me. Tristan gently laps up the evidence of my pleasure as I ride the high he just gave me. Once my body is sated and has stopped buzzing, I open my eyes, and there Tristan sits between my legs. His lips are wet and he's wearing a look of adoration.

I've always wondered about something. "What do I taste like?" I ask.

"You taste like mine," he declares before he stands up, strips off the rest of his clothes, and climbs onto the bed. His cock hangs heavily between his legs, and I lick my lips and reach for it. I can't decide what I want more: to suck him or to have him inside me. He shakes his head, understanding my dilemma. "I need to be in you right now." Excitedly, I scoot up the bed and spread my legs. "Slow down, Steph. Let's get you naked."

Slowly, he drags my shirt off, and I'm left in just a lace bra. Tristan growls, "You are so fucking sexy." Then he places his mouth over my nipple and gives it a nibble, which makes me squeal. Reaching behind me, I undo the clasp of my bra and pull it free to give him full access. Kneeling between my legs, he palms my breasts and gives them a tug and twist before he sucks on them individually. It's insane. I just orgasmed and I can already feel another one building.

"Tristan," I moan.

Lifting his eyes to mine, I know he can see my desperation. Lining himself up with me, he thrusts his cock in deep, bottoming out completely. We both groan.

He stills, wanting to give me a moment to adjust, but I shimmy my hips, trying to encourage him to move.

"Steph," he growls as he pushes my hips down, limiting my movement. "So tight. You've got my cock hugged tight and I'm not ready to move yet. You feel so amazing."

"Please," I beg. And that's all the encouragement he needs before he rolls his hips, pulling himself almost completely out before he drives forward. I raise my legs to wrap around his waist and he speeds up his thrusting. I match him, and in minutes we're both panting. "Right there," I demand as I snap my hips, chasing my high.

Tristan leans his head down and sucks on my

breast, adding a nip. "Ahh!" I shout. My muscles squeeze tight and Tristan roars above me. He collapses on top of me in a sweaty heap. After he catches his breath, he confesses, "Shit, Steph. I've never come that hard before."

"Guess what they say about make-up sex is right." I giggle.

"Damn right!" he confirms. He kisses my lips again and then my nose before he says, "Baby, in all honesty, that was amazing, but having you not mad at me is a thousand times better. I love you."

"Love you too," I whisper, my eyes getting heavy. Tristan laughs before he climbs over me and pulls me in to be his little spoon.

Relieved that we aren't fighting anymore, I realize how exhausted I am. With him snuggled up behind me, I pass out.

Chapter 11

Tristan

After our fight in November, I try to be more aware of all the things Steph has pulling her in so many directions. During Christmas break, she travels home to see her dad and brother while I remain in Boston. As soon as I finish my games for the year, I head home to Concord too. Arriving home is almost like traveling back in time. We're sleeping in our childhood beds alone instead of with each other. On Christmas morning, Steph, her dad, and Jeremy come over to our house for brunch. When I meet her at the door, she's panicked. Her dad, who's been here several times, heads off to the kitchen to say hello and offer assistance. Before my parents see Steph, I sneak her off to my room to find out what's going on.

I pull her to my chest and kiss her as soon as we're behind the door. Pulling back, I ask, "What's going on? You look worried about something."

She drops her gaze and nervously looks at her feet before mumbling something that sounds like, "I don't want you to get mad."

Mad? About what? My stomach sinks. What isn't she telling me? "Steph, remember the last time we didn't talk things out? How'd that end?"

"Epic sex, if I recall," she deflects.

She's not wrong. Smirking at her, I say, "There is no way we aren't talking this out. And then we can have epic car sex. Later."

Laughing, she smacks my chest and whines my name. But the worry sits heavy in her eyes.

Holding my hands up, I say, "I'm kidding. Well, mostly. Yes, I want to have epic car sex with you, but first we need to talk about what has you upset. Then we probably have to have brunch with our families. And after that, we can take a walk down memory lane. What do you say?"

Steph nods, blows out a big breath, and confesses, "Your mom is driving me crazy. I love her, but every time I see her in town, she presses me about the wedding, making 'helpful' suggestions. I haven't had time to plan anything, and her asking just stresses me out."

Taking her hands, I kiss her knuckles before pushing a lock of hair behind her ear.

"Okay, if it's all too much, why don't we make it simple?" I suggest.

"What do you mean?" she questions.

"I mean simple. All we need is you, me, rings, and a witness or two, right?"

Confused by what he's saying, I mumble, "I guess, but your mom wants to make it a big event."

I laugh, catching Steph off guard. Then I step closer, cupping her cheeks in my hands. When I trace my thumb down her chin, her eyes soften and she smiles. I tip her head to me before asking, "But what do *you* want?"

Thinking for a moment, a flash of emotion travels through her bright eyes and a smile dusts her lips before she answers. "You. That's all I want."

I pull her in for a kiss, then suggest, "Then, let's do that."

"Are you serious? That would be amazing." She beams at me.

Grabbing her hand, I say, "Let's go tell them now, enjoy brunch, and celebrate by steaming up the windows at our spot. It's been two weeks since I've been inside you, and I'm getting desperate."

Steph squeals her excitement, and I lead her out of the room, down the stairs, and toward the dining room.

"There you are," my mom chides when she spots us. "I was wondering where you went off to before even saying hello."

"Hi, Connie. It's so nice of you to have us over. Where's Jeff, Jeremy, and my dad?" Steph asks. *Apparently, she's ready to share the big news.*

"Well, of course, darling. You're family now." Mom

smiles at her, then adds, "I think they're out back. Someone thought it would be a good idea to deep-fry a turkey." Mom sighs and then turns back to the kitchen. We follow behind dutifully, waiting to be assigned some random task.

"Tristan, dear, can you set the table? And Stephanie, can you help me finish the fruit salad?" We both fall into line, doing what's asked and stealing glances across the room. *Man, I love that woman. I can't wait until she's officially mine.*

After another half hour, we sit down to eat and everything is delicious. I definitely look forward to my visits home, and a big part of that is the food. If I ate like this all the time, I'd have to spend a lot more time in the gym. When I was drafted to the Storm, my diet was one of the first things they revised. It wasn't that I ate too much junk food, they just had some retraining to do with me on the types of foods that were optimal for a professional athlete. And most of the time, I'm strict with it. Today, I plan to fall off the wagon, running headfirst into a food coma.

While eating, my mom starts her twenty questions. Thankfully, I did mine when I got home last night. Now it's Steph's turn. *Oh, man.*

"Stephanie, how did classes go this semester? Still on track to graduate this summer?"

She wipes her mouth before she answers. "All my classes were great, and yes, graduation is still set."

Mom smiles at her. "Oh good. Do you mind if we come?"

"T-to graduation?" Steph sputters. "Are you sure? They're really boring."

Steph's dad chimes in with, "The more the merrier. Plus, it'll be nice to suffer with someone I know." Then he laughs. My dad joins in, and soon everyone is laughing but us.

I whisper in Steph's ear, "I'm going to tell them and let them know we plan to do it graduation weekend in front of the Justice of the Peace. Okay?" I pull back to look into her eyes. They are sparkling and a smile marks her beautiful pink lips. When she nods, I know I have her permission.

Clearing my throat, the laughter dies down. "It would be great if you came to Boston for Steph's graduation, because it will be a big weekend."

"Really, what else is happening?" my dad asks.

Steph smiles when I look at her. "Steph and I are getting married that weekend. We don't want anything big, so we are going down to the courthouse." Everything goes silent except for the gasp I hear from my mother. *Dramatic, much?* Next to me, Steph looks worried. Patting her hand, I try to offer comfort.

Her dad looks at her, and it seems like a silent conversation takes place. Finally, he speaks up. "I think that's terrific. If that's what you want." Steph nods. He smiles at her and then adds, "Then that's what you should do. I'm looking forward to it." He then turns to me. "You're right, Tristan, that'll be a big weekend. I get to watch my baby girl earn her degree and gain another son too." Looking back at Steph, he lowers his voice and says, "Your mom would be so proud of you, Sunshine."

Wiping a tear away, she says, "Thanks, Dad. I appreciate that." Then she smiles and squeezes my hand. *It's official, we're getting married.*

Chapter 12

Stephanie

The week of graduation finally arrives, and I can hardly believe it. The classes that stretched me to my limits are finally over. As I think over the past year, I'm grateful I didn't plan some big elaborate wedding too. Final projects and exams were tedious, but I survived. And now that that's over, I can focus on my future with Tristan.

He and I went shopping a few weeks ago to select our wedding rings and special outfits for our big day. Our parents arrived in town last night. Dinner with them was nice, but because Tristan was out of town for hockey, it wasn't as comfortable as usual. The Storm is vying to maintain a spot in the Stanley Cup bracket, and he returns late Thursday night.

We're getting married Friday morning, and graduation is Saturday. He and our parents leave on Sunday. Because he's in the playoffs, we're postponing our honeymoon and staying in Boston. When he's in town, we plan to do touristy things. Although we've been here for years, we've never really explored much. The only reservation I made was for a brunch cruise. I also planned for a picnic in the Public Garden. Maybe I'll even convince Tristan to go for a ride on a swan boat. We just want to spend some undisturbed time together. Once the season is officially over, we'll be heading back to Maui to enjoy some sun and relaxation.

Stretching my arms high above my head, I look around my cluttered bedroom. I scattered books all over my desk to prepare for finals and I haven't cleaned them up yet. My graduation robe is hanging in my closet, pressed and ready for tomorrow. Moving boxes are leaned against the wall, and I just need to assemble and fill them. But that's not on the agenda today. No, today I'm getting married.

"Ahhh!" I squeal out loud in the empty room. It all feels surreal. We've been together so long, it seems like it's the next step for us. Don't get me wrong. I love Tristan and there's nothing I want more than to be his wife, but today has a somber feel to it, and I can't figure out why.

Ding, ding.

My phone chimes from its charger. Grabbing it, I see a text from Tristan.

TRISTAN

> Good Morning, Love. I can't believe in a few hours you'll be Mrs. Murphy. See you at the courthouse. I'll be the handsome guy wearing a perma-grin. I love you, Steph, and I can't wait until you are officially mine.

My heart flutters in excitement. *Mrs. Murphy.* I don't know how many times over the years I have doodled that exact name over every surface I came across. Since shortly after we started dating, I knew Tristan was my forever. Our future is so bright, and I can't wait to see where it's headed.

I type back a quick response before I shower and get ready.

ME

> I love you too, Tristan. Today, you are making my dreams come true. Thank you for loving me. I'll see you at the courthouse. I'll be the woman wearing a dress, and a matching perma-grin.

Slipping from my nice, cozy, warm comforter, I head down the hallway to the bathroom. I take longer than usual, making sure everything is perfect. After I shower and do my skin and hair routine, I return to my bedroom to do my makeup. After that's done, I don a white dress. The final touch is the hockey-themed garter. *I'm getting married.* Standing back, I take in my reflection staring back at me. Turning around, I see something that stops me dead in my tracks. A sunburst sits high and proud on my shoulder. The warmth it puts off mimics a hand resting there, and that instantly makes me think of my mom.

Over the past five years, I've missed her so much. But especially on important days, her absence weighs heavily on my heart. For years, I'd pushed it away, refusing to think of how much it hurt to have her gone. Just as tears well, a familiar ringtone sounds. "Butterfly Kisses" by Bob Carlisle surrounds me. I close my eyes, savoring the moment. When it stops suddenly, I have to remind myself that it's just a ringtone. Picking up my phone, I select the missed call, and within moments, I hear the familiar drawl of my dad.

"Hi, Dad," I whisper.

"Stephanie, my darling girl, how are you? I know I'll see you soon, but I just wanted to check on you."

Hesitating, I answer, "I'm doing okay. I miss Mom a lot today. She should be here with me. With us. Celebrating."

Dad's quiet for a moment, and I know he's thinking the same. "You're right, and I'm sorry she's not here to celebrate. I know she would have been beside herself, filled with so much joy, love, and excitement. Even though she isn't here in person, know she's with you in spirit. I believe that since leaving us, she'd been a guardian angel. I feel her near me all the time. Even with things that happen, I know she's part of it."

"What do you mean, Dad?" I ask, wondering if he's talking about things like the sunburst.

He chuckles to himself. "Well, sometimes I see things that instantly make me think of your mom, and I think that's her way of staying involved in my life. Does that make sense?"

"Maybe. But do you have any examples?"

"Sure. This morning when I went down to the hotel's breakfast, the flowers on every table but mine were yellow tulips. My table alone had pink tulips—your mom's favorite. And when I asked for jam to go with my toast, you know the only kind they gave me?" He pauses, letting me answer.

"Raspberry?" I whispered. It, too, was Mom's favorite. Sure, you could always get strawberry, grape, or orange marmalade, but never raspberry. "A-anything else?" I stutter, half believing everything is a coincidence.

"When I checked in, all the tea packets in my room were Earl Grey. And then after dinner last night, I grabbed a nightcap at the hotel's bar, and you want to know what song was playing when I entered?" Again, he pauses, waiting for me to catch up.

I've heard the story of their song a thousand times.

"No?" I whisper in disbelief.

"Yep," he says, popping the p. "'The Lady in Red.' Our song." I can hear the smile in his voice. My parents were so in love with each other. Their story ended far too soon. But what I saw between them was truly magical. And it's what I want for Tristan and me.

The emotion of it all is swirling around me, and I'm finding it tough to breathe. A shiver moves through my body. She's here, I know she is. "Dad," I croak.

"What?"

"I think Mom is with me right now. Ever since I put on my dress, a sunburst has stayed on my shoulder. As soon as I saw it, she immediately came to mind." Do I sound crazy? Maybe. I know that if anyone else heard our conversation, we'd both be off to the psych ward.

"I know you're right. She wouldn't miss today. I know she's incredibly proud of you, and she would have loved Tristan too. I am so happy for you and the life you are building together."

"Thanks, Dad. I probably should go. I need to finish getting ready. You're still planning to give me a ride to the courthouse?"

"You bet. I'll be there soon to get you. I can't wait to see my little girl all grown up and ready for the biggest day of her life. I love you, Sunshine." *He's called me that since I was little.* Not wanting to get too lost in that thought, I say goodbye.

A short while later, Dad arrives and we head to the courthouse to meet up with Tristan and his parents.

Standing in a crisp, black suit with a yellow tie is the man of my dreams. *He's wearing yellow.* That's my mom's and my favorite color, and he wore it today. I'm unbelievably touched by his thoughtfulness.

Although he's deep in conversation with his parents, his head is on a swivel, seeking me out. When his eyes finally find me, his casual smile morphs into a soul-stealing gaze that lights my body ablaze. Heat creeps up me as his eyes trace from my feet to my head. His eyes darken as they cross over the deep neckline of the dress. He's cradling a simple bouquet of wildflowers. Saying something to his parents before he turns away from them, he heads to me.

"Steph. Babe, you look so beautiful," he croons as he gets closer. When he licks his lips, I feel my composure wane. I want to run to him and jump in his arms, but that wouldn't be acceptable.

When we reach each other, we stand toe-to-toe. Tristan grabs my hand. "Hey, babe. You ready to do this?"

Squeezing his hand back, I answer, "I'm so ready." He places a chaste kiss on my lips, and my knees go weak. *This man is about to be my husband.*

"Let's go change your last name," he says while leading me into the stone building. Our parents trail behind as we search out the judge's chambers.

The judge wastes no time performing our simple ceremony. When it's all said and done, we've both promised to be faithful and true through the good times and bad. Exchanging rings and a kiss to seal the deal is all we need before we are officially married. *Mr. & Mrs. Tristan Murphy. Finally.*

Chapter 13

Tristan

After the excitement of tying the knot, we head to a celebration lunch. Unfortunately, I can't stay the entire time because Coach ordered a light practice for us. He says that we have to keep ourselves ready. Coach pushes us hard, reminding us that just because we worked hard all season, doesn't mean we can afford to slack off now. *But, fuck, today?* Today, of all days, I want to. Instead of playing hockey, I'd rather take my wife home and ravage her the rest of the day and night. *Wife.* I love the sound of that.

Returning home after practice, I see Steph's car in the parking lot. She finally moved in. My heart kicks up and I excitedly race up the stairs to our condo. It's much nicer than the one I originally rented when we first moved to Boston three years ago. My hefty paycheck has afforded us a nice unit in a magnificent building. We even have a doorman. Before opening the door, I try to loosen all the pent-up aggression from practice. I shake out my hands. I don't want to come in too strong. After all, it's our wedding night. *Shit. Why didn't I think to get a fancy hotel room for the night?* Too late now. My wife is just on the other side of that door. I notice my palms are sweaty, and my stomach tightens in excitement. *Why am I so fucking nervous?* When I open the door, heavenly smells waft around me. *What is she cooking?* It smells divine.

"Hey, honey, I'm home," I call out while entering the kitchen. There she is, loading food onto two plates, wearing... only an apron. *Damn.* Forget dinner, because she looks good enough to eat. How did I get so lucky?

"Hi, my husband," she answers with a sultry smile on her red-painted lips. If this is how she's doing dinner every night, I'll never miss it.

I step up behind her and place kisses on her shoulder and trace my tongue up her neck. When I reach her earlobe, I suck it into my mouth. She shivers and I wrap my hand around her hip, pulling her into me. "Ohhh," she breathes out when she feels my erection pressing between her finely sculpted ass cheeks.

"Everything looks and smells divine, babe."

Leaning herself back into me, her head rests against my chest and I let go of her hip and trace my fingers up the curve of her waist. It reminds me of an hourglass. Her silky, soft skin is decadent. When I reach her ribs, I make a detour and tickle my fingertips under her breast. "Tristan," she moans. I move to her nipple where I tug and flick it. Her breathing picks up, and soon she's slumped against me.

"Am I making you feel good, babe?" I ask, just before I lick and nip at her neck. Knowing she doesn't want hickeys on her neck for graduation, I remind myself not to suck.

"Mmmm," she hums.

Needing more of her, I spin her around in my arms and back her against the counter. I lift her chin and seek out her lips. It turns incendiary in seconds. *So good.* It's not our first kiss as husband and wife, but it's still special. Needing air, I pull back. I look over to the dinner she made. And squash the selfish desires coursing through me. "Looks like you made dinner. How about we enjoy that first, then get back to what we were doing?"

"What were we doing?" She plays coy, laughter dancing in her eyes.

Scratching my head, I answer, "You know, before I take you against the fridge, across the countertop, or have you ride me on our new dining room chairs?"

Steph snort laughs. "I'm not sure the chairs could handle our combined weight and the force of our movements."

Knowing she's probably right, I give her a kiss on the nose and reach for the plates she's already assembled, then I head to the dining room table. During dinner, we run through our plan for graduation the next day. I am so proud of Steph. Not only did she graduate with honors, she completed her degree in three years, just like she planned.

Following dinner, after we clean up the kitchen together, we spend the rest of the evening wrapped around each other. This is the life. I couldn't be any happier than I am right now. Thinking over my life, I realize I have everything I ever wanted. And my future looks perfect.

Chapter 14

Stephanie

Beep, beep, beep.

"Make it stop." Tristan groans from beneath the blanket, making me smile. I'm sure I look like a loon.

Last night we made our wedding night epic. I'd lost count of how many orgasms I received and on what surfaces. It's a good thing I remembered to set my alarm, because after the night we shared, there was no way we were going to wake up before noon, and graduation starts at ten. We didn't get to sleep until four a.m., and it's going to be obvious when I finally get up and look in the mirror.

Turning off the alarm and getting out of bed, I hear another groan as Tristan burrows deeper under the covers. Stepping onto the cold tile of the bathroom floor works as effectively as throwing back a triple shot of espresso. Now wide awake, I flinch when I see my reflection. *Hello, raccoon eyes.* Although the shower last night washed most of my makeup off, my mascara had run, making me look ghoulish. My straight blondish hair, which had always been problematic, has volume I never knew was possible. Apparently, sex hair is a thing, and it isn't always a bad thing. This morning my boring hair looks styled like I walked off the cover of a sixties doo-wop record photoshoot. It looks like it had been back-combed and teased for hours, then secured with Aqua Net. Reaching up, I touch it and it doesn't move an inch. Laughter falls from my lips as I shake my head, trying to get my hair to move at all. *No luck.*

"What's so funny in there?" a mumbled voice calls out.

Smirking into the mirror, I call back in between giggles, "My hair."

"Yeah? If it's that funny, I gotta see it," Tristan answers.

Rubbing his eyes, he enters the bathroom. "Holy shit. Babe, what happened?" He stares at me with wide eyes.

I shake my head a few times and his mouth falls open. "What, you don't like it?" I ask. "This is how I'm doing my hair for graduation. Isn't it perfect?" Trying to keep a straight face, I smother a laugh. *He's right, it's terrible.*

"Really?" he hesitantly questions as he scratches his head.

Mesmerized by the solid mass on my head, I finally answer him. "No, this isn't my hair for graduation. I went to bed last night with wet hair after you nearly killed me in the shower. And this is the result. Thank you very much."

Tristan smirks, wraps himself around me, and offers, "You know, we could start our morning the same way."

"I wish. But we have to be there at nine because the ceremony starts at ten." Tristan's face falls. "Raincheck?" I offer. He gives me a sad smile. "What's going on, Tristan?"

Pulling me into his arms, I try to aim my beehive so it doesn't cause damage. "I just wanted to make our first morning as a married couple special."

Hugging him tight, I coo, "You made this morning and last night very special. You rocked my world, and if that is what married life looks like, I can't wait." Pushing up on my tiptoes, I place my lips on his. At first, he just stands there, still grumpy. So, I playfully bite his lip, triggering something wild in him. Pretty soon he has me pushed up against the wall, and I wrap my legs around his naked waist. "Shower," I mumble.

Ensuring he's got me supported, he walks over to the shower and turns on the water. After it warms up, he steps in, soaking us both while we continue kissing.

I'm wet all over. Pulling his hot, heady lips from mine, he quirks his head. "Do we have time for a quickie?" His puppy dog eyes plead with me. I answer him by grinding my hips into him. Tristan moves toward the wall, pressing me against it, then lines his hard cock with my center before sliding home in one thrust.

"Ahh. So good." I groan and he slowly pulls out, pushing back in with force. He's driving so deep and already I feel my orgasm building. Using my legs, I pull him even tighter to me. The delicious slap our bodies make when they come in contact is driving me insane. My hips thrust wildly, seeking more friction. Tristan moves one hand to my clit and starts making circles on my needy nub. "Almost there," I gasp out as my orgasm builds. His movements become wilder, and I can tell he's close too. I thrust my chest up and Tristan latches on to my nipple. He bites it and I explode. My muscles squeeze as I arch, moan, and pant.

"Tight." I hear him mutter as he pumps into me at a feverish pace. Then he goes still, buries his head into my neck, and pants. His warm breath tickles my skin and sends a shiver down my spine. I wiggle my hips and Tristan thrusts back. Unfortunately, we don't have time for round two.

Thirty minutes later, after we've both showered and dressed, we're ready to head to the school's gymnasium where the ceremony is being held. Once we arrive, I'm ushered away to a section for graduates while Tristan waits for our parents so they can all sit together. *I'm a graduate.*

We celebrate with another lunch, and again Tristan has to leave early for a team meeting. The team flies out tonight for the next series they have to play.

Chapter 15

Tristan

After battling for a position in the Stanley Cup bracket, we're knocked out after the second round. I was disappointed, as I'd been dreaming about this since I was a kid, but I'm determined to use that to motivate me to work harder next season. We'll get there, I know it.

When the dust settles and I finally move past the disappointment, I realize it isn't all bad. Being out of the playoffs means I can finally take my wife on our official honeymoon. We haven't been back to Maui since I proposed, and we're both excited to relax and enjoy spending some undisturbed time together.

We haven't been married long, and we're settling in as best as we can. Steph started a job working at a non-profit whose goal is to feed the community's hungry. And I'm playing for a professional hockey team. With such different schedules, we're bound to have some tense times as we try to navigate newlywed life.

When we finally arrive in Maui after fifteen hours of travel, I'm ready to sleep. That is until I step off the airplane. The warm Hawaiian air wraps me in a hug as I walk through the open airport. Any tension I was carrying is instantly forgotten as my body relaxes. Breathing in and being surrounded by eau de Tropics, an island aroma that is specific to, and can only be found in, Maui, has my body humming with excitement and anticipation for the days ahead.

"This is the best," Steph exclaims as she rolls her carry-on bag next to me. And she's right.

"Let's get out of here," I say with a wink. She squeals, and my heart thumps beneath my flower lei that we'd been gifted when we arrived.

Wanting to embrace the island culture, I reserved a Jeep with removable roof panels. This time on the island, we intend to explore. I'm determined to find a hidden waterfall to ravish my wife under.

We opted to stay in one of the premier resorts in Wailea because we fell in love with that side of the island last time. Since it's late and there isn't much to see, we head straight to our hotel to check in. Since I informed the hotel it was our honeymoon, we're greeted with another lei welcome. This time, I receive a kukui nut one.

"Nice nuts, but I like yours better," Steph whispers to me as we head to our room.

Giving her a sly smirk, I lower my voice and growl, "Well, they've had a long day and desperately need your attention."

"I look forward to that." She grins at me, and my cock grows hard beneath my athletic shorts.

Our suite is spacious and luxurious. The last time we were here, we had a mediocre vacation rental, but this feels like a palace. Our view is stunning and over-looks the ocean. Opening the door to the lanai, the sound of the waves crashing on the shore is hypnotic. "I can't wait to see a sunset from here. I know it'll be magical," Steph says. Pulling her in for a hug, my lips find hers, and before I know it, I'm itching for more. Before I scandalize any hotel guests with a peep show, I spin Steph around and duck-walk her toward the master bedroom. But when we pass the bed, she asks against my chest, "Where are we headed?"

"Take a shower with me, babe." Pressing my hips forward, I know she feels my erection, and there's no doubt what I want to do. The bathroom is larger than I expected, housing both a walk-in shower and a soaking tub. I turn the water on in the shower and spin Steph around to remove her clothes. She opted to travel in comfort. She's wearing sexy-as-fuck leggings, a tank top, and a sweatshirt. I remove each item in no time. Then, I drop my athletic shorts and pull my t-shirt over my head. Steph runs her hands up and down my chest. Every time she goes past my nipples, she tugs on my barbells, which sends desire racing through my needy body. Rolling my head back and enjoying the sensation, I growl, "Get in the shower."

Steph smirks, tugs on the barbells again, and saunters into the shower, swishing her hips back and forth. I bite my fist. *Is she trying to kill me? A man can only take so much.* Dialing down my caveman urges, I enjoy her show before following her in. *Have mercy.* My cock leads the way, seeking her warm, wet body. It doesn't take long to have her wrapped around me as I'm pressing her against the tiled wall with my swollen cock rubbing against her clit.

"Oh, Tristan, right there," she moans.

Trailing my hand down, I check to see if she's ready for me. Running my fingers through her folds, I find her soaked. When I dip one finger in, she groans. Sliding back, I place the tip of my cock at her entrance and slowly push forward. "Fucking perfect, Steph. You were made for me."

Using her thighs, Steph moves up and down my cock at a mind-blowing pace. My fingers dig into her luscious ass, helping her when she appears to fatigue. "Almost there," she shouts. I push and pull her body as if she weighs nothing, forcing our pleasure out into the stratosphere. Steph shakes and her muscles lock down, putting everything she's touching into a tight squeeze. My cock, waist, and hair are the recipients of her strength, and I'm not complaining one damn bit. It's sublime to watch and feel her come. A taste of Heaven on Earth. Thrusting up into the tight hold she has on me, has me hurling toward my own orgasmic finish. When it hits, my knees go weak and I place my hand on the wall behind her to stabilize myself.

"Holy shit." I pant in her ear after it tears through me. I lean my weight into her so I don't collapse from instability. That orgasm rocked me to my core.

Chapter 16

Stephanie

Ever had your world rocked so thoroughly, you temporarily forgot who you were? Yeah, me neither. That is. Until. That. Shower. Can I even call it that? At no point did I actually wash myself. There was water, and I got wet, in more ways than one, and in the end, I was relaxed and warm. But I will admit, soap and shampoo weren't used at all. As soon as we stepped into the shower, Tristan had me distracted with his tongue, fingers, and cock in the most amazing ways.

Turning off the water, he reaches for a towel, and I can see he's panting. *Good, it isn't just me.* His eyes are dark and mysterious, and I can't help but wonder what happens next. After toweling me off, he wraps a clean dry towel around his waist and leads me toward the bed. He picks me up and sets me on the edge, steps between my legs, and kisses me passionately. Our tongues duel mercilessly and when I feel dizzy, I anchor my hands to his waist and squeeze, encouraging him. Needing air, I pull my lips from his and gasp. After a few labored breaths, he gently pushes my chest until my back hits the bed. He drops to his knees, and his still-wet hair drips on my thighs.

Knowing what's coming, my body shakes with giddy excitement. He flicks my towel open and then lifts my legs over his shoulders and then skates his hands up my thighs. Goose bumps chase his delicate touch. When he reaches my apex, he blows mind-numbing hot air on me. *It feels so good.* My eyes flutter closed and my head drops to the bed. Tristan's first lick sends me flying. From back to front, he drags his hungry tongue through my dripping-wet folds, flicking my clit when he reaches it. "Ahhh," I moan loudly. He growls and nips my clit before soothing it with languid strokes of his tongue. Returning to my folds, he traces his fingers through them, opening me wide. He circles my entrance with his tongue a few times before finally thrusting in. Another moan falls from my lips. He removes his mouth and replaces it with his fingers, curling at just the right depth. He lays kisses on my hips and inner thighs, and I love the scratch of his scruff. It all brings me higher, faster.

It isn't long until he lowers his mouth over my clit again and begins to suck, lick, flick, and nibble it. Before I know it, an orgasm crashes into me, and I reach down to run my hand through Tristan's hair. I tug tight when he continues to hit the magic spot. Shifting my hips, I thrust my pelvis at his mouth. *He's incredible at this.* In just a few rotations, I'm again seeing explosions behind my eyes as another orgasm rips through me. "Tris-tan!" I scream.

Tristan pops his head up. "You hollered?" he asks with a sexy smirk. *This man is my husband.*

Completely sated, I stammer, "T-that w-was incredible."

Tristan stands and unhooks his towel, revealing himself fully. *I will never get sick of that sight. My husband is so hot!* The towel drops to the floor and his erection juts out, almost like it's reaching for me. I lick my lips and smirk. He clenches his teeth and grabs his cock, squeezing firmly before giving himself a few languid strokes. Once I'm able to feel my body, I scoot back on the bed. Within seconds, he's hovering over me, his stiff cock bobbing between us. Reaching up, I circle the darkened head, and he groans. "Babe, I'm so close already. Please don't tease."

Instead of answering him, I raise my legs and line his throbbing cock up to my center. He pushes in slowly, and when he bottoms out, he says, "You always feel so perfect." Lowering his lips to me, he kisses me senseless before he begins to move. Our pace is slow at first, but I need more. I squeeze my muscles and he clenches his teeth, rasping, "You got tighter. That's amazing. Can you do it again?" I do and his hips thrust into me harder, hitting just the right spot. Wrapping my legs around him, I lock my ankles, making it so he can only withdraw so far before he thrusts back in. The rapid movement lights my body on fire and, like a bullet train, I hurtle toward orgasm station. Everything tightens and I explode around Tristan's cock. My hips jackknife, lifting us both off the bed and shifting the angle of his thrusts. "Damn, baby," he grits out as he releases into me. Once he's done, he collapses on me and my fatigued body drops back to the bed. *So good.*

Tristan rolls to my side. We lie on the bed as the sounds of the crashing waves fill the surrounding air. It's peaceful and relaxing. "What a fantastic start to our honeymoon," I say.

Tristan lifts his head up and smiles. "And it's only the beginning." The hazy look in his eyes tells me he's as weary as I am. "Wanna order dinner and we can eat and snuggle the rest of the night?"

I yawn while nodding my head.

Chapter 17

Tristan

I hadn't known what to expect on our honeymoon, but I plan to have a lot of sex with my wife. And I'm determined to do said act outside of our suite. Thankfully, Steph's on board with my plan, because that makes it even more exciting to find just the right locations for our tropical trysts.

On our first official day on the island, we plan to take our Jeep out exploring. I'd heard from the concierge that Big Beach is incredible. Knowing we're on our honeymoon, he also suggests Little Beach, mentioning it's clothing optional. *No, thank you.* There is no way I'm sharing my wife's delectable body with anyone else. We'll just have to be creative at Big Beach.

Stepping into the suite with a to-go cup of macadamia nut flavored coffee, I almost swallow my tongue. Steph is all wrapped up in a brightly colored sarong tied perfectly to hint at all she's hiding under it.

"Holy shit," I growl. I know what she's covering up, and I'm salivating, thinking about getting my hands back on it. My cock angrily presses against my board shorts, and I'm grateful I grabbed them instead of my swim trunks. Otherwise, I'd be dealing with a completely different situation. Would it be a medical emergency if the mesh lining of your swimwear strangled your cock? *Let's not find out.*

"Steph, you look amazing," I say, stepping toward her. I tug on the ponytail she has tucked beneath her Boston Storm cap. Just seeing her support for my team, I want to pump my arms in the air. My gorgeous wife makes me absolutely wild with desire. A fantasy I've always had is for her to dress in only black stilettos and my jersey. *Holy fuck.* That would be hot.

"You like?" she asks, pulling me out of my lust-driven fantasies. She's holding the edge of the brightly decorated wrap.

I still can't figure out how she put it on. Genuinely confused, I ask, "Are you going to be able to get yourself out of that when we get to the beach?"

She smacks my t-shirt-covered chest and laughs. "Of course. I know how to get out of this. I watched several YouTube videos on it before we came."

I laugh. "Of course you did."

Thirty minutes later, after we packed everything for our day at the beach, we head toward Makena (Big Beach). My body is shaking with excitement. I'm beyond eager to spend a day at the beach, swimming in the ocean, and staring at my breathtaking wife in whatever bikini she's chosen. Before we left, she informed me she bought some new ones but has been keeping them a secret. *I can't wait. I'm giddy like a kid on Christmas.*

Once we carefully walk through the hot sand to a less busy section of the beach, I pull out the sun tent I purchased from Amazon before we left. It doesn't close, but I think if I'm inventive with a few extra towels, I can give us some privacy. *Let's hope anyway.* Setting up the tent is easy, and in no time, I've got everything inside, then all that's left to do is... watch my wife disrobe. *Yes, please.*

Like a good boy, I sit quietly and wait for the show. Steph pushes her ponytail to the side, revealing the long line of her neck. She reaches up and works at the knot tied there, and the sarong droops, revealing glimpses of her soft skin. *Is that magenta I see?* Focusing my eyes on the exposed gaps, my mouth waters and my shorts tighten. Gripping both ends of the sarong, Steph pulls it loose, and my jaw drops open. Before me stands the sexiest woman I have ever seen, clothed in a magenta string bikini that looks like it was painted on her. I lick my lips when I see her nipples have pebbled. I want nothing more than to have them in my mouth, lavishing her in pleasure until she screams loud enough that the lifeguards at their hut a few hundred feet away can hear her.

"Goddess," I mumble with the limited amount of blood left in my brain.

Turning around, she asks, "Do you like it?"

"You are stunning."

She smiles widely at me. "Ready to go play in the ocean?"

Looking down at my crotch, I see I have a problem. "Give me a minute. You kind of blew my mind with that swimsuit and things have to calm down so I don't scare any kids."

Steph giggles. "Okay," she says before lying down on her towel outside our tent.

Twenty minutes later, after much deep breathing, picturing wrinkled old ladies, and imagining Coach barking orders at me, I'm deflated enough to stand up without causing a scene. We walk hand in hand down to the waves, and I don't miss all the eyes my wife is attracting. Thankfully, she's none the wiser. When we finally reach the water, we stroll into the surf. It doesn't take long for the waves to hit our knees and then our thighs. When it's chest level, we swim and duck under the waves so we aren't thrown around too much. Making it past the break zone, I pull Steph into my arms.

"Isn't this perfect, Tristan?" she gushes while wrapping her body around me.

Grabbing her ass with one hand, I rub my cock against her. "It doesn't get better than this."

It's then that I realize I've made a grave error. I

can't touch the bottom; we're too deep to have sex. *I can fix that.* Releasing her ass, I trail my fingers around her hip and drop between her legs. "Are you wet for me?"

Steph looks at me. "Of course I'm wet. We're in the ocean." Just as I'm about to protest about meaning something different, she smirks at me.

"You brat," I admonish her as I plunge my finger into her hot, needy center.

"Mmmm." Her back arches, pressing her breasts into me. I feel her nipples rub against my chest and my cock becomes even harder as I pleasure her. "Ahhh," falls from her plump pink lips, and nothing has ever sounded sweeter. While working her, a plan forms in my mind.

Moving us farther away from people but closer to shore, I'll be able to stand. Removing my fingers from Steph, she groans at me. I kiss her passionately. "Ready for me?" Her bright smile is confirmation enough for me, and I slide her bikini bottoms to the side. I shift her up while I pull my pulsating cock out. Steph adjusts her hips and lines up with me. She slides down my shaft, taking me to the hilt, and I'm knocked off balance by how amazing it feels. Once I'm sure I'm steady, I give her ass a squeeze and she begins to ride me.

At first, it's slow and her movement matches the surrounding waves, like she's bobbing along their surface. It's fucking amazing, even though it feels sort of taboo. The element of potentially being caught makes it even more exciting. My orgasm builds quickly, and I reach down to rub circles on her clit. My woman has to come first.

Her speed picks up and her movements become choppy and frantic. Looking around, I wonder if anyone will notice. A millisecond is all I pay to that worry as I feel myself about to tip over the ledge. I squeeze Steph's clit, setting her off first. Her back arches like a dancer lost in the music of us, and I move my hands to support her. She is breathtaking. Reminding me of the living marble sculptures created by Bernini. After taking a moment to bask in her glow, I resume pumping into her and, after only a few thrusts, my orgasm rips through me. Pulling her up to my chest and digging my toes into the sand below me, I pray I won't tip us over.

"That was amazing, babe," Steph whispers in my ear, and I couldn't agree more. Sliding her off me, I fix her swim bottoms as best as I can. As I tuck myself back into my shorts, I can't help but glance at the beach, checking to see if we caught anyone's attention. Thankfully, it doesn't appear we did.

We fill the rest of our day with lazing in the sun, more trips into the ocean, a picnic lunch, and round number two in our tent. I secure a few towels to block out any potential prying eyes and we try our best to keep it silent. But right after we both climax, we hear the rumble of the lifeguard's four-wheeler getting closer. We scramble to get dressed and take down the towels just before he arrives.

I stick my head out of the tent as he approaches.

"Good afternoon," he offers.

"Same to you," I say.

Steph joins me with some food in her hand, making it look like we were enjoying a snack in our tent. The lifeguard looks at us both and smirks.

"So, this isn't the type of conversation I love having, but we're in Maui and it happens... so here goes." He scratches his head, looking amused. I nod and he continues, "We got a complaint of some weird sounds coming from your tent, and policy requires that I check it out."

Both Steph and I look at each other. "Weird sounds?" I question, pretending to not know what he's referring to.

"The lady who made the complaint said it was sexual. Now, I'm not accusing you of doing anything. I'm just here to remind you that this is a public space and there are a ton of kids around. Maybe leave the sexy times at your hotel?"

Steph puts her hand to her chest. "I'm so sorry. My husband was tickling me, and I am extremely ticklish. They probably heard that. But we promise no more tickling while at the beach. Right, honey?"

The lifeguard scratches his head, "Tickling... uh, sure... we can go with that. Please, just remember to keep that to a minimum while you're here at the beach, surrounded by people."

I nod my head. "Will do. Sorry you had to come all this way for that."

"Okay. Thanks for your time. You have a great rest of the day." After bidding us goodbye, he climbs back on his four-wheeler and returns to the lifeguard station. He approaches an older woman who's just standing there with her arms crossed and a scowl on her face.

"Guess we know who narced on us." I laugh as I pull her in tight against me. She giggles against my chest before I let go so we can get back into the tent to clean up. Smirking to myself, I wonder if the lifeguard noticed my shirt was on inside out. We spend another hour at the beach before we pack up and head back to our hotel.

The rest of our week in paradise is nothing but adventures, glorious weather, and amazing sex in a variety of locales. We're almost caught a few more times, which makes the entire experience more exciting. When it's time to go home, neither of us is ready. Escaping real life and spending undisturbed time together is just what we needed.

Chapter 18

Stephanie

Returning home from Maui, I'm not sure what to expect. We've always had so many other things demanding our attention. And then in Maui, I had one hundred percent of Tristan's attention and it was addicting. But I soon learn that isn't possible at home. Married life is a constant juggling act.

I'd always dreamed of being married, and this is not at all what I imagined. This is... well... if I'm honest... it's awful. When we were dating, I assumed I'd see Tristan more if we were married, but that isn't the case. I miss him. With eighty—yes, that's right, eight dash zero—plus games a season and travel time, it feels like I never see him. During college, I'd been so preoccupied with classes and schoolwork, I hadn't noticed as much. I don't remember ever feeling this lonely. The few friends I made while in school moved away to pursue jobs. But this is my home, and with Tristan playing for the Storm, I have a feeling we'll be here for a while.

The one amazing thing about Boston is I absolutely love my job. It isn't exactly what I wanted, but I'm learning so much and it's beyond rewarding. Right after graduation, I was hired by a non-profit that's mission was to end hunger in the community. They work with local food pantries, schools, and other programs to reach out to the community and ensure no one goes hungry. Since my job is in accounting, I don't often see the clientele we work with and the impact we have on the community. Over the last few months, I've volunteered for opportunities to help on the front lines, since I have plenty of free time with Tristan being gone so much.

The people I work with are incredible. I have never met so many generous people in my life. Seriously, I know many of them would give you the shirt off their backs if you needed it. During my first weekend helping, I'm assigned to stocking the warehouse. My bosses explained that we have a grant that enables us to buy bulk food at a cheaper rate because we're distributing it out in the community. It's incredible to see the amount of food given out each week. Until now, I didn't realize there were so many hungry people in our community. Volunteering made the problem tangible. Helping is fulfilling, and something I need in my life. Before I know it, I'm spending every Saturday volunteering wherever I'm needed.

My alarm goes off at seven, like it has for the past month, and I roll over to silence it when a muscular arm wraps around me and pulls me into a hard body. "Where do you think you're going?" Tristan growls at me.

Snuggling into him, I reply, "It's Saturday."

He rolls on top of me and I feel his hard cock push into my stomach, and it sets my body on fire. "Exactly. That means it's sexy time before I have to go skate." Then he dips his mouth to mine. He places a gentle kiss on my lips and nibbles.

I pull back. "Tristan, I'm volunteering at the food pantry this morning. I already told you this." *Hasn't he listened every time we've talked? I've been doing this for weeks now.*

He pouts at me. "I know you do that while I'm gone, and that's fine, but I expected you'd want to stay in bed with me when I'm home."

Really? I don't need his permission to feed people. And I am not waiting in bed naked for whenever he has time for me. What is this 1920? Annoyed, but trying to hold my tongue the best I can, I grit out, "Excuse me?"

Tristan registers my tone and his eyes grow wide. He climbs off me and hangs his head, sulking. "I just figured we would have a lazy morning before I have to leave for the arena. You know, since I'm hardly here."

Counting down from three to one, I curl my hands into fists. "I am more than aware you are hardly here, which is why I've started volunteering. This work makes me happy and keeps me from feeling lonely because you're always gone. It's all I have, and I'm not going to not show up to a commitment I've made because you've decided you want to be screwed."

Tristan turns toward me, glares, and spits out, "Nice welcome home, Steph. This is bullshit."

Crossing my arms, I scoff. "I didn't realize I was supposed to just serve your every whim when you were finally here. Next time, I'll clear my calendar so I can be at your beck and call. Of course, naked, too, so you can use me as you see fit." *We have never talked to each other like this. What is happening?* Sadness clouds my anger.

Not wanting to be part of this conversation any longer, I get out of bed and head to the bathroom. Once I'm behind a closed door, my emotions crash into me and it feels like my heart is being torn from my chest. Big tears fall as I step into the shower. Lost in my pain, I don't hear Tristan step into the shower. His warm, strong arms hug me from behind. He tenderly kisses my shoulder and says, "I'm sorry, Steph." My whimpering is my answer. He pulls me in tighter. "Talk to me, please."

It feels so good to have his arms wrapped around me. It's been so long. I didn't realize this would be this hard. Finally, I admit, "I've missed you. I've been so lonely, I started volunteering. And I love it, and now you're expecting me to give it up."

When he turns me around, I keep my eyes lowered. I'm not sure I'll be able to maintain my poor composure if I look into his eyes. Tristan realizes that and tips my chin up, forcing it. "Steph, I've missed you too. I'm not expecting you to give it up. I just hadn't considered it, and I'm disappointed we don't get to spend hours in bed."

He kisses my forehead. "I'm sorry I took out my frustration on you." His apology is like a Band-Aid to my soul, covering all the cracks and splinters, but ultimately, not enough to fix the deep fractures that were already forming. "Do you have plans on Sunday morning?"

Shaking my head, I say, "I'm free." He lets out a throaty growl, and my blood pressure spikes, making me feel lightheaded. Then he places a possessive kiss on my lips while squeezing my ass.

"It's all mine, then," he proclaims against my lips. The excitement of that and the possession in his voice ignites the desire I have for him. I push things deeper, suddenly feeling wanton. I want him. Now. Gripping his cock, I stroke it slowly. He breaks the kiss and nibbles against my ear. "What do you need, Steph?"

"You," I pant, already feeling lust ooze through every pore of my body.

"Have time for a quickie before you go?"

"Please," I beg.

He bends down and lifts me in his arms, and I wrap my legs around him. We kiss feverishly while he spins me toward the wall of our large tiled shower. When my back hits it, I arch, and he grunts, pushing his hard cock against me. He pulls his lips from mine and in a hoarse voice asks, "You ready for me?"

"Always," I answer before he lifts me higher and effortlessly slides inside, grunting again when he bottoms out.

"You feel so damn good," he says, his deep voice strained and raspy while he pumps into me at a steady pace.

The next thing I know, an orgasm is overtaking me. "Right there, Tristan," I pant as his hips pound into mine. After a few more thrusts, he follows behind me, collapsing against me and pinning me to the wall.

After our breathing has steadied, I say, "I hate to cut this short, but I really have to get to the food pantry." He groans as he pulls back. Once back on my feet, he steers me under the warm water so I can clean up. Taking the quickest shower ever, I kiss his lips before I step out.

"We'll have more time tonight. Okay?" I say when I'm dried off. Tristan gives me a lazy smile and nods his head.

The food pantry is busy when I arrive a tad late. Clients are already beginning to line up and the doors don't open for another forty-five minutes. "Sorry, I'm late. Tristan got back into town late last night. Where do you need me, Charles?" At 6'3", he looks over his clipboard and smiles at me. His worry lines and short-clipped military cut that's peppered with gray speak of his age. Charles has been the director for the past five years, and the pantry runs like a well-oiled machine.

"Can you help Susanne with boxing?" he asks.

"On it, boss," I answer while heading toward the other side of the gymnasium, where we actually distribute the pre-packed boxes of food.

The day passes quickly, barely allowing for a bathroom break, but we distribute food to two hundred hungry families. And it feels amazing.

"Hey, Steph, you want to go get dinner?" Christie, a friend I made when I started volunteering, asks.

Shaking my head, I reply, "Sorry, I can't. Tristan got home last night, and he's waiting for me. Rain check?"

Grinning, she says, "Totally understand. Go home and have fun."

"I plan to," I tell her with a smile plastered on my face.

Heading home, I'm on cloud nine. I spent my day giving back, and my husband is finally back in town. Only when I arrive home, he's not there.

ME

Hey. Just got home. Where are you?

TRISTAN

> Didn't know how long you'd be, so I'm out watching the game and having a beer with the guys.

Didn't they just get home from a road trip where they were all together?

ME

> Okay. Do you know when you'll be home?

TRISTAN

> Game still has thirty minutes on the clock, so maybe an hour, give or take.

Really? Why the guilt trip this morning? I don't understand. I'm confused, angry, and sad.

ME

> Oh. Okay.

Slouching down on the couch, I want to cry. Why isn't he rushing home? He'd rather be with the guys than his wife? What does that mean? Forcing myself to get up, I head into the bedroom and pull on the comfiest clothes I can find: a pair of oversized joggers and an old holey t-shirt. Then I pop a bag of popcorn before selecting a random chick flick on TV. When Tristan arrives home an hour and a half later, the ending credits are just finishing. I turn it off, grab my empty popcorn bowl, and head to the kitchen. He follows behind, and I do my best to hold my tongue because nothing good will come from it. My mom, may she rest in peace, always told me if you can't say anything nice, don't say anything at all. Once I'm done with the dishes, I start the dishwasher, flick off the lights, and head toward the bedroom.

"Steph," he calls out, still standing in the hallway. I keep moving while tears well up in my eyes. Getting ready for bed is a chore because I'm trying to brush my teeth and clean my face all while tears are streaking down my cheeks. Crossing to the bed, Tristan finally comes into the room and comes close. He smells of beer, and that instantly turns my stomach. *When did he start drinking more than just one?* Unease washes through me. "Steph," he tries again. This time his voice sounds pained, kind of like my heart feels.

"I'm tired, Tristan. It was a long, busy day, and now I'd just like to go to sleep." Not even waiting for an answer, I climb into bed and close my eyes. But Tristan remains standing there. I can feel the tension and heat radiating off his body, and it's disorienting, but I'm not in the right space for a discussion. I know for sure it would turn into a heated argument that would leave me a sobbing mess. *Nope.* I'm just going to lie here and hope he walks away, sooner than later.

Chapter 19

Tristan

Being on the road absolutely sucks. My first year in the league wasn't so bad because I was excited to see all the cities I'd be traveling to. However, in reality, we didn't get to see the cities at all. They'd bus us from the airport to the hotel to the arena and back. Because Steph was in school, I was happy something distracted her during my absence, but I still missed her like crazy. And over the years, I just accepted that was how it was going to be.

Then our first months of marriage happen, and it sucks on a whole new level. Even though I love playing hockey, I want to spend 24/7 with my wife. And that isn't a possibility. Because we're newlyweds, it seems like when I'm home, we have incredible sex, but there isn't time for anything else.

The distance and time apart put an immense strain on our relationship. It feels like we're becoming strangers, and coming home fills me with anxiety and uncertainty. It seems like Steph has built a life for herself that doesn't include me, and that hurts more than I can admit. Instead of talking about it, I just ignore it, hoping I'm wrong. But after a weekend home where I have to schedule time with my wife, I'm annoyed.

Steph's text this afternoon asking where I am arrives after I've already had a few beers with the guys. I'm not drunk, but I am nicely relaxed. Seeing that the game isn't over, I know I'll be fine to drive home when it is. Even though her texts give me the sense she's off, I continue watching the game. What I come home to later that evening is the silent treatment. *What the fuck?* Each time I try to engage her in conversation, I get the cold shoulder. When she tells me she's tired and going to bed, I remain silent, even though my body shakes with anger. I think about calling the guys to see if they're still at the bar, but I'm already home. Pissed off, I return to the living room and sulk on the couch. I don't understand what happened. I figured we were fine after the amazing quickie we had just before she left this morning. *What had happened to make everything go so wrong?*

At two in the morning, I'm still angered and decide the couch is comfortable enough for the night. Stretching out my over six-foot frame, I pull the fleece throw from the back of the couch and over me, then fall asleep. I'm woken the next morning by the noisy

Keurig coffee maker gurgling. Trying my best to wake up, I pop open my eyelids one at a time, when a heavenly coffee aroma invades my nostrils. It smells like the coffee we had on our honeymoon in Maui. It's all chocolate and macadamia nuts, and my mouth waters.

Yawning, I lift my hands above my head. "Morning," I say, sounding rough, like I'd chewed on gravel. Not angry anymore, I reconsider if my sleeping on the couch last night was a smart decision. Not only was it uncomfortable for my enormous frame, but I missed the nearness of my wife.

"Sorry, did I wake you?" Steph asks, startled to see me awake and on the couch. *I don't know where else I'd be.* I look over and she won't make eye contact. *What is she avoiding? Me?* I mean, we didn't end the evening on very good terms, but we need to talk about what happened. She finally looks at me, and her worried eyes scream she is hurting.

Standing, I slowly make my way over to her and answer, "It's all good." When I reach her, I pull her into a tight hug. I don't care if it makes her angry or combative. She is my wife and I'm going to let her know I missed her. I still don't understand everything that happened the day before, but I chalk it up to nerves and declare today a better day. Thankfully, after a moment of resistance, Steph melts into my arms. And I just hold her.

"We need to talk, Tristan," she whispers against my chest, and my stomach drops and dread sinks in. *Those words no man wants to hear.* What will she say? I assure you, I probably don't want to hear them. Instead, I want to pretend we don't have any problems. I don't want to hear how many times I've messed up and let her down, and I sure as shit don't want to confess that I feel alone in our marriage, especially when I'm home.

The air surrounding us feels heavy, suffocating. I need a moment away from it. "Okay. Can we grab breakfast first?" I ask, knowing my stomach will start protesting soon if I don't feed it. Plus, it will give us a chance to reset. Before she can even answer, my stomach growls, and she laughs.

"Yes, we can get breakfast."

Half an hour later, we're seated at a nearby café that offers the fluffiest pancakes and best scrambles. It's easy to keep everything surface level when we're at the restaurant, and we have a nice meal. It's reminiscent of the old days, and that gives me a spark of hope.

I'm not sure how our conversation will go when we get home, but as soon as we arrive, I feel things shift, and the happy, carefree feeling I had at the café is gone. Sitting together on the couch, we look at each other, both uncertain about how to start the conversation we need to have. Dread sits heavy in my gut.

Finally, Steph breaks the silence. "Yesterday was not a good day. The morning started poorly and then the evening was a complete disappointment."

"Is that why you wouldn't talk to me?" I question.

She nods. "When I got home yesterday, and you

weren't here, especially after you'd been upset about me going to help at the food pantry, I was confused."

I hang my head. "Yeah. I can see that. I just didn't know when you'd be back and I was getting stir-crazy. So when Brayden called, I jumped at the chance to hang out with my guys."

"But then when I texted you I was home, why did you stay longer? Why didn't you rush home? Didn't you start the day complaining about how we don't spend enough time together?" Her words are precise, just like a surgeon's blade, revealing the damage. Yes, I made that accusation, and yes, I still feel that way.

I take her hand in mine. "Honestly, Steph, I didn't know what I'd walk into. I knew when you left, even though we had sex, things weren't fixed. And with the guys, I know exactly what to expect. With us, I'm not sure anymore. Things between us seem strained, and I'm not sure what to do."

"You could have come home. That would have made things better. But instead, you stayed out." Her accusation stings. But she isn't done. "I felt like I didn't matter to you. You spend all your time with your teammates, and there you were, choosing them. Again."

Groaning, I say, "I wasn't choosing them."

Steph pulls her hand away and chuffs. "Really? Didn't you stay out with them?"

"Yes, I guess I did. But I really was watching the game. They were still at the bar when I left to come home to you," I grumble, feeling incredibly defensive.

When she crosses her arms against her chest, my heart rate skyrockets. *This isn't good.* A scowl settles on her face, and I notice her chin wobble. *Oh shit!* "Tristan." The pain in her voice breaks me and I lunge for her, pulling her into my arms as the tears begin to fall. My stomach drops. This isn't our first time jumping through these hoops, and I suspect it won't be our last. But how do I make things right? I feel like I'm losing her, and that's the last thing I want. We need to get back on track.

"Steph," I whisper as I hold her tight to my chest. "I'm so sorry. We'll figure this out. I promise."

Sniffling, she pushes back to look up at me. "What if we can't?" *Please don't say that.*

"Do you want to fix us?" I ask, trying to keep the anxiety out of my voice. *Please say yes. It'll break me if you say no.*

She nods. "I do."

Kissing her head, I pull her in tight. "Me too."

Sitting back on the couch with Steph cuddled into me, I try to make a plan. Our uncertainty of one another's feelings combines, weaving together a chaotic snapshot of unspoken heartache. *Isn't there a fix?* I need more information if I'm going to figure out how to fix us. Starting small, I ask her questions. "Are you unhappy?" Her answer is a nod against my chest, but I need to see her eyes. Nudging her chin up, her red, puffy eyes plead with me. *Fix us, Tristan. I'm trying to, babe.* "For how long?"

A minute passes, and I'm not sure I'm ready to hear her answer. When her lips finally part, the truth burns. "Probably since we got back from our honeymoon." *Fuck, that's only two months.* How is that possible? I mean, I've noticed things have been strained, but I thought it was just growing pains. You know, just adjusting to married life and finally living together. I rub at my temple. Her confession hits me like a sledgehammer to the head. When everything stops ringing and I have calmed my breathing, I look at her.

"I'm sorry, Steph. Why didn't you tell me?"

"Because then I would've had to admit failure. And I don't want to do that."

"Unless you're ending our marriage, we can consider it a learning curve or a speed bump. Every relationship has them. It's how you handle them that determines your success or failure."

"Oh," she says, looking at me. *Did she already think we were over?*

Sucking in a breath, I ask, "Are you trying to end this?" *Please say no.*

Steph pauses for a moment and my heart pounds in my chest. My body is pulsating with nervous energy and I can't sit still. Instead of pacing, I bounce my leg, trying to control myself. "N-no," she stutters when she finally answers. I wait a moment to see if she's going to say more because 'no' isn't really giving me a lot to go on.

Finally, she shakes her head. "No, I don't want to

do that. It's just these last couple of months have been..." Her words trail off, and I just want to scream. Her confession has pierced my heart, and she isn't giving me any information. I have no words. I'm not sure what to do to make things right between us, so I just hold her.

Chapter 20

Stephanie

January 2010

After the trials of the past year, I feel like I'm finally getting myself into a good place. I'm still volunteering at the food pantry and loving it. It is beyond rewarding, and the friends I've made keep me sane when Tristan is out of town.

With the big blowup Tristan and I had in the fall, we have been working on our relationship and healing the hurts we inflicted on each other. I can admit it isn't always easy. Our focus has to be on making each other a priority. Being apart is still a strain on our relationship, but that isn't going to change, so we've had to figure out how to not let it ruin us.

When Tristan is home this weekend, we spend every moment together after his hockey commitments are over. He volunteers at the food pantry with me and sees how incredible it is. We go on some impromptu dates. He even convinces me to take off a few days before he heads out to another series in Florida when the current home series wraps up.

I meet Tristan in the players' hallway outside their locker room following the game. They just won against the Mississippi Magic. Tugging me into him, he sucks in an enormous pull of air. "You smell so fucking good." Then he kisses me.

When he pulls back, I laugh. "I better smell better than a room full of stinky hockey players."

Tristan smirks. "Thanks for coming to my game. Are you ready to get out of here?" As we're heading toward the exit, one of his teammates approaches.

"Tristan, that goal was killer. The way you skated circles around their defenders and had that one on one with the goalie. It was like art, man. And then you turned it up with the perfect over-the-shoulder shot. It was perfection," he says.

Tristan hugs me tighter to his side. "Thanks, Roger. I wouldn't have had that play without a stellar pass from Williams."

Roger nods. "It was a thing of beauty from when the puck dropped to you scoring the winning goal."

I squeeze Tristan's hand, then whisper in his ear, "I'm so proud of you." He grins and puffs out his chest. Patting it, I say, "Okay, let's go home, big guy. It's been a long night."

"Good morning, sleepyhead," Tristan says as he wanders into our bedroom Monday morning.

I crack one eye open. "You better have coffee," I

grumble. He laughs and then his lips are on mine, giving me a deep, passion-filled kiss. When he pulls back, I'm lightheaded. "Good morning to you, too." I smile as he sits beside me. The smell of hot coffee wafts past my nose and I'm suddenly awake. Lifting my hands above my head, I stretch my body across our bed and yawn. Tristan runs his hands down my sides, tickling me. "Tristan, stop that," I warn.

Holding up his hands, he laughs. "Okay, okay."

"What's the plan for today?" I ask, knowing it's our last day before I have to go back to work and he goes back on the road.

"Well, seeing that you almost slept through breakfast, we'll have to do brunch or lunch."

Setting down my coffee, I enthusiastically throw back the covers. "Do I get to pick what we're having?"

Tristan eyes me. "Sure."

I squeal my excitement. "Okay, I want a lobster roll by the harbor."

Tristan stands up from the bed. "That we can do, but you have half an hour to get ready. Your time starts now." Before he even looks at his watch, I'm out of the bed and sprinting for the bathroom. It's doesn't take me long to get ready, but it's been two days since I washed my hair and it's in desperate need of cleaning. After taking the world's quickest shower with hair washing and conditioning, I speed dry. Getting dressed is a bit of a challenge since I'm still somewhat wet. Next, I add mousse to my hair and scrunch it. Brushing my teeth,

I'm done with a few minutes to spare. When I enter the living room, Tristan slow claps with a giant smile plastered to his face. I just shake my head as I grab my purse and head for the door.

The Waterfront Co.—the best seafood restaurant in town—is already packed at eleven a.m. Thankfully, our wait for a table isn't long. Tristan gets recognized and they show us to a magnificent table on the deck. While talking through his schedule for the series in Florida, our server walks up with our order. I bite into my lobster roll, and the taste of butter and lemon hits my tongue first. It is divine, and as if it couldn't get any better, it does. The sweet taste of thick, juicy fresh lobster follows it. Looking over at Tristan, I see he's wearing the same contented look I'm sure graces my face. This is the life.

Chapter 21

Tristan

I've got shit for luck. We just arrived in Florida for a series against the Copperheads, and the air conditioning in my room is broken. *Nice hotel.* It's so fucking muggy here, my sweat is sweating. My hair is plastered to my head like I just got out of the swimming pool, and my suit that I traveled here in is soaked. Guess I'll be sending that out for dry cleaning. I'm praying that practice comes soon so I can escape the sweatbox the hotel staff is calling my room and cool off. My body always craves the coolness of a hockey rink, but now, even more so.

About an hour after we're given our room assignments, they bus us to the arena for an early skate. We have a game tonight, so it won't be too rigorous. Hotel maintenance is supposed to be fixing my air conditioning while we're gone, so by the time I return, my room should be cool, just in time for my pre-game nap.

On the way to the rink, I text Steph.

ME

Good morning, gorgeous. How'd you
sleep?

STEPH

I slept well, but I miss you already.

ME

I miss you too. Thankfully, this is a
quick series and we'll be home in a
few days.

STEPH

Who are you rooming with this time?

ME

No one, but I'd take a roommate over
the single room any day.

STEPH

Really?

ME

Yeah. My air conditioner is broken,
and my room is doubling as a sauna.

STEPH

I'm so sorry. Can they fix it?

ME

They're working on it now. Hopefully,
it'll be fixed by the time we're done
with light practice.

STEPH

Crossing my fingers.

ME

You and me both. Pulling up to the
arena, so I gotta go. I love you and
will call tonight after my game.

STEPH

I love you too. Good luck with your
game. I'll be watching.

The game against the Copperheads started with them dominating the play. But then the intermission between the first and second periods happens and Coach lights a fire under us with a motivational speech. Okay, really, he just yells a lot. However, he's right. We need to step up our game and prove we deserve the W.

Pumped up and ready to go, our backup goalie, Woodsy, fist-bumps everyone before we take the ice. The second period is the opposite of the first and we tie up the score. When the third period starts, it's anyone's game. Whoever is the hungriest will walk away the winner. My second shift in, as I'm skating backward toward my net, the Copperheads center, Joseph Kristoph, plows into me. Our bodies become intertwined, and we both go down. In the process, my left knee gets tied up with his right leg and I hear a pop just before I feel the most agonizing pain.

"Fuck!" I shout. Being sandwiched between him and the ice puts more pressure on my knee and I grit my teeth, trying to deal with the throbbing pain. After he extricates himself from me, all I can do is lie there motionless. If I didn't move, I wasn't in excruciating pain.

Brody, one of my teammates, skates up and asks, "You okay, man?"

"No," I rasp. His head whips toward our bench and he motions to our trainers. Soon, I'm surrounded by trainers, referees, and teammates. Joseph skates up, getting as close as he can. His face looks pained, and he gazes at me with sad eyes.

"Sorry, Tristan. I didn't mean to take you out." I nod at him with my teeth still ground together. I know the hit hadn't been intentional, but the uncertainty of my next days and weeks makes me nauseous.

Before long I'm carried off the ice by stretcher and put in a training room. The Storm's trainers evaluate me, deciding to send me over to the hospital for an MRI. After stabilizing my knee, we do just that. In conversations with the trainers, I know I won't be back to play that evening or the next. They hypothesize on the way to the hospital that I tore my ACL. Without confirmation of that and its severity, they can't say if it will be weeks or months before my return.

There are some perks to being a professional athlete, and not having to wait for care is one of them. Within moments of arriving, I'm whisked away from the general population and put into a private section of the ER. As quickly as possible with a bum knee, I change into a hospital gown before shucking my clothes into the empty chair near my hospital bed. The attending doctor arrives and, after briefly talking with me, he agrees with the recommendation of my trainers. Before I can even get bored, I'm being helped onto the MRI table for my scan. I'm given a headset so I can listen to music while I'm in the machine for images of my knee.

Sixty minutes and an IV of dye later, I'm wheeled back to my room. An hour after that, an on-call orthopedic surgeon enters my room with my diagnosis. According to Dr. Ben Bishop, I suffered a third-degree tear of both my left knee's ACL and MCL. He recommends surgery and gives me some time to think about it. Before I decide, I need to talk to the trainers, the GM of the Storm, my manager, Troy, and Steph.

Our head trainer, Jack, arrives after the game. He informs me he's spoken with our GM. "We've looked into Dr. Bishop and can assure you he is a top-notch surgeon. The organization would feel comfortable having him perform the repair. However, if you'd rather return to Boston first, we'll get you in with Dr. Jacobs immediately. He's a surgeon who works closely with the team." I nod my understanding, but I'm struggling to commit. *I want the guy who fixes my knee to guarantee I'll still be able to play hockey.*

"Tristan, after the game, I spoke with Dr. Jacobs and told him about your injury. He recommended that if he were in your shoes and Dr. Bishop was the surgeon, he wouldn't hesitate to have it repaired here," he explains.

Still processing everything, I ask, "Can I have a moment to call Troy and Steph?" Jack steps out to give me some privacy.

My call to Troy goes exactly how I expected. He's gruff and to the point. He tells me he's sorry this happened but that I'll get past it. Before hanging up, Troy says, "Let me know what you need from me. I won't lie to you. It's going to be a long road, but you've got this."

I let out the deep breath that's held me hostage since I was laid out on the ice. Over the past few hours, it feels like a million things have happened and my mind is spinning. I close my eyes and lay my head back for a moment. I try to gather myself before I call Steph. I know she was watching the game, and she's probably freaking out, desperate for information. I hate to make her wait, but I wanted all the facts before we talk.

My heart thumps in my chest as the phone rings.

A panicked Steph answers, "Tristan, is that you?"

"It's me, babe." I can hear her break into sobs, and I wish I could hold her.

After a few moments, she sniffles. "I was so worried. I saw the hit and then you didn't move. Are you okay?"

I don't know. Hanging my head, I tell her, "Yes and no. I've torn both my ACL and MCL and need surgery. The team highly recommends the orthopedic surgeon here. They've told me it's better to have the surgery here so that I don't risk further injury, but they've left the decision up to me."

"Okay. Will they rehab there? How long will you be gone?" I can practically hear the wheels turning in her head, and her anxiety is palpable.

"They can schedule me for surgery the day after tomorrow and I'll be in the hospital for a few days. Then a few days later, I can travel home. Once I'm cleared, I'll start rehab with the ortho office the Storm contracts with."

"Who will help you travel back? Can I come to be there for your surgery and trip home? I don't want to get in the way."

Concerned, I say, "I'd love to have you here with me for this. Will your work give you time off?"

Without a second passing, Steph answers, "Already texted my boss, and he's in total support. He wishes you a successful and speedy recovery."

I'm relieved that Steph is coming because I need her more than I can admit. I shift on the bed, trying to get more comfortable. But the slight movement pulls on my knee. "Fuck, that hurts." This entire experience has been a complete mindfuck. I'm uncertain of what I'll feel from one moment to the next. Slight movements can make me grit my teeth and curse the heavens, while supported movements are just an uncomfortable throbbing. And don't even get me started on the muscle flinches. *What the fuck!* Those shitty movements aren't controlled, and usually, they're agonizing. Sharp like a red-hot fire poker ground into my knee. All I have to say is I hope once I have surgery and they stabilize my knee, this will all get better.

"What happened?" Steph's worried tone fills my ear.

"I just shifted, and apparently my pain meds are wearing off." As if on cue, a seasoned nurse who reminds me of my mother pops in to check on me.

"Mr. Murphy. How are you doing?" she questions.

"Honestly?" I ask. She quirks her head and nods.

"I just tweaked it again when I moved, and I don't think the pain meds are doing anything anymore."

Walking over to the moveable computer, she opens my chart. "Well, it looks like you're almost ready for another dose. Let me check with the attending as to his plan. He'll be in shortly."

"Thanks," I mutter as she heads out.

"Hey babe, it's going to get busy here in a minute when doctors come flooding back in with my trainer. I need to let them know I'm having the surgery here. I'll have Troy call you with all the details. If you need help to get here, let him know, and his assistant can help. Thank you for coming. I love you."

"I love you too. I'll see you soon."

After hanging up, it seems like my door is constantly opening. The doctors and my trainer come back in. I call Troy and put him on speakerphone to listen as we discuss the surgery. It's two in the morning and I'm beat. Basically, I want more pain meds and a nice enormous bed to crash in.

After they stabilize my knee, I'm discharged from the hospital with a few pills to get me through the next day until surgery. Troy plans to call Steph and get her on the plane. Jack helps me get back to my room at the hotel and sleeps in a roll-out bed the hotel has put into my room. It isn't long after I power down a protein bar, sports drink, and pain pill that I pass out. Sleeping on my back with my knee propped up isn't comfortable at all, and my night of sleep has been rough. The next day is a haze of sleep, managing the pain, forcing myself to eat and drink, and, of course, fielding visits from my worried teammates.

That afternoon, a knock at my door has Roland, one of the junior trainers, jumping. Jack had to be at the game tonight in case any other players suffer injury, so Roland, a hysterically funny middle-aged man who's worked for the Storm for a decade, is with me. Lying with my eyes closed, I feel the dip of the bed and a soft kiss placed on my cheek. My eyes flicker open, and there is my beautiful wife, who, despite all the worry she's wearing across her face, is as gorgeous as ever.

"Steph, you're here."

She taps my chest and warmth spreads over my body. "I told you I would come. You aren't facing this alone." Her strength and determination speak volumes about the woman she is. Threading our fingers together, I wonder how I got so lucky.

"How do you feel?" she asks while her eyes trace the room, no doubt noticing all the medical supplies.

"Mostly tired, and I have to pee," I confess with a laugh. Because of my situation, Steph doesn't know how to help me yet. She looks at me as if she expects me to swing my legs over the side of the bed and stand up. We look at each other and I suggest, "Maybe Roland can help this time and you can see how it goes."

"Yeah, sure," she says before stepping away. Roland moves into her abandoned spot and I slowly and carefully move my leg off the stack of pillows. The slight movement causes immediate pain and I suck in a breath and grit my teeth.

"Breathe, Tristan," Roland reminds me. Forcing the air out, I take short, stunted breaths while I continue to get myself in position. Sweat trickles down my back like I've just finished a 5K. Minutes later, I'm ready for an assisted lift to my crutches. In the day since my accident, I've become quite proficient at this. Once I'm up on my crutches, Roland makes sure I'm stable before he moves in front of me. He makes sure my path to the bathroom is clear. Already the crutches have worn tender spots in my armpits, and I wince as I stand, waiting.

"Are you okay?" Steph asks from across the room.

I nod. "Yeah. I'm good, just in pain." I attempt a smile for her, but I'm sure she's not convinced when I see her slight frown. Shaking my head, I try to reassure her. "Babe, I'm good, all things considered." She forces a smile, but I don't miss the tears welling in her eyes.

"All clear," Roland tells me as he moves in front of me. The trek to the bathroom is agonizingly slow, but when I finally pee, relief has never felt better. When I finish up, Roland and Steph help me back to my bed.

The rest of the day passes by slowly. Between naps and trips to the bathroom, I watch mind-numbing cable TV. Surgery is scheduled for early the next day. So after watching the game, I go to bed, hopeful everything with my surgery will be successful.

Chapter 22

Stephanie

While watching Tristan's game against Florida, I'm impressed with how well the team is playing. They're on fire. Not only do they dominate possession of the puck, but the goals are magical.

At the moment of Tristan's accident, my world freezes. Chills overtake my body as he lies motionless on the ice. Seeing the faces of his teammates and the trainers, I know something is very wrong.

Hockey is a dangerous sport and injuries aren't uncommon, but usually, the player leaves the ice without assistance. This isn't the case with Tristan. When a lift team carries a backboard onto the ice and nears my husband, my stomach drops. How will I get to him? He's all the way in Florida.

For the rest of the game, I remain glued to the television, hoping for any information. My cell phone sits silently next to me as I'm overwhelmed with worry. A few hours later, I pace our condo. I'm curious if the hospital has called Tristan's parents. *You're his wife. They'd call you first.* At least I hope that is the case. But all I get is radio silence. I text my boss and tell him about the situation and that I may need a few days off. He grants them and tells me he hopes everything goes well. Finally, in the early morning hours, Tristan calls me. He tells me about his injury and that he'll need surgery.

I book a one-way ticket to Tampa so I can be by Tristan's side. I don't know what to expect when I arrive, but it's difficult during the flight to prepare myself for what I'm walking into. I'm so scared, and when I finally talk to Tristan, my worries only amplify. He's always been so strong, but he sounds broken right now, and I haven't seen that before. We're entering unexplored terrain, and I'm fearful of the uncertainty of it.

On surgery day, Roland and I help get Tristan ready and to the hospital. Before leaving the hotel, Coach Phillip Jameson and Jack stop us in the lobby.

"Good morning," Coach says as he approaches us.

"Morning," we all answer, our voices full of hesitancy. *How will today go?*

"Are you all set for today?" Jack asks as he looks at Tristan, who is sitting in a rented wheelchair, looking pale and fatigued. He shrugs his shoulders, as he hasn't been very talkative today. Not that I blame him.

Roland jumps in. "Yes, we're all set. Surgery is at ten, so hopefully late this afternoon, I'll have an update for you."

"Sounds great," Coach says as he lowers down to a squat in front of Tristan. "I know you've got this. You are one tough son of a bitch, and I know right now sucks, but you'll get through this with the strength and determination that got you into the NHL."

Tristan forces a smile and mutters, "Yeah." Coach stands up, pats his shoulder, and moves next to Jack again.

Jack looks at me. "Stephanie, thank you for being here. Roland will be with you until you get back to Boston. You have the full support of the Storm behind you. Let's get through this and put this horrible chapter behind us. Okay?"

I nod, they both say goodbye, and we're left alone. Looking at my phone, I notice the time. "We should probably head to the hospital."

When we arrive, they rush us through the check-in process because of Tristan's VIP status and then escort us to pre-op. Roland stays with me the entire time.

At nine-thirty, Dr. Bishop pokes his head through the curtain with a wide smile. "Good morning, Tristan. How are you?"

Tristan lets out a weak laugh. "I'm here, so I'm going to answer... not so good."

Dr. Bishop nods his head. "Yeah, I can see that. Any questions for me?"

We all shake our heads no.

Dr. Bishop slaps his hands together. "Okay. Then let's mark your knee, get you back to the OR, and fix you up."

Tristan looks at Roland. "Can I have a moment with my wife, please?"

Roland nods. "I'll be right outside."

Curious about why we need privacy, I look at him, confused. When we're alone, Tristan gazes at me with weary eyes. My heart tugs.

"Babe, I just wanted to say thank you for coming to Florida to be here for the surgery. It means a lot to me to have you here. You know I've never gone through this before, and just having you by my side takes away some nerves and fear." *He's scared too?*

Grabbing his hand, I lower myself closer to him and say, "There is no place I'd rather be. This is scary, and my nerves are frayed, but I'm relying on the good recommendation the team gave for Dr. Bishop, and because of that, I'm confident you will be just fine." I lean closer and kiss him gently on the lips.

The anesthesiologist comes in next and gives Tristan a nerve block in his leg. The meds take effect quickly, and I'm not prepared for the jokester my husband turns into. Because of his injury, the nurses gave him a disposable urinal so he can empty his bladder before surgery. After he uses it, he thrusts it at me and, in a very serious voice, warns, "Do not drink what's in this." Then he looks around as if he's being watched and side whispers, "It's not lemonade." Then he bursts into laughter as if it was the funniest thing he's ever said. I look at Roland, and he snickers.

Shortly after, the hospital staff comes and collects Tristan for surgery.

"I love you," I tell him while kissing him on the forehead.

Tristan lays his head back, then dazedly answers, "Love you too, babe. See you on the flip side." *Oh my. Those meds are bonkers.*

Four hours after they rolled him back, Dr. Bishop finds Roland and me in the waiting room. "Mrs. Murphy, everything with Tristan's surgery went great. I made repairs to both his ACL and MCL, and because he's injured both, his recovery will be longer. He'll need to stay the night tonight, and if his pain is controlled and he can move around with assistance, he'll likely be ready to go home tomorrow. I know that home is a hotel room right now and you are probably eager to get back to Boston. But I'm asking that you stay here in Florida for a few more days to make sure Tristan is healing well and there is no sign of infection." I nod my understanding. "I will also talk to Dr. Jacobs and send him Tristan's scans and my op notes." He asks if we have questions, and I can't think of any. I just want to see my husband.

Finally, after another hour, Roland and I can see Tristan in recovery. Lying in a hospital bed, snoring, is my pale-faced husband. He's covered in a blanket with his knee propped up. Machines next to him beep and chime. I look at the attending nurse, wondering if everything is okay, and she smiles.

"Tristan's just waking up from surgery. His body is working hard to process everything that just happened. When he finally wakes up and is alert with all his vitals stable, we'll move him to his room," she kindly explains.

"Okay, thanks," I reply. Standing back so I'm not in the way, the nurse again looks at me.

"You can talk to him and touch him. Let him know you're here."

Setting my purse down, I move to his bedside and lean over his face. I place a kiss on his lips, and they seem chilled. "Excuse me. Is he warm enough?" I ask.

"He should be. I just put a warm blanket on top of him before you came back. Check his hand." Untucking his hand, I notice it's plenty warm, and I squeeze it, although I'm careful to avoid the IV. Tristan squeezes back. Surprised, I look at his face and see his eyelids flutter.

"Tristan. You're out of surgery and the doctor said it went well," I tell him as I stroke his hair from his forehead. When his eyes finally open minutes later, they are glazed over. He's higher than a kite. *This ought to be fun.*

"Welcome back, Mr. Murphy. How are you feeling?" the nurse asks.

Slurring, he answers, "Never been better. Can I go

home now?" My mouth falls open and I look at Roland and mouth *"He's wasted."*

Roland nods and says, "They gave him the big drugs. He's happy now, but in four hours he'll be singing a different tune."

"Done this before?" the nurse asks with a smirk from across the room as she enters more information into her rolling computer.

"Not the knee surgery, but I have definitely been a caretaker before," he answers. *Oh good. That makes one of us.*

She smiles at us both. "Then this should be a piece of cake. How about I get Tristan ready to move to his room?" she asks as Tristan sings something incoherent. All I can do is laugh. I wish I could record this. He won't believe me. At least Roland is here to witness his live concert.

"Visiting hours are eight to eight," the new nurse tells us after she gets Tristan settled into his room. When she hands him the combo remote that controls everything from the television to calling the nurses' station, he happily smiles at her. She walks to the doorway to enter information into her rolling computer, and he presses the call button.

"How can I help you?" someone from the nurses' station responds. Our nurse turns around to see what Tristan's doing.

"I've got to pee and I can't walk," he grumbles. Roland snickers. *Why?*

His nurse walks farther into the room. "It's okay, Julie. I've got him," she says.

"Thanks, Sara," Julie answers.

Nurse Sara moves to Tristan's bed and asks, "You need to go to the bathroom?"

Tristan, looking stressed, nods frantically.

"Then just go," Sara tells him.

Tristan's mouth falls open, and he sternly informs her, "I'm not peeing this bed. I just need someone to help me to the bathroom. Can you help me?"

Roland again snickers, and I'm still lost. *The nurse told him to pee the bed? That can't be right. What am I missing?*

"Tristan, you still have your catheter in from surgery. It'll allow your bladder to drain without making a mess," Nurse Sara explains.

Confused, Tristan stares at her. I look back to Roland, and he points to the bag attached to Tristan's hospital bed that has yellow liquid in it.

"Just relax and go," she tells him again.

Agitated, he scowls, crosses his arms, and tells her, "Fine, I'll just go, and when I get pee everywhere, you'll have to clean it up."

Sara smiles at him. "Deal."

Tristan relaxes, and the bag begins to fill. He calls out, in a strained voice, "I can't pee."

Stepping forward, I grab his hand. "Babe, you are peeing right now. I can see the bag filling up."

His head whips to me. "Bag?"

I point to it. "Yes, right there."

He looks along the side of the bed and sees the bag. "Oh."

Roland and I stay for another few hours until visiting hours are over. Returning to the hotel, we are emotionally exhausted, and we both head to our rooms for the night.

Early the next day, I meet Roland in the lobby before we head back to the hospital. *I hope Tristan had a good night.* When we arrive, he's sitting up, eating his breakfast and watching sports. I'm relieved. *Of course he is. Tristan puts a hundred percent into everything he does, and if he's determined to not let this stop him, then it won't. It feels great to see a smile on his face again after the frown I've seen the past two days.*

"Morning," I say as we enter the room. Tristan gives me a lazy smile, and I know the pain meds are doing their job. *Oh, maybe that's why he is smiling?* I'm still counting it as a win.

Approaching his bed, I ask, "How did you sleep? How are you feeling?"

"I slept great, and they finally let me pee in a bathroom like a civilized person." He forks his rubbery-looking omelet. "But this food is..."

Grimacing, I say, "Interesting?" Tristan laughs. His deep rumble registers, settling my heart and letting me know everything is going to be fine.

Roland steps forward and asks, "Have you seen your doctor today?"

Tristan shakes his head. "The nurse who brought breakfast said he'd be by sometime this morning."

When the doctor arrives an hour later, he asks Tristan a series of questions to get his thoughts on being discharged. Tristan is all for it. Roland and I go back and forth, asking what to expect the next days. After we've exhausted all our questions, he excuses himself to see other patients and to get Tristan's discharge paperwork ready. From what I now understand, the next days, weeks, and months will be busy. Looks like I'll be talking to work about taking some time off until Tristan can move around independently.

Since we've been together, we haven't ever spent as much time together as we are about to. I'm scared to admit I'm nervous. I love Tristan and I want to be there for him in every respect, but it's all uncertain. The worst I've ever seen him is with stomach flu or a cold. This is so much worse. Logically, I know I can handle the yuck factor of it all. The thing that makes me most conflicted is not knowing how he's going to deal with being limited in movement and ability. Tristan has always been a go-getter, and I can't imagine it will be easy for him to lie around for weeks healing until PT starts. And then that's a whole other beast to deal with. What if he's frustrated with how slow recovery can be and the thought of just because you're fixed doesn't mean you're one hundred percent again?

Chapter 23

Tristan

I survived the surgery, but I feel weird. I'm exhausted. I don't have much pain yet, but my nurse has told me several times I'm on strong pain meds. I notice my mind is relatively blank. The only thoughts consuming me are that I am dying of thirst and I know someone promised me a popsicle, but I've yet to receive it. It feels pretty nice not having to worry about anything else. I guess that's Steph's and Roland's job now. *Suckers.*

It's day two, and they discharged me yesterday. Steph and Roland have alternated caring for me at the hotel. I have an appointment with Dr. Bishop in a few days, and if all is going well, he'll give me permission to travel home. For now, it is ice, rest, and repeat. We have fun ordering from local restaurants and trying things that aren't in Boston. Steph loves the Cuban food, and Roland and I have eaten our weight in soul food. The days are long and boring, and I'm more than ready to get home. When that day arrives, Steph acts like a seasoned nurse and Roland only assists with transfers. As long as we stay on schedule with the ice and pain meds, I'm fairly comfortable. Steph has talked with her boss and started her FMLA paperwork so she can stay home with me for a few weeks. I'm lucky it's my left side because I can start driving sooner than if it had been my right.

Knock, knock.

"That must be Roland," Steph says as she moves over to the door. Roland comes in wearing a giant grin.

"What are you so happy about?" I ask while I lift myself to my crutches, wincing when they push into my raw skin.

Placing his hands on his hips, he asks, "The real question is, why aren't you smiling? Are you ready to go home?"

Looking around the plain hotel room, I laugh. "And leave this paradise?" Roland chuckles and Steph rolls her eyes.

"Let's get this over with," she chides as she ushers us to the door.

Thankfully, the ride to the hospital is short and fairly smooth, as I am rather uncomfortable having my knee bent more than it's been in days. *How's the plane ride going to go?*

Once Dr. Bishop's assessed me and answered all our questions, he tells me I'm clear to travel. He cautions me about the added stress it'll put on my body, but to me, that far outweighs the cost of staying here any longer. Don't get me wrong, I'm grateful that Dr. Bishop was my surgeon, but I want to be back in my bed, wearing something other than a few pairs of shorts and tees that Steph grabbed from the hotel gift store. I feel like a walking advertisement for Tampa, and all I've seen is the ice arena and hospital.

After we get back to the hotel, Roland, Steph, and I have a conference call with Coach, the GM Michael McCarthy, and Jack to give them an update.

"Tristan, I'm glad your surgery went well. I spoke with Dr. Jacobs here, and he wants to get you into his office soon so he can evaluate you and decide on the best course of action going forward. I imagine you're still uncomfortable and moving won't be easy. Because of that, I'm having my assistant book all three of you in first class for your flight back. She'll be sending that information to you soon. You are important to our organization and we want to assist you in all ways during your recovery. If you need anything, please don't hesitate to let us know," Mr. McCarthy says.

Looking over at Steph, I notice her shock. *Must have been the first-class comment.* "Thank you, sir. The extra leg room will make for easier travel, and I will contact Dr. Jacobs's office once I'm back in town."

"Tristan, this is Jack. I can set up that appointment with Dr. Jacobs for you. And Roland can be available to go with you."

Roland sits up. "I can do that. Once we're back in Boston, I'll help Stephanie get Tristan all settled before I leave."

"Sounds good. Thanks," Jack says.

"Hey, Tristan, it's Coach. How are you feeling?"

Sitting back against the headboard with pillows propping my leg up, I think for a moment before answering. "I'm okay. Steph and Roland have taken good care of me. They've stayed on top of my ice and pain needs, but I am so bored and I miss hockey."

"Understood. When you're back, let me know when you're up for visitors. The guys have required daily updates and, thankfully, Roland provided them. I heard Jonesy even bought the latest NHL game for the PlayStation to bring over for you."

Tristan laughs. "Visitors would be great. Give me another couple of days. Maybe after your next road trip."

After the call, I need a nap. Steph sets me up with an ice pack, a peanut butter and jelly sandwich, and another dose of pain meds, and Roland excuses himself to his room. I try my best to get as comfortable as possible. As I'm about to drift off, Steph curls up next to me. I lean over and kiss her head. "Thanks, babe, for coming down here to take care of me." She snuggles in closer.

"This is where I want to be, taking care of you. Now, get some rest." I fall asleep with a smile on my face.

Hours later, I wake up to Steph packing our room up. "What are you doing, babe?"

Startled, she answers, "Mr. McCarthy's assistant got us all on a flight tomorrow morning, so I'm packing up what we have. Coach took your gear with them on the team plane, so we don't have much. Do you want me to run out and get you something better to travel in?"

I laugh. "What, you don't like my tourist travel wear? Are you saying this isn't sexy?"

Rolling her eyes at me, she says, "You know I think you're always sexy. It doesn't matter what you wear. In fact, I saw a sweatshirt in the hotel gift shop that would complete your look and make you irresistible."

"Oh, really? What does this sweatshirt have on it?" I ask in a deep, gravelly voice.

Steph puts down the items she's holding and steps closer to the bed. Running her fingers up my uninjured leg sends shivers down my spine. And despite all that my body's been through the last week, my cock is desperate for her touch. My blue cotton shorts tent, and Steph stops and looks at me. All I can do is grin. Smirking at me, she palms my cock. The tight grip wrapped around it is divine. My balls tighten as my lust clouds over any rational thought.

"Come here, babe," I beg.

"Tristan, we can't. Have you forgotten you're injured and you just had surgery?" Her words register, but it's tough to care about their importance when she's stroking my cock.

"Babe," I whine.

Steph leans over my body and grabs the waistband of my shorts and slides them over my hips. My cock springs forward like he's reaching for her. She laughs before she slowly circles the head with her tongue. I moan at the sensation. *Temptress.*

"Stay still," she cautions, then moves to the end of the bed.

"Wait, where are you going?" I ask.

She seductively crawls up the bed, ever mindful of my injured leg. When she's again at my hips, she leans over and wraps her hand around the base of me and gives me a few pumps before she lowers. Instinctively, my hand goes to her hair. I gather it in a messy ponytail because I need to see her face. The way her eyes smolder and the expression she wears are sexy as fuck. Excited anticipation zings through my body as she lowers her mouth and blows on the tip of me. Smiling, her pink tongue darts out to lick my slit. *This is ecstasy!* I suck in a sharp breath and remind myself to remain still. I'm not feeling my knee right now, but that doesn't mean I won't if I get too crazy.

"Hold still, Tristan," she chastises, as if she can read my mind. "I'm going to blow your mind." Then she swallows me whole. When I reach the back of her throat, she swallows, and it squeezes my cock.

"Steph." I groan. Slowly, she pulls her mouth back

up my pulsating shaft with her teeth bared. It isn't painful, but it certainly makes me aware of what her capable mouth could do to me if she wanted to inflict torture. I'm undecided if that would be good or bad. We've never really tried anything too risqué involving pain.

When she reaches the head of my cock, she wraps her teeth around it and sucks hard while also reaching inside my shorts and fondling my balls. My breath becomes labored and I want to thrust my hips, but I know that won't be good for my knee or her dental work. As my orgasm builds, I feel myself tighten the hold I have on her hair. Steph massages my taint and I warn, "Babe. I'm going to come." Again, she swallows me down and I grunt. My orgasm shatters my tension and I explode into her mouth, following it with a deep groan. *Holy shit. I haven't come like that in forever.* Steph squeezes my balls again before she removes her hand from my shorts. My eyes flash to her mouth, and the way she licks her lips is sexy as fuck. Lost in lust and panting, I pull her to my lips and kiss her with all the desire coursing through my body. My wife has a deliciously dangerous mouth that wipes my mind clear of everything except how fantastic I feel.

It's easy to fall asleep after that, as Steph has sated me. I'm only upset I can't reciprocate, but she reminds me it won't be forever. Then she tells me she's more than happy to pleasure me in the meantime. *Hell yes.*

The next morning, our trip back to Boston is

uneventful. Because I'm obviously injured, they give us ample space and time to get around the airport and onto the plane. Roland is a whiz with a wheelchair, and he gets me through the airport faster than I do at my normal walking speed. Security is even easy. The agent wands me and the wheelchair and then lets me through.

When we arrive home, Roland helps us get set up in our condo. He even runs to the nearby Target to buy extra pillows and a pair of rubber-soled slippers I can wear around the house. He also uses hockey tape and some washcloths to make my crutches more comfortable to use.

If things keep going the way they have been so far, I see my recovery going pretty smoothly.

Chapter 24

Stephanie

The first day we're home from Florida is a blur. Jack gets us in to see Dr. Jacobs just a day later, which also coincides with Tristan's post-op. I do my best to help him with what I can, but besides being much larger than me and hard to shift, he's as stubborn as an ox. More than once this week we've exchanged heated, ugly words that leave him snarling and me crying. Last night was the worst. During his post-op, Dr. Jacobs delivered some grim news. Since the injury, Tristan has been looking at his recovery as a checklist. Surgery. Check. Rehab. Check. Return to play. Check. And from what I understand, that is still an appropriate outlook for the next six-plus months of our life. Tristan, however, is impatient and doesn't agree with what Dr. Jacobs said. He becomes angry when the doctor explains that it'll take longer to heal because his injury involves two major muscles and ligaments in his knee,. Everyone is still considering Tristan's return to play as a viable option. But his recovery will dictate everything.

The first few weeks are hairy. During week two, while Tristan is still banned him from rehab, I get up early and help get him ready before I head to work. In those first days, Tristan was still awkward with his crutches, but we figured out how to most effectively move him with my assistance. He spends his days resting, hydrating, and recovering. The week before physical therapy begins, we have it all down to a science.

At the first session of physical therapy, when they are assessing his ability, strength, and range of motion, he becomes frustrated. "Why can't I be squatting right now?" he complains to his therapist, Kelvin.

Kelvin stops what he's doing, rolls his chair back, and looks at Tristan. "Man, I get it. You're a professional athlete and you aren't used to putting on the brakes. You give one hundred and ten percent at what you do. Am I right?"

Looking tired, Tristan's shoulders slump in defeat. He doesn't even bother to answer with words, just nods.

"I get you're frustrated and probably angry, but in order to make sure you heal correctly, we have to do things in the right order. There are no shortcuts in rehab. First, we have to assess your ability. Second, we need to gauge your healing. Third, and finally, we form a plan for action. Okay?" I'm blown away by the kindness and support he's offering to my husband, who looks like he's ready to attack. "I'm here to help you in any way I can and answer questions you may have. I will warn you that you may not always like my answers, but I'm a straight shooter with a heart full of optimism. I will be one of your biggest cheerleaders." Tristan hangs his head.

Not wanting to interfere, I remain in the periphery, just observing. Next week, Tristan will be on his own. The team has arranged a car service to get him to and from rehab. I wish I could be here with him, but I don't have the flexibility in my job.

After a few moments, Tristan finally looks up. "Kelvin, how long will this take until I'm back out there?"

Kelvin offers him a friendly smile. "I don't have a definite timeline to give you. I know we are looking at months to let you finish healing. Then we have to work on building your strength, endurance, and skills back after a long hiatus."

"Months?" Tristan questions. "So I'm out the rest of this season, but I might be ready for next season?"

Please, please, please say yes.

"You are definitely out the rest of this season. But a great goal for us would be to work toward returning to the team in the fall, maybe not for preseason, but hopefully before October."

Tristan nods, looking more confident. "Okay, let's

get started. The sooner we begin, the sooner we finish, right?"

Kelvin laughs. "That's the spirit. Let's show your teammates what a beast you are."

Following Tristan's session, we go out to lunch. He's still in a mood that puts me on edge. We don't talk much, because I can see he's still processing what Kelvin said. And I can agree it was a lot to take in. But I'm grateful Kelvin is so optimistic. I can't help but believe that Tristan is going to return to the ice sooner than they expected, faster and stronger than when he left. *Or I hope so anyway.*

The first month of rehab for Tristan moves painstakingly slowly. When I get home in the evenings, while I make dinner, he complains about all the simple exercises they have him doing and what a waste of time it is. A few nights ago, I suggested he ask Kelvin to explain his thinking behind them. When I ask him about it days later, he tells me he forgot and then continues to complain. He believes they are holding back his recovery and prolonging his absence from hockey.

Another month passes, and even though he's moved on from basic moves and exercises to more complex work with balance and strength, it isn't good enough for him. I know he wants to recover and get back to hockey, but he's unwilling to listen to the professionals when they explain why this takes so long.

I hope that soon he'll be able to see the light at the end of the tunnel.

Unfortunately, the next few months follow the same pattern. I try my best to be supportive and encouraging, but it always falls on deaf ears. In fact, we don't talk much anymore because I'm never sure which Tristan I'm going to get. Angry one or Eeyore one. Neither is enjoyable. Either way, I seem to end up in tears. It's all emotionally taxing and consuming. Stressed about how I'm handling everything—or not handling it, as the case may be—keeps me awake at night, and no matter what I do, I feel like I'm failing. I'm not enough for Tristan. I'm not as productive at work because I'm exhausted. My days never seem to end. I deal with a full day of work, then come home to be met with the mood swings of my husband. *When will it end?* It's taking its toll on me, and I'm feeling like I'm disappearing.

It's been five months since he began rehab, and although Tristan may have improved physically, emotionally, he's regressed by miles. On most days, I can tell by how he responds to me, how my evening will most likely end. Even his teammates have a similar reaction to him when they stop by. I'm not always there, but the few times I have been, the interactions are short, snappy, and frigid. It's like he can't stand to see them healthy and able to still play hockey. I only imagine it will get worse when the season officially starts. Maybe then they'll be too busy to visit and I won't have to watch him push away his friends and coaches. Those guys obviously care for him despite the way he treats them. When visiting, the guys are always great about checking in with me. Each time I've seen them, they've offered to grab Tristan for an outing. But every time I approach him with that, he snarls at me as if I'm suggesting something incredibly awful to him. He's become unpredictable; someone I don't even recognize.

"Hi, honey, I'm home," I call out when I enter our condo. It had been a taxing day, and I'm desperate for a distraction. Listening hard, I notice there isn't any response. Moving through the space, I'm looking for Tristan. *Maybe he has his headphones on and can't hear me.* When I get to our bedroom, the door is only open a smidge. Pushing it open, I notice everything is pitch black. The blackout shades have been pulled tight, and no light is visible. To see, I step back and flip on the hallway bathroom light and it casts light into the room. Slowly, I make it over to our bed and I see a large, unmoving lump. "Tristan," I whisper. *I hope he isn't getting sick.* Reaching for his forehead, I check to see if he's warm. He isn't, but he must be sleeping really deeply.

Tiptoeing back out into the hallway, I pull the door closed. Making my way to the kitchen, I decide to make a pot of chicken noodle soup in case he isn't feeling well. Pulling out all the things I need, I set them on the counter. Grabbing the peeler and a carrot, I reach for the trash can. I don't know why, but I look down and it feels like I've been sucker punched. Sitting in the trash can is an empty bottle of Jack Daniel's. My stomach sinks and my mind refuses to accept that he drank it all, but there are no other explanations.

Since he's been home, he's pushed everyone away and grown depressed. I've tried talking to him about it, but the conversations always end the same—in a massive argument. It feels like I can't do anything right. No matter what, he'd rather just ignore me. All day long, I tell myself he's been through something traumatic, and I just need to give him space, support, and love. But if he's drinking, this is a new low. After losing a friend in high school to drinking and driving, we both opted not to overdo it. Then, suddenly, the truth of it hits me. Tristan's not sick and sleeping. He's passed out, drunk. *He's never been drunk.* Anxiety and fear tear through my body. *What is going on?* My stomach cramps like I'm going to be sick. Not feeling like making soup anymore, I tuck the trash can away and put all the ingredients back.

Stepping out of the kitchen, I look around, feeling lost. Making my way to an oversized chair, I collapse into it. My teeth chatter and I realize I'm freezing. Pulling the blanket off the back, I wrap it around myself, hoping to get warm. Sinking deeper into the chair, I pull my knees up to my chest and hug myself, lost in my head. My thoughts are a chaotic mess, and I can't figure out which way is up. Racking my brain, I'm unable to come up with the answers to my questions. The most important being, how do I help Tristan? *That's if he wants my help.* Lately, I haven't felt wanted or needed, and no matter what I try to convince myself otherwise, it still hurts. This injury has caused irreparable damage to our relationship, and I wonder if we've experienced the worst of it yet. *If not, I'm not sure how much more I can take.* My mind and body are so weary.

The next morning, I'm startled awake. My eyes shooting open, I force myself to focus. Standing in front of me is Tristan. Alarmed, I jerk myself up. My entire body aches from cramming myself into this chair all night. "Did you need something?" I mutter.

"Why did you sleep in the chair last night?" he gruffly asks me. *Do you even care?* I look at him and notice his haggard appearance. His hair has grown long and desperately needs a wash. It appears he hasn't shaved for days. He also has deep circles under his eyes and the permanent frown he's worn since his injury.

Not wanting to have an argument, I say, "I was exhausted last night and must have fallen asleep." Folding my blanket, I ask, "What time is it?"

Tristan pulls his phone from his pocket and I notice the screen of his new iPhone is cracked. Staring at it, a myriad of thoughts race through my head. *How'd that happen? Do I even want to ask?*

"It's nine." Tristan notices the attention I'm giving

to his phone and quickly tucks it away, saying nothing about it.

Tipping my head to the side, I ask, "Have you had breakfast? Do you want me to make something for you?"

He shakes his head. "No, my head and stomach are killing me." *Serves him right.*

I'm at a crossroads. Do I push the obvious, save it for later, knowing I will probably just drop it, or play stupid, hoping he'll admit it?

Turning my head to the side, I question, "Why do you think you feel so bad? Are you getting sick?"

Tristan flops down on the couch and lies with his arm covering his head. It is so obvious he's hungover. A few moments pass and he says nothing. Instead, he lets out anguished breaths, flops about as if he can't get comfortable, and groans. He's acting like a man-baby. You know... drama, drama, drama. I can't help it. I roll my eyes. His behavior has been unrecognizable lately, and I've grown tired of it. It's a struggle to muster any empathy for him when he's making everything so much worse than it has to be.

"Tristan, why do you feel so bad?" I hear the snark in my voice, but no matter how much I try, I can't curb it. Slowly, he removes his arm from his eyes and props himself up. Still, he remains quiet, providing no answer. A flash of emotion crosses his face, and it hits me. He's in pain. Not just physically, but emotionally too. *Why doesn't he talk to me? Why is he doing every-*

thing to push me away? Why is he treating me like he doesn't care? Maybe he doesn't. Maybe he'd rather be alone or with someone else. My insecurities weigh heavy on my heart, each one acting like a slice to it. I feel my eyes grow wet with tears. Desperately, I try to wipe them away before Tristan notices them. When all is said and done, if he sees them, he doesn't react. Which further shreds my tattered heart. He just sits there, staring at me. It's strange and makes me uncomfortable. Needing some space, I get up and put my folded blanket away before turning to him. "I'm sorry you don't feel well, and if you can't tell me what's wrong, I can't offer any solutions. I'm going to take a shower and then run a few errands if you need anything."

When I emerge from our bedroom, clean and dressed, I'm not feeling any better. Tristan is still on the couch. His eyes are open, but he looks like he's far away. I lean over the back of the couch and say, "I'm heading out. Do you need me to get anything? Cold medicine, chicken noodle soup, Gatorade?"

He grumbles words that sound like, "those won't help." Leaning in closer, I ask, "I didn't quite hear you. What?"

Tristan scowls, then growls, "Never mind." The bite in his voice has me whipping my head back as if I were slapped.

Chapter 25

Tristan

"Fuck, my head hurts," I mumble to myself for at least the twentieth time since waking up this morning. *In my bed, alone.* Although just sitting up has me wishing for death, I need to find my wife. While I sit on the edge of the bed, waiting for the spinning to slow, I rub at my temples, wondering when I took the blunt end of an ax to my skull. My mouth feels like I played chubby bunny with cotton balls instead of marshmallows. And my stomach is threatening a mutiny. Basically, I feel like complete shit, and all I can trace it to is the half bottle of Jack I nursed all afternoon after I returned from my physical therapy appointment.

I've never been drunk, but I'm pretty sure that's how I ended up last night. I passed out hard and am suffering from my first-ever hangover. Besides that, I've lost my wife. Had she been drinking with me? No, I don't think so. Had I seen her last night? I'm not sure about that either. Before pushing off the bed, I make sure my knee brace is on correctly. I don't need any more stumbling blocks to my recovery. From what my therapist said yesterday, this injury is proving to be more complex than they all assumed. He didn't use the words "career-ending injury," but that's the feeling I got as he updated me on my recovery so far. It was a blow, and all I wanted to do was forget about it. I have a meeting with my coach, the team's GM, and the team's owner next week, and after yesterday, there is no other way to feel about it but worried. The writing is on the wall. Next week, I'm sure I'll get my walking papers.

Holy fuck, it's bright. My head throbs in protest and I struggle to keep my eyes pinched almost shut. When I finally stumble to the living room, I see my wife, and my heart calms instantly. Curled up in our oversized gray chair, she is clinging to a blanket. Studying her, I notice how small and vulnerable she looks. *Why did she sleep out here?* When she finally wakes up, I ask, and she responds as if it's nothing. I would have believed her, but her eyes hint at some-thing more. *What isn't she saying?*

Unable to handle the constant throbbing in my head and churning of my stomach, I lie on the couch, covering my eyes with the crook of my elbow. I'm attempting to block out the piercing light. Unable to get comfortable, I move around until my body isn't constantly aching. I'm not prepared for Steph's inevitable inquisition. *I can't tell her the truth. Not yet anyway. I'm not ready to believe it.* Then her face softens, and she asks if I'm sick or getting sick. *No, not sick.* I know exactly what's wrong with me, but I'm ashamed. Yesterday was a tough day. It isn't the first one, and it won't be the last. However, yesterday I did something I've never done or wanted to do. I got drunk. The emotions following therapy were intense, and there wasn't anyone to talk to. *No one would understand. My teammates aren't injured and can still play. Steph doesn't understand what it feels like to be a professional athlete. My parents... they would just try to coddle me.* I don't want people's sympathy or pity. Really, I just want to escape the pain, anger, frustration, and sadness I'm struggling with. I know I need to talk to Steph about it all, but we haven't really connected in months, and honestly, I'm not sure how it would go. It seems like every time we discuss my situation; I turn into an asshole and she ends up crying. It makes me sick to my stomach knowing that I'm hurting her, but I can't seem to control it. I miss those early days when everything was carefree and easy. Now our days are filled with pain, doubts, questions, and confusion. I don't have answers to ease either of our worries or concerns, so I figure why stir shit up if I know it's going to leave us worse off than before.

When Steph leaves—did she have to shut the door so loudly when she stormed out of here?—it eerily feels like she was trying to convey another message. *Is she planning to leave me?* I know we've struggled since my injury six months ago, but that isn't all my fault. Nothing I do is good enough. I'm not excelling in anything. And for someone like me, that bit of truth is a fucking horse pill. Impossible to swallow. *She can't leave me.* I won't survive.

But Steph is colder... more distant. She won't talk to me, and I can't seem to reach her. What about in good times and bad, in sickness and health? I know I hold most of the blame. I know I haven't been the same. I'm not so dense that I can't see the writing on the wall screaming at me that something needs to change or I'll lose everything. I want to change, but it feels like I'm drowning. Those were our vows. I know our wedding wasn't a big event, but neither one of us cared. Instead, we focused on what being married meant. But like my career, I feel the promise of it slipping away. *But what can I do?*

Lying on the couch turned to sitting, then to pacing. I need to come up with a way to fix things between us. I can't lose Steph. She is my everything. I will never get through this next stage of my life without her. But I can admit, ever since my injury, I've treated her terribly. On my third lap around the living room, it hits me. I need a starting point for a conversation where I tell her everything that is going on. It won't be easy, but hopefully, it will fix some of the damage I've already inflicted.

By the time Steph returns hours later, I'm feeling much better. My headache is mostly gone and my stomach no longer feels like I rode the Kamikaze too many times in a row. I showered and shaved and look more like myself. I washed dishes, stripped the bed, and remade it. I started the laundry, vacuumed, and did some prep work for dinner.

"Tristan." The concern in her voice makes me panic. Stepping out of the bedroom, my gaze takes her in. Despite her tired, sad eyes, she is still the most beautiful woman I've ever met.

"Hi," I tentatively say and see her eyes go wide when she notices I cleaned up—both the condo and myself.

"Y-you c-cleaned up," she stutters as she scans the room.

Smiling at her, I reply, "I did. I know I've been a lot to deal with lately. This whole situation has been a nightmare. And yesterday was the worst." I'm not sure I can even form the words to explain more, so I just stop talking.

She stays frozen by the door with her shopping bags gripped tightly in her hands. "Yeah?"

Her question stuns me. Surely, she recognizes I wasn't acting the same. "Sarcasm?" I question.

She nods her head. "I didn't know how to have that conversation with you, so I didn't." Her words penetrate my heart, registering deeply. *I pushed her away. This is my fault.*

I step toward her. "I'm sorry, Steph. I know things haven't been easy lately, and I don't know how to fix it, but I want to. I feel you slipping away and I can't let that happen. I love you. I know we've never really been big drinkers. Last night I got a taste of it and I won't let that happen again, I promise." A ten-pound weight lifts off my chest. That was an apology I've been needing to make for months, but I haven't been strong enough. *Maybe it's desperation?*

Tears fall from her long eyelashes and her body slumps like she's been carrying the weight of the world. *Is my drinking last night the only thing that's bothering her? Why does she look like she's so broken?* I can't stand the thought of causing that. The realization that it might be true slams into me like a defenseman in his corner.

Rushing as best as I can with my knee brace, I catch her and cradle her in my arms. Her bags drop to the floor just before she wraps her arms around me, sobbing into my chest. Placing a kiss on her head, I murmur, "I've got you, babe. I'm so sorry." The discomfort of watching her in pain claws at my heart, leaving it ripped and tattered. All I want to do is make it better for her.

It's unclear to me how long we stand there holding each other, but a thought crosses my mind. *How long has it been since we touched?* We are still newly married, shouldn't we be humping like bunnies? I don't know. All I know is she feels amazing in my arms. And as far as I'm concerned, it's the only place she's meant to be.

When she stops sobbing, she pushes against my chest, and I lessen my hold on her. Looking down into her deep, dark-chocolate eyes, I question how badly I've messed things up. *Are we fixable?*

"We need to talk, Tristan," she says in a scratchy, strained voice.

I shudder. *There are those words again.*

Unease swirls in my gut, and my heart pounds irregularly fast in my chest. I've never been so scared in my life. Trying to be strong, I lean down and kiss her forehead. "I understand." Leaving her abandoned bags on the floor, we make our way over to the couch. Dread weighs heavily on me. *Is she ending us?* Not wanting to think about that, I do my best to push it away and listen to what she has to say. No matter what, I know that if she ends us, I'll be destroyed.

We both sit silently on the couch, waiting for the other to start the uncomfortable conversation. Finally, I reach out and grab her hand. I trace over it with my fingers, as if I'm memorizing the look and feel of it. *Will this be the last time I get to hold her hand?* Despair comes rushing back into my body, and my shoulders sag, my stomach tightens, and my breathing becomes shallow.

"Tristan, I don't know how to say this without hurting you." My heart flinches and my body tightens, waiting for the blow I'm sure is about to be delivered. *Here we go.*

"Just say it," I beg, my voice strained as I struggle to get those words past my lips.

I sense Steph's eyes on me, although I'm finding it impossible to look at her. If she admits we're over, I don't think I can handle the devastation on her face. Hell, I don't want her to see my devastation.

"You know, since your injury, things have been strained between us. I feel like I'm not helping or doing the right thing, and that you don't want me around. When I try to encourage you, you snap at me, telling me I don't understand. This experience has been scary because the uncertainty of it has controlled the narrative. Holding us captive. No matter what's happened or how long everything has taken, I've always been hopeful of you and your full recovery. That is, until last night. As soon as I walked in, I could sense something had changed. It's almost like the air was heavy and suffocating. It felt supercharged with hopelessness and dread. When I finally found you and checked to see if you were all right, I grew concerned you might be sick. However, shortly after, it became apparent that you were just drunk."

Beyond ashamed, I don't know what to say. Instead, I squeeze Steph's hand, which is still cradled in mine. Silence surrounds us, and no matter how uncomfortable that makes me, I can't seem to form any words.

Steph pulls her hand from mine and goes to stand up. Panicked, I reach for her. Wrapping my fingers around her delicate wrist, I beg, "Please don't leave me. I need you." The emotion of the last forty-eight hours weighs heavily on me and I slouch against the pillows. I know she deserves an explanation, an apology, and a commitment to do better, but just the thought of that makes me weary. Steph stands near but not next to me, and the distance is notable.

"Tristan, what is going on?"

Motioning to the couch, I ask, "Can you please sit back down? I'm really trying to figure out how to explain what's been going on with me."

Turning myself so my feet are flat on the floor, I rest my head back on the couch cushions. My headache has returned. Right now, I'd rather go to sleep than admit all my faults over the past six months, but the fear that Steph is going to walk away propels me forward. Blowing out a deep breath and rubbing my temple, I resolve myself to tell her everything.

"The past six months have been my own personal hell. Ever since I was a kid, I wanted nothing more than to play hockey in the NHL. Every day, I worked and trained hard to make my dream a reality. And in a few seconds, it was all taken away."

"After surgery, I found myself angry, scared, and confused. My mind was constantly running rehab scenarios, wondering when I could get back to the job I love so much. I hadn't given much thought to the success of my surgery. I just assumed it would be done and within a few months, I'd be working on regaining my strength and speed. I didn't consider any other option."

Looking at the ceiling, I hear Steph clear her throat. I turn my head toward her. "Are you saying that isn't an option anymore?" Concern is etched across her face, and it's tough to deny how weary she looks too. These months have not only worked me over, but they've also done a number on my wife.

Shaking my head, I confess, "I-I d-don't know."

Always the rational one, she crosses her arms against her chest. "Well, what *do* you know?"

Shrugging my shoulders, I'm not sure what to say. "I have a meeting with Coach, the GM, and the owner next week." Dread pools in my stomach at the uncertainty of it all.

"Okay. That's not exactly telling. You've met with them before, right?"

"No, not all at once. I got the call right after my PT appointment, where Kelvin basically told me I've plateaued." My heart squeezes in my chest and my throat feels tight as the emotion of it all acts like cancer, spreading out all over my body. "My career is finished," I say in a throaty rasp. Leaning forward, I rest my elbows on my thighs. The couch dips, and a warm hand rubs comforting circles on my back.

Steph murmurs, "It's going to be okay, Tristan." *How can she know?* The desire to lash out and question her is strong, but I know it won't help our current situation, so I focus on my breathing and getting past this moment. It's hard to picture a future without hockey. I've been playing since I was small, and I'm not sure what comes next for me. For us. Since meeting Steph, I'd known what my future looked like, and I was so looking forward to it. Now it's full of uncertainty.

Chapter 26

Stephanie

Sitting the closest to my husband I have in weeks, I try my best to console him by rubbing his back. He just dropped a major bomb on me, and I can feel the sadness and anger emanating from his body. I want to lower to my knees, crawl between his legs, and force him to show me his face. I know it's tear-stained. Ever since he mentioned his fear about the team cutting him, he's hidden his face from me. *Is he ashamed?* He has nothing to be ashamed of. He can't help being injured. Or that he had a complex surgery and a hard recovery. All of it is out of his hands, no matter how hard he works or how much he wants it. Despite the awkwardness between us, I don't want him struggling. Thinking back, I can see why last night happened. He drank to forget his feelings instead of sharing them. That is certainly something we need to talk about because, as far as I'm concerned, alcohol is not an effective coping mechanism.

Not understanding how things work in the NHL, I turn to him. "Do you want me to go to that meeting with you?" He lifts his head slightly, a look of surprise stretched across his face.

He shakes his head. "I appreciate the offer, Steph. I really wish you could be there, but as far as I know, family isn't allowed in these meetings."

I nod my understanding. *At least he wanted me there. That's something, right?*

"I'm here for you. Please let me know how I can support you. Let me help you," I say. True, I'm pleading with my husband. I don't want us to drift further apart. For him, hockey is life. It would be detrimental to everything Tristan is if it's taken away. And I know if that is the outcome, he can't handle it alone. I want to be here as long as he proves he needs and wants me.

That night, we spend a lot of time in silence. Hurt hangs over us like a rain cloud waiting to unleash its downpour. The next morning when I get up around seven, Tristan is already awake and in the kitchen making breakfast for us. *This is a change.*

Before his injury, this had been a common occurrence I absolutely cherished. On the weekends he was in town, he'd start our Saturday mornings off with breakfast. On his menu is always hot coffee and pancakes. But ever since his injury, he's barely made it out of bed before noon unless he has therapy.

"Need any help?" I offer after I get over the initial shock of seeing him in low-hung shorts and a bare chest. Despite him missing the last few months of continual exercise, he is still in amazing shape.

Turning to me, he gives me a smile, and my heart thunders in my chest. His normal eight-pack has shrunk to a six-pack, but I'm not at all complaining. His abs still beg for my touch. With him standing there with a metal spatula, I run my eyes up his chest until I get to my favorite part. His stupidly sexy silver barbells drive me wild. I want to kiss and suck on them. Blow cold air on them and tug them until he can't do anything but lift me onto the countertop and ravish me. Because of his surgery and recovery, we've been on a sexual hiatus. Actually, that isn't one hundred percent accurate. We've drifted apart, and never even realized how far until the other night. The surgery had been a convenient excuse. Truth is, I found it hard to want Tristan when I felt stuck on an emotional tilt-a-whirl. I can't speak for him, but I miss his touch, his closeness. I'm beyond needy.

"Why are you looking at me as if I'm breakfast?" he asks with a saucy wink. A hint at his playful side I haven't seen in much too long and absolutely adore.

"What?" I ask, feigning innocence.

He pulls the final pancake from the griddle, turns it off, and stalks over to me. My heart rate climbs higher the closer he gets to me. My stomach flutters as if a colony of butterflies has taken flight. My center throbs in anticipation of what I think is happening. Within moments, Tristan is standing in front of me. Looking into his eyes, I see they're filled with heat. And they're focused on me. It feels amazing to be the object of his attention.

"Good morning," I whisper, looking at his pink lips. *It's been so long.*

As if he can read my thoughts, he reaches out, tugging me closer before he kisses me. Soft, tentative kisses turn into pure madness. Soon we're licking, biting, and thrusting into each other's mouths. Tristan pulls on my lower lip. "I've missed you so much, babe." His confession, although nice to hear, doesn't prove we're on the right path.

Following his confession, I want to share my feelings with him. *Tristan, I've missed you too.* The words are there, but I can't bring myself to say them. These past few months have been really hard. They've shaken us to the core. I gave my whole heart to Tristan, and it feels like he used it as a punching bag. I'm not ready to repeat that, so for the time being, I'll keep my emotions close.

Pressing his athletic body against mine, he growls into my ear, "Just say no and I'll step away. But if you say yes, I'll give you the best damn wake-up call you'll ever get."

My cheeks heat, and I'm sure they've gone pink, giving me away, but I still nod my head.

He grabs the waistband of my sleep shorts and drags them down my legs.

"No panties?" he questions while licking his lips. I laugh because I've never done that before. *Maybe subconsciously I was trying to get his attention.*

Reaching down, I palm his enormous cock. When I squeeze it, he growls before I even can pull it out. Not wasting any time, he steps back and rips off his shorts and boxer briefs. Kicking them away, he slides his hand between my legs. *Touch me, I'm wet.* His fingers move through my slick heat with reverence. His touch is commanding, yet gentle.

Leaning his forehead to mine, he growls, "You feel ready for me."

Desperate for him, I whimper. He pushes himself in on one big thrust. At first, all I notice is how full I feel. At the tinge of burn from being stretched, I open my legs wider, welcoming him deeper. "You feel so good, babe," he breathes out. "I've missed this. Missed *you.*"

Flicking and circling his hips absolutely drives me wild. In no time, I pant, commanding him, "Don't stop."

Gritting his teeth together, his strained voice utters the words I most want to hear. "I don't plan to."

After kitchen sex, we share the cooled pancakes before moving on to another round in the shower.

Round three is in our bed. Following our full-day escapades, we're both famished. Ordering takeout for dinner is a necessity because neither of us has any energy. When it arrives, we sit on the couch and watch a movie while we replenish. My body's tired but eager for more. Even if my brain is screaming we need to talk. *Sex won't fix us.* No, but it's the best I've felt in weeks. So right now, I'm going with it. Maybe when my lust-soaked brain sobers up, I'll be able to approach everything more rationally. Right now, I'm going to savor these moments.

The next morning, I wake up in bed, unable to remember how I got here. Looking over, I see Tristan lying next to me, looking at his phone. The despair on his face is alarming. *What happened?* Reaching out, I lay my hand on his naked chest. I consider playing with his barbell, but he doesn't look to be in the mood.

"Morning," I whisper. Lost in thought, he doesn't answer. Sitting up, I turn to face him fully. In a sterner voice, I ask, "Tristan, what's wrong?"

He looks over while trying to mask his emotions. "It's nothing, really."

I don't believe him. Why doesn't he want to share it with me? We used to tell each other everything. When did that change?

Instead of saying anything, I tilt my head sideways.

"Really, Steph, it's nothing. I just got a message from my agent, Troy, saying he wanted to meet with me before the meeting with the Storm executives.

And... it caught me by surprise." He holds his hand out to me and I take it. As he pulls me into his chest, I feel conflicted. I'm thankful we're connecting, but I don't want us to ignore or sidestep what the past few months have been. I understand that marriage isn't perfect. Each one has its highs and lows. But unless we're both willing to examine the problems we've been having, I don't see us being able to move forward. I'm unwilling to maintain a relationship that is this destructive and unhealthy.

Cradled tightly in his chest, I nuzzle his small patch of chest hair, hiding my face. "We need to talk," I whisper. *Why was that so hard to admit? To say out loud?* I'm scared. Scared we might be over. Scared of his reaction. Scared of the decisions I might have to make. There's no denying it. Tristan is my forever love, and I want no one but him. But I also love myself, and because of that, I refuse to stay in an unhealthy relationship. So, although I'm terrified of what's happening to us, I have to push forward, demanding better.

Chapter 27

Tristan

Steph and I both agreed that we'll talk after I meet with Troy about the upcoming meeting. Every time I think about it, knowing they hold my hockey future in their hands, my stomach spins and I feel nauseous. Since the meeting with the Storm's executive team isn't for a few days, waiting is inevitable. And the stress and worry about it does me in. Troy comes over Sunday morning, and his grimace instantly puts me in check. *Shit.* Does he know already? Are they benching me permanently?

"Troy, come in," I say as I shake his hand. Steph sticks her head out of the kitchen.

"Hey, Troy. How are you?" she chirps.

"I'm good. Thanks for asking," he answers, then he turns to me and utters, "We need to talk." The tone of his voice chills me instantly and sends shivers down my spine. Showing him to the dining room table, we both sit down. My nervous system is in an uproar. My leg bounces and my hands shake. Even waiting for the draft, I don't remember feeling this uneasy.

Steph steps up to the table. "I'm leaving so you can have your meeting in private. Do either of you need anything before I head out?" We both shake our heads. As soon as the front door shuts, I feel the surrounding air shift. It is heavy, almost suffocating. *Is this a predictor of what's coming? A snapshot of what my future looks like?*

Troy looks at me and attempts a smile. But all I see is a grimace. "Tristan, I wanted to meet with you to talk about a few things."

"Okay, shoot," I say, faking a confidence I don't actually possess. What's that saying? Fake it until you make it. That's me right now. Terrified, I look at him, waiting.

"I want to be prepared for that meeting, so I need to know about PT and how you think you're doing."

Swallowing hard, my mind flashes back to my last PT appointment, where Kelvin told me exactly what he thought. "Well, my therapist said that I've had a tough recovery. I haven't progressed as quickly as he had hoped, but I'm not done. I still have some range of motion, strength, flexibility, and endurance I need to gain back. He also told me he'd given a summary report to the Storm executives, and that it said I was probably eighty percent recovered. He also told them he knew I would recover eventually with enough PT, but he didn't have a prediction about when that would be. Basically, I still have work to do before I even get back on skates as a professional player."

Leaning back in his chair, he pushes his chubby hands through his thinning hair. "Wow. Okay. That gives me an idea of what they might say. What's your gut say?"

Afraid if I speak it out loud, it will come true. I whisper, "They're going to let me go."

Troy's eyes go wide. "Really? You've played for them for five years and you think they'll toss you aside? That's harsh, man."

"It may be harsh, but it's a business. At the end of the day, they want healthy players who can perform and bring in more fans. While I'm injured, I can't do that. And without an idea of how much longer my recovery will take, it makes sense to let me go. I'm not a guaranteed investment. I may never return."

Troy glares at me. "You'll return, Tristan. Mark my words. The NHL hasn't seen the last of Tristan Murphy."

I laugh because, at this moment, that's all I can do. No matter what I do or how many wishes I make, I can't make my recovery go any faster. "Anything else you need to know about before the meeting?" He shakes his head and stands up. We walk to the front door and shake hands before he leaves. *Why do I feel heavier and more burdened now that he's gone?* Maybe speaking the words out loud made them real. *Has doing that forced my destiny?* I don't know, and I'm tired of trying to talk myself in or out of anything. I want a definitive answer so I can move on. But I won't be getting that for a few more days.

Sitting on the couch, I palm my phone. I need the one person who's always been there.

ME

Troy is gone. It's clear to come home.

STEPH

I'm just a few minutes away. Do you need anything?

ME

Actually, it feels like the walls of our place are closing in on me. Do you want to go out?

STEPH

Sure. I'll let you know when I'm back and you can come out.

ME

Sounds great. Thanks, Steph.

STEPH

No problem. See you soon.

That afternoon, we stop by a deli and grab lunch, then head over to the Commons. It's September, so the weather is still in the seventies. We sit on the steps of the Parkman Bandstand and eat while we people watch. I remembered to wear both a sweatshirt and a ball cap to keep from being recognized. I haven't been out a lot since my injury, and when I have, I avoid fans like the plague. I'm not ready to handle questions about my return, especially now, seeing that it feels so uncertain.

After we finish our lunch, we walk through the park. As we walk side by side, our hands brush and I feel a bolt of electricity surge through my body. Even though we recently reignited our sex life, holding hands feels more intimate, and I'm not sure Steph would be okay with that. We're in a delicate place, and I'm a coward. The fear of rejection is more than I can handle, considering what the previous days have done to my emotional state.

When we make our way down to the public garden, we see they've removed the swan boats from the lagoon, and Steph sighs her disappointment. Looking it up on my phone, I find their months of operation. "We just missed them. They closed for winter a few weeks ago. We'll have to come back in the spring." *I hope we're still in Boston next spring, and that I'm still a member of the Storm.*

"It's okay. Let's hang out here for a bit and enjoy the sunshine." Grabbing my hand, she leads me over the suspension bridge to a patch of grass under a monstrous weeping willow. "How about here?" Steph asks nervously. *Why is she nervous?*

Lying down, side-by-side, we remain quiet. *It hasn't ever been this uncomfortable between us.* "Tristan," Steph says, pulling me from my reverie.

"Yeah?"

"Will you tell me what Troy had to say this morning?" It's obvious her nerves are wound tight based on the staccato delivery of her question.

I take her hand and weave our fingers together. Then, I fill her in on what we discussed, the concerns I'm having about the upcoming meeting, and what comes next.

"Wow," is all she can say, but I don't miss the heaviness in her response.

"Yeah, it's been a lot to take in." Although that confession is hard to make, I notice relief in my shoulders once it's left my lips.

Moving closer to me, she wraps her arm around my middle, giving me a side hug. "I'm sorry. This must have been terrible to shoulder all by yourself. Why didn't you tell me what was going on?"

Leaning down, I kiss her head. "I didn't think it was fair of me to dump that all on you when I didn't have definitive answers." *Plus, I'm scared you'll walk away because, without hockey, I am nothing. I can't offer you anything. I'm not even sure how I'd support us.*

"My job as your wife is to be here for you, help you carry the load. If you'll let me." Her words are sharp, poking my still fragile heart.

"I'm sorry, Steph. I wanted to tell you, but it felt like I'd be complaining."

"It's not complaining if you're seeking a probable solution." The truth of her words is jarring, like I'd been hit with lightning. I haven't complained that much about my situation. And it's been a lot. Dealing with PT three times a week, doing at-home exercise, sleeping, and eating healthy. It's not only taxing physically but emotionally as well. Honestly, I don't know what I could have done differently.

Days later, dressed in a Tom Ford suit, I'm sitting in the executive offices of the Storm, filled with dread. Waiting has never been my strong suit, but today the anxiety and nerves coursing through me are making things unbearable. My knee bounces rapidly, I'm sweating buckets, and my stomach has tightened into a knot. *Breathe. Relax.* That's tough to do when you're waiting to hear about your future. My time with the Storm is uncertain, and the emotions whirling within me are hard to grasp. Troy comes into the office at exactly ten o'clock, looking cool as a cucumber. *Man, I want to be that relaxed.* But of course he is. It isn't his career and livelihood on the chopping block.

"Tristan. Good morning," he says while extending his hand.

I shake it and grumble, "Not sure it's a good morning."

"I get that. Let's just see what they have to say before we draw any conclusions. Okay?"

I hear what he's saying, and if I weren't so worried and anxious right now, I might even consider listening. But I can feel my career slipping through my fingers, and right now I can't seem to find it within me to be optimistic. "Sure."

We sit in silence until the office door cracks open a few minutes later. The GM appears. His stoicism doesn't give me any hint about what my fate will be, and my stomach sinks further.

"Tristan, Troy, come on in and let's get started."

My feet feel like dead weight as I trudge into the office. Seated around the table are the Storm's owner, Martin Shielding, Coach, Kelvin, and Jack. *Oh, joy!* Looks like everyone is here to take part in my firing.

"Geez, this looks like an intervention," I mumble. Mr. Shielding laughs. *Whoops. Thought I said that in my head.* Troy and I take the two open seats around the large conference table, and I immediately fidget. I can't get comfortable, and although it hasn't in weeks, my knee throbs. *I wonder if that's telling.*

Mr. Shielding clears his throat before he speaks. "Tristan, I'm sure you're wondering why we called you in today."

"Yes, sir."

He smiles before leaning back. "To be honest with you, we're in a tough place. You've been on this team for five years and you've done well. Not only are you an exceptional player, but you are also a leader on the ice and in the locker room. Your injury has left a hole in the team and not having you on the ice has not only affected our level of play but also the team's optimism.

There is no doubt in anyone's mind that you were the heart of the Storm."

My head whips up. "You said 'were.'" Frantically, I look around the room to confirm if anyone will verify what I know is coming next. Mr. Shielding nods his head.

"Unfortunately, we are at a crossroads. I have had many conversations with Kelvin, Jack, and Coach Phil over the last few weeks, and it seems that your recovery has stalled. They can't tell me if it'll be weeks, months, or years until you get back on skates. And because of that, I have to make a very hard choice. We, the Storm organization, are letting you out of your contract."

His words are a direct gut punch, pushing all the air out of my system. I feel light-headed. Trying to suck in enough air so I don't pass out is a monumental task. Sadness and anger rush through my body, and all I want to do is leave. I look up, and no one will make eye contact with me. *Fucking bunch of cowards.*

Pushing back my chair, I stand up. It feels like sharp claws are slicing at my chest, and my throat is tightening. "Thank you for your time. Please give Troy all the details for the transition. I need to go," I rasp before I leave the suite.

When I'm in the hallway, I glance at the clock and notice my *former* teammates will be on the ice practicing. If I'm lucky, I can get down to my locker and clean out my personal items before they're done. Within twenty minutes, I have all my things and I make it to the players' parking lot undetected. Climbing into my car, the weight of what I've lost hangs heavy on my back. My phone rings, and it's Troy. I press decline, because there is no way I want to talk to anyone right now. My phone dings, letting me know a text has arrived.

TROY

You okay, man?

ME

Great.

TROY

Bullshit. Where are you?

ME

Just cleared out my locker. Sitting in my car and about to head home.

TROY

I'll handle all the other stuff. Going home sounds smart. Will Steph be there?

ME

Yeah.

Or she will be in a few hours after she finishes work-ing. And now I have to tell her I'm unemployed and unable to get a job since I have no degree or skills. *Oh, happy day. My life is fucked.*

Chapter 28

Stephanie

All day long, I've been a nervous wreck, waiting to hear how Tristan's meeting went. I haven't heard from him and that has me worried. Normally, I'm the last one out of the office, but at exactly five o'clock, my desk's cleaned up and I'm logged out of my computer. The drive home is typical, full of impatient drivers who think their time is more valuable than yours. *Maybe that's why I always left work later... to avoid this ragging group of idiots I'm now sandwiched between.*

I notice Tristan's truck in his spot when I pull in. Walking past it, I notice he's still inside. *Maybe he just got home from somewhere.* Coming closer, I see his expression, and my heart pinches. A mix of emotions covers his handsome face: despair, disappointment, anger, and sadness. His shoulders slump and his eyes are puffy, like he's been crying.

Knocking on his window breaks his trance, and he slowly turns to me. When he recognizes it's me, I notice his chin wobble. My handsome husband is truly, utterly broken. My heart breaks for him. Pulling open his door, I whisper, "Oh, babe." Taking in the man before me, I know he's in pain, and I bite my lip to stifle my reaction.

Then he makes an unrecognizable sound, conveying his despair. "Let's get you upstairs and then you can tell me all about it." He comes willingly, but he's awkward. Slowly, he puts one foot in front of the other, taking forever. By the time we get upstairs, my back is screaming and I'm drenched in sweat. Because it's obvious he's distracted with something, my first task is to get him to the couch. Tristan drops like a sack of potatoes and tips over, landing with his head in the pillow crease. *That can't be comfortable.* I know things are dire when he doesn't immediately correct it. I squeeze in next to him, pulling his head onto my lap, and I rub circles on his back. Unsure what to do or say, I remain silent but keep my hands on him to let him know I'm here. In no time, I notice the rhythm of his chest has leveled out, and I can hear a faint snore. Sitting in silence, I consider all the probable outcomes, and my only conclusion is the team must have ended his contract. Only that would make him like this.

Hours later, my bladder screams at me, and my stomach threatens mutiny. Reaching for my phone, I order a pizza. When it's expected to arrive, I try to slip out from beneath Tristan without waking him. Unsuccessful in my endeavors, he sits up and rubs his eyes. I jog to the bathroom before I'm dealing with another situation, and pee while Tristan is still waking up. When I walk back into the room, I retrieve my purse from the floor where I must have dropped it when we arrived home. I pull out the twenty dollars for the pizza and a tip and set it by the front door. Looking over at Tristan, he's again slumped on the couch.

"Babe, I ordered a pizza and it should be here soon. Are you hungry?" He shakes his head just as the doorbell chimes. After retrieving the pizza, I head into the kitchen for plates, napkins, and water bottles. When I get to the couch, I set dinner on the coffee table, plating a piece for me and one for Tristan. I'm halfway through my first piece when I notice he hasn't even taken a bite.

Wiping my mouth, I ask, "Babe, are you ready to tell me what's going on?"

His weary, sad eyes look from the pizza up to me. *If he doesn't, I'll understand and give him some spuce.* He opens his mouth, then closes it, no words coming out. My heart squeezes. I hate to see him like this. I offer him a smile, reminding him I'm here for him. Again, he opens his mouth; his lips move, but I can't hear him. Leaning forward, I catch the tail-end of what he says.

"I'm not part of the Storm anymore." Tears appear in his eyes, glistening and threatening to fall. Angrily, he swipes at them.

"Oh, Tristan. I'm so sorry." Setting down my pizza, I move his plate before I wrap my arms around him. His large body trembles, and I just hug him tighter. Leaning my head to his, I whisper, "I'm so sorry." *I don't want to promise everything will be all right because, in all honesty, I don't know what the future will hold.* Tristan is still young and can do anything. Sure, he opted to go straight into the NHL, but he could always go to college. Or maybe he could coach? His future isn't limited. But first, he has to deal with the heartache he's feeling. And I'm going to do my best to help him through it. "I love you, Tristan. I know this hurts, but I've got you. Lean on me."

Chapter 29

Tristan

Even though I'm not with the Storm any longer, I know I need to keep going to PT. I have to find a new physical therapist though since Kelvin works for the team. Because I'm now on Steph's insurance, benefits aren't what they once were, and it is a struggle at first. After a few weeks, I find someone I connect with. Actually, he's a lot like Kelvin.

And speaking of Kelvin, he calls me to check in and see if I'm continuing with PT. He tells me he's glad to hear I am. Hearing from Kelvin is nice, despite feeling like I'd been sideswiped at that meeting.

Yes, I suspected I might be let go, but I question management's loyalty. I gave them five years of my life, couldn't they have invested a bit more time? To make matters worse, the team brought in my replacement only a week after they let me out of my contract. Every time I think about it, anger boils in my veins and questions fill my mind. *How long had they been planning to replace me? Will I ever get another chance with the NHL? What am I supposed to do now?* I don't have any answers. Several of my former teammates try reaching out, but I don't want their pity. Plus, it's like a slap to my face. They still get to play, and I'm jealous.

One month after I'm let go, my new therapist, Taylor, gets me up on skates again. Sure, I look like a fawn taking its first steps, but the rush of being back on the ice is incredible. That afternoon, I return home to share the good news with Steph, and remember she won't be home until late because of a commitment at work. Bummed, I sit in our condo, wondering what to do with all the extra hours. I want to share my good news, but with whom? Reaching out to my parents is a good idea since they always have my back.

Ring, ring.

"Hello. Murphy residence." My mom's familiar response makes me smile.

"Hey, Mom."

"Tristan, my boy. It's been forever since we talked. How are you?" The concern in her voice is palpable. Since my injury, every time we talk, all I seem to share is bad news. *She expects it.*

Hanging my head, I squeeze the bridge of my nose. Forcing myself to perk up, I say, "I had a fantastic day, and I want to share it with you and Dad."

She squeals, and I pull the phone from my ear. "Let me get your dad. He'll want to hear too." I hear the clunk as she sets her cell phone down. And I laugh to myself. She forgets sometimes that she can take it with her. She's so used to the phones of yesteryear when you could only wander so far before your cord reached its limit.

A few minutes later, I hear the familiar banter of my parents as they walk back into the room. I hear a bunch of beeps and I realize they're putting me on speaker. My dad is definitely more tech-savvy than my mom.

"Tristan, my boy. Are you there?" My dad's scratchy voice comes across the line perfectly.

"Still here. Hey, Dad," I answer.

"What's this your mom is saying about you having a good day and you want to share it?"

Clearing my throat, I say, "I did. In PT today, Taylor got me on skates and onto the ice. I'm not doing much more than gliding, but it feels amazing to be out there again.

Listening to my mom sniffle in the background breaks my heart. "Don't cry, Mom. I told you it was a great day."

"That is amazing. In no time, you'll skate laps around everyone, and the Storm will look like putzes for letting you go. Have you seen the guy they brought in to replace you? Pathetic. You left some mighty big skates to fill, and I'm sorry to say, but he's not cutting it." *Thanks, Dad.* I appreciate the support, but leaving the team is still raw. It's all been a bitter pill to swallow.

In fact, Steph and I have had multiple discussions—okay, arguments—about it, and the only conclusions I've come to are that it isn't fair and I'm not ready to put it behind me.

Catching up with my parents is nice, but I'm eager for Steph to come home so I can share my good news with her. Watching the clock, I waste time with dinner and some random TV show on. When I hear the front door unlock, relief washes through my body. *Finally.*

Chapter 30

Stephanie

I t's been a hellacious day. Nothing has gone right at all. And I agree to stay late and volunteer in the food pantry. Usually, that isn't a problem, but when a migraine struck about noon, I dreaded the rest of my day. I try everything I can think of, and no matter what I do, I'm unable to curb it. So, with my head throbbing in protest, I help stock shelves and get clients the items they need to feed their families. At seven, we run out of food and close the pantry. It always feels horrible turning away people who depend on us for their survival. But sometimes that's how it goes. We don't always get enough deliveries or donations to provide enough food for all those who need it.

When I finally make it back to our condo, all I want is more medicine, an ice pack, and my bed. Focused on that, I make sure my sunglasses are on straight to avoid all the excess light and march forward with my head bowed. Walking into the kitchen, I don't notice anything around me. Tristan clears his throat from behind me, startling me. Whipping around, pain shoots up my neck, piercing my skull. There stands Tristan.

"Ahh," I cry as I clutch my head.

"Hi, babe. How was your day?" he asks nervously. Even in my incapacitated state, I notice a touch of excitement in his voice. But right now, I struggle to care.

"It was horrible and I have a migraine from hell," I grumble while reaching into the freezer. My fingers land on my trusty ice pack, and my heart drops. It isn't cold. *What? Is the freezer not working? Everything else looks fine. I don't understand, and my head hurts too much to consider any other possibilities.*

"Oh, shit. Do you need an ice pack? I just put that one back after icing my knee. I'm sorry. Can I get you anything else?" Tristan says in a rush.

"Nope," I snap, knowing the other ice packs are probably warm and sitting on his nightstand, where he constantly leaves them. Feeling defeated, I drop the warm ice pack back in the freezer and walk out of the kitchen toward our bedroom. The next best thing is a blacked-out room and bed. And then I'll sleep this off. *I hope anyway.*

Already on edge, it annoys me when I sense Tristan behind me. Usually, when I'm like this, he gives me plenty of space. But today, he's doing the opposite, and I'm not enjoying it. When I reach the bedroom, I strip off my clothes and drop them on the floor. *I'll deal with that later.* Climbing into bed in just my panties, I feel a chill tear through my body. Burrowing down deep into the covers, I plan to hibernate until the stabbing, sharp pain has subsided. Even though I can't see him through the blankets, I feel him nearby.

"Tristan." With my eyes pinched shut, I can picture him hovering over me.

"Yeah, babe. What do you need?"

Using all my energy, I force out a deep breath, and then answer, "I took my meds already. And now I just need darkness, quiet, and sleep. Same as always. Okay?"

"Okay." I can hear the disappointment in his voice, and I don't know why. But I don't have the bandwidth to care. "We'll talk tomorrow. Sleep well," he whispers before making his way out of our room. I hear him close the door, and after a few relaxing breaths, I drift to sleep.

I wake up still feeling foggy the next morning. And the painful band of tightness from yesterday still refuses to let go. "Ugh," I moan while massaging my temples. Thank goodness it doesn't feel as bad as yesterday. *Small victory.* But I know if I don't deal with it now, it's only going to get worse.

Calling my boss, I tell him I still have a migraine. He saw how miserable I was yesterday, and he tells me to stay home and rest, telling me he'll see me on Monday. Rubbing my eyes, I stumble toward my bathroom, where I splash cold water on my face. *That's refreshing.* When I'm finally able to fully pry open my eyes, I notice the light isn't as bothersome. *That's a good sign.* After brushing my teeth, peeing, and taking another med, I head out to the kitchen for some water and my ice pack. *Hopefully, it's there.*

"Morning, babe. How are you feeling?" Tristan asks when he sees me. He seems more cheerful than in weeks past. *Why? As soon as I'm feeling better, I'll ask. His behavior is odd, because for months he's been a grumpy monster who only got worse when the Storm let him go.*

"Still dealing with a migraine. I'm headed back to bed after I get a few things," I inform him. He nods, and I retrieve my ice pack and return to the bedroom. After draining the sixteen ounce bottle of water, I climb back into bed. Once I'm finally settled, I pull the covers back up over me, tucking them around me tightly. Then I align myself perfectly on my ice pack. "Ahhh," I cry out, startled when my skin comes in contact with the ice pack. Because of the coolness on my neck, it takes longer for me to fall asleep.

It's late afternoon by the time I wake up, and I've got a full bladder and a growling stomach. Sitting up slowly, I evaluate my head, and while it still feels sluggish, the pain is gone. Throwing back the covers, I head to my bathroom to take a shower. Once I'm dressed, I head toward the living room, looking for Tristan. He's gone, but I find a note he left for me.

> Babe,
> I checked on you before I left and you were sleeping so peacefully. I had PT today at three. I should be home at five.
> Love you, Tristan

Looking at the clock, I notice it's almost four. My stomach rumbles, and I fix myself a small snack before I settle on the couch. Still leery of my migraine, I keep the lights and the television off. Two hours later, Tristan returns, but he's wearing a scowl. *What now?* We'd clung to the hope that Tristan could return to playing for the NHL, but when he was dropped from the team, that hope dwindled. Because of the uncertainty of recovery timelines, we can't even get a good estimate on what to expect. As far as I know, his recovery has somewhat stalled despite how hard he works.

"How was PT today?" I ask.

Still scowling, he shrugs, then answers, "It wasn't as good as yesterday."

"What happened yesterday? I'm sorry I didn't get to ask."

He hangs his head and his long hair sweeps past his high cheekbones. On his way to the couch, I notice he's limping, and my mind goes crazy with worry.

"Yesterday, Taylor got me on skates," he says, but something is wrong. He isn't excited like I thought he'd be. Instead, he's frowning, and I don't understand why. Just as I'm about to ask, he continues. "Then today, we tried again, and even though we were barely gliding, I fell. I haven't fallen on skates since I was five and first learning." His voice is heavy with emotion. His posture is rigid and tight and he's clenching his jaw.

"Did you get hurt? When you fell?" I ask, wondering if that's why he's limping.

"Yeah. I fell on my knee, and my therapist insisted I get x-rays, which is why I'm late. Thankfully, everything looks fine, but according to Taylor, we have to take a few steps back before we try skates again. This is such bullshit. No matter what I do or how hard I work, I'm not getting better." He slumps back on the couch. "This is taking forever, and I want to be done now." The anger in his voice is tangible and has my body tensing up. It's not like I'm afraid of him, but I've never seen him this angry.

He pushes off the couch and storms into the bedroom, slamming the door. Looking around, I'm not sure what to do. I don't want to chase him down and force him to talk. Obviously, he's angry, and we'd probably end up in a fight. Thirty minutes later, he comes storming out of the room, dressed in a pair of jeans and a sweatshirt. He heads toward the front door and I all I can do is watch. Tristan says nothing to me as he leaves, and I'm left alone in our condo wondering where he's going, how to help him, and what to do.

Twenty minutes later, when he still hasn't returned, I send him a text.

ME

You have me worried. Where are you?
When are you planning to come
home?

Thirty minutes later, I still haven't gotten a response, so I try again.

ME

I'm planning to order something for
dinner. Do you want me to get you
anything?

Five minutes later, my phone dings.

TRISTAN

Don't bother.

Staring at his reply feels like I've been punched in the heart. Where is he? Using his contact, I look up his location. When it registers, my stomach rolls. He's at a bar a few streets over. After last time, he'd sworn he wasn't going to try to drink away his problems. But obviously that's what he's doing. *Do I go down there and drag him home and cause a scene? Do I go there and wait for him to come out and drive him home so at least he isn't drinking and driving? Or do I just hope the bartender takes away his keys and makes him take a cab home?* It's times like this that I wish I had a group of close friends to call, or maybe his dad nearby. It's not that I want to tattle on him, but I can't do this by myself, and the promise he made to me last time isn't proving to be worth shit. Anger boils up within me. *How dare he!* Tristan's behavior is so fucking selfish. He isn't considering me at all. I understand that he's in pain, emotionally and physically, but he hasn't even given me the chance to help him.

Sitting on the couch, staring at the television screen that's playing some documentary I stumbled onto hours ago, I notice it's midnight. Tristan has been gone almost six hours. Worries fill my mind and my gut churns. I never did order dinner. At nine, I found a sleeve of crackers and nibbled on those for a while until they started to taste like paste.

Reaching out for my abandoned phone, I wonder if Tristan sent me anything. But no messages appear, so I check on his location and it still shows him at the bar. *This is ridiculous.* I toss off the blanket I've been snuggled in all evening and grab my coat and purse. Within ten minutes, I'm at the bar. I see my husband's truck and I give thanks he's not trying to drive it.

The door to Sidewinders is stained wood with a tree-knot handle. Tugging it open, the stench of stale beer wafts out. My stomach rolls. *Just find Tristan. Maybe the bartender will help you get him to your car.*

Scanning the bar, I don't see my husband, and my heart drops. His location said he was here. Walking up to the bar, I spot the bartender. Marching over, I feel the adrenaline pumping through my body.

"Excuse me. Can you tell me if this man has been in here tonight?" I ask, while thrusting my phone at him with a picture of Tristan and me.

He smirks at me, and I grit my teeth, trying not to snarl. "Is that your boyfriend or husband?"

Glaring at him, I growl, "Husband. Now, has he been in tonight?"

Not intimidated by me at all, he leans in. "Oh, honey, he's a regular, and yes, he was in tonight, but he left a while ago."

My face drops. *Regular? Already left?*

"What?" I squeak. My mind swirls with unhelpful thoughts.

The bartender motions to someone across the room before answering me. I feel someone come up behind me and I step to the side. "Hey, Rhonda. When did T leave?" *T? Who the hell is T? They have to be talking about another person, right?* To my left is a beautiful woman wearing a low-cut top that definitely accentuates her assets, and short jean shorts that show off all her curves.

Tapping her red nails on the bar top, she answers, "T probably left about half an hour ago, but he left his phone behind." Dread fills my heart as I recognize the cover of the phone she's holding. T is apparently Tristan, and they say he's a regular. My mind swims with information that I'm unable to process.

Pain squeezes my chest. My stomach mimics a rock tumbler trying to get a good polish on a stubborn stone. My hands shake and I start sweating as my breathing becomes labored.

Stuttering, I ask, "D-do you know w-where he w-went?" *They obviously know him. Maybe even better than I do these days.* Swallowing hard, I add, "Was he with anyone?" Fear weighs heavily in my gut, making me want to sink to my knees and curl into a ball. *I don't want to hear the answer.* I'm not sure I can take any more tonight.

The woman looks at me. "Oh, no, darling. He isn't one of those guys. He's infatuated with his wife." Her eyes grow big and she points at me. "That's you, right? I've seen your picture a ton of times. He always talks about you." *How is that possible?* I'm so confused. On most days, I'm not even sure he likes me. *Is she talking about another husband who comes here to drink?*

I shake my head in disbelief and mumble, "You must have him confused with someone else."

The waitress looks me dead in the eye. "Honey, I've been at this a long time. I've seen and heard everything your little heart could ever imagine and more. There are two things you need to know about me. I hate liars and I never forget a face. So when I tell you that T always talks about you, it's the God's honest truth."

Shyly, I nod my acceptance, saying nothing because I still can't seem to get my head wrapped around the thought that he talks about me and how much he loves me. Apparently, he has no trouble telling strangers about his feelings. *Why can't he tell me?*

"Okay, you said he left. Can I have his phone back, please?" She hands the phone to me and then digs in the fanny pack I hadn't noticed her wearing.

"Here, you'll need these too." She hands over his keys.

Shocked, I question, "You have his keys?"

She nods. "Sure, honey. I wasn't going to let him drive drunk, so I had Charlie over there help me get him in his truck and then locked it up tight. I was fixing to call you around closing time to see what you wanted me to do with his phone and keys."

"R-really?" I sputter. Relieved, I throw my arms around her. "Sorry, it's just been a crazy couple of months, and I don't know what's happening to him, but I surely wouldn't want anything bad to happen."

The waitress looks at me. "He seems like a decent guy. I hope he figures it out."

"Me too," I mutter before she walks away.

The bartender, whose name I didn't get, wipes the bar in front of me. "Anything else you need?" he asks with a smile.

"Think that's enough excitement for one night. Thank you for keeping an eye out for him."

Exiting back out into the parking lot, I walk past Tristan's truck and, sure enough, he's passed out in the driver's seat. My heart flinches, and a sigh of relief falls from my lips. A surge of emotions overwhelms me, making it impossible to breathe. I rest my arm on the door frame of his truck and tuck my head against the cool metal exterior as I try to control my breathing.

In the past hour, I have been worried, angry, disappointed, disgusted, relieved, heartbroken, and exhausted. What is he doing? Is this what I have to look forward to? Is it our new normal? *I can't do it.* Tears fall down my cheeks, and I reach for my purse and start to dig. I find a piece of paper and a pen. I scribble a note to him.

I have your keys. Met some lovely friends of yours in the bar. We need to talk.
Steph

Then I turn off his phone to save his battery and put it in the cup holder with the note. I lock the doors before I walk back to my car with my heart a tattered mess.

Chapter 31

Tristan

Before I even open my eyes, I run my body through a mental scan. My knee hurts from the fall I took in PT. My stomach is churning and my head is throbbing. I can feel the heat of the sun, so I must be sleeping on the couch in our living room.

Last night, I'd gone out for a drink. The setback in therapy had me enraged, and I didn't want to feel anything. I didn't want to see pity on Steph's face, so I just walked out. I only intended to have a beer or two, but at some point, I lost count of the time and the number of drinks I'd had.

When I got up to leave, I felt my body sway, but I'm sure that was just my knee reacting from the fall I'd taken earlier. It didn't have anything to do with the fact I'd spent a few hours sucking down bottle after bottle of whatever pilsner they had on hand.

Yawning, I notice my mouth is exceptionally dry.

Maybe that, with everything else, suggests I have a hangover. One way to check. I crack open my eyes, and the tiny amount of light that sneaks in feels like a direct hit to my temple from a hammer. *Shit. This isn't good.* I force my eyes open a bit more and notice I'm staring at the logo on my steering wheel. *Okay, I'm in my truck. But where?* It takes effort to get myself righted in the driver's seat. Once I've corrected the seat settings so I'm upright, my eyes fall on a familiar building. Sidewinders, a bar that I've been secretly visiting the past few weeks while Steph is at work. *How did I get in my truck? And where are my keys?* I look in my pockets, under my seat, and flip down the visor. No luck. Then I look at the cupholder and see my phone tucked in it with a piece of paper. My already churning stomach heaves when I recognize the handwriting. *Steph.*

She has my keys, and all she's requesting is a conversation. *Fuck.* I pound the steering wheel and the vibration from it travels up my arm, shaking my body. "Ahhh. I feel like shit," I shout into the cab of my truck. *I need to call my wife.*

Grabbing my phone, I power it back on. In no time, I see all the messages she sent me last night that I ignored. Disappointment weighs heavy. *I'm an asshole.* I promised Steph I regretted getting drunk a month ago, and I was telling the truth. But lately, I've discovered a few beers in the afternoon have taken the edge off things. I can admit I didn't handle yesterday well, but it was too late. And now I need to face the conse-quences.

Ring, ring.

Is she going to answer? I don't even know what time it is.

Looking at the clock, I see it's eight, and she's usually up. *Why isn't she answering? Because you fucked up again.*

The phone rings again.

"Hello," a raspy voice answers. *Why does she sound so bad?*

"Steph, it's me. Can you bring my keys to me so I can get home?"

"Tristan, you just woke me up. I didn't sleep well when I finally got to bed around one, thanks to you. So you're going to have to wait until I've at least showered and had a cup of coffee. I'll be there when I get there," she growls before she hangs up. *Damn, she sounds pissed. This ought to be fun.*

An hour later, she pulls into the parking lot. I hesi-tantly step out of my truck and slowly make my way over to her. *I screwed up again.* Her anger is coming off her in waves. My balls shrivel up. *This isn't good.* She chucks my keys at me without a word and drives off. Hanging my head, I mutter, "Fuck" *How am I going to explain I know I messed up, but that I couldn't help it?*

I knew after the first beer I should've gone home, but I was still so angry, so I stayed and ordered another. Before I knew it, hours had passed and empty bottles surrounded me. Even through my alcohol-soaked brain, I knew I wasn't making a smart choice. I even recognized that it'd hurt Steph, but I couldn't force myself to get up out of that chair, call a cab, and head home. It didn't matter if I was on the first beer or tenth, I fucked up.

Picking up my keys, I walk back to my truck, grumbling about how much of a dumb fuck I am. I fear going home and facing the wrath of my wife. I know I deserve anything she has to say, but I'm not ready to hear it. I know her words will be full of pain and disappointment. Hell, I'm disappointed in myself too. I've let everyone down, especially her. I'm not a professional hockey player anymore. I'm not sure who I am anymore. Ten minutes later, I pull into my parking spot. Moving at the speed of a sloth, I trudge up the stairs to our condo.

Pushing the door open, I'm not sure what I'll find. An eerily quiet space isn't what I expected. Nor are the bags next to the door. My gut sinks.

"Steph," I call out as I head toward our bedroom. It looks like a hurricane has torn through the space, leaving only destruction in its path. Sinking onto our bed, reality starts to sink in. *She's leaving me.* It's hard to tell how long I sit there, but when Steph finally returns, I sense her even before I see her. The air in our condo shifts and, suddenly, it seems like the surrounding temperature has dropped dramatically.

Goose bumps cover my skin and my body does a full-on shiver.

"Tristan," she calls from the front room.

Scared to move because I don't want to make the situation any worse, I call out to her, "I'm back here."

Steph appears in the doorway, and even though I thought I was at my worst, seeing her tear-stained face crushes me further. I want to leap up and hold her, but her eyes stop me in my tracks. She's never looked at me this way before. Like I'm a stranger to her. Like she doesn't know me. Like she... doesn't love me anymore. There are so many emotions battling for dominance in her expression—rage, sorrow, hurt—and I put them there. The thought guts me and renders me immobile.

"Last night I learned some things about you that absolutely broke me. You don't trust me, and now I know I can't trust you. My heart's been shattered and I need some time away from this toxic environment you have surrounded us with.

"You have been my best friend since we met in high school, but I don't even know you anymore. You've been the love of my life for so long, and I question if you are anymore. I'm sorry I let you down and wasn't more for you. If I had been, then maybe we wouldn't be where we are today." Her voice cracks on the last sentence.

What? My brain stutters and I can't speak. Rather chaotic pleas overwhelm my grey matter. *Please don't leave me. I'll fix this. Don't give up on me. I love you.*

Paralyzed by fear, the words I desperately want to say remain stuck in my throat. I grind my teeth in frustration. *Say something, you idiot.* I open my mouth, willing anything to come out. But nothing does. Panic sets in. My body shakes and my fists clench. The rapid thud of my heart is all I hear.

Every minute that passes between us weighs me down with more and more regret. I want to comfort her and tell her all the things she needs and wants to hear, but I'm stuck. She patiently waits, her eyes pleading with me, and my heart aches, knowing I'm letting her down yet again.

Another few minutes pass and the air becomes thick and suffocating. I look at Steph to gauge if she's having the same reaction. Her tense lips have fallen into a deep frown and her eyes are heavy with tears. She nods, and it feels like it's a sign of defeat. *Ouch!* I rub at my chest because it feels like I've received a direct punch to my heart from a championship MMA fighter. *What's going on?* It feels like things just took a turn for the worse.

Steph breaks eye contact, whispers "goodbye," and is gone. When I hear her roll her bags to the front door and then finally shut it, I collapse on the floor and sob. *This is all my fault. I am solely responsible.*

Chapter 32

Stephanie

After I gave Tristan his keys, I drove to the closest four-star hotel to my work and checked in for an undisclosed amount of time. Is it practical? No. But Tristan has been smart about his paychecks from the NHL and we've been responsible, not spending frivolously, and this separation is warranted. I can't trust my husband right now and because of that, I need some distance to figure out my next step.

I cry like a baby the entire way back to our condo to grab my bags, which I packed this morning before I brought Tristan his keys. I don't even know if he'll be at our condo when I return. If he isn't, I guess I can leave another note. My heart squeezes in my chest when I think about the past six months and how everything has gone to hell after his injury. I don't fault him for that. It's out of his control, but I can't look past the behaviors he's been in control of since then and how he's surprised me by doing things I never thought possible. His actions have sent me into a downward spiral. He has me questioning our entire relationship, and the only way I feel I can gain clarity is by allowing myself room to breathe. And if we stay in the same space, I'll suffocate.

Walking away from Tristan is the hardest thing I have ever done. Emotional and physical pain seeps out of every pore in my body, making me feel weak. I desperately wish my mom was still alive so she could hold me and tell me it would be okay. She never met Tristan, but I always thought she would have loved him. My dad and brother sure do. Our separating will destroy them, and so I know I have to keep it quiet until I decide what to do.

I feel like a failure when I push into my hotel room alone. I've never stayed at a hotel by myself. And now I have this giant room all to myself because my marriage is on the rocks. Dropping my bags as soon as I'm past the door, I make my way over to the queen-sized bed and crawl in. Thankfully it's Saturday, and I still have another day before I have to show up to work, acting as if everything's normal. My coworkers know about Tristan's injury, surgery, and recovery. They even know about his dismissal from the team, but everything else I've kept closely guarded. Rationally, I know his decisions are why we're in this situation, but I can't help but feel personally responsible for not being able to fix it. To make life easier for him. With that guilt on my mind, I drift off to sleep.

The next morning comes much too early, despite my fitful sleep. I try to untangle myself from the sheets, but it proves a challenge before five o'clock and with a full bladder. When I free myself, I stumble into the bathroom, stubbing my big toe on the door frame. "Shit!" I holler. My weak voice echoes off the bathroom walls as I hop over to the toilet. Once I'm done, I walk carefully back to the bedroom and survey the damage. Lying right next to the door are my two still-packed suitcases, purse, discarded clothes, and cell phone. Flipping over the phone, I'm not sure what I'll find. No one but Tristan knows what happened yesterday. Not expecting any missed calls, I flip the phone over. The confirmation of that is jarring. I didn't have a single text or missed call, and the realization of that hits me hard.

The first day in my hotel room is dark—the room and my mood. I don't want to be here. I want to be home, but I don't recognize the man my husband has turned into, and I don't want a VIP ticket to his self-destruction. Because right now, it seems inevitable. Every time I think about him, my stomach twists, my heart aches, and my body breaks out in shivers. Tristan hasn't hit bottom yet, but I don't think he'll have much farther to fall. It takes everything within me not to grab my bags and head home. But I know doing that won't be best for either of us. No matter how much that decision hurts, or the knowledge that I'm shredding my own heart, I know if I return, I won't survive what he's doing. Heavy tears fall as I wonder what's going to happen to us.

Things go well at work that first week of staying at the hotel. I expect to have more emotional moments, but my boss has kept me incredibly busy and distracted. I haven't told him what's happening, but it's like he has a sixth sense and knows something is off. By Friday night, when I'm sitting in my bed eating a salad I picked up after work, I reflect on how comfortable I've become in my new surroundings. No matter what, though, I still miss Tristan. And I haven't heard a peep from him since I left. When I allow myself to think about that, it feels like I'm being crushed alive. My breathing becomes stunted, my chest feels tight, and I get dizzy. *What is he doing? Is he still going to PT? Is he still drinking? Is he as miserable as I am?* On multiple nights, my fingers dance over his contact while an internal battle rages inside me. Not only do I want to see him, but I want to talk to him too. During these weak moments, I scroll through my photos and remember what we had, and that always makes me cry so hard I can't breathe.

It's been a month, and I still haven't heard from my husband, so I consider other options. I move out of my hotel room and into a short-term, furnished apartment. Until now, I thought Tristan might come racing in, beg my forgiveness, and save the day. But our life isn't a romance novel, and instead, he's done nothing. I'm talking no phone calls or texts, no attempts to see me. Nothing. The lack of his response stings a thousand times worse than why I left. And the realization that my leaving doesn't affect him, shreds my broken heart.

With Christmas right around the corner, I make plans to go home to Concord. I need to see my dad and tell him what's happened between Tristan and me. And I need to do it in person. As far as I know, Tristan's parents are still planning to come to Boston for the holiday season. *That'll be a shock.* With them being here, I'm relieved I won't run into them while I'm at my dad's.

Flying home the night before Christmas Eve, I'm excited to see my dad. His plan is to meet me at the luggage carousel, but he told me he'll call if things change. Taking my phone out of airplane mode, I see I have a few missed calls. When I look to see who it is, my stomach drops. It's Tristan's mom. Dread sets in and I start to sweat. *Do I call her back? Is something wrong?* Stepping out of the way of the crowd, I send my dad a quick text.

ME

We just landed and I'll be there shortly. I just need to make a quick call.

DAD

No problem. See you soon.

Suddenly nauseated and hot, I jet off to the closest ladies' room, where I splash cold water on my face and take a few deep breaths. Once I feel a bit better, I listen to the message Tristan's mom left.

Hey, Steph. I know we haven't talked in a few weeks, but I'm trying to get ahold of Tristan. I've tried calling all day, and he's not answering. We just landed in Boston, and while Jeff is getting the rental car, I thought I'd try you. But you aren't answering either. And now I'm starting to worry. Did you two get off to an impromptu holiday vacation and forget we were coming to visit? I hope that's the case and you are somewhere tropical, enjoying the sand and surf. We're going to head to our hotel. As soon as you get this message, can one of you call me back? Thanks so much, dear.

My heart breaks at the worry in her voice. Obviously, Tristan hasn't been in communication with his parents. They don't know we're separated. I stop at one of the empty gates and fire off another quick text to my dad, telling him I'm going to be another few minutes. I drop into one of the empty chairs. My hands shake as I do something I told myself not to do weeks ago. I track Tristan's phone. After a moment, his location shows that he's at the bar where I found him the night before I moved out. *This isn't good. How often is he going there?* Breathing out deeply, I open up our joint credit card and look at the past months' charges. The detailed list feels like a sucker punch. There are so many charges at bars and liquor stores. Fear curdles in my gut and I clutch my stomach. *What is he doing to himself?* With tears in my eyes, I close the web browser and look back at my missed calls. *How am I going to call his mom and tell her this?*

My phone rings. It's my dad.

"Hi, Dad. Sorry, I'm coming right now." Looking around, I make sure I have all my things before I step onto the escalator.

"It's okay, Steph. I wanted you to know I grabbed your bag. I was just worried about you." His concern makes his voice deep and thick, like molasses.

"I'm on the escalator. I see you now."

Rushing off toward him, he opens his arms wide and I lunge at him. Being wrapped in his big, strong arms is exactly what I need. My heart's broken, and until just now, I didn't realize how badly it hurt. For the past few months, I have tried my best to ignore the ever-constant ache. No matter how much sleep I get, I'm exhausted. And on top of that, I'm chronically weepy.

Hugging me tight, my dad whispers to the top of my head, "Let's go home and we can talk over a cup of coffee." Reaching up, I swipe at my tear-soaked cheeks before I push back.

"Okay," I say before we walk out to the parking garage.

Looking out the window at the snow-covered ground, my body feels heavy. Weighed down by an invisible force. I don't say anything as we drive to my childhood home. Occasionally, I look at my phone, wondering if I should call or text Connie back. *They're his parents.* Shouldn't he be the one to tell them we're separated? I haven't seen him in months. I don't know what he's been doing. That's not exactly true, now that I've seen the credit card statement. *He's been drinking a lot.* I wonder if that's all he's been doing.

Pulling up to my childhood home, memories overwhelm me, and I start to tear up again.

"How about we go inside, Sunshine?" Once inside, Dad heads off to the kitchen for that cup of coffee he mentioned. After hanging up my purse and coat, I follow him.

After setting two mugs of hot coffee on the table, Dad goes to the fridge and grabs a small container of French vanilla creamer for me. He smiles at me when he sets it on the table. "Thanks, Dad."

Quietly, he sits down to join me. "Can I ask you a question?"

While playing with the handle of my mug, I nod.

"Sunshine... Why did you come home for Christmas? And why isn't Tristan here too?"

Looking down at the table, I hide my eyes from him before I speak. "Tristan and I are separated. The injury and recovery have been tough on him, and over the last six months, he changed. Then the team let him go and things spiraled even further. And I moved out."

Rubbing his beard, he looks lost in thought. I'm worried about how he'll respond. *Will he be disap-*

pointed? He and my mom had something special, and it isn't fair that she was taken from him early. Tristan and I had something good when we were younger, but apparently, it isn't strong enough to endure hardship. Yes, I chose to walk away and take a break, but he never once reached out or tried to make any effort. That was my deciding factor, and after the new year, I have an appointment with a divorce lawyer. If Tristan had made any effort, I would have seen it as a sign to fight for us. But during our time apart, I haven't heard from him, and that absence in my life has destroyed me.

"Separated," my dad says, as if he's trying it out to fully understand its meaning.

"Yes, separated. I know that isn't what you want to hear, but he and I haven't talked since I left months ago, and his silence has spoken volumes. I have an appointment with an attorney in a couple of weeks. And I've started looking at jobs in other cities. I need a change, and getting out of Boston and away from my failed marriage is part of my plan." This is the first time I'm saying it out loud, and I'm a mess of emotions.

My dad looks down at his coffee and, in a gravelly voice, asks, "You think that is the best option?"

I shrug. "At this point, I'm not sure. But it seems like Tristan doesn't seem to care. He didn't reach out once, and he's started drinking heavily. To make matters worse, Connie is calling me because she can't get ahold of him, and I don't know what I'm supposed to tell her."

My dad's eyes grow wide. "What do you mean? You tell her the truth." *I can do that. I just don't need to tell her everything.* His sad eyes confirm his words, and I know he's right. I nod.

"You're right. I'm exhausted, Dad. I'm going to go call Connie and then go to bed. Thanks for picking me up at the airport." I give him a hug before I grab my suitcase and trudge up the stairs to my childhood bedroom. Pushing the door open, it still looks just like it did when I was young. Sitting down on the patchwork bedspread, I glance around the room. My dad hasn't changed a thing. My bulletin boards covered with pictures of friends, dried corsages from dances, and of course, concert and movie tickets.

My phone dings, alerting me to a message. Although I just left him, it's my dad.

DAD

> I know this will be tough, but Connie is worried about Tristan, and you can give her some news, even if it isn't what she'll want to hear. She cares very much about you, and just knowing you are safe will ease some of her worry. She and Jeff can sort Tristan out now that they're in Boston. I love you, Sunshine.

ME

> I know you're right. I love you too, Dad.

Selecting Connie's contact, I pray our conversation goes well.

Ring, ring.

I'm not ready for panicked Connie when she answers. "Steph, is that you?"

Clearing my throat, I timidly answer, "Yes, it's me."

"Where are you? Tristan isn't answering his phone, and no one answered at your condo. We looked in the windows and it looks like you were robbed. We've been so worried. Are you okay?"

Her rapid-fire questions catch me off guard and my answer stutters out. "Y-. I'm o-okay. I'm n-not with Tristan, though."

The line goes silent. "You aren't? Where are you? Where is he?"

"I'm visiting my dad. As for Tristan, he's still in Boston." I take a deep breath before I continue. "Connie, I haven't seen Tristan in a few months. We separated right after the team released him, and he hasn't made any attempt to contact me since. I'm sorry you're finding out like this."

Connie's crying fills the line. "What do you mean you're separated? Are you getting divorced? Steph, what is going on?"

Sitting on my bed, with tears streaming down my face, I pick at a stray string on my bedspread. *How much do I tell her?*

Before I can answer her, Jeff gets on the line. His

voice is full of worry. "Steph, you and Tristan are separated?"

I reach for a tissue and wipe my nose. "We are," I answer.

Ever calm, he asks, "Can you tell me why?"

My heart splinters more. Whispering, I answer, "This injury. His recovery. It changed him. He's become someone I don't recognize anymore."

Jeff lets out a deep breath, digs deep, and asks, "What's he been like?"

I dab at more tears. *I still love him, and this is killing me.* "I don't want to speak poorly of him, but I think he's in a terrible place and needs help. He showed me multiple times he doesn't want it from me, so I gave him some space. And he hasn't reached out, so I assume things are over. I hope you have more luck than I did. I still love him, but I can't stand by and watch him destroy himself."

Jeff must have put me on speakerphone because I hear Connie sobbing in the background.

"I'm so sorry I wasn't enough. I do love him, but I wasn't what he wanted." Admitting those things out loud forces my last wall to crash down. My body crumples onto my pillows, and I pull myself into the fetal position, seeking solace and protection from the misery I'm in.

"Steph," Jeff says.

"Yeah," I whimper, sounding as broken as I feel.

"Do you know where I can find him?" The despair

in Jeff's question makes me cry even harder. *How do I tell them he's probably at a bar, drunk?* I didn't want to get in the middle of this, but I want Tristan saved. He will always be the love of my life, even though we aren't meant to be.

"One second, let me track him." Pulling up Tristan's location, I see it still shows him at the bar. "He's been drinking the past few months and spending a lot of time at this bar by our condo." Connie makes a strangled noise, and I give Jeff directions to Sidewinders, Tristan's apparent new favorite hangout.

I hear rustling in the background of the call. "I've got to go. Thanks, Steph," Jeff calls out.

"Good luck," I say right before the line goes dead. Hugging myself even tighter, I send up a prayer that Jeff finds Tristan and they can help him. *Maybe they'll be just what he needs.*

For the first time in months, I have hope for Tristan's future. It may not include me, but I don't want anything bad to happen to him.

Chapter 33

Tristan

Waking up the morning after the team let me go, passed out in my truck with a note from my wife was a new low for me. That was until the day after that, when I woke up and realized I'd gotten drunk again after my wife walked out on me. That was months ago, and it feels like I'm stuck in a loop of repeating days.

Well, I think I just discovered my greatest low ever. I wake up with a horrendous hangover in a room I don't recognize. *Where am I?* Peeking my eyes open as much as I can before pain stabs through my head, I gather enough information to conclude I'm in a hotel room. *Shit, what did I do?* I'm terrified of not only the pain but of the truth when I finally pry my eyes open.

Sitting across the room, I see what I think is a woman, but my eyes are fuzzy and she just registers as a blob. *Did I go home with a strange woman last night?* Regret sinks low in my stomach and I feel like I want to throw up. I may be in a pretty low spot right now, but I am not a cheater. It's never even once entered my thoughts. There is only one woman in my life. Not that my wife seems to care anymore. She walked out on me and I haven't heard from her since. A Christmas carol is being hummed by the woman and then I remember what day it is. *It's Christmas.* A nagging in my brain reminds me that my parents are supposed to be in town, not that I bothered to answer any of the calls they've made to me recently.

Pushing myself up to sitting, my stomach flips and flops, and I swear I'm moments away from puking. I lick my lips and realize my mouth is dry like the desert. And the taste of my breath is like rotten assholes that have been sitting in the sweltering sun for days. "Fuck me," I say on a groan, forgetting I'm not alone.

"Excuse me?" the woman calls out, and her voice registers as familiar Then, like lightning striking, it hits me. *It's my mother.*

"Mom," I rasp out. If it's really her and not a figment of my imagination, she's going to kill me.

"Tristan Alexander Murphy." Her stern tone sends shivers throughout my body, and my already churning stomach quivers. *Oh shit.*

Rubbing my eyes, her image becomes clearer. "Good morning," I say.

She purses her lips. "Not for you." I don't know if

she means it's not actually morning or if it's not good. Because, let's face it, I'm screwed in both scenarios.

Scratching my head, I'm not really sure how to respond, so I try for light, hoping we can ignore my current state. "Merry Christmas?"

A deep growl comes from another area of the room, and I whip my head toward it. *Shit, that sucks.* Now I'm dizzy on top of everything else. But when my vision clears, there stands my dad, with his hands on his hips and a deep frown on his face. "Do you think this is funny, Tristan? Do you think this is how we wanted to see our son or spend our Christmas?"

My life has collapsed, my body is revolting against me, and now my parents are chastising me. *It's too damn early for this.* "I don't know, Dad. Is it?" I spit back, annoyed that they're even here. *How'd they find me?*

I've only seen my dad angry a handful of times, but this right here terrifies me. Because it is so much more. Not only is he angry, but he looks disappointed too. And that's worse. *Fuck me.* I slap my hand to my head. *Shit.* That hurts.

Looking at my mom, I see she, too, is wearing a frown, and her eyes look sad. It's undeniable I've hurt them, and I don't know how to make things right. I have the same problem with Steph. And since I don't know, I don't do anything but drink. Then I can be numb and I don't have to think about all the people I've hurt or disappointed.

Feeling like it can't get worse, I ask, "Why are you here?"

My mom's gasp makes me instantly regret my question. But I still want the answer. My dad steps closer and sits next to me on the bed. "Well, son, we came to celebrate Christmas with you and Steph." I put up my hand to interrupt, but he pats it down before he continues. "But neither of you were returning our calls. Finally, your mom got through to Steph last night and we learned what's been going on between you two."

I hang my head in embarrassment but say nothing.

"Is it true... you've been separated for a few months?" His voice is now calm and steady.

A lone tear sneaks out, and I angrily swipe at it with the back of my hand. "Yeah, that's true." Those words sink deep and wrap around my chest like a stranglehold, making it tough to breathe. I drop my head between my knees and suck in a few deep breaths. A large, warm hand rubs circles on my back.

"It's okay, Tristan. We'll figure this out." I hear his words, but I find it impossible to believe them. I did this. I pushed Steph away, and now I've lost her. She hasn't told me as much, but I'm dreading that the next interaction we have will be our last. And the thought of that kills me. It's as if my still-beating heart has been torn from my chest. The pain I'm experiencing is unbearable. I rub at my chest, trying to ease the sharp pain within it. When it doesn't subside, I feel even more desperate and emotional than ever. *What is happening to me?*

"Breathe, Tristan." My mom is now next to me. I shake my head. If I'm dying, maybe that's for the best. At least then, I'll stop hurting the people I love.

Two sets of arms wrap around me and hug me tight. Where once I felt dark, a light, warm energy chases it away, stretching across my entire body. Squeezing tight, Mom whispers against my ear. "Don't give up. We'll help you. It's okay. You're going to be okay. We love you." Her words are like a balm to my fractured soul, providing comfort and love when I need it most.

My parents hold me for a few more minutes before they unwrap their arms from around me. I know I look less than desirable, and a shower sounds amazing after the last few days.

Taking in the hotel room, I wonder where we are. "Is this your room?" My dad nods. "How'd I get here?" Dad winces at first, but then he fills me in.

"We talked to Steph last night. We told her we'd been by the condo and you hadn't answered there or on your phone. We knew we needed to find you and so she offered to track your phone. Which is how we found you at Sidewinders last night. You were passed out in a corner booth, and from a conversation with the bartender, it's become your regular spot the last few months. He even shared that you'd been by every day since Steph showed up looking for you months ago." *Okay, that's not the worst thing that could happen.*

Then mom elbows me. "Rhonda says to stop screwing around and go after your wife. Apparently, she thinks Steph is a badass." My mouth drops open. *Connie Murphy does not use swear words or anything like it.* And Rhonda needs to shut up. She and Eddie, the bartender, have been riding my chops for months about going after Steph and winning her back. But what can I offer her? The answer is always the same... nothing. So nothing is what I do.

Dad suggests a shower for me and hands Mom the room service menu. "Looks like fine dining today. I bet nothing else is open." So, after a shower and tugging on a pair of my dad's sweats and a t-shirt, we dine on a smorgasbord of breakfast options. My hangover subsides after popping a few pain relievers and hammering down a stack of pancakes, a pile of hash browns, and a few slices of bacon. My folks drive me to Sidewinders to pick up my truck, which thankfully hasn't been towed but has a nice covering of snow. They sit in their warm rental while I clean it off and then they follow me back to my place.

When I open the door, the state of my condo makes me immediately embarrassed. Takeout boxes are scattered everywhere, and it smells like a combination of stale fried food and beer. I didn't go to college, but I'm imagining frat houses smelling similar the day after hosting a party.

"Tristan," my mom chides. Looking over at her, she looks horrified. "It's disgusting in here."

My dad laughs. "Reminds me of college." The goofy grin on his face tells me he's fond of whatever memory he's reliving.

Mom clears her throat. "That's before you met me."

Dad laughs again. "And the best thing that's ever happened to me."

My parents share a look, and I can't help but frown. I'm happy for them, but Steph and I used to share looks like that. I imagined our future often. And it was never this.

Needing a moment by myself, I head down the hallway toward the closet where we keep all the cleaning products. I pull out the bleach, trash bags, rubber gloves, and anything else I'll need to clean up this pigsty. Returning to the living room, I dump everything on the coffee table. I don't ask my parents to help, but they do. In an hour, the place looks brand new. "Thank you. I'm sorry you came all the way to Boston to find me like this. I know it's disappointing. I'm just having a hard time adjusting to losing both Steph and hockey."

My parents again share a look, but this one makes me pause. Confusion sets in. "What?" I ask.

"Are you sure you've lost them both?" my dad asks.

Really, Dad? Squishing up my face in disgust, I spit out, "Well, considering I've been fired from the team and my wife has left me, I'm pretty sure I've lost them both. Thanks for questioning my sanity."

He puts his arms up in defense. "Now, son, hear me out. Let's just focus on hockey first. Yes, you're done playing professionally, but does that mean you have to be done with hockey altogether?"

"Okay, Dad. If I can't play, what else is there?" I question.

"What about coaching? Have you ever considered that?" *Interesting.*

My mom claps her hands together excitedly and then chimes in. "That would be so lovely. You always loved to help teach the younger, less experienced kids at all those camps you attended." *I don't want to be a kids' coach unless it's my kids' team, and seeing that my wife left me, the chance of that seems improbable.*

"Dad, I don't want to coach a kids' team. Plus, that's volunteer. How else am I going to support myself? I don't have a degree," I say gruffly.

My dad shakes his head. "Not kids. What about the AHL? You'd be a natural."

Taking a minute to consider his suggestion, I wonder if it's possible. For the first time in months, I feel hopeful. I smile as the warmth I'm feeling spreads throughout my body. "Okay. That might work." Both parents smile at me. "But what about Steph? How do I get her back?" My mom's face falls and my stomach does too. *Did she say something to them?* "What?" I beg.

Mom's eyes grow misty, and it feels like I'm

inflicting torture on her, just asking her to talk. "Tristan, Steph is the hard part of this problem. I'm afraid you may have taken too long to decide you still want her. She said the distance between you two has become too vast..." Her voice trails off.

I sink down onto my couch, pull the blanket that still smells faintly like her over me, and let my mom's words flow through me. I feel hollow and empty. I think I could survive without hockey, but Steph? That's unfathomable. "W-what did she say exactly? Did she say it's over? Is she going to divorce me?"

Dad puts his hand on my shoulder, his fingers curling in, gripping me tight. He's offering silent support. *Obviously, he knows more.* "Son, I don't know how to say this, but..." He hesitates, and I whip my head to look at him, willing him not to say what I think he's going to. "From talking to her, it sounds like it. I'm so very sorry, Tristan." He squeezes my shoulder, letting me know they're here for me.

But my world has just imploded. A sharp pain rips through my chest and I feel the air sucked from my lungs. *Am I dying?* Panicked, I grab the blanket tighter to my chest and inhale it. And the faint scent of her perfume hits my nose. *Is this the last I have of her? Of us?* My chest tightens and my breathing becomes labored. *Am I having a heart attack?* Concerned, I look at my parents and croak, "My chest hurts and it's difficult to breathe. Call 9-1-1. I think I'm having a heart attack." My mom gasps and dad leaps into action.

Within ten minutes, EMTs are surrounding me, assessing my condition. One EMT points out that my blood pressure and heart rate are high. They get me ready for transport to the hospital and then I'm whisked away. Hours later, when I'm discharged from the ER, the doctor concludes I didn't suffer a heart attack. *Thank goodness.* After having my blood drawn and being given oxygen, aspirin, and hydration, he suggests maybe I had a panic attack. He explains many of the symptoms are similar. After showing me my EKG was normal, it's obvious I was fine. *And now I'm crazy. Great!*

Exhausted from the emotions of the last few hours, my parents grab dinner from the hospital's cafeteria before we head back to my condo. Once we've eaten, I plan to crash and sleep for days. My heart still throbs, and every time I think of Steph, it only gets worse. Maybe sleep will give me some relief from it.

"Sorry about all the trouble today. Thanks for being there for me. But I'm exhausted and I just want to go to bed." My parents nod, then look at each other, and an entire conversation I'm not privy to takes place between their eyes. "What?" I ask.

Mom looks at me with a worried expression. When she looks at Dad, his face morphs to match hers. *What?* "You're just going to bed?" he nervously questions.

"Yeah. Where else would I go?" I say, feeling dead on my feet.

My dad shifts his stance and grabs my mom's hand.

"We wanted to make sure you didn't go out drinking."
Dread settles in my gut. *That is how they found you.*

Annoyed, more with myself than anything, I snap out, "I'm not going out drinking. I just want to go to sleep." Their weary eyes grow large in surprise at my sharp response.

"Okay," is all my dad says before they shuffle over to the front door.

"Sorry, I'm just tired and my mind is a mess." Walking up to them, I pull my mom into a hug. "Love you." Her shoulders shake and then I feel her nod against my chest. When she pulls back, her eyes are filled with tears. My dad holds out his hand to shake and I reach for him. "I love you too, Dad."

He smiles. "Same, Tristan. We'll see you tomorrow. It'll be better." *Let's hope.*

Chapter 34

Stephanie

After spending the holidays with my dad, I return to Boston lighter than when I left. I did some major thinking over the week and sadly concluded that my marriage is over. It hasn't been a simple decision, but when I think about the last year of our marriage, I have to be honest with myself. We struggled even before Tristan's injury. Was our love only ever puppy love? Did we ever have what was necessary for a successful marriage? It was like Tristan didn't want to be part of a life with me, and I took that as a sign that I needed to move on, no matter how bad that felt. I wasn't going to force him to love me or stay married to someone he didn't want. Those are the thoughts that floated through my mind when I cried in my childhood bedroom.

Most days, my eyes were red, sore, and puffy. My poor dad checked on me often, offering tea and food.

Nothing sounded good. I just needed to work through my feelings and make some decisions. I was still young, and I had a lot of life to live.

Right after the new year, I visited a divorce lawyer who made the process fairly simple. Tristan and I hadn't signed a prenup, and I didn't want anything from him. I wanted to start over completely, and he'd need his salary from the NHL to get back on his feet, if he ever got himself back together.

By the beginning of February, the papers are filed and we have a court date for August. Through our attorneys, I work out a time to visit the condo and move the rest of my stuff out without Tristan there. I don't have much that I want, but saying goodbye to this life takes longer than I expected. Just as I'm grabbing the last box, Tristan comes through the front door, surprising me. "Oh, hi. I didn't realize you were still here." His eyes dart around, finally landing on my purse that's lying on top of my box labeled "romance books." "Do you want me to leave and give you more time?" He smiles.

Stunned by his arrival, I look over at my things. *This is the end.* The weight of that hangs heavy on my weary body. My mind is in utter chaos. *I've missed him so much. It's been months since I've seen him. Why doesn't he look as broken as I feel?* Seeing him hurts so much, and I recognize I need to go. I shake my head at his question, forcing out a smile I don't feel before answering him. "No... I just have this one last box and

I'm officially moved out." Tristan frowns, and I wince at how callous that sounds. I've learned to deflect my hurt for humor, hiding my pain.

Looking closer at Tristan, I'm drawn to his eyes. They're filled with pain and sadness. Not wanting to deal with that, I drop my focus to the box. "I'll just grab this and be on my way."

Tristan steps forward. "Here, let me help you. If it really is your romance books, I know it's heavy." His playful demeanor tugs at my heart. *Am I doing the right thing?* We step out of the condo, and a beautiful woman approaches. Instantly, I'm on edge at the way she's looking at my husband as if he's her next meal. What am I thinking? *He's not mine anymore. We're getting divorced.* But the more this woman eye-fucks him, the more jealous I get. I want to claim him as my own.

"Hey, T," her high-pitched voice calls out. It's like nails on a chalkboard, and instantly I despise her. *She isn't good enough for him. Why am I concerned? I wasn't either. Maybe this is what he wants.*

"Hey, Jaycie. How are you?" he calls back in a tone that makes my blood boil. I can feel my fingers curling tightly around my purse straps. *If they like each other so much, why don't they just do something about it? He's a free man, after all. Well, not really until August. But maybe that's why he wanted to help get my stuff out. Maybe she's coming over after I leave so they can fuck.*

My mind spins, and I know I need to get out of

here quickly before I melt down in front of my soon-to-be ex and his new fuck buddy. Grabbing the box from Tristan's hands, I say, "I got this. Thanks for your help." He refuses to let it go.

"Steph, I got it. Where are you parked anyway? I didn't see your car."

Noticing the petite blond still nearby, my body tenses even more. Turning to my new car, a year-old Audi Q5 I've got on lease, I stop, point at it, and answer, "I'm right here."

Tristan's mouth drops open. "You got your dream car."

Proud of myself, I stand taller. "I did. You can give me that box. I can carry it the rest of the way. Plus, it seems like your friend is waiting for you." I can't help the snark I use. *If he wants to fuck around while we are still technically married, that's on him. From what I know, a lot of the hockey players do that during the season. I always assumed Tristan was faithful, but maybe I was just being naïve. He did a lot of things I didn't expect.*

"Huh?" Tristan questions, his eyes still focused on me.

Setting the box in my car, I turn back to him, roll my eyes, and say, "That girl you said hi to looks like she's waiting for you, and you probably don't want to keep her waiting. Right?" He stares at me. Then he shakes his head and shrugs. *Great, a non-answer.* Why do I even care? *Because I still love him. And I always will.*

I climb into my car and give Tristan a wave before I drive away. My heart squeezes tight in my chest the entire time, and once I'm sure he can't see me anymore, I finally let my tears fall. Being in the space we shared for so many years wrecked me. Every time I turned a corner or looked through a drawer, memories flooded my mind. Moving out took longer than I'd expected because I'd spent far too long standing in the closet sniffing his clothes. I'd laid in the bed until I couldn't take the pain spreading through my body. Finally forcing myself up, I realized something. This process felt like I was ripping myself apart and then using scotch tape to put myself back together. All the edges were jagged and ill-fitting. Nothing felt right.

Tristan

When I'd finally accepted that Steph was divorcing me, I felt absolutely destroyed. I'd promised my mom and dad that I was done drinking, and giving it up was surprisingly easier than I'd thought. After I'd been served the official divorce papers, I gave myself a few days to grieve, but I reminded myself that we were over and I needed to move on. *Okay, that's not really true.* Moving on from the love of your life isn't possible, but I wasn't willing to hold her hostage when all she wanted was her freedom. From me.

Our attorneys arranged a time for her to officially move out. And although I want nothing more than to stay there, parked on the couch and force a conversation—make her admit that she still loves me—I don't. I felt a little comforted that she'd at least admitted that to my parents when they'd talked. Unfortunately, they also said she didn't feel that was enough.

So here we are. Me sitting at a diner a few blocks away, drinking lukewarm black coffee while she packs up the rest of her belongings from the home we'd shared. Over the last few weeks, I realized just how far I'd fallen and how horribly I'd treated her. I wasn't a monster by any means; I hadn't been abusive, but I'd been dismissive and absent. I'd lied to her and done things that were out of character for me.

When I got sober, I could see those things, but it was too late in her eyes. Still feeling crushed, I stare into my empty ceramic coffee mug at the grounds sitting alone at the bottom. Do they have special powers like tea leaves? Can they tell me about my future? If they did, would it be worth finding out? The gray-haired waitress returns and asks if I need a refill or anything else. I just shake my head, so she leaves my bill and moves on to another table.

Looking at my watch, I see it's been three hours, and Steph's lawyers said that was more than enough time. Pulling a five-dollar bill from my wallet, I drop it on the table before I show myself out. Walking back to my condo, I notice the day has grown gloomy. An icy wind blows past me and makes me shiver. It wasn't too cold when I left. I'd only pulled on a coat. Now I wish I had a beanie because my ears are freezing.

Shoving my hands deep in my pockets, I tilt my face toward the sky. It looks like it's going to snow. "That's just great," I mumble.

The usually ten-minute walk takes twice as long as I drag my feet the entire way. I'm not ready to face my new reality. Life without Steph isn't a life at all. When I finally reach our complex, *my* complex, everything sinks in and it feels like my body is solid lead. Attempting to drag myself up the stairs, I mutter, "The only woman you've ever loved is leaving you." And I can't really blame her. It was my fault.

The sight before me when I open the door to the condo, leaves me momentarily speechless. Steph is still here. *Has she decided to stay?* My heart pounds at the thought of that. *No, she hasn't.* She wouldn't be moving out if she were staying. There would be no need for attorneys either. Looking around, I see she has a single box sitting near the door. *She must be done.*

After I carry her last box out to her new car, she drives away, taking my fractured heart with her. I'm not sure what I expected of our interactions now that everything has shifted between us, but it's hella awkward. Thinking back, Steph seemed closed off.

That is until Jaycie said hi, and that's when I saw a flash of emotion. *Was it jealousy?*

Jaycie's a new neighbor that I helped a few weeks earlier. She and her boyfriend Todd were moving in. They needed help to lift a dresser up a flight of stairs and I was just getting back from a workout. They promised me dinner some night in return, and that had been all she'd wanted. Nothing about it was nefarious. But it intrigued me how reactive Steph was to the interaction. "It doesn't matter, anyway. She's divorcing you, dipshit," I mutter as I watch her taillights disappear. "I love you, Steph," I confess quietly into the frigid air.

I'm not sure how long I stand there, but I finally notice my ears, fingers, and toes have gone numb and small snowflakes are falling. Shoving my hands in my pockets, I turn back to the condo building, wondering what's next for me. The urge to go drink hits me, but the image of Steph driving away from me reminds me of the cost.

Chapter 35

Tristan

I t's been a month since Steph officially moved out, and I've been working hard on my PT and staying sober. I've also gone and visited several members of the Boston hockey scene, and today I'm starting a volunteer job with the local AHL team, the Stingers. From what I've researched, they have a decent team and record. Their coach, Matty Jacobs, was one of my biggest fans when I played for the Storm, so when I came knocking, he jumped at the opportunity to bring me on board.

Walking into the arena they practice in affects me more than I expected. I practically lived in hockey arenas since I was a kid. They've been a home away from home. But everywhere I look brings back a flash of memories that stabs me in the gut. Leaning over, I force myself to take in a few deep breaths. *Get yourself under control.* While bent over, a large hand appears on my shoulder.

"Tristan, is that you? Are you feeling all right?"

Looking up, I see Matty, but instead of wearing a smile, he looks concerned. *Don't screw this up.*

Rubbing my knee, I smile. "Yeah, I'm great. Just making sure I put my brace on tight enough." I stop talking to gauge his reaction. When he smiles, I know I'm in the clear. "Excited to be here, helping you and the Stingers."

Squeezing the hand he still has on my shoulder, he says, "Glad to hear that. When was the last time you were on skates?"

"Just a few days ago. It was part of my PT goals. I'm solid," I proudly tell him.

His smile grows. "Then let's go. Do you have your skates, or do you need to borrow some?"

Tapping my bag, I answer, "All set."

He leads me to the locker room and introduces me to the coaches and support staff before the players.

Standing in the middle of the room, I watch as Matty knocks on his clipboard to get everyone's attention. The noise of the locker room dies down and everyone stares at their coach. "Listen up, guys, I have an announcement. You may recognize this guy next to me. If not, you must have been living under a rock the last few years. Tristan Murphy, the greatest player the Boston Storm has had in a decade, received a career-ending injury last year. And because of that, we are fortunate enough to have him as another coach. Since he's played at such a high level, he is well-versed in drills, plays, and what it takes to be a successful player. I expect you to give him your attention and respect. I know with his help, each of you will become a better player." Matty's words are lively and complimentary. They make me stand a little taller. Since my injury, I've constantly questioned if I'd play again or if I will become a washed-up has been. Thanks to this opportunity, I can see something more for myself. I may not play anymore, but I haven't lost my love or passion for this game. I'm not ready to hang up my skates, and even though the rest of my life is in shambles, I feel hopeful that my career in hockey isn't over. *I wish Steph could see this.* She hasn't been far from my thoughts since she left, and I doubt I'll ever get over her. But if I can be happy in one area of my life, it's better than nothing.

Coach turns to me. "Tristan, would you like to say anything to the team?"

Nodding, I look at this group of young men, and I see myself. They are excited, hungry, and determined. Just what it takes. "Hey, guys. I'm really glad to be here. Thanks to Coach Matty for bringing me on. Over the next few days, I'm going to be doing a lot of observing, so show me what you've got. After that, I will teach you some new drills and make recommendations for plays. I'm not here to mess with your team or the chemistry you have. I just want a chance to help you reach even higher. Please come talk to me if you have any concerns or questions. Thanks for having me."

Coach raps on his clipboard again. "Finish getting dressed. See you on the ice in ten." Then he turns and heads to his office.

All the players fist-bump me on the way out of the locker room. Making my way to the stands, I grab a seat halfway up the bleachers, lining myself up with the middle of the rink. While the assistant coach takes them through drills, I make notes of the players' speed, agility, puck handling, and awareness. After a few drills, the guys scrimmage and I jot down who I'd like to see paired up on a line. Matty said he was excited about my thoughts and recommendations. The Stingers have been successful, but he wants to take them to the next level. *I hope I can help do that.* My insecurities overwhelm me, reminding me I've never coached before. Just then my phone dings, alerting me to a text message. It's from my dad.

DAD

Good luck today. The Stingers are lucky to have you. You read the game better than most professional players. Your skills on the ice are unmatched. Yes, you were given a bum deal with your injury, but you were made for more. Show them what you got. Your mom and I love you, Tristan.

ME

Thank you, Dad. That was exactly
what I needed to hear. Love you too.

The next few months fly by, and I feel like I'm finally getting my stride back. The team is responding nicely to the suggestions I recommend and we're excited to see how this next season goes. I think we've got something great here. These guys have worked really hard, and they are definitely faster, smarter, and more focused than they were months ago.

It's Friday night and I'm ready to chill. Just as I'm leaving a particularly long practice, my phone rings. It's my attorney.

"Ugh," I moan out as I get into my truck, answering the call when the door is shut. "Hello, Mr. Jackson."

"Hello, Tristan. I hope this is a good time." He hesitates, like he's going to say something else, and I wait. Moments pass with nothing but silence being exchanged.

I clear my throat and say, "Now's fine. What's going on?" I know we've settled everything and Steph didn't accept anything I offered. All she wanted was to remove me from her retirement account and the savings account she had when we'd gotten married. Even though I'd offered alimony, she rejected it. I don't know why, but I couldn't force her, so in the end I dropped it.

We're supposed to meet at her attorney's office next week to sign the decree. Once it's recorded by the courts, we'll be officially over. Thinking about that makes my stomach cramp and my heart thud. I don't want to be over. I still love her and want her in my life. But she's done.

I saw her at the grocery store a few weeks ago, and instead of approaching her like I wanted, I stayed still and watched as she moved around the produce section. She looked radiant. Her hair's cut and styled. She had makeup on too. Her clothes were form-fitting, but not revealing, and she looked absolutely stunning. Every part of me perked up when I saw her. It pained me to know she was no longer mine.

Mr. Jackson interrupts my daydream. "Just calling to remind you of our meeting next week to sign the papers."

I grumble, "Yes, I remember."

"Okay. I'll see you then. Have a nice evening," he says.

"You too," I reply, then hang up.

The skies darken and fat raindrops pelt my truck the entire thirty-minute drive home. When I get there, my mood resembles the turbulence above me, and I want to hit the bar and get wasted. The desire to drink is still there, and I've done a fantastic job of avoiding my triggers, but our divorce is a major one. I feel like a failure. Drinking myself into a stupor sounds ten times better than feeling empty and destroyed, which is exactly what I feel every time I think about it.

Hockey and coaching have proven to be a worthwhile distraction. Add in working out and PT, and usually by the end of the day, I'm exhausted and have no energy left to think about her and what happened.

Before I let myself get sucked into something I'll regret, I get out of the truck and head inside. After kicking my wet shoes off, I head into the bedroom to change clothes. I can release some aggression by jogging to the gym. And once I'm there, I can work out my pain on the machines and strengthen myself at the same time. It's a win-win.

Zipping my raincoat up tight, I set off at a nice pace for the few-block jog to the gym. I end up resembling a drowned rat when I finally push through the entrance. Waving to the front desk clerk, I swipe my membership card. Working my way through the club, I keep my head down, hoping to avoid everyone. Just as I exit the locker room, a familiar voice calls out, "Hey, Tristan."

Whipping my head around, my eyes land on Kelvin, my physical therapist when I was with the Storm. "Hi, Kelvin. How are you?"

He rubs his chin while studying me. "I'm good. How's the knee? Still doing PT?"

"My knee is great! Regarding PT, yes and no."

He gives me a side eye. "What do you mean?"

"Insurance only covers so much, and since I'm not with the Storm anymore, I can only get a few more sessions. I continue to do the things I learned, and my knee has gotten stronger."

Kelvin looks down at my knee. "That's great. Can I

see where you're at? Maybe show you a few new exercises to add to your lineup?"

"Sure, man. That would be great."

After spending a couple hours together, where Kelvin evaluates my knee and explains new exercises to me, we part ways. My body's fatigued from all the paces he put me through, and a sauna sounds heavenly.

Coming to the gym tonight was a much better idea than visiting a bar. Are my problems gone? No. But I received great feedback from someone who saw me at my worst physically, and he couldn't stop mentioning how far I've come and praising me for the hard work I've put in. I'll sleep easier tonight knowing I chose something better for myself than just drowning in my miseries.

The weekend passes quickly, and as I get ready Monday morning for the signing of the divorce paperwork, I have a strange desire to look my best. To show Steph what she's missing. So I pull on soft-washed jeans and a button-up. I roll the sleeves up my forearms because she said that always drove her wild. I somewhat mess with my hair, making it resemble bedhead. I don't shave, leaving my scruff to make me look rugged.

Entering the Law Offices of O'Callahan, all I can think is, *eat your heart out, Steph.* A smug smile appears on my face when I see her reaction. Her eyes grow wide as soon as they trace my arms. Then they darken when she reaches my messy hair. I can still read her like a book. She still wants me. I love the feeling of control that washes over my body, until her attorney scoots closer to her, places his hand on her arm, and slides paperwork to our side of the table. He's opportunistic and creepy, and I don't like him one bit. He's touching my wife and is too close to her. Steph seems unaware. Her gaze is still fixed on me. I lick my lips, and her pink tongue darts out of her mouth. We're locked in a staring contest, and I refuse to fold first.

Out of the corner of my eye, I see my attorney roll his eyes. He's known from the beginning that I still love my wife and I don't want to get divorced.

The slimeball attorney keeps touching her, and I'm livid. All I see is red. I stand up, stretching to my full height of 6'3". Steph's attorney doesn't even flinch. "Get your fucking hands off my wife," I growl loudly. Steph gasps and the asshole just smiles at me. I push my hands fist down on the conference table, posturing at him. *Hit me, prick. I dare you!* I chance a glance at Steph, and her eyes have gone wild as they shoot around the room. I grit my teeth and sneer at Captain Doucheface. He still doesn't move. *Does he have a death wish?* Out of the corner of my eye, I see Steph stand up and reach for me. Her touch is like a warm salve to my tattered heart, and I know without a doubt, I will do whatever she asks of me.

"Tristan," she says in a timid voice.

Shaking my head so I can focus on her, I mumble, "Yeah?"

Making sure she makes eye contact, she says,

"Please sign the papers and let me go." As if a semi-truck just ran into me, my whole body shifts off balance and I fall back into the chair behind me. Boom! With eight words, she decimates the rest of my heart.

Captain Doucheface adds, "Here, you can use my pen."

Snarling, I flick my eyes back to Steph, who's now seated and refusing to look up at me. Knowing that can't be good, I sign the paperwork as she asked.

Pushing back from the table takes all my strength. When I get to the door, her attorney spouts out, "Good doing business with you folks." Instantly, I'm a raging bull and I want to pummel him until there is nothing left. Steph moves away from her attorney and takes a step closer to me. Then she stops herself.

I can see her warring emotions, and all I can offer is, "I'm sorry, Steph." I desperately want to drop to my knees and beg her forgiveness, declare my love, and show her I'm a changed man. But she's ready to move on, and I can't be the selfish asshole who stands in her way. Just as I'm about out the door, I hear her attorney ask when her new job starts and when she's moving. I don't linger to hear her response. *It doesn't matter anyway.*

Chapter 36

Stephanie

oving to Chicago is my chance to start a new life. My boss had noticed I'd been uneasy and restless. He's actually the one who suggested a move and to use it as a restart. I felt stuck until he mentioned it.

I need to move on from my past and start fresh. And I can't do that in the same city as Tristan. What if we run into each other? What if he's with someone? Nope, I need a new environment where I don't know anyone.

Packing up my things and preparing to leave the state I've lived in my entire life is easier than I thought. I'm ready for a change. Sure, I'll miss being only a few hours from my dad, but he's never been to Chicago, and he's excited to explore the city with me. In fact, he's coming to Boston this week to help me pack up and drive to my new home.

I flew to Chicago a month ago for a job interview as a senior accountant with Embrace You, a non-profit that brings awareness to the fight against breast cancer. I am thrilled with the opportunity. It also helps that I'm already in the non-profit sector, so the taxes, grants, and specific regulations are familiar. It's my dream job.

For months, I watched all the wonderful people caring for my mom as she bravely fought her battle with breast cancer. Their kindness brought comfort and solace to me, my dad, and my brother, even after we'd lost my mom. And since then, I've wanted to work with that community in some capacity. Palliative care nursing was too close to it, bringing back too many painful memories. But being able to raise funds to help provide for those in need of nursing, care, and pampering was something I could be passionate about.

The last days of work at the food bank are full, including a send-off potluck and volunteering at the weekly pantry, so I can say goodbye to some of the regular clients that I've come to know.

When Dad arrives on Thursday morning, I pick him up from the airport. He elected to fly because we are driving my car to Chicago. Afterward, we grab the U-Haul trailer I rented and pack it and my car for our drive. By that afternoon, we hit the road.

In planning my move, I gave myself plenty of time to get to Chicago and get settled before I have to report to my new job the week after next.

When we get to my new place, Dad helps me

unload, unpack, and get situated. For his final two days in Chicago, we explore the city. We go to the Navy Pier, a Chicago Cubs game, and to the Riverwalk. The apartment I'm renting is in downtown and isn't far from my new job.

When I take Dad to the airport on Tuesday, my eyes are heavy with tears. He pulls me into a warm hug and whispers against my head, "Don't cry, Sunshine. This is a new beginning for you. Time to shake off the chains of the past and live a full, rewarding life."

Clinging to him like I'm a little girl with a skinned knee, I mumble into his chest, "I'm scared, Dad."

Pushing back so he can look into my eyes, I see only love reflecting back at me. "Stephanie. I know this isn't the path you had planned for your life, and sure, it's scary, but it's also an adventure, full of possibilities." I can't help but be fearful. Once he leaves, I'll be all alone. Just a stranger lost in an enormous city, hoping for something better than what I left behind in Boston. Dad pulls me in again. "You got this. I am confident in your ability to adapt and conquer. Make this city your own. I love you, Sunshine, and I am so proud of you."

Hugging him as tight as I can, I say, "Thanks, Dad. I love you, too."

And then he's gone. Off through security while I stand near the coffee shop, wondering what I've gotten myself into.

* * *

Before I know it, I'm celebrating my first year at Embrace You. So far, everything about it has been amazing. The CEO, Justin, is just ten years older than me. He started the non-profit to honor all the women in his family who've had breast cancer. Because of advancements in treatment, his mom and sister were victorious in their fight with the disease. They diagnosed his mom when he was still in high school, and we shared many similar experiences. His mom's doctors discovered her cancer early and her treatments were not as extensive as what my mom had endured. His older sister, Jennifer, who is the CFO, was diagnosed while he was in graduate school. After he graduated and doctors deemed her cancer free, they joined forces and started Embrace You. Jennifer's husband, who designs impressive technology that made him a billionaire overnight, gave them the seed money to start Embrace You. He'd seen what she'd been through and was more than willing to help. It was an incredible non-profit that not only encourages research and education, it also provides support for those dealing with breast cancer.

At Embrace You, I'm not just an accountant. I'm fortunate to take part in all community outreach programs. My favorites are the charity 5K and the beauty workshop we host with local estheticians and stylists who pamper survivors for a day. Our goal is to help them step outside the box breast cancer places them in and show them they are so much more. We want them to feel as beautiful as they are.

With Embrace You being so busy, I've barely had any time to focus on myself. *Okay, maybe that's a lie.* I've busied myself with Embrace You so I don't have to deal with all my unresolved emotions of the previous year. *Sounds about right.* In those quiet moments I sometimes get, I struggle to find peace. Unwanted emotions, worries, and insecurities surface.

Chapter 37

Tristan

Volunteering for the Boston Stingers has been an incredible experience that came at the absolute perfect time. It's been almost two years since I learned my dream of playing professional hockey was a bust and close to a year since my divorce was final. My life when I came to the Stingers was in shambles and needed direction. And being with this team certainly has done that. Not only does it foster my desire for coaching, but helps me embrace my limitations and work toward being the best I can be. I've learned a lot about successful coaching. The Stingers have grown and developed, and I'm proud to have been part of that. With all this growth, I've also learned I'm ready for a new challenge.

Just like winter turning to spring, I feel a change in the air, and it excites me. Last week I did a preliminary phone interview with the owner of the Aurora Anacondas, an AHL team in Illinois. It couldn't have gone better. My in-person interview with the team's owner, Steve, team manager, William, and various members of the board is tomorrow. You'd think I would be nervous, but I'm not. I'm ready for this. It helps that the whole Stingers organization is behind me.

My visit to Chicago is quick. I see the airport and then get straight on the road to Aurora. I'm glad I did a little research before I left, so I'm prepared for all the tolls. Don't need tickets following me home to Boston.

The interview is in a private room at a restaurant downtown. After dining, those in attendance grill me about all things hockey. We discuss my goals, my philosophy of coaching, and my feelings about my career in the NHL and how it had been cut short. You'd think after all the years passed, I might not be so sensitive about it, but I am. I didn't just lose hockey; I lost the love of my life, and for me, those things were interconnected. I can't think about one without the other. So, for me, I just avoid and deflect as best I can without causing unnecessary suspicion. The in-person interview really gives me a chance to see what type of organization the Anacondas is, and I'm hopeful they feel I'll be a good fit for their team.

Flying home later that evening, I feel confident about where my life is headed. The only regret I have is I'm doing it alone. I still miss Steph every day and wonder what she's up to. Did she find someone new? Thinking about that is painful. I still have no interest in replacing her with another woman. Because the truth is, there is no replacing your soul mate. And I still believe that's what we are.

As the days pass with no word from the Anacondas, I grow nervous. *Did I misread the situation?* When I'm leaving practice at the end of a tedious week, my phone rings. It's Steve. My heart thumps dangerously hard in my chest, stalling my breath and making me sweat.

"Hello," I answer, my voice straining with nerves. *What is he going to say?*

"Tristan, it's Steve, the owner of the Aurora Anacondas. Do you have a moment to talk?"

Leaning up against my truck, I try to control the anxiety racing through my body. *Sound confidant.* "I do," I firmly answer.

"Great. We've finished all our interviews with the prospective coaches, and I apologize it took so long to get back to you. We wanted to take the time to make the right decision for our organization." I nod my head as I listen intently to his words. *What's the decision? He isn't hinting either way.*

"Tristan," he says, stopping my chaotic thoughts, "the Anacondas would like to offer you the position of Head Coach for the next season. If you're still interested."

Excitedly, I fist pump the air like a madman. Pushing all the stale air from my lungs, I pull in a refreshing breath before I answer him. "I would be honored, sir."

Steve laughs awkwardly, like he wasn't sure what my answer would be. "That's great to hear. I'll have our HR department reach out next week to begin the paperwork and explain the benefits package to you. I'm really glad you said yes. I look forward to seeing what you can do with our team."

I run my hand through my hair and stare up at the sky, giving a silent thanks. "Thank you to you, Steve, and the board for your faith in me. I won't let you down. And I appreciate this opportunity more than I can express."

"Well, I've got a few more calls to make. But I wanted to make the best one first," he explains.

"Thanks again. Talk to you later," I say before I hang up. Smiling to myself, I look up just as Coach Matty comes toward me, wearing a look of confusion.

"Tristan," he calls out on approach.

"Yeah."

He points to my face. "Why are you grinning like you won the Stanley Cup?"

I laugh. "Next best thing?"

Even more confused, he scratches his head, unable to come up with an answer.

"Matty, I got the job!" I confide.

His face instantly morphs into a smile. He sticks out his hand, offering it to me. When I shake it, he says, "Congratulations, man. No one deserves it more than you." Humbled by his words, my stomach twists. *I'm not sure about that.* I shake my head no. "Come on, Tristan. You deserve some good in your life. I know the last couple of years have been tough, but here's your chance to start fresh."

"Thanks, Coach. I appreciate it and all you've done to get me ready for my future."

He offers me a kind smile. "You're ready for this. Now, when do you leave?"

"Ready to get rid of me?" I mock frown at him. He smirks. "You bet your ass I am. I can't wait until our teams face each other in the league." He laughs again. There he goes, throwing down a gauntlet. His one negative coaching flaw is his incessant need to win.

Months later, when I'm in Aurora showing my new team a drill, I think back to how far we've come. When I first came on, there was a decent group of players. They just needed better direction and focus. Since coming to the Anacondas, this has been my primary focus. And it's been exactly what our team needs.

* * *

Our first year together was filled with growing pains and plenty of development opportunities throughout the entire organization. But the past four seasons have been noteworthy, leading our division with an impressive record as we fought for the Calder Cup. We won it the last two years, beating out the Texas Comets and then the Philadelphia Wolves. Each time, I can feel the spotlight of the sports world on me and it reminds me of my days in the NHL. We'd gotten close to the Stanley Cup a few times while I played for the Storm, but in the end, it remained out of reach. I didn't think I'd ever get my name on that cup, so seeing it on the Calder Cup twice is incredible.

Following our second cup win, I'm called in for a meeting with Steve. Showing up at his office is still nerve-racking, even after all these years. He holds my career and my future in his hands, and I don't want to do anything to jeopardize that. I've worked hard to rebuild my life.

After arriving, I'm shown into a conference room. Another man is seated on the opposite side of the table. He looks vaguely familiar, but I struggle to place him. I at least recognize him from the hockey world. "Am I in the correct room?" I ask hesitantly. From behind me, Steve laughs, putting me somewhat at ease.

"Tristan, thanks for coming in. Please take a seat. I'm sure you're curious about why you're here." I nod my head, then sit down, eyeballing the other man. Steve clears his throat and I focus my attention back on him. "You are here because there are changes on the horizon." *What?*

I can feel my stomach drop and my eyes bulge. Suddenly parched, I rasp, "Changes?" *We just won our second Calder Cup. What is he talking about?* I stare at Steve, willing him to divulge more information, and he smiles. I'm completely confused. My heart is pounding and my palms are sweating. Wiping them on my slacks, I chance a look at the other man, and he's smiling like the Cheshire cat. *What the ever-loving fuck is going on?*

"Steve, what is going on?" I croak, unable to take the panic racing through my body.

"Tristan, do you know Timothy McConnell?" *I frantically run this man's name through my memory.* A bulb of recognition sparks, and a smile spreads across my face.

"He owns the Chicago Steel, right?" I answer. *But why is he here? Meeting with me?*

Mr. McConnell's smile grows wider, and he leans forward. He looks impressed that I know who he is.

"Yes, you are correct. Mr. McConnell is the owner of the team and he wants you as his new coach," Steve announces.

Dumbfounded by what I've just heard, I pinch myself to make sure I'm not dreaming. "Ouch," I mumble. Mr. McConnell and Steve both laugh. My eyes fly between the two as I try to absorb what I've just been told. But it's no use, it isn't sinking in. "What?" I question.

This time Mr. McConnell speaks. "Tristan, our organization needs a change, a fresh perspective, and we—the board, management, and I—think you are the right fit. If you're interested."

I look at Steve, and he nods. *"Thank you,"* I mouth before turning back to Mr. McConnell. "Yes, I am definitely interested."

He rubs his hands together. "That's great. What do you say about going out to dinner and discussing things in a more comfortable environment? Boardrooms make me itchy." *Wait. Doesn't he practically live in a boardroom?* I've heard he's a shark, and I can admit that's slightly terrifying.

Over dinner, we discuss the ins and outs of the Steel organization. I'm warned that I'm inheriting a team that's been together for a long time and have gotten stagnant. The management thinks I'll come in and shake things up and, according to Mr. McConnell, that is just what they need.

Accepting the job is a dream come true. I'll get another taste of the NHL without the risk of injury. *What could be better? Having Steph by your side.* Every time I think about her now, my heart aches a little less. Over the years, the pain has dulled but never subsided completely. I've finally realized that there is nothing I can do. I can't make her love me or force her to be with me. I can only accept that she's moved on, even if I can't.

When I get home from dinner, feeling on top of the

world, I call the people who've always had my back, whose support has never wavered: my parents.

Ring, ring.

"Murphy residence," my mom answers, and I can't help but laugh. "Tristan, is that you?"

"Yeah, Mom, it's me. How are you?" I ask, noticing how tired she sounds. Then I hear a snore. *Shit. Did I wake them up?* Looking at my watch, I notice it's after ten and rush out an explanation. "Sorry I called so late. I have really great news that I couldn't wait to share with you and Dad."

"Let me get him." I hear the rustle of sheets as she wakes him up. "Tristan's on the phone with good news." I hear my dad grumble, and before long they've got me on speakerphone.

"I accepted a head coaching position with the Chicago Steel."

Thinking about it, I realize some things. Yes, it will keep me in Illinois, but they've known since I was six that I wanted to be in the NHL. Sure, this differs from my original dream, but I have a rare opportunity, and I would be foolish not to jump at it. Right?

"Tristan, that is incredible," Mom squeals while my dad claps his hands next to her. "Well done, son. You earned this and you deserve it." Without a doubt, they are my biggest supporters. I can't wait to get them at another professional hockey game where they can enjoy it without worrying I'll hurt myself. I hear my dad yawn, and I quickly finish up the phone call so they can go back to bed.

As I sit there on my couch, looking around the condo I'll soon be vacating, I see another puzzle piece fall into place. It's taken me years to rebuild my life. Through grit, determination, hard work, focus, and time, I'm finally getting what I wanted.

Chapter 38

Tristan

eaving the Anacondas is bittersweet. It's been my home, my sanctuary, for the past five years. I've grown comfortable and can accurately predict the problems we will encounter before they arrive. I don't have the same luxury going to the Steel. It's something I'll have to learn, but I'm excited about the challenge. I've spent a great deal of time reviewing tapes of the last few years, analyzing who my players are, and building the resiliency I'll need when I shake things up. From the meetings I've been in, the entire management team wants to see things go sideways so I can evaluate what needs my attention first. According to them, I have an enormous task in front of me. All I know is I have a lot to accomplish to get this team where I want them. From thorough analysis, I recognize which players I think will work on a line together. I've also identified where the holes are on the team, and I'm determined to patch them.

Just pulling up to Steel Arena, I'm in awe. It's not my first visit here, but today feels different. I'm officially the coach, and the weight of the success of this organization drapes heavy on my shoulders. In the past week when I've visited the arena, I've been mindful of my position, but until now I hadn't fully grasped the importance of it.

Exiting my truck, I stare at the stylish, state-of-the-art building and feel my body fill with reverence. This organization has the power to change lives, and I'm now a part of that. At the realization, a shiver travels through me. *I hope I make them proud.* I know picking me as the coach was a gamble, but I'm determined to succeed here. To prove I have a right to be here. The press has taken its shots, putting voices to all the insecurities I have churning in my head. In times of doubt, I cling to the fact that not only have I played at this level; I am a coach with a winning record.

To introduce me to the team, Mr. McConnell hosts a dinner, where he's invited the players and their families, the management team, and the board. Most everyone has been welcoming. Only a few players seem unhappy, but I'm more than aware that I'm not everyone's pick. I'll work hard to show all the naysayers that I'm here for a reason.

Days later, when I finally step onto the ice for our first official practice, I know I'll be asking a lot of the team. But, overall, I'm confident they are up for the challenge and they'll respond appropriately. Well, most of them. Those who aren't as agreeable to my plan will either come around or find themselves a new home. I have one hundred percent support from those who make the big decisions.

My shrill whistle pierces the air, silencing everyone on the ice.

"Morning, guys. Welcome to our first official practice. I'm guessing you probably came to practice today assuming I'll spend the first few hours with you by watching you run drills and plays, right?" Most of the guys nod their heads. "But that's not going to happen. For the past few weeks, I've been studying tapes, and I have some ideas. Things I believe will make each of you a stronger, smarter, and more dynamic player."

"I've rearranged your lines to evaluate the chemistry you might have with other teammates, to judge whether we have the most effective shifts. Coach Jones is going to call them out, along with the drills I think we need to practice. If you have any questions, feel free to ask."

Low grumbling happens to my left and right, but no one voices an actual question. *Okay.* Shrugging my shoulders, I head over to the visitors' penalty box with my clipboard in hand, ready to take notes on what I observe. Coach Jones calls out the lines and drills, and the men get to work. Halfway through practice, I've seen enough. Most of these guys play with great skill, but it seems like they've lost their love for the game. Long and short of it, they're just going through the motions.

I blow my whistle.

The play stops and everyone looks my direction. I step from the penalty box and make my way across the ice to where the guys have gathered, grabbing water and wiping the sweat from their faces. The team captain, Magnus Berg, clears his throat, and the chatter and side conversations come to a halt. "From what I've seen, this team is full of talent. But I see one major thing missing. Does anyone want to guess what it is?" Looking around, I see no one wants to answer. *Great. I need to shake them up a bit.* "Magnus, who is the newest player in this squad?"

His deep, smooth voice carries over the heads of everyone as he answers my question. "Josh Logan is our most recent acquire."

My eyes land on the one guy who looks like he climbed off his surfboard to come to practice. His deep tan and bleach-blond hair scream *I spend all day in the sun.* "Josh, I know you aren't a rookie, but you are new to this team."

He smiles. "Yes, sir. I played in Arizona for a few years before I joined the Steel."

Nodding, I ask, "Can you tell me in the short time you've been practicing with this team what is missing?"

He scratches at his chin. "Missing? I'm not sure what you mean."

I'm not surprised he doesn't understand what I'm alluding to. After all, he's been in the NHL for a few years. He understands how to play the part of a professional hockey player.

So I tell them. "The missing element is fun. You guys don't seem to enjoy yourselves out there. Do you love this game anymore?" Although they are all looking at me as if I'm certifiable, they nod in response to my question. *Well, that's a good sign and something I can work with.* "That's great. I'm ending practice early, but tomorrow we're going to try something new that will require you each to step outside your comfort zone a bit. At first, it will seem strange, but there's a purpose behind it. Thanks for working hard today."

The next day, I show up ready. I'd spoken to Kit, my assistant coach, and he's on board with my plan.

"Today's practice is all about having fun. We won't be focusing on speeds, plays, or even precision. Instead, your only goal is to laugh. Sound easy?" I tell the team.

I fill the practice with relay races, shooting games, finders keepers, 3x3 cross-ice with a football, and dodgeball. By the end of four hours, we are all exhausted but laughing. The smiles on everyone's faces confirm that fun is just what they need. They need to adjust their focus and remember why they play hockey in the first place—for the love of the game.

After practice, I'm more convinced than ever that our team has a major case of burnout. Without making fun a requirement, we will continue being mediocre.

As I watch them, I identify their strengths and weaknesses. I know as the head of this team, I have to get them to stop taking everything so seriously and enjoy the game again.

* * *

The next two years coaching the Steel are a definite learning experience. One month I feel like I've been getting through and we'll be having fun and be on a winning streak. And then something happens and we lose all the momentum we built.

By the end of my second year, I'm confident I'm making headway, but we need some fresh blood to stir things up. I talk with Mr. McConnell about the draft and bringing in someone with charisma who challenges the status quo, but he isn't interested. According to him, we already have a winning team, I just need another year or two to turn them into magic. I agree with him that our roster is filled with talent, but I still feel we need someone to tie it all together.

Unfortunately, Mr. McConnell passes away before it comes to fruition. I've heard rumors that his son Trey will inherit the team, and I'm hoping he'll listen to my pleas. However, Trey remains mum to any roster changes until the end of the season when he comes to me. He informs me he's traded an underperforming rookie for an impressive veteran player for the upcoming year. When I find out who it is, I can't wait to get him on my bench. When the trade is finally announced, it seems Trey receives an unnecessary amount of criticism. But I feel strongly in my gut that he made the right decision, and it is going to change the entire Steel organization.

Chapter 39

Stephanie

After I've been with the organization for almost ten years, Jennifer steps down as CFO and I'm named as her replacement. Since the organization started with her and her brother, she remains an active member of the board.

I love the challenges of my new position. The first goal I set is for Embrace You to host a breast cancer awareness gala. In brainstorming how to make this event huge, the event planning team and I list all of Chicago's highest rollers, as we'll need their support. Unfortunately, we realize after looking at the list, we don't know any of them personally. Slightly discouraged, I still pitch the idea to Justin and Jennifer, who absolutely love it. Jennifer also discloses that her husband Brian has known Trey McConnell since they were kids. Win!

Jennifer's husband secures a lunch meeting with

Trey, and we pitch my idea of a joint fundraiser hosted by Embrace You and the Chicago Steel. It will be an elegant event that will raise awareness and funds to support breast cancer research, education, and assistance in our community. Thankfully, after we share my vision, Trey agrees. He especially seems to like the name of the gala I suggest: Steel Your Heart. Following our lunch, I busy myself with everything gala related. I want this event not only to be the talk of the Windy City, but to be the first of many we host.

* * *

Less than a year later on the afternoon of the gala, I meet with my event organizer, Rachel, to ensure that everything is set. We decided early that the event would include dinner, dancing, and a silent auction. As I expected, Trey didn't give me carte blanche. He wanted to be a part of the planning. He also had his organization donate many items for the silent auction, including season passes, autographed Steel paraphernalia, and a lunch with him. I'm confident each item will earn a lofty donation. Trey also reached out to other big names in the city, requesting donations. The items I've seen come across my desk are mind-blowing. Good thing our guest list includes wealthy patrons because I'm not sure how the average Joe can afford to bid even the starting price of some items.

In all the hustle and bustle of pulling the gala off, I

failed to do something major. Before the event, I meant to familiarize myself with the names and faces of the Steel players. But I ran out of time. The idea of not recognizing someone of importance scares me shitless. But ever since leaving Tristan, I avoid anything hockey related. And the idea of jumping back into it, even if it is just learning names for my job, makes me nauseous.

Greeting the guests with Trey, Justin, and Jennifer before the event begins makes me a sweaty, nervous mess. Just as the line is thinning out, I'm called to the kitchen to check on something. When I return later, I notice guests mingling and fawning over the silent auction items. Some are even dancing. Standing against the wall, watching, my heart flutters. "I miss that," I whisper to myself. The last person to hold me like that had been too long ago. I've had a few casual flings over the years, but nothing serious. After Tristan, my heart never mended enough to give any other man a real chance. Eventually, I just gave up and put all of my effort and time into Embrace.

The song ends and when the next one comes on, the air in the room changes, sending a shiver through my body. A shadow moves to my left, and I whip my head in that direction to see what's coming closer. When my eyes register the sight before me, my mouth opens, and a squeak falls from my lips. Recovering quickly, I wipe at my gown as if I'm ironing out invisible wrinkles.

"Tristan. What are you doing here?"

Before he even answers, Trey appears, looking handsome in a perfectly fitted tuxedo. "Stephanie. Tristan. Have you two met?" Trey asks. Stunned silent, I can't respond.

Tristan offers his hand to Trey to shake, smiles, and answers, "Yes, we've known each other for years. Isn't that right, Stephanie?" My proper name on his tongue sounds so impersonal. So wrong. I shudder and goose bumps pop up on my arms as if I'm cold. I wrap my arms around myself while glancing around. *How can I politely exit this conversation?* I don't want to explain to Trey how we know each other, and I don't think I'm ready to be in the same room as Tristan. Especially when he looks like he just did a photo shoot for *GQ*. And especially if he has a date somewhere. I think I'd rather die. Shifting forward, I think I see an exit.

Trey looks at me and asks, "Stephanie, are you all right?"

Forcing a smile, I say, "I just need the powder room. If you'll both excuse me." Jetting off before either says anything, I catch bits of Trey's comments raving about me and this gala I'm responsible for.

When I finally reach the bathroom, it takes multiple tries to lock myself in a stall because of the tremor in my hands. In my dress, I can't bend over, so I grab at my waist and do my best to suck in deep breaths. My nerves are on edge and I can't seem to calm down. *Why is he here? It's been twelve years.* "Get it together," I tell myself just before the door opens and a group of ladies enter the space, talking loudly and laughing. *At least someone is having fun.*

Once I'm sure my breathing has returned to a regular pattern, I let myself out of the stall and go to the mirror to check my makeup before rejoining the gala. I'm careful to avoid Tristan. Just our brief encounter has stirred up a whirlwind of emotions I'm not prepared to handle.

I move to the front of the room, knowing I'll need to MC soon, and Justin approaches. Feeling edgy, I jump when someone touches my elbow. "Oh, goodness, Justin, you scared me," I say, and he laughs.

"You should be relaxed. Everything turned out amazing."

I smile. "Thank you. I hope it raises a lot of donations to help those in our community who need help in their breast cancer journey."

He squeezes my arm. "It'll be a success, Stephanie. I can feel it."

Following dinner and dancing, we spotlight the silent auction right before the dessert tables are revealed. Everything looks delicious, but it's plain and generic. Next year, I plan to step up my game and find a baker who offers something truly exceptional and unique. And I think I know just who to ask.

Last week, I'd been leaving an appointment, and I'd been lured off the street by the most heavenly smells coming from a small brick bakery. Everything in the display case was unique and scrumptious looking. I purchased a few items to take home, knowing they'd be delicious. Before I left, I introduced myself to the owner, who also is the baker. Her name is Kenzie, and from the moment we met, I knew she was something special. With any luck, next year her edible works of art will be on display at our Steel Your Heart gala.

Sipping on a cup of coffee, I let myself relax for a moment. It seems like the gala has been a hit. I can't wait to see how much we've raised. Lost in thought, I don't hear someone step up next to me. I jump when I feel a warm hand on my shoulder. Turning my head, I see it's Tristan.

"Can I join you?" he asks. Nervously, I nod. Pulling out the chair Trey abandoned much earlier, Tristan lowers himself next to me. My entire body tenses. *What is happening?*

"Steph, you look absolutely stunning. I haven't been able to keep my eyes off of you."

Unable to help myself, I evaluate his words, and I'm shocked to find them full of truth and sincerity. Throughout our relationship, Tristan never lied to me. Until the end, when he broke his promise about drinking. *But was that a lie?* Either way, I found it tough to distinguish. I felt deceived. *This is too intense.* Unable to handle the moment, I make eye contact and whisper his name. It hurts to have him so close. I still want him, but he isn't mine anymore. *It's been so long.*

Tears prick my eyes, and I look away. "I'm sorry I've upset you, Steph. I just wanted to see how you are.

I've missed you. But if you don't want me here, you can tell me to go, and I will." The sorrow in his voice is like an arrow to my heart, piercing and sharp. *I don't want you to go, but this hurts.*

Turning back to him, his eyes are clouded with emotion. I tentatively reach over and place my hand on his arm. At the moment of contact, I feel an electric surge shoot through my body, sucking the air from my lungs. "I missed you too," I admit, my voice straining. Then we both sit in silence. *What now?*

After a few moments, he clears his throat and says, "Trey told me you're responsible for all of this." He looks around, his eyes wide. "You did an incredible job. I don't think I have ever been to anything this fancy before. I had to go out and get a tuxedo." At the thought of that, laughter bubbles up within me. My shoulders shake, giving me away. Tristan nudges me. "What's so funny?" I pinch my lips tightly to stifle anything from sneaking out. But I'm not so lucky because a handful of unattractive sounds escape. Mortified, I quickly turn away. *This is not happening.*

"Steph, please turn around," Tristan begs, his voice smooth. Not a trace of humor can be detected. *He wasn't laughing at me?* Slowly, I turn back to him, and I'm met with a warm smile. "Hey there," he offers.

"Hi," I answer back.

Another smile. "How are you?" he asks.

"Embarrassed. You?"

He reaches for my hand and clasps it in his. *That*

feels so good. I've missed him so much. "Come on, over the years, we've had more embarrassing things happen to us. I'm just glad you're here. You've never been far from my mind, and I've wanted to reach out a million times to see how you were. Where you were. But I always stopped myself, believing you wanted your space."

Tilting my head to the side, I ask, "Yeah? What about tonight?"

He chuckles to himself. "I tried to keep my distance, but in the end, my heart refused to just stand by any longer."

My eyes grow misty. I haven't seen this tender side of Tristan for a long time, even a year or two before our divorce. His drive to succeed in the NHL took precedence over everything else. "What now?"

Tristan leans back in his chair while still cradling my hand. "I'd like to give a friendship a chance. You see, twelve years ago, my best friend walked away from me, and her absence has been felt every moment she's been gone."

"Really?" I'm stunned and thrilled at the same time.

He stares at me and answers, "Really."

Chapter 40

Tristan

All week, management has been telling me that tonight is an epic night and extremely important to Trey. Taking the warning seriously, I purchase my first tuxedo. In all my years, I've never worn a penguin suit, and shortly after dressing in it, I know why. It is extremely uncomfortable. Relaxed is normally my style, but... this is the exact opposite. I'm not a slob by any means. I can look nice. As the coach of the Steel, I dress up for games, usually in slacks, a button-up, and a sweater, not a suit like some.

By the time I make my way through the bright lights and intense flashbulb circus of the red carpet, I'm in desperate need of some peace and quiet. Slipping into a corner to go unnoticed for a minute, I scan the large room, making note of who's in attendance. Never one who is comfortable in the spotlight or at events like this, I naturally shy away from the crowds. I'm here to support our organization. I don't know much about the non-profit it's co-hosting with other than its focus on breast cancer. Standing there, I remember the destruction breast cancer had on Steph's family. Over the years, I've donated to multiple organizations to support those on the front lines.

Pulling at my sleeves, I adjust the cufflinks so they're not so tight on my wrist. Swiping at my leg, I notice I'm itchy too. But the worst of all is the death grip my shirt has around my throat. I can't take a full breath. Well, maybe I can, but my breath becomes short the minute I spy my ex-wife across the room. She looks ravishing, and I notice not only is my breathing labored, but my pants have become tight too. "Not the time," I warn my severely deprived dick. *But we like her,* he chimes in as he flinches. I grit my teeth, willing him to behave.

Thoughts of her flood my mind. *How easy would it be to steal her away and demand a conversation?* I'm desperate to know what she's been up to since we divorced. Why is she in Chicago? And here at the gala? Does she have a new husband, partner, or lover? Has she in the past? Even though the thought of that makes me insanely jealous and angry, I want to know. I can't blame her if she did. We're divorced, and in our time apart, I haven't exactly been celibate. But I can count the number of hookups I've had on one hand. I have needs, and occasionally my right hand isn't satisfying. But none of them ever got serious. *Did she do that too?*

Moving closer to her, my body relaxes and grows warm. I haven't had a reaction like this in years. Just after I approach, Trey appears and Steph runs away, taking all her warmth with her.

All evening, it feels like she's always out of reach, helping or answering questions for staff. *Maybe she's avoiding you?* Finally, toward the end of the evening, I see her sitting alone at a table. *Now or never.*

Having a conversation with someone you haven't seen in over a decade is uncomfortable. But when you were once married to that person and you're still in love with them, it becomes almost paralyzing. After stumbling through the first bit, we seem to connect again. When she asks me what's next, my heart dances a samba in my chest. It takes everything within me to restrain myself. All I want to do is pull her from her chair, throw her over my shoulder, and catch a cab to my place, where I can worship her all night long. Instead of actually doing that, I offer her friendship. *Start small, right?*

Her shock at my suggestion isn't surprising. I mean, how often do you see exes being friends? Better yet, how often do you see them rekindle something? Okay, okay, I know, the odds are stacked against me. But if I never try, I'll always wonder. Steph has always been, will always be, my everything. Letting her go has been my biggest regret. I know now that I hadn't honored my vows. I'd abandoned her when she needed me most. She'd walked away without a fight from me. And

I would be a moron if I let that happen again. I know I can't control or decide for her, but I will do my best to win back her heart. Even if friendship is all she can manage.

"In the spirit of friendship, would you like to do dinner next week?" I ask, excited about the opportunity to take her out. *It's not a date,* I remind myself.

Steph thinks for a minute before answering. *Shit, did I rush this? Is she questioning this already?* My anxiety kicks in and worry fills my veins.

She smiles at me and it brings me to my knees. "How about we do coffee first?" she offers.

I nod enthusiastically. "That's great. Does this weekend work? Tomorrow, maybe? I can pick you up." *Do I sound desperate?*

Shifting in her chair, she grabs her clutch and pulls her phone from it to check her calendar. "Can we meet at Grinders? Say nine? I have something at noon, so I'll need my car."

"You bet." I stand up, but then I remember I don't have any way to contact her. "Can I get your number?" After exchanging numbers, we say our goodbyes. I need to get home before I screw things up. Tonight looks to be a success on all fronts.

Arriving home, my brain is so active that it makes sleep a struggle. The next morning, I wake up at six, excited about coffee with Steph. Having more than enough time before then, I head to my building's gym. Normally, I work out at the Steel's facilities, but I don't want to commute when there is a gym a few floors below me. Even though it's been years since I was in PT, I still practice my knee exercises religiously. In an hour, I squeeze in a 5K on the treadmill and a leg routine that doesn't make my quads feel like Jell-O.

Half an hour later, I've showered and shaved, and I'm standing in my walk-in closet wondering what to wear. Casual is my vibe, but I don't want to appear lazy. Reaching for a pair of uber-comfortable jeans, I also select a short-sleeve button-up, leaving it untucked. Pulling on my Jordans and my Tag Heuer watch, I'm ready.

After pacing my condo for an hour, I head to Grinders to meet Steph. My nerves are shot. I'm bursting with so many emotions. Hopefully, I don't make things awkward.

The aromatic scent of roasted coffee beans fills my nostrils when I pull open the door to the café. I've never been here before. My brain is overwhelmed by all the colors. They're everywhere. I could describe this place in one word: eclectic. It's so different from the coffee chains that dot almost every city block.

Turning toward the line of customers waiting to order, I see Steph. Like last night, she is stunning. Her blond hair is tied in a knot on the top of her head, displaying her long, sexy neck. I want to trace my finger down it, only stopping at her ear before whispering what I'd like to do to her before giving her earlobe a nibble. She's wearing black yoga pants that put the curves I've always found irresistible on display. A magenta crewneck sweatshirt with an oversized opening reveals a hint of a creamy, naked shoulder. My fantasies continue as I imagine tracing down from her earlobe to her clavicle and across to her exposed shoulder with my tongue.

"Next, please," a long-haired, grungy barista shouts out, breaking me from my reverie. Looking at the register, I see Steph is next. I step up behind her and touch her elbow.

"Please let me pay for that. I invited you, after all."

Steph gives me a sweet smile and says, "Okay. Thank you, Tristan." After placing our order, we find an offset table that gives us some privacy.

With drinks in hand, we stare nervously at each other. "Ever play twenty questions?" I ask.

"Yes. In speech class in college, we used it to gather information about the partner they paired us with before we had to give an informative speech."

I smile. "Maybe that's what we can do… to get to know each other again?" I know my suggestion is odd, but we already know so much about each other. Just the last decade is a mystery. "Want me to go first?"

Steph nods, almost relieved that I volunteered.

What to share? Keep it light.

"I've been the coach of the Chicago Steel since June 2017. Your turn."

Steph laughs. "Wow. Almost five years. I always knew you'd get back to the NHL. Maybe it isn't how you imagined it, but you've obviously worked hard to get there. What to tell you about me?" She takes a drink of her coffee while she thinks. "I know. I've worked for Embrace You since August 2011. After ten years, they promoted me to CFO when the former stepped down."

My jaw drops open. "CFO?" *Holy shit!* "That's impressive. And its mission is to assist those dealing with breast cancer. Your Mom would have been so proud. I bet your dad sure is." I see Steph flinch when I mention her parents, and for a moment I regret bringing them up, but then I reconsider that. I know her past, and it speaks volumes she has dedicated her life to an organization like Embrace You.

"Thanks, Tristan. Dad is proud, for sure. And when I visit my mom's gravestone, I tell her about all the good we're doing and all the advancements in treatments that have happened since her death." The air is heavy with sorrow, and I want nothing more than to lighten the mood.

Leaning forward, I ask, "Did you hear that the Chicago Steel won the Stanley Cup last year and we are in an excellent position to make a run for it this year too?"

Steph's look of sadness quickly morphs into happiness. "Really?" she asks excitedly. Pulling my phone from my pocket, I open up my pictures from last year and show her the one I had taken with the Cup and my name engraved on it.

"You always dreamed about that. I'm so proud of you."

Her words cover me like a warm blanket, heating my entire body. "Thank you. It's been a long road. The few months before you filed for divorce were the worst I've ever had. As soon as you left, I really started drinking, and I was a complete mess. On Christmas Eve, my dad had to drag me out of a bar, passed out drunk. They saved my life. Since then, I haven't had a drink. I fought my way back and made sure the past stayed the past. I got serious about what was next and pursued it with everything I had."

I go silent. I hadn't intended to share so much with her right now. But I guess that's good. I'm laying all my cards out, showing her I'm a different man. A few more quiet moments pass between us, and instead of letting it become awkward, I ask about her.

"So, the gala last night... that was your pet project?" Steph nods her head. "Was it everything you imagined? Did you meet your fundraising goals? Will you do it again?" I sit back in my chair and take a drink of my coffee, waiting for her response.

She takes a drink, then smiles. "Yes, it was something I proposed shortly after being named CFO. It was actually part of my contract negotiations. I dreamed about working for a company like Embrace You, and hosting an event like the gala became a bonus dream. Justin and Jennifer, my bosses, who started the non-profit, loved my idea and gave me their unwavering support."

"That's amazing. It's a great feeling to know your boss has your back when you want to change things up. I had a similar situation with the Steel and the AHL team I coached right before." Steph smiles, and I finally feel free of anxiety and worry.

"Oh yeah? Where did you coach before the Steel?" *Wonder if she'll find it just as ironic as I do that we've both been in or around Chicago for the last ten years.*

Chuckling, I answer, "You won't believe this, but I was with the Aurora Anacondas from 2012 until 2017, before the Steel hired me."

Steph gasps. "You've been living in the same area as me for the past decade and I didn't know. Your parents said nothing. I'm assuming they know?"

I take another sip of my coffee and then smirk at her. "They know, all right. But I didn't know you were still in contact with them."

Steph's eyes dart around like she's nervous about what she'll say next. And I hear myself growl, "Steph, tell me." She licks her lips, and I never wanted to be a tongue so badly.

"Ummm... you see... well..." she stammers. *What is she keeping secret from me?*

"I've been talking to your parents every few weeks since I left. They never told you?" Her words register and I wince like I've been hit with something. Resting back in my chair, I'm confused about how to feel. On the one hand, I'm upset with my parents because them choosing to stay in contact with Steph feels deceptive. But then, on the other, I'm glad that their relationship remained intact even if mine didn't. Actually, when I really think about it, I'm jealous of them. It took me a long time to accept my role in everything that went wrong between me and Steph. How my selfishness and hurt feelings tore my marriage apart. Us not working was because of me. Sitting here, I know they didn't remain close or in contact to hurt me. My parents have loved Steph almost as long as I have. It makes sense, even if it's tough to hear.

"Wow. That's a surprise," I admit, my voice thick with emotion.

Steph reaches out for my hand. "I'm sorry, Tristan. I wouldn't have kept in contact with them if I knew it would upset you." When she tries to pull her hand away, I don't let her. I intertwine our fingers and hold her tighter.

"I'm not upset," I insist. She gives me a look that tells me she doesn't buy it. "Really, I'm not upset. I'm more... hurt. But it's probably not why you think." *How do I explain myself?*

"You felt like they were picking sides?" she asks cautiously.

I shake my head. "It sounds dumb," I say. Steph looks at me, so I continue. "I know we were divorced, and that everything was final with us, but they still got a part of you, while I was completely cut off."

Steph squeezes my hand. "You sound jealous."

Hanging my head, I admit, "Yeah. I am." *Is admitting that the right thing to do? When we're just starting out?* Worry sits heavy in my gut like a ton of lead. *What would she think of me?*

Steph's worried eyes speak volumes. "Your parents have been like a second mom and dad to me for so long. It feels natural to keep in touch. I'm sorry I never considered how that would make you feel. Please don't be upset with them."

"I'm not. I just feel like I missed out on so much."

"You didn't, really. And we're here now. You can ask me almost anything." She offers a smile as an apology.

"Okay. D-did you ever... ask about me?" Finally, I get the question out. *Has she been as curious about me all these years?*

Watching her closely, I see her withdraw. *Shit. Too much, too fast.* "You don't have to answer that if you don't want to."

When she looks up and makes eye contact, I know she's going to answer. "At first, I was so worried about you. That's why I called your mom back that Christmas Eve and told them they could find you at Sidewinders." I swallow hard. *She didn't know it, but she saved my life.* Before that night, I was headed down a dark road. My parents pulling me out of that bar was the wake-up call I needed to stop drinking. I nod, encouraging her to go on.

"Before long, hearing about you was too hard, and I stopped asking. In fact, for months I just didn't call them. Every time I thought about you, it hurt, and it was impossible to talk to your parents and not think about you.

"Once I moved to Chicago and got settled, I reached out again. I missed them, and every time I talked to your mom, it felt a little like coming home. She was the motherly influence I was missing in my life. And she figured out that I'd pulled away when she talked about you, so she didn't. We built a friendship based solely on us and what was currently happening. We sort of ignored the past."

I look at her, stunned. "How did I not know about this? I talk with both my parents weekly, and neither one ever mentioned it, even when I moved to Chicago." I scratch my head. "They didn't even give me a heads up, like 'watch out, Steph lives in Chicago too.' I mean, this is an enormous city, and the likelihood that we'd run into each other is small, but I would have liked to know you were doing well."

Chapter 41

Stephanie

As I look at Tristan across the table, the realization of our situation sinks in.

My heart flutters. He does still care for me, and because of that, I have to keep my feelings locked down. We can't travel down that road again. I hardly survived last time. This time would surely destroy me.

"Friends," I whisper to myself. A reminder of all that we can ever be.

"What was that?" Tristan asks as he leans forward.

I clear my throat, then say, "It's good to have you as a friend again." I don't miss the wince he makes or the wrongness I feel in every pore of my body when those words fall from my lips. But it's all we can ever be. And I have to be okay with that, or there is no use in trying.

The rest of our coffee date, or whatever friends call

it, goes well. We make small talk for another twenty minutes, then say goodbye and go our separate ways.

I told him last night I have something to do at noon, and that's half-true. It's a hot yoga class. But right now, as I sit in my car, I'm debating skipping it. This morning has been more emotional than I expected, and I just want to go home and take a nap.

Everything with Tristan had been so easy. The conversation flowed comfortably, almost like no time had passed. We didn't miss a beat. I knew a friendship would be easy between us; it always had been. *But would that be enough?* Having more with him is something I want but can't have. I have to prepare myself to build up sturdy walls to protect my feelings from his impossible charm.

* * *

Before the next series in the Stanley Cup playoffs, we meet up a few more times for coffee. The meet ups are never long, but they're always enjoyable. I'm starting to once again see those personality characteristics that I'd fallen for as a teen. They are still as charming as ever, but now they're more mature and purposeful. Other than that, we stay connected by texting. And it's through that, he asks me out on our first official date.

TRISTAN

Hey, Steph. How are you?

ME

Good. How are you?

TRISTAN

I'm great. The guys won another game, so we're leading the series 3-1.

ME

One more and you're in the finals, right?

TRISTAN

Yes.

ME

Good luck!

TRISTAN

Thanks! I have a question…

ME

Okay.

TRISTAN

After the cup, can I take you out to dinner? I had a really great time at coffee.

I stare at my phone, uncertainty coursing through my veins. I type out a half-dozen replies, deleting them before I send them. "Yes" is on the tip of my tongue, but what if he's only looking for friendship? My heart wants more.

TRISTAN

Or coffee. We could do that again. I miss you. You were my best friend, and I want that back.

ME

I want our friendship back too.

Actually, I want more, but if that's all he wants, I guess that'll have to do.

TRISTAN

So that is a yes to coffee or dinner?

ME

Yes, to either? Friends do both, don't they?

But I want more than friendship.

TRISTAN

I think they do. We can make better plans in a few weeks when the series is over.

ME

Sounds great. Good luck tomorrow. I want to see the Steel in the finals.

TRISTAN

Good night, Steph. Talk to you tomorrow. Happy day.

ME

What's with the camel?

TRISTAN

Tomorrow is Wednesday.

ME

Yes. So?

TRISTAN

It's hump day. Get it? Camels have humps. Happy Hump Day!

ME

Okay. Night.

Great. Now the only thing I'll be thinking about tomorrow is the word hump and how much I wish I could hump Tristan. But I can't. "Ugh," I groan.

* * *

When the Steel wins the cup for the second year in a row, I know he'll be overjoyed. I'm thrilled for him. Because I know he'll be busy with Steel functions and media events, I send him a congratulatory text.

ME

Tristan!!!!! Congratulations on the Stanley Cup! I am so happy for you and your team.

TRISTAN

Thank you. It's very exciting. The team played so hard and they earned this. I'm proud of them.

ME

I know you're probably celebrating in the locker room, but I wanted to offer my congratulations before everyone bombards you.

TRISTAN

I appreciate it, Steph. The guys got carried away with champagne in the locker room, and now I look like a drowned rat. I should have expected this; the jokers did the same thing last year. I still avoid alcohol because I don't want to travel down that road again. But evenings like tonight, celebrating the Stanley Cup, you can't avoid being doused in it.

<Selfie of Tristan>

ME

You're right. You look absolutely dreadful. NOT. Still handsome as ever.

I hit send before I think.

TRISTAN

Handsome, huh?

I reread my previous text. Whoops. Didn't mean to give myself away.

ME

You caught that?

What is he thinking? Am I flirting with Tristan? Yes, it appears I am. Now, how is he going to react?

TRISTAN

I did. Hey, what are you doing later? Feel like celebrating with me?

ME

I have work tomorrow, so it's probably not a good idea. How about when it calms down a bit?

TRISTAN

You know that your boss, Justin, loves the Steel, and even he wouldn't miss an opportunity to celebrate the Stanley Cup with the winning team. Work be damned. Plus, aren't you the CFO? Don't you have a flex schedule?

ME

I'm sure he'd be more agreeable. I could give his number to you. But you're right, he would definitely join you. I, on the other hand, would rather avoid the loud ruckus.

TRISTAN

Can't blame a guy for trying. I know I'll be busy for a couple of days with a media blitz. I'll call you when it's done and we can go out and celebrate. Okay?

ME

Sounds like a plan. Have fun. Talk to you later.

TRISTAN

Talk soon.

Before I close out of the text feed, I see the dots bounce like Tristan is writing a message. I stare at the screen for longer than I care to admit, excited for his next message. But it never comes. To distract me from my disappointment, I turn on the television to watch an episode of whatever I'm bingeing on Netflix, but the news is on. They have live footage from the Steel's locker room, and it is wild. My eyes find Tristan. He's right; he looks like a drowned rat, but he's still incredibly handsome. His light brown hair has darkened from the champagne and it looks even sexier than normal. I focus in on the beard he's grown in the last few weeks, and damn, does that make my body feverishly hot. It's groomed well and I want to touch it and see if it's as soft as it looks. My core clenches. I'd really like to feel it brush against my thighs as he satisfies my needs. *What am I doing?* Sitting back on my couch, I close my eyes. Fantasies of Tristan flood my mind. Obviously, my libido has been severely neglected, because she's screaming for freedom, like Mel Gibson does in *Braveheart.* I squeeze my legs together, hoping to temper the throbbing I feel. I'm suddenly craving a bath with my trusty BOB.

Just as I'm about to turn off the news and take care of myself, I realize the mistake I made when I said we could only be friends. I thought I was protecting myself, and now he's free to move on. *Shit. What have I done?* My stomach tightens as a myriad of worry fills my head. *Will I be able to be friends with him if he has someone else in his life?* The first tear falls. I know it isn't fair of me to feel this way, but I do. He seems like he wants to pursue something more with me again, and

I'm always the one dodging it. I can't blame him for listening. Knowing if he moves on, it will shred me. I grab a pillow, curl into a ball on my couch, and cry. "What am I going to do?"

My phone dings, alerting me to a text.

It's another picture of Tristan. This time he's holding the Stanley Cup with a giant grin on his handsome face. He doesn't send any message with the picture, but you can't miss the happiness radiating off him. It's so fucking beautiful. Finally, he got his dream. I am so proud of him. I just wish I were part of it.

I text back exactly what I'm feeling in a single emoji. A heart. I love this man so much it hurts. *What am I going to do now?*

Chapter 42

Tristan

I'm on top of the world. The Steel just won their second Stanley Cup and other than the team, the only person I want to share that with is Steph. Since we rekindled our friendship, I've tried to hold my feelings close, but there is no denying it. I still love her. Every time I talk to her, I want to confess it, but she seems scared, and the last thing I want to do is frighten her away. I've already lost ten years because of the mistakes I made. I don't want to lose any more. I'm electing to give her space, biding my time, hoping that eventually she'll come around.

When the Cup makes its way around the locker room, I have one of my players take a few pictures of me with it. Knowing Steph will think it's cool, I send the best one to her. I'm not expecting a reply, but the one I get makes my night even better. She sends a heart. My heart thumps in my chest, wondering what it means. Is she loving the picture, the experience, or me? I can't wait another minute to find out.

When I breeze out of the arena ten minutes later, I'm desperate to see Steph. Am I being presumptuous? Maybe. I can't let any more time or opportunities pass between us. I need to know how she feels. Now. The drive to her place is quick. And in no time, I'm knocking on her door. I haven't been here before, but she gave me her address weeks ago. We planned to hang out once the playoffs were over. And now they're done.

Knock, knock.

My heart gallops in my chest, and I wipe my sweaty hands on my still-damp pants. worry increases as I wait for her to answer the door. Seconds feel like minutes. *I hope she's still awake, and that she's happy to see me.*

Steph pulls open the door and gasps. "Tristan. What are you doing here?"

I move in closer and say, "I had a question for you." Her beautiful blue eyes go wide.

"You do?"

I lick my lips and nod. "Can I come in, or would you rather I stay in the hall?" Steph opens the door, showing me inside. Instantly, I feel warm and cozy, the chill of my soaked clothes having less of an effect. *Should I have changed before I rushed over? Maybe, but*

I probably would have talked myself out of coming. Looking around, I see the space is full of color. It's vibrant and inviting. And nothing like our old condo. Her home is a perfect representation of her.

Steph closes the door and then turns to me. "What did you need to ask me?"

Stepping closer, I reach for her hand and thread our fingers together. Her cheeks flush. "Well, it's more of what I have to say, but there is a question in there too."

"Okay," she hesitantly says.

Is this a mistake? No.

Pushing aside my nerves and fears, I clear my throat. "Steph, I need to know what the heart you sent meant." She lowers her head, hunches her shoulders, and begins to pull away. I grip her fingers tighter, pulling her into me, and then lift her chin with my other hand, forcing her to make eye contact. Her brown eyes are swimming with uncertainty. "Please talk to me, Steph."

She lets out a deep sigh and forces a smile.

"Please?" I beg as I squeeze the hand I'm still holding.

"It's hard to say," she whispers.

I smile, trying to encourage her. "Can you try? For me?"

She takes a deep breath before she goes on. "These last few weeks, as we've gotten to know each other again, I've realized how much I've missed you and how much I still care for you." Her confession is the best thing I've ever heard. "But I need to take things slow. I don't want to get hurt again."

I nod in understanding. What we went through was painful for everyone involved, but I know if I don't try for something more, I'll regret it forever. "So, what are you saying? Do you want to give this, us, a shot?" I nervously ask.

"Yes, I do," she whispers. Reacting without thought, I hug her fiercely. Finally, she wraps her arms around me, and it feels so fucking good to have her in my arms again.

"Tristan," she mumbles into my chest.

"Yeah," I answer.

"When you showed up, you said you had something to say and a question for me. I'm assuming the heart was the question. So, what did you need to say?"

I laugh, then answer, "Easy. You already did it for me. I wanted to know how you felt." When I finally pull back from her, I make sure I've got eye contact before continuing. "I feel the same way, Steph." I really want to kiss her, but I'm afraid that's moving too fast, so I just go back to hugging her.

She turns her head sideways and squeaks, "Oh."

I don't know how long we stand there hugging each other, but eventually, she asks, "What do we do now?"

"I just want to hold you, if that's okay. I've missed ten years, and I'm not ready to let go. Then I want to take you on a date and get to know you again." My stomach turns as I anxiously await her response.

Finally, she speaks. "That sounds good."

And I'm overjoyed. I don't know what our future holds, but I'm excited for another chance.

Chapter 43

Stephanie

Today is a big day. Tristan and I are going out on an official date. Since confessing our feelings three weeks ago, we've spent a lot of time talking to each other. Because the team won the Stanley Cup, management expected him to take part in various social media activities. But the first Saturday he has free, he reserves just for us. Even though we've both been in Chicago for years, neither one of us has done much exploring. It's strangely like when we lived in Boston.

When I ask what he has planned, he doesn't say much other than that I'm supposed to dress comfortably. When I open the door, I'm rendered stupid. Tristan is the epitome of relaxed and sexy. His brown hair is messy, and I want to run my fingers through it. He has on khaki cargo shorts and a form-fitting t-shirt that hugs his biceps perfectly. He looks devastatingly handsome.

"Hi," I breathe out.

"You look gorgeous, Steph," Tristan tells me when he sees me. I'm wearing a pair of soft denim capris and a tank top, and I feel underdressed, but I'm not sure what I'd do differently.

"Thanks. Ready to go?" I ask while grabbing my bag. When he leads me to a shiny new truck, my mouth gaps open. "Is this you?" I ask, shocked. He nods. "It's so... so big."

"I guess. I don't really notice," he says before he helps me into the cab. Good thing he has running boards and a grab bar, or I might have had to jump. *Of course he doesn't notice. He's substantially taller than me. To him, this is probably normal.*

After driving farther into the city, he takes me to Millenium Park. I've been here for a few events, but mainly just on the Great Lawn. It is absolutely gorgeous, especially the giant stainless steel ribbon bandshell designed by Frank Gehry. However, we don't go there. He leads me to the Lurie Garden, that is in full bloom. Closing my eyes, I savor a slice of nature that's surrounded by skyscrapers and the hustle and bustle of an active city. Inside this space, I hear birds chirping a beautiful song. I feel the gentle breeze, and I smell lovely flowers. It's a perfect escape. Tristan reaches for my hand, and when I open my eyes, he's pointing out a few butterflies he spots dancing around the purple and white flowers.

"This is so peaceful," I tell him.

He smiles and squeezes my hand. "I thought you might like it. There's still more to see. I read about all the different varieties of tulips they have, and I know those are your favorite."

My cheeks grow warm. "You remember that?"

"Of course I do. I remember everything about you," he confidently states.

Swallowing my surprise, I ask, "You do?"

He pulls me to his side, and I melt. *This feels so good. So right.* Leading me to a bench, he answers, "Yes, I do. Ask me anything and I'll answer it."

Laughing, I remember how competitive he is. *This could be fun. I just need to think of some hard things.* Biting on my lip, I filter through possible question ideas. *I better start off easy and work my way up to harder ones.* "Okay, hotshot. What's my favorite place to eat?"

He laughs. "That's easy. Texas Roadhouse." He slaps his hands together and rubs them. "What's next? Give me a hard one."

I think a little more. "Favorite chip," I challenge. Smirking, I watch as his eyes go wide. I love chips of all brands and kinds, so this is definitely hard. He stares at his shoes for a minute, as if they'll give him the answer. After a minute of silence, he sits up straight, snaps his fingers, and smiles like the Cheshire Cat. *I can't wait to wipe that smug smile off his face.*

"That was a hard one, but I think I have it. First off, you classify chips in the broadest sense. You include all kinds of salty snacks, including pretzels and popcorn. Your favorite chip of all time is the Maui Onion kettle chips. When you're on your period and you're craving salty and sweet, you want chocolate covered pretzels. When watching a movie, you love popcorn; mostly butter, but you like kettle corn, cheddar, and caramel too. Last, when you're at a picnic, you want only barbeque flavored chips, although they can either be regular, wavy, or kettle." *Damn, he's right.*

He's still wearing that annoyingly handsome smile, and I roll my eyes. "Okay, you got that right, but there are plenty of other things you'd probably get wrong." Tristan just laughs at me, letting me know that my attempt at being snarky was just foolish.

Leaning closer, he gets his lips inches from mine. *Is he going to kiss me? Am I ready for that?* Before I can process that, he says, "Try me." He's throwing down the gauntlet.

Never one to take too kindly to being challenged, I accept it fully. *We'll see about this.* I'll pick something I never did while we were together. *That'll show him.* "What's my favorite drink in the morning?"

Without hesitation, he answers, "Earl Grey tea. Either hot or cold." Then he smiles. I mirror it but shake my head no.

"Yes. I love Earl Grey tea, but I start my morning with a matcha."

He looks at me in shock and stammers, "Y-you... don't drink matcha." Even his pouting frown is adorable.

Grabbing his hand, I say, "Yes, I do. I started drinking matcha when I moved to Chicago. One of my work friends dared me to try it, and I've been addicted ever since. In the past ten years, some things have changed for me. Are you saying that you're the same as you were years ago?"

"No, things have changed some." Tristan looks at our joined hands, then up into my eyes. When I see them darken, then drop to my lips, my heart beats a frantic pace. *He's going to kiss me, and I want him to.* I smile at him. And he leans in and places a tentative kiss on my lips. Pulling away, he reminds me of what he looked like in high school: shy and lacking confidence. "Sorry," he apologizes.

"For what?" I ask, genuinely confused.

"I shouldn't have kissed you. It's too early, and I don't want to mess things up between us. But I couldn't help myself." His admission sets off a million butterflies in my stomach. Without using words, I answer him by pulling him closer and pressing my lips to his. After a few awkward seconds, he lets go of his worry and begins kissing me like he's been missing me for over a decade. And I can't help but feel the same way. Everything about this moment feels so natural and right. And I have to remind myself that it's just the beginning for us. We have a lot to learn about each other, and what went wrong originally, before we throw ourselves into another relationship. It's taken me a decade to consider moving on, and coincidentally, that decision is perfectly in time with reconnecting with Tristan. *Is that fate or karma?* Either way, I'm grateful.

I pull back from the innocent get-to-know-you-again kiss, my lips still buzzing. Not only did that kiss reignite my desire, it also felt like something more. It seems like Tristan was offering an apology, and I answered back with forgiveness.

Following our day in Millenium Park, Tristan whisks me off to the next adventure he's planned. He's cooking dinner for me. Count me surprised. In all the years we were together, the only things I knew he could successfully make were pancakes and grilled cheese.

Once he's shown me around his clean, well-kept condo, I offer to help make dinner. Instead, he makes me Earl Grey tea while he prepares dinner. Within no time, delicious scents fill the air and my stomach growls. When he plates the mouth-watering food, I'm excited to see what he's made. It's roasted chicken with rosemary, homemade mashed potatoes, and asparagus.

That evening we dine like kings. Everything is delicious. Too full, I pass on dessert. But I'm not ready to go home. "Want to watch a movie?" I suggest. *Snug-*

gling up to him had always been one of my favorite things.

"I'd love to," he says, then leads me over to the couch and grabs a blanket for me before sitting beside me and pulling me into his side. *This is the start of something great.*

Chapter 44

Tristan

Steph and I have been spending a lot of time together the past few months, getting to know each other again through trips to undiscovered parts of Chicago, dinners, and movie nights. We've taken excursions to local tourist traps like the zoo and the Field Museum. And even joined the hunt for the best deep-dish pizza Chicago offers. It's been incredible.

However, I discover that even though I've always been in awe of her, she's become even more amazing in the last decade. Now she's more confident and determined than she ever was when we were younger. And I have to admit, it's sexy as hell.

Speaking of sex, we're taking things slowly. Neither one of us wants to endure another breakup, and before we get too physical, we've been cautious, putting the physical relationship on the back burner.

Instead, we focus on the entire relationship. We've had multiple conversations about when we were married and what went wrong. We both admit that we made mistakes, but I know I carry most of the burden of why we ultimately fell apart. My injury was tough, not only physically but emotionally too. It had been brought to my attention that I didn't handle the loss of hockey well. Looking back, I can see that was true. At the time, I didn't want to hear it. Steph shouldered the brunt of my anger, sadness, disappointment, and frustration. Like a soldier, she kept showing up, ready to help fight my battles, only I was too self-centered and arrogant to allow her to help. She explained that in the end, she felt completely alone, and the reason she'd left was because she couldn't watch me further self-destruct. Her words—her confession, her truth—pierced my heart like a sharp dagger. I'd known I'd hurt her, and that I didn't deserve a chance to make it right. But I'm so thankful she is giving me one.

When the next season starts, we aren't able to spend as much time together, and that's tough. It feels different from previously. I guess this time I know what I would lose and how that feels. It isn't something I ever want to go through again. But I'm not sure how or what to say to her about that.

For weeks, Mika has been stopping by my office

after practice. At first, it seemed kind of odd, but then word got around that he and his girlfriend Shiloh had broken up and he was struggling. Usually, we just talk, but today feels different. Heavier.

"Mika, do you have plans tonight?

Hanging his head, he mumbles, "No, Coach."

I slap my hands together. "Now you do. After your workout, come find me and we'll go grab an early dinner." He doesn't say anything but gives me a nod before he leaves.

When he's done for the day, we head to a nearby restaurant, and once we're settled, I notice him fidget like he's uncomfortable.

"Mika, all your fidgeting is making me nervous. Do you have something on your mind?" I wait for a minute and he remains mute. "Wouldn't it feel better to get it off your chest? Maybe tell someone?" His eyes flick to mine, and they look stormy. *What is going on? Is this all about Shiloh?* Mika crosses his arms over his chest and remains silent. *Is he challenging me to make him talk?*

"Really? You aren't going to say anything?" I ask.

"What? I'm fine," he scoffs. *I don't know who he thinks he's fooling, but I know he's miserable.* Even if his teammates weren't talking about it, his pain is painted across his face.

I shake my head at him. "You're something... but you are definitely not fine. You are the moodiest SOB in the NHL right now, and that's saying something.

"If you're not hitting something, you aren't happy.

Killing the gym equipment during workouts has become your modus operandi. And anyone who tries to talk to you gets their head ripped off. You, my friend, are miserable with a capital M."

He winces. Apparently, my words hit hard. "Maybe," he finally mutters. And all I can do is shake my head in disbelief. *Stubborn. Kind of like someone else I know.* Me.

Clearing my throat, I admit something I've held close to me for a decade. "You know, Mika, I see a lot of myself in you. I'm trying to help you avoid some of the pain and heartache I've had to deal with because I was too stubborn to push my ego aside. From what I know, Shiloh and her boys are good for you. When you got together, there was a change in you both as a person and as a hockey player. You became unstoppable. It was like we were finally seeing the real you. Then the New York drama happened, and it knocked you down. And I get it. What went down was not fair or your fault. But how you choose to deal with it is. You can step aside from your anger, ego, and hurt, and you can make things better. I once lost the love of my life because I let all those things control the outcome for me, and I've been miserable since. I don't want the same for you." *Well, that's mostly true.* Steph has given me another chance, and I will not be making the same mistakes I did so long ago. I'm not giving her a chance to walk away.

Following dinner, I find myself knocking on

Steph's door. Standing there in a tank top and leggings, she's breathtaking. Seeing me, she blushes. My visit was unexpected. She touches her messy bun, then looks down at her feet and laughs. "Pedicure night in progress," she says. I can't help but smirk when I look down. She has some foam torture devices crammed between her toes, forcing them apart, and she's resting back on her heels.

"Hey, beautiful," I say before leaning in for a kiss. Then I pull her into my arms so she doesn't tip back and fall with the way she's trying to balance. She throws her arms around my neck, hugging me close and deepening it. Before I know it, I have one arm wrapped around her waist and the other holding us against the door frame. I hear someone clear their throat behind me, and I freeze. And Steph speaks across my lips. "Hi, Mr. Johnson. Taking Fluffy out for a walk?"

"I am, dear. And whatever you are doing... should probably be done inside your unit." I swallow a laugh, but my shoulders shake. Steph hits my chest and mumbles for me to stop.

"I will take that under advisement, Mr. Johnson. Have a great night." Before he can reply, she pulls us both into her apartment and shuts the door, giggling.

"You are such a bad influence on me," I chastise.

"Me?" She feigns innocence.

"Yes, you," I tell her while kissing the tip of her nose. We filled the rest of the evening with Steph's pedicure, a movie, and some heated snuggling. While I'd like to take things further, I understand her concerns. I just remember how good we were together, and the memory of that makes things hard. Literally and figuratively.

Chapter 45

Stephanie

Planning for the second annual Steel Your Heart gala is well under way. Last year was an enormous success, but I want to blow this one out of the water. Justin and Jennifer have again given me their blessing, and that is the ultimate compliment. I'm working with Kenzie, the baker I found last year right before the first gala, and she is absolutely amazing. Not only does she make delicious edible art, but she has a heart of gold, and we've became fast friends while deciding on the dessert menu. It seems like I stop by her bakery, CakeStop at least weekly for some new treat.

Jingle, jingle.

"Good afternoon. Welcome to CakeStop. How can I help you?"

Looking at the display case, I zero in on my choice. Smiling, I approach the counter. "Hello. I'd like a sixteen-ounce mocha and a dozen triple chocolate cookies. Thank you."

"Name, please?" the employee I've never seen before asks.

"Stephanie."

"Steph, is that you?" a sweet voice calls from behind the swinging doors to the bakery's kitchen. Moments later, Kenzie appears with her enormous smile. She's adorable, with her blond hair tied up in a red paisley handkerchief and flour-dusted cheeks. She's wearing her usual well-worn apron that looks more like a tie-dye art project from years of food coloring shenanigans than a baking one. She clops over in multi-colored Crocs and gives me a hug.

When she pulls away, her face contorts and she frowns. "I didn't forget a meeting, did I?"

"Order for Stephanie is ready," another new employee shouts.

Retrieving my items, I take a sip of the heavenly mocha before turning back to Kenzie and laughing. "Kenz, I just met with you a few days ago and we finalized the menu. We're all set."

She wipes her hands on her apron nervously. "It's just... this is the biggest job I've ever done. I'm nervous I'll mess it up."

Locking our gazes, I say firmly, "You've got this. You are going to knock it out of the park."

She rocks on her feet. "How do you know?"

I offer her a smile. "Kenz, I think I have tried just

about everything on your menu and it's all been magical. You are a baking genius, and I can't wait to introduce you to the world. The Steel Your Heart gala will be like your coming-out party. Are you ready for that?"

She gives me a small grimace before she answers. "Yes and no." I understand, but I have faith in her and her ability, and I'm confident she's going to do amazing.

Although almost a decade younger than me, our friendship is more sisterly than anything. Honest to goodness, she's probably become my best friend. Well, other than Tristan, who's secured that spot again.

I set my coffee and bakery box down on the table next to me and pull her into a hug. Normally, I'm not like this with vendors, but she needs reassurance right now. "I know this is big and scary, and you're worried you're going to fail, but that's why I'm here. We have run through the menu and made sure that you can provide all the desserts. We've figured out how to transport them all, and you'll be at the event to make sure everything goes off without a hitch." I squeeze her tight. "You've got this. I believe in you."

"Thanks, Steph. I appreciate it. I don't know what I'd do without you. Obviously, I wouldn't have this amazing opportunity, but I wouldn't have you as my best friend either."

"Other than making my clothes snugger in certain areas, you're pretty great yourself." I laugh at her while looking at my bakery box. *Why did I order a dozen cookies? Tristan isn't even in town this week. He's defi-*

nitely not complained about my curvier figure, but he hasn't seen me naked again, so maybe I do a good job of hiding it.

Kenzie looks much more relaxed than she did minutes ago, and I need to get back to work. I stopped in for an afternoon pick-me-up and got so much more. A dozen cookies and a visit with my friend. "I've got to get back to work, Kenz." She smiles and walks me to the door. No doubt she is prepping for tomorrow. I'm not sure when she sleeps, but her kitchen is pure magic. I leave CakeStop with my heart full.

April arrives a month later and, of course, Kenzie pulls everything off beautifully. She and I even squeezed in a date for dress shopping for the big event. And just like I thought at the shop, she looks amazing tonight in her bubble gum pink gown. I've even noticed she's getting extra attention from some of the Steel players. One in particular, their captain Josh, seems completely smitten with her. He's been to the dessert table a handful of times. Every time he grabs a plate, he talks to her and seems to make her smile. Then he excuses himself, walks away, delivers the dessert to a teammate, and repeats the process a few minutes later. From my perch, I think I've seen him take six trips so far. It's adorable to watch, but I want to protect her. She doesn't have a lot of experience with dating and I don't want to see her get hurt. I'll have to ask Tristan about him later, because we're still keeping our relationship quiet. As far as anyone knows, we've known each other for years, and we're friends. It's nice not being in the spotlight, but when I see beautiful women approach him, it's hard not to get possessive and want to claim him. *That was your call.* But I have to remind myself that I was the one who pushed us to take this slowly. So, I have to accept what that looks like.

Just like last year, the event is a success. The silent auction makes a killing, and with Trey in charge of it, he acquired some incredible items. Hopefully, he'll want to keep that job for the foreseeable future because there is no way I could secure even a tenth of what he manages. He is amazing. I've heard through the grapevine he's still single, and that baffles me. He seems like a pretty great guy to me.

* * *

The Steel is gearing up for their next run at the Stanley Cup. May is a busy month in the hockey world, especially for those who've earned spots in the playoffs. About a week before the games are to start, Tristan shows up at my apartment wearing a gigantic smile. Usually, he's stressed at this point with the playoffs looming, but today he looks as though he doesn't have a care in the world. *That's strange.*

"Hey," I say as I let him into my apartment.

"Hey yourself, beautiful," he replies while pulling me in for a kiss.

"Are you ready to celebrate earning another spot in the playoffs?" I ask when we break the kiss.

"I am. Can we do dinner in tonight? I just want to be alone with you." *Swoon. This man.*

After devouring a delicious meal from Mateo's, we snuggle on the couch to watch something on Netflix. I drape my legs over Tristan's lap, and he mindlessly runs his hands up and down my thighs. Every time he gets close to my center, my stomach flutters and my blood pressure spikes. He's awoken the beast, and squeezing my thighs together does nothing to satisfy the desire growing within me. My body feels hot and wanton.

Overheated, I pull the blanket off us, and Tristan looks at me with curiosity. My eyes land on his hands, and suddenly I'm desperate to have them all over me. I look at him to see if he's feeling as needy as I am. His brown eyes are wide and wild. He licks his lips, and I'm about to lose my mind. *I want him so much.* His hand settles on my hip and he tugs me closer. Our lips crash into each other. *I need more.* Shifting my body, I move to straddle his lap. I can't miss the hard, throbbing cock against me. Desperate, I grind down on him. He lets out a deep throaty moan that imprints itself on my soul, giving it a direct shot of adrenaline. My heart rate thumps in my chest as I continue to grind against him. He plants his hands on my hips, firmly locking me in and ensuring our contact isn't broken. Then he nudges my head up with his nose. "Kiss me, Steph," he rasps. And that is all it takes to set off the orgasm building within me. Our tongues wrestle as we fight for control over the kiss. I slide one hand around the nape of his neck, forcing him closer while I tug on his hair with the other. He lets out a deep, throaty growl, and my hips flex furiously. In seconds, I feel like I'm flying as another orgasm tears through my body. My hips keep chasing the high and my back arches. Tristan bites my lower lip, and I gasp out his name. When the orgasm subsides, I relax against his chest. *I just dry-humped my ex-husband to two orgasms, and it was fucking fabulous.*

He picks me up, secures my hips around his waist, and heads for the bedroom. "Where are we going?" I squeak, excited at what I think is ahead.

"That was just round one. Don't you remember how this goes? Once on my tongue, once on my fingers, and once on my cock. That just now was the bonus round. Better hope you are well-rested and hydrated for what I'm about to do to you."

I squeeze my legs tighter around him. "I can't wait," I say against his lips before he nips me again.

Chapter 46

Tristan

Striding toward her bedroom, I feel like I'm walking on air. For months, I've wanted Steph. Okay, that's a lie. Since I saw her at the gala last year, I've wanted her. Don't even get me started about all the years we were separated. That doesn't need to be rehashed. But tonight, the dreams and fantasies I've had for too long are coming true. And I can't fucking wait.

When we finally enter her bedroom, it's like passing into the inner sanctum. In the last decade, her style has transformed. It's transitioned from country chic plaid to dark, rich, sultry colors. She has a boudoir picture hung above her bed that makes my already rock-hard cock jump. And it's in black and white, making it classic and even more intriguing and enticing to me. Although her face is shielded by her light hair, her full body is on display, scantily clad in lace lingerie. She is a goddess, and I can't help but stare. This woman knows she is beautiful and sexy. And tonight, I'm making her all mine. Again.

Setting her on the bed, I spread my hands wide on her thighs. "Steph, that picture is amazing. It's my favorite piece of art. It captures what a goddess you are." Shyly, she dips her head. Taking my finger, I tip her chin back up to me. Softly, I kiss her, keeping it chaste. Pulling away, I make eye contact as I say, "You. Are. So. Beautiful. Don't ever hide from me."

We've both changed so much, and it's been mostly fun relearning each other's habits and tendencies, and discovering new ones. I assumed because we've waited so long that Steph is still meek and reserved in the bedroom. She's confessed she hasn't been with many men since me, and just hearing that makes me over-joyed. But this picture makes me believe that during our time apart, she's explored her wants and needs. She knows who she is, and that is so damn sexy. No one could ever compare.

I look at her and it all falls into place. I love her. I always have. But I've been holding back admitting it because I don't want her to feel pressured. But maybe thinking that is wrong. My eyes flick from the picture to the beautiful love of my life in front of me. "Steph, I... I don't know how to say this, but I can't hold it in anymore." She sucks in a breath, and her eyes frantically look around the room. *Is she scared?* "What's the matter? Are you scared? Did I do something wrong?"

She looks down and lets out a deep breath, then whispers, "I'm afraid of what you're going to say."

Curious, I ask, "What do you think I'm going to say?"

Still looking at her lap, her shoulders shake. *Is she crying? This isn't how I thought this would go.* "Can you please look at me? Are you crying?"

Wiping the tears from her eyes, she lifts her face to mine. "I'm afraid you're breaking up with me." Her confession is painful to hear and surprises me after how close we've gotten again.

"Babe, I'm not breaking up with you. I'm trying to get enough courage to tell you I love you."

Her eyes go wide and she swipes at a few rogue tears. "Really?"

Pulling her into my chest, I hug her and kiss the top of her head. "Yes. And apparently I fumbled it."

"Tristan, you didn't fumble. I allowed my fears to overwhelm me. If I had been paying attention, instead of harnessing my worries, I wouldn't have jumped to that conclusion. I'm sorry. And I kind of have a confession too." I separate us so I can see her fully. Now worry fills my gut. *Did I make a mistake telling her? I can't take it back now and wait for a better time. My thoughts are a chaotic storm inside my head.* "What I want to tell you is that I feel the same. I love you too."

Relief floods my brain, washing away any trace of my doubts or worries.

I pull her in for a kiss, and just before our lips meet, I growl, "You. Are. Mine."

She nods, and in a breathy voice answers, "Yes."

Holy shit. I won back the love of my life.

Although I want to scream that from the highest building or announce it on the Jumbotron at the Steel's next game, I'd rather savor the moment, making new sexy memories with the woman in front of me.

"Lie back, Steph. I'm about to show you a glimpse of heaven." She does as she's told, and I waste no time stripping the leggings from her curvy body. Tracing my hands up her legs, I reach her hips and lean over to kiss her mound softly through her damp lacy panties. She smells like heaven. I then travel up the rest of her body, gliding my fingertips up her ribs, making her squirm. "Let's get rid of this," I say when I tug up her shirt. Her balconette bra matches her panties, and although I love to see her plump breasts pushed up and presented to me, I'd rather have them in my mouth. "This is next, I say as I slide my hand behind her back and flick the clasp open. Once it's loose, she pulls it down her arms and tosses it somewhere in the room. I put myself in a pushup position above her and look into her eyes. "You are breathtaking. And you're all mine. Are you ready for me?"

She gives me a sultry grin and nods. Making my

way back down her body, I place kisses under each ear, whispering dirty sweet nothings to her. When I get to her chest, I trace her sternum with my tongue until I'm level with her nipples. Approaching the left first, I lap it, making it peak. And soon after, I'm sucking it into my mouth. Steph writhes beneath me. I smile against her breast before I nibble it. "Tristan," she says on a moan, and it's the best sound I've ever heard.

After giving her other breast the same attention, I kiss my way down to her waist. When I reach her panties, I blow hot air over her mound. She flexes her hips up, trying to get my mouth on her. "Patience," I caution in a commanding tone. She shivers. When she's settled and lowered her hips back to the bed, I tug her panties slowly down her legs, prolonging things. I throw them over my shoulder, then focus on what I'm after and spread her wide. She's shiny with her own juices, and I lick my lips. I can't wait to taste her. Blowing on her has just the effect I'm after. "All mine," I growl before I lower my mouth to her center.

"Oh, Tristan," she breathes out.

I finally give her my tongue, dragging it from back to front, and a low, throaty mewl falls from her lips, registering in my cock. Her taste explodes on my tongue. And I can't get enough. She's addictive. After a few more swipes, I focus on her clit. I can feel it pulse and I know she's close. I insert a finger, then two, and curl them into her, searching for her G-spot. Once I find it, I drag my fingertips against it slowly while she writhes beneath me. Watching her is like gazing at a fine piece of art. The flush of her skin, the arch of her back, the faint dusting of goose bumps across her dewy skin. It's magnificent. Seeing it and knowing I caused it fills me with pride.

I keep on my focused ministrations. "Tristan, right there." She gasps as she grips the comforter tightly. In no time, her orgasm thrashes through her body. Then she relaxes into the bed with a sated smile. *I've done my job. And there's so much more in store.*

Climbing over the top of her, I lower my lips to hers and give her a soft kiss. Her eyes flutter open and she looks at me dreamily. "Ready for more?" I ask, eager to be inside her for the first time in a decade.

"Thought you'd never ask," she answers lazily.

I sit up, strip my own clothes off in a hurry, then climb back between her thighs. She pulls her knees back to her chest, opening herself up to me. Just as I'm about to thrust in, she stops me. "Tristan, it's been a long time since I've had sex." My inner alpha male pounds his chest and grunts.

"It's been a long time for me too. Are you sure about this?" *Please say yes. Please say yes.*

Nodding her head, she says, "I want to. I even got tested and started birth control a few weeks ago, just in case."

Swallowing hard, it's all sinking in. "You did?" She

smiles. "I get tested every year with the team, and I'm clean."

Slowly, I slide into her hot, wet, pulsating channel. And it feels amazing. "You feel so good." I grunt as I continue forward. The way her body squeezes my rock-hard cock is overwhelming in all the good ways. When I finally bottom out, I stop, letting her body adjust to mine. "Are you okay?" I ask, panting. *Why am I out of breath?* I haven't even started thrusting yet. *Not that I'll last long anyway.* I don't know how many times I almost already came because I'm so turned on. I know that whenever I do, it'll be embarrassingly fast. Steph wiggles her hips, letting me know she's ready for more.

I retract myself slowly and then thrust my cock back in. Each time I do, I add more speed and force. Pretty soon, Steph is meeting me thrust for thrust, and an addictive heat is building between us. I stop thrusting and pull out, and she whimpers. "Hold on, I want to make this better for you." She looks at me, confused. I reach for a pillow and slide it under her butt, changing the angle of things. Then I push back in. The feeling of her inner muscles wrapping around me tightly is enough to make my eyes roll back in my head. *Nirvana.* Once I begin thrusting again, Steph feels the difference immediately.

"Right there," she pants, and I keep thrusting. "Alllmoooost," she moans out, and I slide my hand between us, finding her clit. Rubbing it earns me a throaty groan, which makes me feel ten feet tall. Steph grabs my butt and pulls me in even tighter, and our hips crash together. The rhythm we have is steady until it isn't. Instead, it morphs into a chaotic symphony of thrusting, moans, and shouting.

"Oh God!" she shouts as her fourth orgasm overtakes her. I thrust a few more times and then release into her. *That was fucking glorious.* Once I'm done, I collapse on top of her.

"That was incredible," I pant.

"It was," she echoes as she lies spread out on the bed. Knowing she wasn't a snuggler in the past, I hop from the bed and go into her bathroom, checking for a washcloth. *Bingo.*

After cleaning us up, I pull her into my arms. Another round will have to happen later. I'm exhausted, and Steph is already dozing on me. *Hell, I'm not complaining.*

* * *

The Steel is knocked out of the playoff bracket. It's a major bummer considering our record and performance this year, but you can't win them all. The one benefit to losing is that I'm not currently traveling or working. And because of that, I can devote all my time and energy to Steph. And, boy, has that been fun.

Last week, I kidnapped her from work at lunchtime and took her to a nearby park for an impromptu picnic. On the weekends, she's been sleeping over at my place, so on those days I try to make things special. Either I wake up early and make breakfast for her, or I plan something for us to do, like movies in the park or neon bowling. We have so much fun together, and I can't imagine my life without her. In fact, if I had my way, she'd never go home.

Chapter 47

Stephanie

Summer is finally here, and the weather is gorgeous. I take a week off work and Tristan and I just hang out. We have lazy mornings, then lunch in whatever clothes we can find. It feels like we're teenagers again. Everything is exciting. We are dating, having fun, and relearning each other. But this time, it feels more mature and meaningful. We experience a lot of firsts, and by the end of the week, we're exhausted but happy. On Saturday night, while doing a quick load of laundry, I'm grumbling to myself when Tristan walks around the corner. "Babe, what are you doing?"

I look at the machines I'm sitting next to, my open bag, and the clothes I'm folding, and answer, "Playing Scrabble. Want to get in on the next round?" His rich laughter filled the small space and makes me smile.

"No, I mean, why are you packing?"

Confused, I remind him, "You know tomorrow is Sunday, right?" He nods his head. "And I have to go back to my place for work next week," I explain.

He smirks at me. "Do you, though?"

I cross my arms. "Do I... have to go back to my place?"

He nods again.

"Yes, Tristan. That is where all my things are for work." I'm still confused by his questions. I've done this same thing every weekend for a month. Why is he pestering me about it now?

He squats down next to me, glares at my bag as if it's offended him, then clears his throat dramatically. *I can't wait for this.*

"Why don't you just stay here?" he offers with a giant smile on his face.

"Because all my stuff is there," I rationalize.

He nods, then smiles wider. "Couldn't we just move it here so you'd never have to pack up again?"

My mind is cluttered with a chaotic mess of thoughts and feelings. Big feelings. And worries. So, so many worries. *What if this doesn't work out? What if we slide back into old behaviors? What if I'm not ready to live with someone again?* Those are all valid questions, but as I confront each of them, I realize something. We're basically living together now, and since we got back together, we've remained committed to not repeating past mistakes.

Surprised, I gush, "You're asking me to move in?"

He laughs and scratches his head, making himself sexier, and answers, "Yeah, I guess I am. How about it? Do you want to?"

I think about it for a moment. *Am I ready for this? Are we ready for this? Yes.*

Turning my body so I'm facing him, I finally answer, "Yes, I want to move in with you." He whoops and then picks me up off the floor, spinning me around.

Slightly dizzy, I use him for support when he sets me back on the ground.

Tristan claps his hands together. "Sounds like a great project for tomorrow."

My eyes go wide. "Wow. Th-that's so f-fast," I stutter.

He shrugs his shoulders. "I've been thinking about it for a while. I just wasn't sure you were ready. We can move some tomorrow and then I can call a moving company Monday to schedule a slot. And I can oversee it all while you're at work."

"You have thought about this. Okay. We can do that. Your plan sounds great. One question, though. What should I do with all my furniture?" I ask, thinking out loud.

"Do you want to keep any of it? Is there anything you'd rather switch out here? We can rent a storage unit for overflow items and then decide what to keep or toss. How does that sound?"

I beam at him. "Sounds like you've thought of everything."

He laughs again and gives me his best smile. You know, the one that makes my knees weak and my heart soar. "Only one thing remains in question."

"Yeah? What's that?"

He looks around his condo. "Will this place be big enough for us?"

It's my turn to laugh. "Tristan, it's just the two of us. Remember when we were first married, we lived in something much tinier than this? Hell, my apartment now is bigger than anything we've ever lived in, and your condo is easily double that." I lay my hand on his arm. "I think we'll be fine here. We might have to rearrange things and purge our closets a bit, but I think we'll be just fine."

He pulls me in for a hug. "So, we are doing this?" Wrapped tightly in his muscular arms, I smile.

"I guess we are."

Early the next morning, Tristan goes to the store and buys boxes, packaging tape, and bubble wrap. When he gets home, he pulls me from his warm, cozy bed, demanding I get dressed so we can get the show on the road.

As I'm pulling on a pair of yoga pants and a tank top, he laughs at me. "Ready?" he asks, and I nod, still half asleep. "Steph, you look tired, but something else on you is wide awake and begging for some action " I look at him cluelessly. He laughs again and points to his chest. Looking down, I see my nipples are peaked and raring to go.

"I must have forgotten a bra." Looking around, I try to spot one.

Reaching into a drawer, Tristan pulls out a Steel sweatshirt. "Here, toss this on. No one will know you aren't wearing a bra, except for me. Plus, it's an incentive. It will make me work faster because all I'll be able to think about is how soon I can get you home and stripped naked." The only answer to that is to roll my eyes.

He smirks. "What?" He pauses for a moment, eyeing me. "Are you also not wearing panties? Because I can't be held responsible for all the times I might try to mount you as you bend over boxes today." He grins and all I can do is laugh. *Really?* Pulling down my pants, I show him my G-string, and he pouts, lip and all. *Poor baby.*

"Guess you'll have to be a good boy today and help me get moved," I taunt him while pulling on his sweatshirt. Hugging it to myself, it smells just like him, and I might never take it off.

* * *

The move goes smoothly. The company Tristan schedules can't come until a week later, but their delay is my gain. Each night after work, Tristan meets me at my apartment with dinner and helps me purge things. By the time the movers arrive, there isn't much left to do. A few hours after they arrive, my things are boxed and transported across town to Tristan's condo. However, unpacking is as awful as you imagine.

While unpacking, we discover we have double of everything, even those uncommon things like a grapefruit knife. While I haul yet another appliance to our large donation pile housed in the spare room, Tristan remains in the kitchen, making loud noises. Returning to the kitchen, I stand and watch him as he lunges at the air with precision as he holds his grapefruit knife like it's a saber.

"What are you doing?" I laugh.

Tristan stops, turns, and, with a straight face, says, "Isn't is obvious?" I raise my eyebrow and shake my head. "I'm sword-fighting an imaginary pirate. Can't you tell?"

I can't, so I just smile at him, suggesting, "How about we save the rest of the unpacking for another day? Maybe give the grapefruit knife a rest?" His arm drops, putting the knife on the counter.

Leading him over to the couch, I turn on Netflix, and the queue for *Pirates of the Caribbean* is highlighted. I grin. *Now it all makes sense.* Selecting to play the movie, I realize that this, right now, is the happiest I've been in years, and it's all to do with the man seated next to me. Together, we have worked on our relationship, strengthening it. Focusing on making each other the priority.

If we keep going like this, the chances are good that this time around, our relationship will last. And that's a goal I think we're both aiming for.

Chapter 48

Tristan

Thanksgiving is just around the corner, and Steph and I are trying out our cooking skills to prepare for the big day. We aren't hosting any big get-togethers, but we want to make a full turkey dinner together. Actually, I'll be out of town at a game on the actual day, so we're celebrating the week after.

Since moving in together six months ago, we have come quite a long way. When we were married before, we ate out a lot or relied on boxed meals that aren't healthy or great tasting. Since living on our own, we have had to learn some basics. I mastered grilling, and she is fantastic with side dishes. Neither one of us can bake, so Steph's going to order a pie and some rolls from Kenzie's bakery. *Yum.*

Since I'm in town now, we're doing a trial run on the turkey. It's the only thing we haven't cooked before. *This will go well, right?*

Walking into the kitchen, I see Steph awkwardly bent over the counter, shouting, "Come out, stupid thing!" I stand back and watch. She's trying to maneuver a slimy, ten-pound turkey. She's obviously unworried about salmonella. *Ugh.* I make a mental note to wipe everything down with bleach when she's done. She wipes at her brow with the end of her fancy decorated dish gloves. She blows out a breath as if she's finished a long race and mutters, "Stay still, you dead bird. I need to pull those thingies out of your big, nasty hole." I try my best to muffle my laugh, because I know she's trying to remove the packet of giblets and neck. If I'm honest, I'd probably have trouble with that too.

She let out another groan. "Need any help?" I offer.

"Tristan. Hi. Uh... I didn't know you were there." She puts her hand on her hip. "Just how long have you been standing there?" The panic in her voice is adorable.

I laugh. "Long enough to see you struggling with our turkey." Coming up behind her, I see she's wrapped the whole sink up with Saran Wrap. Pointing to it, I nudge her and say, "Well, that's one way to protect everything from salmonella." Steph laughs at me, then shrugs.

"I didn't know what else to do." After we get the gut bag out of the bird, we pat it dry, then stuff it with apples, citrus fruits, and herbs. Once it's in the roasting pan, we paint it with softened butter and put it in the oven to roast. Hours later, we both deem it a worthwhile endeavor.

Yesterday, I stopped by CakeStop to grab something for dessert. It isn't pumpkin pie, but it's still delicious. While sipping her coffee, Steph nibbles on her pumpkin chocolate chip cookie, and I take our plates into the kitchen. While there, I pull a small box from where I hid it in a lower cabinet. Flipping it open, I make sure the ring is still inside before I close it and make my way back to the table. When I get there, I push out a deep breath. Steph turns to me just as I lower to one knee. She gasps. *I hope that's a good gasp.*

Clearing my throat, I say, "Steph, I know our path to love has had major hurdles and bumps, and I can't promise there won't be more. What I can promise you is that you are my main priority. I've learned my lesson and I never want to do life without you again."

"I know this might seem rushed, but when you know, you know. I've loved you since we were teens and never stopped. Please be my wife again. Let me show you what a great friend, lover, and partner I can be. Will you marry me?" Silence fills the room, and all I can hear is the rapid beating of my heart. *Please say yes.* Desperately, I look into her eyes, pleading for the answer I want to hear. Her mocha-colored eyes look bright and clear. Looking down at her mouth, I see she's wearing a smile.

"Yes, Tristan. I'll marry you." I jump up and pull

her into my arms. "Again," she adds with a giggle, and all I can do is laugh with her.

We clean up our dishes and cuddle on the couch for the rest of the night. After we escape our turkey coma, we celebrate our engagement in the best way possible. I strip her down and give her multiple orgasms with my mouth before she rides me. By the end, we are completely sated. Spooning her, I say, "So... about this wedding thing. What do you want to do?"

Steph reaches back and runs her fingers through my hair. "Let's do something small. What do you think about a destination wedding?"

Tilting her chin to me, I place a soft kiss on her lips. "I'm up for anything, especially if it involves a vacation and sex with my wife." I squeeze her tight. She's going to be my wife again.

"Mmmm, that sounds good. When do you want to do it? That'll probably determine the where."

I reach for her hips and pull them into my hardening cock. She nuzzles her butt against it, making it grow harder. "The sooner the better. I can't wait for honeymoon sex."

She laughs. "Honeymoon sex. Is that better than regular sex?"

"No, it just sounds really hot. You'll be mine officially, and I can't wait for that. Just thinking about it makes me incredibly hard. Can't you feel that?" I grind into her.

She wiggles loose, rolls over, and straddles me. Her hands sweep against my chest and she tugs on my barbells. *That feels so damn good.* I thrust my hips.

Like a vixen, she shifts backward, making sure her pussy slides all the way down my cock, and dips her breasts in my face, whispering against my lips. "We could have a New Year's Eve wedding. You know, new year, new start."

I nod, agreeing with her suggestion, and she again tugs on my barbells.

Possessively, I wrap my hands around her hips, and growl, "I need you to ride me now before I explode."

Dutifully, she lifts her hips and lines us up. Her slipping down my cock is complete bliss. "So. Fucking. Good."

When she's settled so our pelvises are kissing, she rotates her hips and asks. "Where should we get married?"

She feels amazing rubbing up against me, but I need her to move up and down my painfully hard shaft. "I don't care where we marry. Timbuktu, courthouse, or Hawaii, as long as we do it. And soon." She giggles and swivels her hips. My desire is pumping through my veins, threatening to erupt if I don't find my release soon. "Babe, please ride me," I beg in a strained voice. At first, her speed is slow, like she's teasing me, and I groan. When she picks up the pace, I feel myself bottoming out.

"Oh, Tristan. That feels so good." Using force, I

flex my hips up while pulling her into me by the grasp I have on her hips. It isn't long before we both climax.

Lying there, sated, we decide on one last thing. We want to invite our parents to Chicago for Christmas. They still don't know we're together. It'll be a surprise for everyone, and I know they'll be overjoyed. I think they took our divorce almost as hard as we did. I didn't remain close to Steph's dad. But she's tight with my mom, and every time they talk, it kills Steph not to divulge our relationship. All Mom knows is that Steph is seeing someone, and it's serious, or that's what she tells me every week when she calls. I'm not sure if she's calling to check on me or to remind me that Steph, the love of my life, has moved on with someone else. I can't wait to see her face. It's going to be good. Her dad may scowl at first, but I know he'll come around.

It's Christmas Eve and our parents are in town. Even though we're from the same smallish town outside Boston, we got them on different flights so they wouldn't see each other. As far as they know, they're invited to dinner. My parents know they're coming to my house, but her dad thinks he's going to Steph's serious boyfriend's house. We figured we'd dump all the surprises on them at once so we could soften the blow.

My parents arrive first. "Mom. Dad. Good to see you. How was your flight?" I ask.

Dad grumbles, "It was fine. Little bumpy but survivable."

I turn to Mom as she laughs. "It was fine, Tristan. Need any help before dinner? I know my way around a kitchen."

I smirk at her. "I think it's covered. We have one more person coming and then we should be all set."

"Who else is joining us?" Mom asks, and before I have to answer her, the doorbell rings again.

"Honey, that's probably your dad. Do you want to answer it?" My mom gasps next to me, confused at what's happening.

She elbows my dad and loudly whispers, "Did he say *honey*? He's dating someone? Since when?" I just laugh as Steph comes out of the kitchen.

"Hi, Connie. Hi, Jeff." I look to my side to see both my parents' mouths are gaping open. They're stunned silent. *It's amazing.*

The door opens and there on the other side is Steph's dad, Mike. And as soon as he spots me and my parents, his eyes go wide. Steph throws her arms around him.

"Dad, I've missed you so much. I'm so glad you're here." He pats her back and comes inside.

He nods his head at me. "Tristan. Jeff. Connie. Nice to see you all. Merry Christmas Eve." He looks to

Steph, and says, "Sunshine, can you explain some things to me?"

I step forward. "Sir, Steph and I need to talk to all of you, and we wanted to do it together, so this is what we came up with. Talk, then eat a great holiday dinner we prepared for everyone."

My mom's eyes go wide and she stutters, "Y-you cooked?" I nod my head like it's no big deal.

"Actually, Connie, Tristan and I have been cooking a lot together lately, and he's quite good," Steph answers.

My dad elbows Mike and grumbles, "That better not have another meaning, because I don't want to know about it." Mike just shakes his head, and Steph ducks hers in embarrassment.

Once we've all settled on the couches, Steph and I launch into our planned discussion. "So, I'm sure you already guessed. Tristan and I are back together. In fact, we're living together and we're engaged." *That's it, babe. Rip off the bandage.*

Studying our parents, the only person who seems beside themself is my mom. She's wearing the biggest grin, and she's practically vibrating next to my dad. My dad looks at her and smirks. *I wish I could decipher what that look means.* My dad doesn't look upset or delighted. He's a tough man to read. Mike, on the other hand, is frowning, exactly like I thought he would.

I grab Steph's hand, thread our fingers together, and squeeze it. "I know this is a big shocker, and we're sorry we dumped it all on you at once. But we had our reasons. We wanted to keep things quiet until we were absolutely sure we wanted to travel down this road again. Our divorce was difficult on everyone, and I know I am mostly at fault there, but I can promise you that things are different this time around. Our relationship is my top priority."

"Am I saying I won't mess up in the future? I can't make that promise. But I do promise to give us one hundred percent of me. Losing Steph almost killed me, and there is nothing that would ever cause me to do that again. She is my world, and I love her more every day."

Out of the corner of my eye, I see both Steph and my mom wiping away tears. I notice the dads aren't sitting ramrod straight anymore. They've relaxed after my confession.

We answer a few questions they have, like when and where we reconnected and when the wedding is. We, of course, invite them to come and witness us remarrying, and they all vow to be there.

Following dinner, they head back to their hotels for the night. They plan to return in the morning so we can have brunch together before their evening flight back to Boston.

A week later, we meet our parents in Maui for our destination wedding. We're planning for a small ceremony on the beach at sunset, followed by a fancy steak dinner. Because this is an impromptu ceremony, getting all the state's paperwork is challenging, but in the end, we manage it. We're also lucky to find an available pastor and a photographer at the last minute. We might be paying double for their services, but it's worth it. The photographer also puts us in contact with an incredible florist for Steph's bouquet and my Ti Leaf lei.

The day before the big day, we head into Wailea, hoping to find something other than matching Hawaiian fabric outfits. Our dads want to get matching Hawaiian shirts. My mom will steer their choices based on the few dresses she brought with her. After a few hours of shopping and, of course, Cheeseburger in Paradise for lunch, we head back to Keihi with our wedding clothes. I didn't see Steph's dress, but I know it's some shade of blue. I lucked out and found a relaxed white button-down shirt and some sand-colored pants.

The next day, Steph and I wake up wrapped around each other. "Good morning, my soon-to-be wife," I say, while placing a soft kiss on her lips.

"Good morning, husband." Okay, I know it isn't official yet. That's actually tonight, but I love hearing the word husband fall from her kissably soft lips. Because the condo we're renting has two bedrooms, I move to the other to get ready. Not even ten minutes later, I'm sitting on the wicker couch waiting for my beautiful wife.

When she finally steps out of the bedroom, she's a vision. Her azure-blue dress hits her mid-thigh and looks incredible on her tanned, smooth skin. "Babe, you look stunning."

She blushes and says, "Thank you. You look so handsome."

I take her hand and we head out to the car. We have to arrive early for pictures. This is so different from our first wedding.

The pastor and our parents show up just as we're finishing up with the pictures. A few minutes later, we're facing each other on the beach, fingers entwined, making our vows to each other.

We both recite the short vows we wrote together: "We've been given a second chance. Because of you, I smile, I laugh, and I dare to dream again. I look forward to spending the rest of my life with you, no matter what is in store for us. I vow to be faithful and true for as long as we both shall live."

After the vows, we exchange rings and then are pronounced husband and wife. Holding Steph's hand, it feels like we've come full circle. Obviously, I don't know what the future holds, but I know what life is like without Steph, and I never want to experience that again.

* * *

Steph and I have been married for six months, and it has been the greatest experience. I won't say it's always easy or we don't have disagreements, but we always communicate and work through things. This time around, I am much more aware of her needs and the importance of what I put into our relationship since my job takes me away from her so often. That has been the hardest part. I'll never get used to my schedule. Not being able to see her and touch her when I want is torture. However, because of the time apart, we have perfected phone sex, and it's a regular occurrence when I'm away. Nothing gets me more revved up than knowing my sexy wife is excited to strip for me at the end of my day. Watching her pleasure herself while she's imagining me doing it makes my cock so hard.

Tonight, I'm in Florida for a series of games. This place always brings up a lot of memories for me, because my injury happened here. With my emotions on edge, I look forward to hearing her calm, loving voice across the screen. Seeing her naked might help too.

Ring, ring.

Not wasting a second, I answer the FaceTime and my gorgeous wife's face fills the screen. I palm my semi-hard cock. "Babe," I rasp out.

"Are you cheating, Tristan? You better not be naked yet," she chides.

I smirk, looking down at my almost naked body. "I'm still wearing something," I offer as I tug down the front of my boxer briefs, freeing my cock.

She sits up excitedly and her breasts jiggle in the silk nightie she's wearing. I lick my lips, wishing I could get my mouth on them. Groaning, I bargain, "I'll show you if you remove that silky nightie and show me what's underneath it."

She lets a strap fall down her creamy shoulder, and I lean forward as if I can touch it. She pushes it back up and smiles. "Tease," I mutter.

"You first," she says.

Fine. Pulling back my iPad, I reveal my lack of clothing. My cock has grown so hard, it's proudly standing tall for her. "Babe, I wish you were here so I could touch you."

"Me too. Me too," she says.

I miss my wife so much when I'm on road trips. In fact, last month was so bad, I calculated when I could stop coaching.

"It's your turn," I remind her.

Steph winks at me before she runs her hands slowly down to where the nightie stops and grabs the hem. Even slower, she lifts the material over her head, revealing that nothing but soft alabaster skin is under it. With the hand that's not holding the iPad, I reach for my throbbing cock. I wish I were touching her, but this will have to do. I'll just imagine it's her small, smooth hand wrapped around me.

When she reaches her breasts, I see them tumble out and settle into a teardrop shape. *Sexy.* "You are so beautiful, Mrs. Murphy, and I am one lucky motherfucker to call you mine." A blush covers her cheeks as the silky chemise makes its way over her head. *Wet dream incarnate.* "Now slide those barely-there panties off and let's get this party started."

While she's pulling her G-string off, I wiggle the rest of the way out of my boxer briefs and palm my cock. I'm already on the edge and I know I'll have to concentrate hard not to come early. "Beautiful," I breathe as she lies back with her legs slightly open, showing me her wet, pink center. *I want to taste her.* Licking my lips, I groan.

"What now, Tristan?" she coos. The power she is giving me makes this experience even hotter.

"Play with your breasts." She fondles and squeezes her breasts, and before long they're peaked and primed. I see her tug on the nipples. "That's a good girl. Now trail your hand down to your pussy and play with yourself. Be sure to miss your clit. I'm not ready for you to come yet," Steph whimpers as she nears her clit, even lifting her hips. "Just like that. Open yourself for me and stick two fingers in your hot, needy center. Squeeze them like you squeeze my cock."

"Mmmm," she moans, and my cock leaks. I fist it firmly, willing my orgasm to hold off. I'm transfixed on the screen as Steph's hips rock back and forth. "Remember to curl your fingers so you hit your G-spot." She nods, and in no time, her body is shaking. "Almost there?" I question. Again, she makes no sound, only nods. Her lips are pinched tightly together and her cheeks are reddening. "Breathe, Steph." A gasp fills the line and then she moans. "You are beautiful. Now take your other hand and start making circles on your clit. Touch yourself just how you like it." A smile blooms on her lips and her eyes roll back in her head. "That's my girl," I say as I stroke myself. The show she's giving me is something I will never forget. My strokes increase in speed, and my orgasm builds. "I'm there, are you?" I ask.

Steph's eyes pop open and focus on the movement of my hand fucking myself. She paces her strokes to mine and continues circling her clit at a rapid rate. Then her entire body quakes and she moans my name. I pump myself a few times before I join her in ecstasy, shooting my load on my abdomen. "So good," I say on a groan.

Normally, I'd slip from bed and clean us up, but with me states away, that's impossible. My eyes have grown heavy, and even though I want to continue talking to my wife, she's well attuned to my inability to do anything after sex. "Babe," I start.

Steph laughs. "I know you have to go. It's bedtime, right?"

Yawning and barely able to keep my eyes open, we end the call. I go to the bathroom to clean up my mess, brush my teeth, and pee before I pull on my underwear and crawl into bed. Two more nights until I'm home and I can see my wife. I drift off to sleep, deep in fantasy about all the things I'm going to do to her when I see her next.

The same cycle repeats itself throughout the season. When I'm on the road, we have phone sex, which is completely hot, but it's no replacement for the actual thing. When I'm home, we get to spend our evenings together. Steph comes to some of the Steel games to support me. Because she sits in the family box, she's gotten to know some of the WAGS. In fact, she's met up several times with Samantha, Shiloh, and Monica, and they always have a great time. Their friendship has become more of a sisterhood.

May arrives sooner than we plan, and with it comes the fight to the Stanley Cup. Last year, we hadn't gotten past the first round of the playoffs before we were out. Some fans felt it was our new goalie, Jersey's, fault, but it wasn't. Yes, he was new to the team, but he wasn't solely responsible for the losses the team took. Our defense struggled with injuries, and the chemistry of our offensive lines was out of whack. With that loss still heavy on our hearts, we worked hard all season to renew our love, passion, and drive for the game. And this year, we're a strong contender for going all the way.

The first series of games is easy, and we breeze through without losing a game. The next series is more of a struggle and requires five games for us to move on. When we finally advance to the final round, we are exhausted. However, making it this far gives us renewed energy and excitement for the series. Only sixteen teams started this journey and we are one of the final two remaining.

Our opponent is the New York Chargers, Lucas and Jersey's old team. Just like all season, we expect to have tough games in store. Not only are the Chargers a solid team, they are one of our biggest rivals, and the games often get chippy. Having two of their former players on our roster seems to stir up negative emotions every time we face-off, and the fact we are facing each other for the Cup means things are about to go crazy.

Walking into our living room, I'm rewarded by a mouthwatering sight: my sexy wife, wearing cropped yoga pants and a sports bra. I stop and stare, tracing her curves with my gaze and holding back a groan.

"I can feel your eyes on me," she says.

Her in downward dog is bringing out the beast in me. Stalking over to her, I slap her ass.

"I didn't know you needed a workout. I could have given you one," I tell her, smirking.

Balancing in a tripod, she waves her hand at me. "You are ridiculous. I'm working on my flexibility and core, if you don't mind."

I make a noncommittal hum in my throat and take a seat on the couch nearest her. "Don't mind a bit. I think I'll sit here and stay for the show." Then I laugh.

Steph switches into a new pose where she's able to see me. She smiles and shakes her head. "Oh, Tristan."

"Yes, wife?" I ask, grinning like an idiot.

"You said the first two games of the series are in New York?" Steph switches poses again, balancing on one foot.

"Correct. The first two games are there and the following two are here. Hopefully, we'll win them all and come away with the Cup, so we don't need to travel back to New York again, but they're a tough opponent, so we'll see."

She's reaching for the sky, and I watch how her delicious body stretches. I wish I could trace every line with my tongue. *Maybe she'd let me after she's done.* Thinking of that, my semi-hard cock pushes against my gray sweats. I move it out of the way before Steph knows I'm thinking about getting her naked.

Looking up, I assume I got away with my sly tuck, but the moment my eyes find Steph's, I know I failed. On her soft pink lips is a haughty smile that tells me she's thinking the same thing. Saying nothing, I rise and walk over to her, bend over, and tuck her body over my shoulder.

"Tristan," she squeals and wiggles.

I slap her ass, and say, "You know that's only making me harder."

Stalking back to our bedroom, I toss her on the bed. Then I tug off her clothes before stripping off my own. Her eyes dance with excitement, and it makes my heart pound in my chest. "Are you ready for me, babe?"

"Always," she answers in a sultry voice.

"That's exactly what I like to hear before I make you moan."

I slide my fingers through her wet folds, coating them in her juices. When I make it back to her entrance, I plunge two fingers inside and her body squeezes them tight. "Tristan. So good," she says, voice dripping with lust. I keep thrusting and curling my fingers into her, brushing against her G-spot before I retreat. Her legs spread wider and her hips flex toward me and she writhes in front of me. Watching her orgasm is the most magical thing I have ever experienced, and that's saying something since I coach professional hockey players. Over the years, I've seen some absolute wizards on the ice, pulling off impossible goals and dusting defenders before deking around the goalies. Some of them are genuine geniuses and have earned my utmost respect.

"Almost there," Steph sighs out, pulling me back to her pleasure. I lower my head and add my mouth, taking deep pulls on her clit, which earns me a tug on my hair. A shiver runs down my body and all I want to do is rip my fingers from her and slide into her warmth, but I won't. No matter how strong that desire is, the desperate need to watch her climax with what I'm doing is overwhelming.

Her muscles pulsate around my fingers and I know she's close. I suck, then bite her clit. Seconds later, I have my confirmation. "I'm coming," she whimpers. Licking the juices from her folds, clit, and my fingers before climbing above her is my reward for a job well done. She reaches up, tugs on my piercings, and then pulls me down for a fierce kiss, making my balls tighten. The tickling of my spine is a dead giveaway to what's coming for me. *Not fucking yet. Hold on, man. Don't jump the gun. You aren't even inside her yet. What are you, fifteen?*

While kissing, Steph widens her legs and flexes her hips up. Blindly, I grab a pillow and slide it under her butt, then I take my cock and line it up. Sliding home has never felt this good. I take it slow so I don't blow my load too soon. It's not like we haven't had sex recently. This is just what she does to me. She drives me wild. Every. Fucking. Time. When I'm finally fully seated inside her, I release her lips and growl out, "You feel so damn good."

Steph pulls at my hips, trying to get us even closer and says, "So do you." Then she swivels her hips and I'm hanging on for dear life. Whatever she's just done has taken us to a new level. And I want to live here forever. However, if I plan to last longer than a double-pump chump, I need to visualize something that will buy me some time. So, I plan the lines for the first playoff game versus New York. But that only distracts me for so long because Steph wraps her legs around me, arches her back, changes the angle of penetration, and lets out a squeal. Knowing I'm hitting her G-spot makes me feel like a king. I increase my thrusting and she falls apart under me. Her muscles give my cock a tight squeeze and I know I can let go.

Only two thrusts later, I cry out, "Fuck," then collapse on top of her. She continues to move below me. I slip my hand between us and rub her clit, and her hips jerk, wringing another orgasm out of her. She keeps up her speed, begging for more, and I happily oblige. Her movements become spastic and I pinch her clit.

"Tristan!" she screams before she goes still. Looking at her, her eyes are closed, she's panting, and a sated smile is stretched across her face. Leaning down, I softly kiss her lips and savor the taste of her. *She's all mine, and I couldn't be any luckier.*

Rolling off so I don't squish her, I kiss her neck. "I'm going to miss you while I'm gone."

She turns her head to me. "I'll miss you too. But it'll only be a few days. And you have some very important games to focus on." I laugh because she's right. I know she'll be right here when I get back, waiting for me. I will never take that for granted again.

After some hard-fought games, we win the series. It takes five games, but in the end, we're victorious. Holding the Stanley Cup for the third time is amazing. It's overwhelming and I can't wait to celebrate with Steph when I get back to town.

She FaceTimes me after the game and rewards me with the sexiest strip tease I've ever seen. My only complaint is that it isn't live. And the outfit that she wears—if that's what you can call it—is virtually nonexistent. *Holy Shit.* She starts off with a satin robe that she teases me with. She gives me peeks of her cleavage, ass, and center. Her hair is tied up tight, but there is something incredibly sensual about it when she lets it down and shakes out her long locks.

"More please, Steph," I rasp. After I beg enough for her liking, she drops the shoulder of the robe, revealing one perfect breast. She found some hockey-puck-shaped glittery pasties. I've already fallen in love with her black-and-white striped tights, but until she loses the robe completely, I don't realize they're hooked to a lacy garter belt. I'm not a stranger to garter belts, as I've played hockey since I was a kid, but this is nothing like I ever wore. It screams seduction, and I'm fully on board with that plan. The last piece of her outfit is pure madness. It's a black leather G-string, and I need my hands on it. Is it soaking up her juices? I know she'll already be wet, and I want to smell it. The heady mix of her and the treated leather make my cock throb and my head spin.

"Are you trying to kill me, baby?" I growl while she stands there with the robe puddled at her feet.

She just smiles wickedly.

Chapter 49

Stephanie

Christmas is over, and we're coming upon the start of another new year, which always serves as a great reminder to get my annual physical checkups scheduled. I secure spots with my dentist and eye doctor, as I'm confident nothing has changed. But when I make my appointment with my OB-GYN, I'm uncertain about how to feel. Last week when Tristan and I were having sex, something concerning happened. While he was pleasuring me, he'd ordered me to fondle my breasts. Eagerly, I did, until I felt something like a dried pea beneath my skin. I didn't mention it to him because maybe I was wrong. We both didn't need to worry. Days later, I walk into my provider's office, convinced what I'd felt was nothing to worry about.

After a quick conversation about my health, I'm instructed to strip down and change into the gown that buttons in the front and then sit on the exam table. I don't mention the lump. I plan to after she's done if she doesn't feel it. Lying back, the nurse starts with a breast exam. With my gown open, I'm fully exposed, my arm raised above my head while she feels my breast tissue. Her fingers circle more times than normal, and the more she circles, the more concerned I grow. "Stephanie, do you do self-exams at home?"

Meekly, I answer, "I try my best."

"You have a regular sexual partner?" I nod, confused. *Why would that matter?* "Did he or she ever mention feeling anything while touching your breasts?"

My worry screams at me. Thinking back, has Tristan ever said anything? *No.* "My husband mentioned nothing, but I thought I felt something small last week. I'm sorry I didn't mention it earlier."

"That's fine. I just remember that you have a family history of breast cancer. Is that correct?" My stomach rolls. *Did she just say cancer?* My brain spins as worry flies through it at Mach speed. *Don't jump the gun.*

"Stephanie. Stephanie, I asked you a question."

I shake my head. "Sorry, could you repeat it?" I hear my voice waiver as I try to keep my feelings on lockdown.

"Don't you have a family history of breast cancer?" she calmy repeats. Then she moves to my other side, lifts my arm and begins palpating my other breast, looking for anything else.

Clearing my throat, I whisper, "Yes. My mom died of it when I was a teen. Why did you feel something?"

She lowers my arm and tells me I can sit up. I feel lightheaded as I pull the gown over myself. Although I'm covered, I've never felt more exposed in my life. The nurse walks to the counter across the room to wash her hands, and when she turns back, I don't miss the forced smile plastered across her face. She sits on the wheely chair and rolls over to the examination table I'm still perched on. "Stephanie, there is no easy way to tell you this. I'm going to request that you have a mammogram done. I felt a lump and I want to have it checked, considering your family's history. Okay?" *No, it's not okay!* I scream in my head. Instead of saying anything, I just nod.

She stands to leave. "Everything else looks great. We'll fax over the order for the test, and once we receive the results, we'll call you. You should be all set unless you have questions for me." Speechless, I shake my head no. When she leaves, I swear she takes all the oxygen with her. *I can't breathe.* Panic sets in.

Stumbling off the table, I wobble on shaky legs over to the plastic chair holding my discarded clothes. When I reach it, I sit down and lower my head between my knees. *This can't be real. Why is this happening to me? Is it really cancer?* Forcing myself to suck in a few breaths of air, I start to feel better. At least the room isn't spinning anymore. Worry hangs over me like a dark rain cloud, threatening to unleash its destruction. My body shivers and goose bumps appear everywhere. Wrapping my arms around myself, I pray that it'll ward off the deep chill I feel permeating me to the bones.

Knock, knock

I freeze. A clinic employee speaks through the door. "Mrs. Murphy, are you all dressed?" *Shit.*

Flustered, I answer, "Almost, but I need another minute or two."

"Okay," she replies in a sing-songy voice. *How can she be so happy? Where does she get off? Doesn't she care that my world is falling down around me?*

Grabbing my bra, I crumple it in my hand, angry with it, like it's at fault for what I am going through. "Great. Thanks," I mumble. Pulling on my clothes as efficiently as I can, I'm ready to go. I stick my head out the door of the exam room and the same CNA that checked my blood pressure and weight at the beginning of the appointment is waiting in the hallway.

She steps forward. "Mrs. Murphy, are you ready?" I nod and she motions for me to follow her. Leading me over to the check-out counter, she hands me a copy of the mammogram order. *I don't want it.* Forcing myself, I take it from her, and I swear it burns my hand.

When I get back to my car, I sit in the driver's seat, wondering how I got here. *You knew this was a possibility. But I'm still so young.* Quickly doing the math, I realize I'm only a few years younger than my mom was when she died. I feel sick again. My breathing is labored and dots are dancing in my vision. Leaning my head against the steering wheel, I squeeze my eyes shut and focus on my breathing. *Calm down, Steph. You don't know anything until you've had the mammogram.*

Ten minutes later, I blink open my eyes. The spots have resolved and I'm feeling clearer. But I'm parched. Reaching into the passenger seat, I pray that the water bottle I left there is still full. Thankfully, it is, and I suck down half the contents. Wiping my mouth with the back of my hand, I let out a deep breath. *What am I going to tell Tristan? He's going to be crushed.* He has firsthand knowledge of dealing with the aftermath following someone's death from breast cancer, but he has no experience of someone he loves actually having it.

My phone rings. Digging it from my purse, I see it's Tristan. My heart thumps. As if he knew I needed him, there he is. I answer the call.

"Hi," I whisper. *Do I sound funny? Can he tell I'm upset?*

He makes a disapproving noise deep in his throat. "What's wrong?"

Do I tell him now or wait until I see him in person? I waiver back and forth.

"Steph," he growls. "Didn't you just leave your doctor's appointment? How did it go?"

Rip the Band-Aid off.

"Yes. I just finished up."

"And... why do you sound funny?" He waits for more of an answer.

Rip the Band-Aid off.

"Well, everything went fine until..."

Tristan clears his throat. "Steph, you're scaring me. Until what?" *This is why I didn't want to tell him.*

"Please, babe. Just tell me what's going on." His voice is full of love and care, but I'm still afraid to tell him. *If I say those words out loud, does it become real?*

I need to face the truth, whatever it may be. It's still too early to conclude my fate. We don't know what we're dealing with.

"She found a lump in my breast, and because of my mom's death from breast cancer, I have to get a mammogram."

Silence fills the line. *Please say something.* "Uh... okay. Did they mention cancer?" he questions, his voice thick with emotion. I nod silently, even though he can't see me, still not wanting to say it out loud.

"They did, didn't they?" he reasons.

"Yes," I whimper.

I hear the blare of a horn through his side of the phone. "Are you driving and talking? What is going on?" I ask, worried.

He lets out a grumble I can't make out. When he finally answers me, he says, "Yes, I'm driving. That honking horn was directed at me because I just did an illegal U-turn."

"You did what? Why?"

"Because I was driving to the arena for something and that's the opposite way from you, so I turned around and am heading your way now."

Really? He's coming for me.

"You are?" I really hope he's using his hands-free option in his car. *I don't want him to get in an accident.*

"Stay where you are. I'll be there in ten," he commands before he hangs up.

Wait. What just happened?

Sure enough, ten minutes later, I'm being tugged from my car by my incredible husband and wrapped in the tightest hug possible.

"Tristan," I squeak. "Can't breathe."

He loosens his hold slightly and whispers against my ear, "You are not alone. We're in this together, whatever it is. We are a united front and nothing is going to take us out. We've been through too much to not have a lot more years together." His words wrap around my heart just like his arms do to my body. I'm cocooned in love. *He's right. Together, we can handle anything.*

As ordered, I go for my first-ever mammogram. *Hello, boob pancake.* A day later, I'm called back for another mammogram and an ultrasound. *Thank goodness for health insurance.* Then I undergo a biopsy because the radiologist doesn't like what she sees on the images. For two days, I sit on pins and needles, waiting for results. And that's on top of the sore boob I'm nursing because those biopsies are painful. The accompanying chaotic emotions leave me a complete and utter mess. Poor Tristan doesn't know what to do. Alone in my office, I finally get the call I'm dreading from my provider.

Glancing down at the caller ID, I see the name of the hospital my doctor works for. Fear and worry settle heavily in my stomach. My body shakes with nerves as I pick up my phone.

"Hello," I answer in a shaky voice.

"Stephanie, it's Hannah from Doctor Blaire's office. She wants to schedule a follow-up for what they found in your biopsy. Would you be able to come in tomorrow morning at ten?" It's tough to form the word yes. I don't know what my calendar looks like, but I know I'll make sure I'm at that appointment.

"Stephanie, are you still there?" the pleasant receptionist asks.

Wiping away tears, I clear my throat and meekly answer, "Yes, I'm here and tomorrow at ten will work fine."

"Oh, good. We'll see you then. Have a great rest of your day."

When she hangs up, I sit back in my office chair, grumbling, "Have a nice day." *Really? What's nice about it?*

The rest of that day, I'm a ball of nerves. I hide

out in my office, afraid I'll break into tears at a moment's notice. When I get home, I remember Tristan won't be home until late because the team has been traveling.

Skipping dinner because I don't have an appetite, I strip off my clothes, tug on a nightgown, and crawl into bed. Sleep is elusive, as my mind is filled with worry. *Do I have cancer? Will I die quickly like my mom? Why did this happen now when Tristan and I finally made it back to one another?*

In the early morning hours, I feel Tristan get into bed and wrap himself around me. The next morning, as I get ready for work, I try to be as quiet as possible. I want him to sleep in. Call it wishful thinking or denial, but I'm hoping to not hear the C word at my appointment. Before I leave, I scribble a note for him.

Glad you're home. I have a follow-up appointment about my scans this morning. Love you. See you tonight.

Arriving to work before anyone else has its advantages, but today, I struggle to accomplish much. At a quarter to ten, I walk into my doctor's office, scared. I'm shown back to an exam room and left alone. After a few minutes, my doctor knocks on my door. "Come in," I whisper.

"Good morning, Stephanie," she says as she takes a seat on the rolling chair. I'm so caught up in trying to read her expression for any clues as to what she has to tell me, I don't respond.

Clearing her throat and rolling closer to where I sit, my gaze whips to hers. Her eyes are sad. My stomach tightens. "Stephanie, I wanted to go over your scans in person because of what they show," she gently tells me as she flashes me an uncomfortable smile. I nod. Pulling up my mammogram, she points to the lump that started it all. "This mass here... it's cancer. See here?" She points to another area of the screen. "While the technician was performing your mammogram and ultrasound, she found another area that is worrisome. I have already reached out to Dr. Peterson, a breast surgeon, for consultation. In my professional opinion, he is the absolute best in his field." I hear her words, although they don't fully register. *She said cancer.*

"Do you have questions for me?" she asks, her voice straightforward now and devoid of any authentic emotion.

"No. It's just a lot to take in," I answer, fear wrapping itself around my body, suffocating me.

Giving me a sympathetic look, she nods. "It is, and I'm so sorry to have to deliver such bad news, but I'm confident about Dr. Peterson." We sit in the silence for a minute, letting the weight of what she's shared sink in.

"Is there anything else I can do for you?" she offers. I just shake my head, because honestly, I don't have any idea. My brain is spinning too fast to process anything else. Before she leaves the room, she hands me a piece of paper with Dr. Peterson's information. It looks like her office has already scheduled an appointment for tomorrow afternoon. "When you're ready, you're free to leave."

"Thank you," I whisper before she's gone. Not wanting to be there any longer, I get up, grab my purse, and head for the exit. When I finally make it back into my car, everything hits me. My body shakes and tears pour from my eyes. An awful wail falls from my lips as I lower my head to my hands. Chaotic thoughts tear through my mind, creating more havoc. *What am I going to do? Am I going to die just like my mother? How am I going to tell Tristan?*

As if he can sense that I need him again, my cell phone rings and I suspect it's my husband.

Pulling it out of my purse, I get confirmation. Wiping away tears, I clear my throat before I answer. "Tristan." My voice is hoarse.

"What's wrong?" I've barely gotten a word out and he already knows something is wrong.

"I'm at the doctor's office," I tell him, not wanting to use the C word.

"Okay..." he slowly drawls. Silence fills the line, but I can't get myself to speak. "What happened? What did your scans show?" he pleads, worry filling his voice.

"I have c-c-cancer," I whisper in a stutter. The silence between us is deafening.

"Cancer," he utters. "Like your mom?" His voice drops as he asks.

"Yes," is all I can say before I sob uncontrollably.

"Steph. Steph. Steph, can you hear me?" he asks firmly.

Nodding my head, I continue to cry. "Babe, if you're nodding, I can't see you. If you hear me, stay where you are. You're in no condition to drive and I'm coming to get you."

I've lost track of time, but at some point, Tristan arrives like a knight in shining armor. He pulls me from my car, carries me to his truck, and buckles me in. After we're loaded, he calls Justin, my boss, and explains that I have a family emergency and won't be in the rest of the week. Then he takes me home.

Chapter 50

Tristan

Hearing Steph on the phone after her doctor's appointment just about broke me. She sounded so scared, and from the moment she answered the call, I knew something wasn't right. I never expected cancer, even though I knew about the lump and her mom's death in high school. I figured fate was on our side and that life wouldn't be that cruel. We'd just found our way back to each other. Our story couldn't be over yet.

Getting her settled on the couch after we arrive home, I try to make her as comfortable as possible. When I see her shiver, I don't know if she's cold or in shock, so I do the only thing I know. I change her into warmer clothes and wrap her up with blankets. While undressing her, I find a piece of paper crumpled in her fist. *Is it important?* It has the information for a Dr. Peterson along with an appointment time for the following day. Leaning down in front of her, I ask, "Steph, who is this doctor?"

Her weary, tear-soaked eyes connect with mine. "It's the breast surgeon. I have an appointment tomorrow to discuss what's next." And just like that, I realize our lives are about to change. Dramatically. Understanding that, I recognize I have some changes to make. But first, we'll see what we're dealing with.

"I'll go with you tomorrow to meet Dr. Peterson."

Steph's eyes widen. "But you'll miss practice. Don't you have a series this weekend?"

She's right, but there's no way I'm letting her deal with this alone. "It'll be fine. I have never missed a practice since joining the Steel. I'll call our GM to let him know I'm dealing with a family emergency and will be out for a few days. My assistant coaches are well qualified to handle my absence. Plus, I won't miss the games."

"Okay, if you're sure. Thank you."

After making a few calls, I join Steph on the couch and pull her into my side. She doesn't have the vacant stare she did when we first got home, but her eyes are still heavy with unshed tears.

"I'm scared, Tristan," she softly admits.

"I'm scared too, babe." *Hell, I'm downright terrified. But I will be strong for her. No. Matter. What.*

Gently, I take her chin and turn her face toward me. I look deep into her brown eyes and speak the truth I wish for her. "You got this. *We* got this." She rests her head on my chest and I pull her tightly to me.

* * *

They fill the next weeks with a mind-boggling number of doctor appointments, meetings, tests, and more bloodwork. We've been exposed to so much information, but the only thing I've retained is that the MRI confirmed cancer. And the genetic counselor confirmed Steph has the BRCA2 gene mutation, estrogen receptor-positive (ER+). Because of that, Dr. Peterson recommended a bilateral mastectomy. He explains that the mutation carries with it a high percentage of reoccurrence. He also mentions that Steph would likely have a hysterectomy in the future. Apparently, ovarian cancer is a high possibility too.

Her mastectomy surgery is scheduled for the following week. Besides all the other procedures she's had to endure recently, they inform us that the day before her operation she has to have four shots of radioactive dye injected into her breasts. Dr. Peterson explains that by doing this, the dye will show if the cancer has affected any of her lymph nodes. She's been warned that it's uncomfortable, but I can't envision it'll be worse than what she's expecting to endure the following day. *Guess we'll see.*

The night before surgery, we have a quiet dinner at Mateo's. She wants comfort food, and I can't imagine anything better. Over her favorite three-cheese ravioli, and my chicken parmigiana, we enjoy the quiet ambiance.

"Are you ready for tomorrow?" I hesitantly ask. *I'm not! I'm scared shitless.* Over the last few weeks, one question has haunted me. And it doesn't matter how many doctors we've seen, or how many degrees they've amassed. Not one of them can honestly answer the one question that refuses to go away. *Will she survive this?*

Steph taps the tines of her fork on her water glass. "Where did you go, Tristan?"

I don't want to tell her I'm thinking about whether she'll survive this or not. *She has to. I can't do this without her.* "I'm just thinking about surgery," I confess, knowing I'm only telling her a partial truth.

"Me too," she admits. "It's kind of surreal. I'm waiting to wake up from the nightmare I've been stuck in the last few weeks."

"If only," I counter. "But we knew with your family history, it was always a possibility." The entire time I've known Steph, her mother has been gone. And from the same thing we are now facing. *Please let her ending be different. Let her live.*

Reaching over, Steph grabs my hand. "We knew it, but it's still a shock. Listening to the doctors over the last few weeks, I'm hopeful for a positive outcome. When my mom was diagnosed so many years ago, such little was known, and treatment was limited. I'm young, they caught this early, and I'm being aggressive with my treatment. I'm confident I'm going to survive this."

Staring at my wife, I am amazed. She's still so full of strength, and her confidence is inspiring.

"I love you, babe. You're right. You are going to kick cancer's ass!" For the first time in weeks, I feel hopeful and not weighed down by her diagnosis.

Chapter 51

Stephanie

Dr. Peterson performs my bilateral mastectomy the next morning and everything goes well. I'm discharged the next day. Pushing open the door of our condo, I'm hit with a beautiful scent and scene. Our condo is filled with various flower arrangements, all in different shades of pink. "Who...?" I trail off.

Tristan smiles widely. "Everyone."

My mouth falls open as my eyes dart around the room, taking it all in. "And they all sent flowers?"

He nods. "Flowers, gift baskets, and gift cards for restaurants."

"Wow. That's amazing." I step toward the beautiful bouquets and falter a bit. Tristan grabs me around the waist, steadying me.

"How about you sit down and rest? I'll get you something to drink and then we can get you more comfortable." *He's right.* I'm exhausted and incredibly uncomfortable. *Who knew?* During the surgery, they'd put in four surgical drains. And what I've learned about them is that yes, they have a purpose. But they are incredibly uncomfortable, making everything from moving to sleeping difficult. For that reason alone, I'm looking forward to the day a few weeks from now when they are removed and I can take my first actual shower.

Tristan has been an exemplary nurse. He keeps my water bottle full, stays on top of my pain meds, and caters to my every need. This evening, I'm craving comfort foods, so he orders loaded potato soup and turkey sandwiches from one of our favorite shops. It's delicious and just what I need after a few days of barely eating anything.

Following dinner, Tristan accompanies me to the bathroom to help with a sponge bath. I know the surgical tubes will give me trouble, but I'm not prepared for the emotions that slam into me when I see myself for the first time. After I unbutton my pajama top, I take the first hesitant look at my chest. Breathing deeply, I pull apart the top. Still covered with medical dressing, I can't see the entirety of it, but what I see is traumatizing. Where I once had breasts, there is now flat terrain. I know under the dressing, my tissue is bruised, battered, and covered with stitches. *I am a monster.* I also know that because I elected to pass on reconstruction, my surgeon has not only removed the breast tissue, but my nipples as well. *I don't look like a woman anymore.* At the thought of that, my knees grow weak. I reach for the countertop to steady myself, and Tristan's strong hands grip my hips. Forcing myself to deal with what is in the mirror is agonizing. I don't feel much like a woman anymore, and the realization of that tears me to shreds. Tears fall as I lightly trace over the dressings. When I reach where the drains have been stitched in, I flinch.

"Are you okay?" Tristan speaks in my ear. Finding his eyes in the mirror, I'm stunned by what I see. He doesn't wear a grimace or a look of disgust on his face. I, however, am wearing a giant scowl. *No, I'm not okay. I don't have breasts anymore. Haven't you noticed?* Sniffling, I shake my head no. He steps closer so I can rest against him. "I got you, babe," he tells me.

"Why?" I whisper. I'm not sure he heard me until I see a frown appear on his lips.

Growling at me, he answers, "You are my beautiful wife, Steph. And I love you."

How can he love me? I'm not me anymore. I'm patched together like Frankenstein.

I scoff.

"You don't believe me?" he questions in a husky tone that gives me shivers.

"It's tough, especially when this is what I see," I answer while pointing to my reflection.

He nods. "Do you know what I see?" I shake my head no.

"I see a warrior. Before me is a woman who's

filled with strength and courage. One who not only has a heart full of love, but one of forgiveness. And she is breathtakingly beautiful. Your breasts don't define you. They never have. Your smile, the way your eyes sparkle, the kind words you speak, and the support and help you lend to everyone speaks of your beauty, both inside and out." Tears well up in my eyes.

He clears his throat. "And if that isn't enough, I still find you sexy as fuck."

A laugh tumbles from my once scowling lips.

Leaning back into him, I turn my head and say, "I love you, Tristan."

He places a gentle kiss on my neck, then murmurs against it, "I love you too, Steph."

My sponge bath goes as expected. I feel slightly cleaner and less smelly. I know I'll be ready for that shower when it finally happens after I've had my first post-op.

* * *

Before the drains are ready to come out, I visit my surgeon, and he confirms he is confident he's removed all the cancer. He also recommends that while the lab still has the tissue sample, it would be smart to send it for Oncotype DX scoring. I agree.

Another few days pass and all I'm allowed to do is rest. Toward the end of my ten-day restriction, Tristan has to go out of town for a series of games. The worst part about being alone is just that—being alone.

When he gets home, some WAGs corner him after practice and inform him I won't be left alone during future away games. His recounting of the story is hysterical, especially when he includes finger waving, high-pitched voices, and head bobbing. I've met many of the ladies over the years, but now it looks like I'll be getting better acquainted with them soon. I'm grateful for them and the lightness and humor they've added to my life. Since the beginning, they have welcomed me with open arms, and I know we're destined to become great friends.

* * *

Finally, the day has come. I have the drains removed. And let me tell you, I feel like a whole new woman. The residual pain is tolerable. While at the hospital, I also undergo a pelvic exam to evaluate any areas of concern. Despite being uncomfortable, I'm glad I'm being proactive about my health.

The next day is filled with good things. I take my first shower, and my doctor's office says my ultrasound looks good. Because of that, we're in a holding pattern until they get my Oncotype DX score back.

Ten days later, I'm meeting with my oncologist, Dr. Mead, again. *Today, I learn the plan for the future.*

After checking in, they show Tristan and me to a

meeting room. *That's odd.* In all the years I've been going to the doctor, I've never been asked to wait in anything but an exam room. When the door finally opens, a man about my age enters the room. "Stephanie. It's good to meet you." His deep voice is gentle and soothing. *Good quality in this profession.*

"It's good to meet you too. This is my husband, Tristan." Once introductions are made, Dr. Mead pulls out the laptop he's carrying. "We received your Oncotype DX score back, and I'm afraid to tell you, it puts you in the high-risk category for recurrence of cancer."

I gasp. It feels like all the air is sucked from the room. Tristan reaches over and places his hand on my thigh, rubbing slowly. "What does that mean for treatment?" he asks for me.

"That means that we have to be really aggressive with the chemo."

"*Chemo,*" I mouth. I lick my dry, chapped lips.

Tristan nods, noticing I've gone mute. "Aggressive chemo... What does that entail?"

"I recommend two rounds of chemo with a different drug for each round. The first round will be once every two weeks, for a total of four infusions. Once that is complete, we'll move on to once-weekly infusions of the second drug for twelve weeks."

I sit up in my chair. "I have a few questions."

Dr. Mead nods his head for me to go ahead.

"Will my hair fall out? Will the side effects of the meds be horrible? Are there any over-the-counter meds that help with the effects of chemo and the chemo meds I'll be taking?" Tristan grabs my hand and laces our fingers together. It's then that I notice I'm shaking. I'm not cold, so it must be nerves. I turn to look at him, and he gives me a smile and mouths, *"I love you."*

Dr. Mead clears his throat, drawing back our attention. "In all the years I've been practicing, I have seen it all. Yes, your hair will fall out, including your eyelashes. Yes, there are nasty side effects to the drugs we put you on, but everyone's reaction is different. We will watch you closely while you're in the clinic receiving the infusions and will administer meds as needed.

"Once you return home, if you need assistance, you or Tristan will call and inform us of the symptoms you're dealing with. Then we will either order prescriptions or recommend over-the-counters that'll aid you during treatment. Does that sound okay?"

The uncertainty of it all is what scares me the most and robs me of the most sleep and time. I even noticed a few gray hairs have appeared. *Guess I don't need to make a color appointment.* According to Dr. Mead, I won't have any hair soon. "Yes, it does," I finally answer. "I'm just nervous." Tristan squeezes my hand.

"That's completely understandable, Stephanie. The cancer journey is tough for everyone on it. I've heard from patients that the best way to combat it besides the meds is to surround yourself with people who love you and maintain a positive outlook."

I smile at Tristan. "I think I can do that." Tristan nods his agreement.

"Great. There's one more thing we need to discuss since your Oncotype DX score was so high. Because of that and because you're a carrier of the BRCA2 gene mutation, I'm recommending that after you finish chemotherapy, you undergo a hysterectomy."

I knew this was a possibility, but until now, I hadn't really given it much thought. Tristan and I hadn't even talked about having children. *Guess that isn't going to happen.* My heart squeezes and my breathing labors.

Tristan rubs my back. "Steph, are you okay?" His voice sounds so faint, even though I know he's sitting next to me. Why is my vision blurry and shaky? I close my eyes tightly, hoping to clear them. Then I feel something shoved in front of my mouth.

I hear someone say, "Breathe, Stephanie. Breathe. Yes, just like that." The rubbing has become more aggressive and agitated. *Tristan, I'm fine.* "Stephanie, keep breathing for me. Good job. She's coming to." That's not Tristan. The voice is familiar, but my brain is foggy and I can't place it. I blink my eyes and notice I'm staring at the ceiling and a handful of people are gathered around me. *What happened?* Panicked, my body freezes.

"Tristan," I call out.

"Over here, babe." My eyes follow his worried voice. He looks concerned as he stands in the corner.

Meanwhile, half a dozen people buzz around me, assessing.

"She's getting color back in her checks and her breathing is evening out. BP and oxygen look great," a woman calls off from next to me. Looking up, I see Dr. Mead standing guard, nodding.

"Is she okay, Dr. Mead?" Tristan asks, and my gaze travels back to him. He's moved closer and reaches for my hand.

"She's going to be just fine. Looks like she just passed out. It's not uncommon, considering all the stress she's under."

After a few minutes, they help me up and back into my chair. Still foggy, Tristan takes over the meeting. "So, a hysterectomy along with her mastectomy are the best ways to prevent Steph from having another bout of cancer?"

"Yes, taking an aggressive approach in treatment may seem radical, but it also reduces the worry you have in recovery and years after. Because of her BRCA2 gene mutation, Stephanie will also need to watch for colon and skin cancers."

Tristan wraps his arm around my chair and then tells Dr. Mead, "We will do whatever is necessary to prevent her from getting cancer again."

As if fainting isn't excitement enough for the week, getting my chemo port placed the next day certainly is.

Here we go.

Chapter 52

Tristan

If I've learned anything, it's that the cancer journey is not for the weary. I'm lucky to be with Steph the entire time she's doing chemo. The Steel didn't make it to the playoffs for the first time in years. And I know that is probably something I need to spend some time thinking about, but right now I'm thankful for the break so I can spend my time with my wife as she fights for her life.

Steph endures the first round of chemo with what they call "the Red Devil," with amazing courage and strength. Her side effects are mild compared to the stories she's told me of other patients' experiences with the drug. She has a few sleepless nights and has been nauseous and emotional, but overall, she concludes it's better than she expected.

Her hair starts falling out about a week after the first treatment, and Samantha offers to come over and shave her head. In fact, she and Shiloh turn it into a pampering party. They kick me out of our condo for hours. I don't know what happened, but when I finally return, I don't miss how gorgeous and happy my wife is. Steph is wearing a long purple wig, and her nails and makeup match. While escorting them out, I want them to know how much I appreciate what they've done. "Ladies, thank you so much for what you've done here this afternoon. You worked some definite miracles. I haven't seen Steph smile like that in months."

"Hey, good looking," I sing while I walk back into our living room. Still wearing a smile, Steph rolls her eyes at me. I join her on the couch. It's been a while since we've been this close. Everything she's been going through with her surgery and treatment means keeping a respectable distance from her. I don't want to hurt her or for her to feel pressured to do anything. I just want her well. But despite the time, our bodies still react to one another, and mine buzzes with anticipation. Turning to her, I run my fingertips up her arm. "What? You don't know that you're gorgeous?"

"Stop, Tristan. I know I don't look the same. Please don't try to pacify me." She rips off the purple wig and tosses it onto the coffee table. Bothered by her words, I need her to hear me. Tugging her arm, I pull her to straddle my lap. When she's settled over me, I tip up her chin, forcing her eyes to mine.

"Stephanie Murphy. Never, and I mean never, will you deflect my compliments. You. Are. Gorgeous. I see you as you are, and I know what you've endured, and all of it makes me love you more. You are still the fierce, sexy woman who drives me wild. Please don't tell yourself anything else. You are a precious jewel with immeasurable value. And I'm proud to call you mine."

Steph collapses into my arms, crying. "It's okay, babe. I've got you." Holding her has been one of the greatest gifts throughout this entire process. As she clings to me, her whimpers die off, and she eventually falls asleep.

While I hold her, I wonder what the next round of chemo will be like. The second drug isn't as scary as the Red Devil, but it's still concerning. What side effects will she have? I refuse to think about survival odds. Dr. Mead has reminded us to remain positive, and I'm doing just that. She is surviving this, and I'm not willing to accept anything different.

Too soon, the next round of chemo starts. Each week, she receives one infusion. Each appointment takes three to four hours. To mitigate her side effects, Steph premedicates with Benadryl, Pepcid, and a steroid, and they seem to help. The weeks fly by and during the few times I can't be with her, I'm lucky to have amazing helpers in Samantha, Shiloh, and Monica.

Steph mentions that the hardest part about the Taxol round is the time sitting in the clinic. Sickness is in your face constantly, and it's tough to remain positive, hopeful, and courageous. I understand exactly what she's saying. It's tough on me being there, and because of the circumstances, it's a million times more difficult for her.

When she rings the bell after receiving her last dose of chemo, there isn't a dry eye in the clinic. Throughout her treatments, Steph has made some great friends, and I have befriended multiple allies in the caretaker world.

* * *

Only weeks before the next Steel season begins, life throws another stumbling block at us. We're set up with an appointment to see Steph's breast surgeon, Dr. Peterson, and her oncologist, Dr. Mead. They let us know that a new provider will be joining us, Dr. Cathy, who is a gynecologic oncologist. I know what this means, but we haven't had a discussion about what it means if Steph has to have a hysterectomy.

"Hey, babe. Got a minute?" I ask as I enter our living room. Steph peers over her Kindle from our oversized chair.

"Yeah, what's up?"

"Dr. Mead's office just called, and they wanted to schedule an appointment with you. They mentioned Dr. Peterson being there and also including Dr. Cathy."

She looks at me, confused. "I know who Drs. Peterson and Mead are. But who's Dr. Cathy?"

Chemo brain is a real thing. "Dr. Cathy is the doctor you need to meet with to discuss whether a hysterectomy is a good idea."

Immediately, Steph's face falls, and she looks down. I move closer and hear her sniffle. Lifting her legs off the footrest, I cradle them in my lap. "Steph, are you okay?" She shakes her head. "Can you look at me and tell me what's wrong?" I rub her feet, waiting for her to look up. When she finally does, I see her eyes are full of unshed tears, and my heart sinks. Nothing about this cancer journey has been easy. Feelings always seem to be large and raw. "Babe. Tell me what's going on. Please?" My request is strained. Seeing her suffer has made me weary. It feels like I'm fighting a losing battle, and all I know is I don't want to lose her.

"It's time to meet with the gynecologist?" she whispers.

Nodding, I say, "It is. And it seems like you have some big feelings about that. Do you want to share them with me?"

Steph sets her Kindle to the side and fidgets with the blanket covering her lap. "I know I have breast cancer, and that makes me feel less like a woman, but having a hysterectomy would take the rest of my womanhood. I couldn't give you a baby," she sobs out. Her words are thick with emotion and heavy with feeling. I don't know what to say first.

I squeeze her feet. "Steph, it's okay if a biological child isn't in our future. I just want a family with you."

"What are you saying, Tristan?" she asks hesitantly.

"Babe, there are plenty of kids who need to be fostered or adopted. As long as I have you by my side, that's all I care about." I smile, knowing my confession is one hundred percent true.

Two nights before the surgery, I take my wife out to a fancy dinner, which forces us to get dressed up. During dinner, we toast her and her recovery. We also say goodbye to her baby-making parts, relieved that we won't pass off any faulty genes to any children.

Steph has the hysterectomy exactly a week before the first puck of the season drops. Just like before, she handles it like a pro. After one night in the hospital, they discharge her home. Again, we're diligent about pain meds. Steph switches to Tylenol quickly and keeps up her fiber intake so she doesn't have any other problems. She also goes online and seeks helpful hints for hysterectomy recovery. Our condo is filled with water bottles to hydrate her and pillows for comfort. Thank goodness for Amazon Prime delivery. Her recovery is slow but steady.

A few months after her hysterectomy, she is invited to a survivorship group and given the no evidence of disease (NED) label and a plethora of information on living a life of recovery and what that may look like. A few weeks later, at the beginning of December, she has her port removed, as it is no longer necessary.

What an emotional day that is for both of us. We cry happy tears and celebrate with a quiet night at home, eating takeout from Mateo's and watching a romcom on Netflix.

Chapter 53

Stephanie

My cancer journey was filled with highs and lows, just as I suspect everyone's is. I am lucky to say I'm a survivor. I met several women and men during my chemotherapy appointments who didn't survive, and with each of their passings, I grieved their loss. Some of those I befriended during the hours we sat hooked up to a cocktail of dangerous meds became some of my greatest cheerleaders and supporters. My medical team was incredible as well. I couldn't have asked for better care during the hardest part of my life. As far as I'm concerned, they're all angels on earth. My dad, Jeremy, and Tristan's parents weren't able to make it to visit very often, but through FaceTime we're able to keep them updated. They're all planning to come to Chicago for Christmas to see us, and I can't wait.

Besides the support of my family and the medical

community, another community kept me encouraged, supported, and loved throughout everything. It was my work, Embrace You. Not only did Justin and Jennifer support me throughout the months of treatment and recovery, my coworkers rallied around me too, with flowers, meals, and offers of help. They also hosted a special 5K for breast cancer survivors. They all wore special t-shirts they'd had made that said "Steph's Army." I was too weak to take part, but I was at the finish line, pink wig and all, to give hugs and say thanks. But the group that took the top honors was the amazing group of Steel players and their wives. I was humbled time and time again by the showering of love they gave me. In fact, tonight is just one of those nights.

"Steph, I'm just about to leave. The ladies are coming over soon to get you, right?" Tristan asks from the bedroom.

"Yep," I answer as I finish tugging on my newest wig. It's incredibly spunky, and the best part is that it's comfortable.

Stepping into the bedroom, I'm wearing nothing but a pair of black lace panties. *Bras be gone.* I've worked really hard to become comfortable with my body after surgery. I have good days and bad. Today is good. Sure, I have a breast prosthesis that I can put into a bra, but on most days I just wear a bralette that is made for someone like me. It's lacy, stylish, comfortable, and, most importantly, avoids rubbing against my scars. It can also accommodate a prosthetic if I feel inclined to wear one. *Win-win.*

"Babe," Tristan grumbles with a telling smile on his face. If I had eyelashes, I'd blink them at him suggestively. But they've yet to grow back, so I lick my lips and smile at him. He rises off the bed, adjusts himself, and saunters over to me. His large, powerful hands go to my hips, and he roughly tugs me closer.

"Are you trying to give me a heart attack?" he asks while staring into my eyes.

I tip my head and whisper, "No," in a saucy tone.

Tristan pulls us even closer, and I can feel his desire for me through his pants. He's hard as steel and emits a heat that makes me want to melt to my knees. He places his lips on mine and says only one word that leaves me panting. "Tonight." Then he pushes back, winks at me, and heads for the door. *So mean.* It's been almost a year since we were physically intimate, and I'm finally feeling better and ready to explore that aspect of our marriage again. Tristan has been incredible through it all, supporting me in every respect and not once complaining about his needs. Well, tonight, after the game, I plan to fulfill every one of them.

A short while later, the doorbell chimes, alerting me that my girls are here.

I open the door a smidge. Thankfully, I remembered to grab my silk robe before answering the door, otherwise, I may have given someone a slightly disturbing peep show. *Hello, scars.* Relieved it's my friends, I pull the door open wider. "Ladies, come on in." They all enter, looking incredible, dressed to the nines in designer jeans and pink Steel logo gear, which I learned was only made for us. *Sorry, folks.*

"Oh my gosh, Steph. Is that a new wig?" Shiloh asks, and I nod. She smiles and gushes, "I love it. It's both sassy and sophisticated. And so... you."

"Thanks. I just got it yesterday, and I wasn't sure how to style it," I admit. I'm still getting used to wigs. On most days, I still wear either wraps or hats to cover the scattering of hair I have coming back.

Samantha steps up. "I wouldn't do anything. It's fun, edgy, and chic."

Monica nods her agreement, then asks, "We know you're wearing jeans and Steel gear, but what shoes are you wearing?"

Hardly able to control my excitement, I squeal. "Wait here and I'll go grab them." Rushing into my closet, I grab the box holding my new lovelies. When I return, all my ladies surround me. Pulling off the top, I'm surrounded by multiple gasps as I reveal a pair of pink suede peep-toe, chunky-heeled boots.

"They are so perfect," Shiloh squeaks.

Smiling widely, I say, "I thought so too."

After getting dressed and applying light makeup, I'm ready to head out. We all climb into a blacked-out SUV and make our way to the arena.

Trey, the owner of the Steel, is dedicating the evening to breast cancer. They've painted the ice pink and the Steel team are wearing a special pink jersey. My husband even donned a pink tie and pink socks to go with a sharp black suit and, let me tell you, he is beyond sexy. All the fans in attendance are receiving a special gift too. I recommended a stress ball that resembled a boob, but I'm guessing my idea was shot down. *Guess we'll see.*

At the start of the game, after the team has warmed up and before the national anthem is sung, Trey walks onto the ice to make a speech. "We here at the Steel are a family, and recently one of our members was diagnosed with breast cancer. She's faced quite a journey, and we are thankful to still have her with us. Tonight, in honor of her and all those fans who've been diagnosed, fought, and survived, we pay tribute to the journey you've faced and overcome. To those who've lost their fight, we pass on our deepest condolences. At the Steel, we are committed to having one game set aside in October to raise awareness and support for this horrible disease. Every dollar dropped in the pink donation pails will be matched up to $20,000. I will send the funds raised to a local non-profit that's at the forefront of battling breast cancer. Thank you in advance. Now, let's play some hockey. Go Steel!"

Watching the game's start, I realize my heart couldn't feel any fuller. I'm surrounded by an amazing group of ladies who have not only encouraged and supported me, but they've cooked, cleaned, and held my hand when I was at my worst. They're not only eager to jump in and help when Tristan isn't available, but they are always available to lend an ear when I need to talk. But my husband hasn't been alone in this battle either. He too has wonderful friends, not only on the bench but also in the team's management.

When we felt like life had speared us in our prime, we rose and went into battle. In the end, we celebrated our victory.

Epilogue

Stephanie

Two Years Later

I guess I didn't consider when I was diagnosed with breast cancer just how long the recovery is. Of course, I expected the extra doctor's appointments to make sure I'm still cancer-free, but everything else is a surprise.

Since they diagnosed me with BRCA2, I have a higher possibility of developing pancreatic or skin cancer. To monitor them, I visit my dermatologist yearly to have my skin checked, and once insurance has given me permission, I'll have an MRI of my pancreas. Besides that, since I had a hysterectomy and started menopause early, I also have to have my bone density checked every two years.

Regarding breast cancer, I'm on lifelong surveillance. During the last two years, I've seen my oncologist every three months. Currently, I've moved to a six-month rotation, and they say once I hit five years, appointments move to annually. Since I no longer have breasts, I am free of the yearly mammogram. The silver lining, right?

Breast cancer hasn't just taken a toll on me physically; it's hit me emotionally as well. Removing both my breasts seemed like an obvious decision, but I wasn't prepared for how it would affect my self-esteem. I knew my hair would grow back after chemotherapy, and it has, but your breasts are just gone. I hadn't elected to do reconstructive surgery because the entire experience was overwhelming and I didn't want to make an emotional decision that I'd regret later. Yes, I'm talking about boob size. What if I'd gotten them too big or too small? Years later, I'm still not really interested. Tristan is supportive either way. He just wants me happy. And he never fails to tell me just how sexy he still finds me.

The ladies and I were joking about what if I got a mastectomy tattoo across that entire region of my chest? Although I've seen some beautiful ones on the internet, it's not really my thing. For now, I try to find cute bralettes that I can either wear with a prosthetic or not.

Another aspect of life that has changed is my relationships. In two years, I've seen people come and go, and I understand that. Cancer can be depressing and taxing. Not everyone is equipped to handle the emotional trials of this journey. And some people are natural cheerleaders, who, no matter what your day looks like or how you feel, are still present and committed to supporting you. These people are invaluable, and I'm lucky to be surrounded by so many of them. These friends and their encouragement, love, and laughter helped me through some of my darkest moments. And while they were supporting me, their husbands or partners were supporting Tristan, their coach.

With our parents in Boston, we wondered in the early days how we'd manage it all, especially when Tristan was on the road. Thankfully, most of my treatment was during the off-season and the Steel organization was one hundred percent supportive. My employer was also amazing. Justin and Jennifer handled all my tasks while I was out on medical leave, making my life less stressful. When I was finally through treatment, Jennifer continued on part-time to assist me in adjusting back to my full workload. It took a few months for me to return to full days, but once I got there, I was unstoppable.

Our parents, who are great supporters as well, just visited to celebrate my second anniversary being cancer free. Although they weren't physically present often, they made sure we at least spoke several times a week. They wanted to keep up to date on treatments and see how we were both coping. I know it was especially tough on my dad, and he has given me more hugs in the last two years than he did my entire childhood. My having breast cancer stirs up a lot of emotions and memories for him, as it does for me. Maybe we'll talk about it one day. For now, I just hold on extra tight when he steps up for a hug.

Tristan is my superhero. He's been at most of my appointments, only missing a few because of road trips. He always treats me like I'm a princess. He's rubbed my feet and my back when I'm nauseous and puking. Whenever I want anything, he gets it for me. And he's loved me unconditionally. I know these last two years have been hard on him, too, and I couldn't have picked a better partner to do this thing called life with. I hope to have many more years of happy, healthy love.

For my two-year cancer-free anniversary, Tristan planned a surprise outing. Sitting in the car, he turns to me with a blindfold in his hand. I waggle my eyes. "Are we doing something kinky?" I ask.

Tristan laughs at me. "Not right now. I don't want you to know where we're going." Pretending to pout, I shift my body closer so he can easily slip it over my eyes. "Can you see anything?" he asks.

I shake my head no. "Everything is black."

"Good. Let's go." After driving a bit, I am completely clueless about where we're headed. I try to pay attention at first, but after the fourth turn, I give up. "Steph, after I park, I'm going to come over to your side of the truck and help you out. You'll need to leave the blindfold on until I tell you."

We pull to a stop, and I feel the flicker of nerves in my stomach. *I hope I don't trip or fall. Where are we? What are we doing?* I listen for any noise around me, and I hear traffic, but no other clues where I am.

True to his word, Tristan helps me from the truck and leads me somewhere, pointing out when I need to pay close attention to where I'm placing my feet. He clutches my hand tightly and leads me forward through a door. Cool air breezes over me, catching me off guard. A shiver runs down my spine, and I mindlessly reach up and tug at my hat. *Sure glad I wore that.* Stepping farther into the building, my nose tickles, and a familiar scent registers. *Are we at an ice arena?* Tristan stays quiet as he leads me over to some chairs. He helps lower me into one, which is quite a feat when you're temporarily blind.

"Okay. Are you ready for me to remove the blindfold?" he asks. I nod excitedly. When the covering has been removed, I blink my eyes a few times to clear them and then a smile spreads across my face.

"Oh, Tristan," I gasp as I look out onto the Chicago Steel ice that is covered with his players and their families. The staff and their families are also there. And they are all wearing pink. Overwhelmed, my eyes fill with tears and I suck in a breath. Tristan grabs my hand and I look at him and whisper, "You did this for me?"

He smiles. "I did, babe. I love you so much. When I

mentioned to the guys that I wanted to do something special for you, they all wanted to be part of it."

"This is incredible," I tell him as I pull him into a hug.

"I'm so happy you like it. Do you want to go skate?" he asks.

Nodding, I stand up from my chair and we head down to the ice. Thinking of everything, Lucas skates up with a pair of skates for each of us. "Congrats, Steph. We are so glad that we get to celebrate this milestone with you."

I hug him. "Thank you."

Throughout the next few hours, I make my rounds, saying hi and thanking everyone for participating in the day. As we all head out to the parking lot, I see a food truck parked at the end of the lot. *That's odd.* Pointing to it, I turn to Tristan and ask, "Why do you think that's parked there?"

He laughs. "Well, when you celebrate something, you have to have cake, right?"

Pulling my hat on tighter, I answer, "Yes, I guess so."

Pointing to the brightly painted truck, he tells me it's a cupcake truck, and he hired it. Kenzie pops out, yelling. "Surprise!" After gorging on delicious cupcakes, we all part ways. Driving home, my heart is overflowing with all the love surrounding me. Just when I thought I would be forever single, life had a way of intervening and showing me I could have what I always wanted.

* * *

Thank you for reading *Speared By You*, the fourth book in the Chicago Steel series. If you'd like another peek into the Chicago Steel world, visit my website at https://907publishing.wixsite.com/my-site and sign up for my newsletter. While there, don't forget to snag the extended epilogue for *Speared By You* and any extras for the rest of the series. Each book in the series is available on Kindle Unlimited. Happy Reading.

If you haven't yet, don't forget to read *Hooked By You*, the first book of the Chicago Steel series with Lucas and Samantha. Keep Reading to check out the World of Chicago Steel.

World of Chicago Steel

Have you read *Hooked By You*, the first book of the Chicago Steel Series with Lucas and Samantha? If not, you can click on the link to start reading. The entire series is available with your Kindle Unlimited subscription.

Hooked By You–Chicago Steel Series Book One

Lucas

She's a goddess in heels. Absolute perfection. Well, almost.

Samantha Fox is the heiress of Fox Sporting, my new management team. As one of the best wings in the NHL, I have never shied away from a challenge, and she is definitely a challenge. But if her company representing me doesn't stop me from wanting her, the fact she's engaged should, right?

But the noticeably absent sparkle from her left ring finger makes me question. I vow to myself that I'll find out what that's all about. And if she's single, I plan to make her mine. Or at least, mine for the night. I just need one taste of the divine.

Samantha

Off-limits. That's what he is. Lucas Bouchard is the prestigious new client acquired by my family's company. From what I know, not only is he an amazing hockey player, he's a humble and generous philanthropist too. Also, he's a walking aphrodisiac.

It doesn't matter that I've just broken off my engagement to a cheating, using loser. Every time our eyes lock, I find myself captivated. But he's not for me. No matter how many times I remind myself of this, though, it doesn't compute. Plain and simple, I want him. And keeping my distance might prove impossible.

Checked By You–Chicago Steel Series Book Two

Mika

She's the uber-sexy, single mother living next door. Everyone tells me to keep my distance. But there's something about her. Specifically, her eyes. They speak to me. Drawing me in like a siren. I want to know her, but she's more guarded than Buckingham Palace. However, after one afternoon in her presence, I find myself addicted and wanting more. Willing to do whatever I have to just to make it past her defenses.

Shiloh

My next-door neighbor is an insanely hot, single professional hockey player. As if that isn't bad enough, he's a nice guy too. After spending an afternoon where he showed my son how to skate and took us out to ice cream, I want to let him in. My past cautions me to put on the brakes, but I find myself going full steam ahead, ignoring all the red flags waving at me.

Clipped By You–Chicago Steel Series Book Three

Monica

She's his.

Or she has been since her freshman year of college.

According to Monica Fields, no man will ever hold a candle to Christian Fox.

Too bad he's completely unaware. Or is he?

Christian

Since meeting her, a sweet dairy farm girl has captivated Christian entirely.

But he's a guy. And he's the one who isn't quite ready to be done sowing his wild oats.

Will he ever be?

In this game called love, sometimes chasing after a woman is just the wake-up call you need. But what if chasing her to her family's farm and following her through a field scattered with cow patties in limited-edition white Nike Air Force 1s is the only way to catch her? And, when you finally do catch her, will she want you? Forever?

Acknowledgments

C.S. Lewis said, "You are never too old to set another goal or to dream a new dream." It only took me forty-two years to figure out what I wanted to do when I grew up, and even now, at forty-three, I don't know if I'll be successful at it. But what is success? Who determines it? What standard of measurement do you use? I've still yet to answer those questions or define the parameters. But until I do, I'm planning to celebrate the journey so far. I've been successful because I not only embraced my dream but achieved it too. **I'm published.** Thank you to all those who've walked alongside me on this path. It has been a wild ride and I know it'll get even better. Thanks for sticking with me.

To Darren - Thank you for always making me laugh. For supporting me fully and being willing to listen to me go on and on about my books, reviews, promos, and anything else that comes out of my mouth. I love you.

To my boys - I am writing today because I want to be an example. I want to show you that you can achieve what you dream for yourself. It may not look exactly how you pictured it, but if you keep working hard, you'll land exactly where you're supposed to be.

To Karen - Words are not enough to express my appreciation for you. You are always so quick to respond with a helpful hint, listening ear, words of wisdom, or support and encouragement. You are one in a million.

To Shauna - Thank you for keeping me on the straight and narrow. I'm sure I have driven you crazy a time or two, but I appreciate you sticking it out with me and offering your guidance and support. Thanks for being available in a pinch to answer my questions.

To Nicole - You stretch me and prod me to ask the important questions. You refuse to let me remain stagnant in a story. You are always pushing me to dig deeper and stretch not only my characters but the depth of the story. And if that isn't enough... you are always full of encouragement and support.

To my friends, family, and readers - Thank you for your support. It has propelled me forward and helped me to celebrate victories, no matter how small or insignificant they may seem.

Most importantly, thank you to my sweet friend, Joye. You are a beautiful warrior. You have a heart of gold and you are constantly giving of yourself. During your breast cancer journey, you made a selfless decision and became vulnerable, opening your life to so many others. At a time when we felt helpless, you gave your friends and family a lifeline, updating us with everything you were enduring. It was a gift, and even years later, when I look back on the entries made on the Facebook site you set up, I am still so touched by it all. Your words made you transparent when many of us would have closed ourselves up tight. Instead of only allowing a few of your closest confidants to see the truth of what cancer did to your body, you let us all in. Thank you for sharing such a deeply personal part of your life with me then and as I wrote Speared By You.

Months before I started this book, I talked with my friend and she was so incredibly supportive of me using her breast cancer journey as a template for Steph's journey. In order to make this story as realistic as possible, I wanted to gain a better understanding of the path this disease took her on. And thanks to her willingness, I am proud of the story I wrote.

Little did I know that by the time I actually sat down to write the heart of this book, I would face my own breast health journey. In the end, my mass was benign, but for weeks, my life was filled with several procedures that left me dealing with a whirlwind of emotions, questions, and fears. But my friend Joye was there, offering unwavering comfort and encouragement.

Ladies, please remember to follow the guidelines for breast screening. Don't put it off. A mammogram could save your life. If

your breast feels or looks different, please get yourself checked out with a healthcare provider. Be an advocate for your health. Flex your muscles. Show the world how strong you are.

Also by Jessica Buss

Chicago Steel Series

Chicago Steel Series

Hooked By You (Lucas & Samantha)

Checked By You (Mika & Shiloh)

Clipped By You (Christian & Monica)

Speared By You (Tristan & Stephanie)

Coming Soon

Delayed By You

Tripped By You

Blocked By You

Chicago Steel Series Novella

Happy Ho, Ho, Holidays (Trey & Nicole)

About the Author

Jessica Buss was born and raised in Anchorage, Alaska. She is married to her high school sweetheart and has two sons. Although she has both her bachelor's and master's degrees in Psychology, she stepped away from that field to be a stay-at-home mom. Now that her kids are growing up and she's getting more time to herself, she's giving this writing thing a chance.

907publishing.wixsite.com/my-site

www.ingramcontent.com/pod-product-compliance
Lightning Source LLC
Chambersburg PA
CBHW071725150726
47998CB00005B/1512